Iain!

— I hope it passes a quiet hour for you!

[illegible]

THE BUSKER

THE BUSKER

Brian McNeill

Macdonald

A Macdonald Book

First published in Great Britain in 1989
by Macdonald & Co (Publishers) Ltd
London & Sydney

All characters in this publication are fictitious and any resemblance to real persons, living or dead, is purely coincidental

British Library Cataloguing in Publication Data

McNeil, Brian
The Busker.
I. Title
823′.914[F]

ISBN 0-356-17943-5

Typeset by Leaper and Gard, Bristol
Printed and bound in Great Britain by
Richard Clay Ltd, Bungay, Suffolk

Macdonald & Co (Publishers) Ltd
66-73 Shoe Lane
London EC4P 4AB

A member of Pergamon MCC Publishing Corporation plc

For my mother and father

PROLOGUE

SPAIN, APRIL 30TH, 1937

MEAT.

Max Bauer sat in the truck, trying not to think about it as he watched the dog.

Nothing, not even the closeness of the machine-gun fire, could disturb the animal. It circled relentlessly, gazing up at the hanging corpse, hypnotised by the proximity of food. The body still swayed with the momentum of the animal's last attempt, bare heels brushing gently against the third letter of the slogan that covered most of the fire-blackened wall. Less than a day dead, Max estimated, everything usable or wearable gone, but the eyes still there; the ravens hadn't had peace enough yet . . . He wondered at his own calm as he watched the thing, until the image of his uncle's butcher shop rose before his eyes: a row of hooked carcasses, the bright blades of the cleavers stuck in the bloodstained wooden block. Suddenly his mouth was dry, and it wasn't just the brick dust.

There was a heavy *crump* of bombardment behind them, far down the valley. Automatically, Max classified it: artillery, ours; bombers weren't due today, they had been told. The machine-gun on the hilltop stuttered in angry reply, but the mongrel never even flinched. It prepared itself for another leap, but the hunger that fed its desperation had stolen most of its strength as well. It sprang, jaws closing on the instep, but without enough force even to tear flesh. Back on the ground, panting, it never took its eyes from the prize above. The dead man's heels bounced against the letter '*z*'.

Von Laer and Vinnie were walking towards the truck, arms gesturing purposefully as they discussed the shot. Their coloured cotton shirts made them bright against the drab brown of the smouldering buildings, the only living things in sight apart from the dog. Max looked again at the slogan behind the grotesque corpse.

Euzkadi. He knew it was Basque, for they'd seen it smeared on walls all the way from Guernica, but he still didn't know what it meant. He turned to the back of the lorry, ready to ask, but Jacky and Bartsch were asleep, and the sight of the pain in Schumacher's drunken face killed the question. One bombed-out town too many, poor bastard . . . Max swung back round again, staring without seeing at the shattered street. They were through the lines now for the last time, the colonel had said. An easy month — away from the front — then they'd be withdrawn. No more Guernicas, *Gott sei dank.* He looked at Von Laer's cropped head, shaking from side to side as he disagreed with the boy about angles. He saw the hand touch Vinnie's shoulder.

Was it true about those two?

Fiercely he decided he didn't care.

The tattered red and yellow Monarchist flag in the smashed shop window came into focus before him, and he wondered if it had bought any clemency for the owner. The scrawled *No Pasaran!* on the church wall would've made it hard, he decided. *They shall not pass*; Franco's troops hated that. He looked at the sign that hung limply from the hanging body's swollen black neck. Did *you* no good anyway, friend, that much was certain; *Arriba España* was a Falangist favourite, they'd seen it everywhere — Toledo, Madrid, Guadalajara. Spain will win . . . But could Spain ever win? Jacky was right, it was all shit. Why the hell were they here? He bit back the thought — he knew only too damn well why *he* was here. Nobody to blame for it but himself, either. Could have been a butcher — a *master* butcher — by now.

'. . . sky, then a slow pan. Ruins on this side of the road, the church, then cut away to our friend here. Has to be better like that, Erich, surely.'

Vinnie pointed at the corpse without looking at it. Wryly, Max noted this little fastidiousness. Be no trouble if it was through the viewfinder, he knew.

'Where from?'

'The square, I think.'

Max smiled. He'd resented it at first. It seemed right now, natural — an equality based on professional respect — but at the beginning it had rankled him to see a twenty-year-old corporal on first-name terms with a colonel twice his age. But now the question nagged at him: Was it because . . .?

'Max.'

'Sir?'

'Would you please bring the Marconi?'

He prised his back from the damp leather of the driver's seat. There was a moment's painful silence while Von Laer studied the hopelessness of Schumacher's face.

'Jacky and Bartsch will help you mount it.'

It took them ten sweating minutes to get the big camera on to the rear of the custom-built Mercedes. Bartsch's grumbling was a persistent drone.

'. . . not even a real bloody newsreel crew, so why the hell bother? Just because these two want to play cinema. And, besides . . .'

Jacky and Max tried to ignore him as they whirred the butterfly nuts tight on the tripod legs.

'. . . if it's anybody's bloody job, it's that drunken bastard's in the back seat. He's . . .'

They looked at each other. Enough was enough; Schumacher was their mate. Jacky stood up and prodded Bartsch's gut with a screwdriver, none too gently. Both men were huge, but Jacky was the younger by ten years.

'Something wrong, Egon? Sale on back at base? Morphia again? Real stuff this time?'

The big wrench stopped swinging in Bartsch's fist, but he wouldn't dare make trouble, Max knew. A month ago he'd been caught selling dud medical supplies to Galician refugees. Von Laer had threatened to have him shot. The screwdriver jabbed again, harder this time.

'You just keep your big mouth shut about Schumacher. In fact, just shut the fuck up altogether.'

For a second Bartsch seemed ready to take him on, but then the boom of the valley guns reached them again, and the tension vanished as they all listened. Once more Max speculated: eighty-eights? Silently, they twisted the last of the nuts into place and jumped down.

All of them watched Vinnie set up the shot, and, as always, Max was torn between envy and respect. The kid was beyond competence, the camera a part of him, an extension of his eyes. Maybe one day I'll find the nerve to ask how you learn, Max thought. I could have the head for it. Be the business, a job like that — something interesting, something to look forward to. Better than a ticket collector on the trams, or driving a bloody Berlin taxi.

Vinnie straightened up from the eyepiece, shaking his head. 'No use, not enough elevation.'

Von Laer turned and pointed. 'Side of the church, Max, would you?'

Max drove the fifty yards or so slowly, careful of the upright load on the vehicle's back. The big motor purred, and his spirits rose with the sound. Engines! He still loved the things, despite all the shit that went with them.

The church stood on the north side of the sloping square. It had once been an imposing white-walled Baroque building with a fine bell tower, but either the shelling or the Stukas had gutted it, and the fires had taken most of the roof. The wall that skirted the road wasn't much more than a jagged ruin, the windows long since gone. Max pulled up beside it and got out of the car. Immediately the head of dark curls bowed over the camera.

Again, Max watched. He saw the lens come down from the pall of smoke in the sky, make an arc across the charred ruins of the street, then begin its slow sweep of the church's rubble-topped wall. *If I ever get out of this*, he thought, *I'll* . . .

'Erich. Max.'

Vinnie's voice was low and urgent. The camera had stopped, the lens pointing through the first of the shattered windows.

They scrambled up on to the platform.

Gathered round the church's altar, perhaps thirty feet away, was a clutch of uniformed figures. In the centre of them, on the marble, was something pale. At first, Max didn't recognise it as a woman's body. She lay nearly motionless, the remains of her green dress hanging in rags, her face hidden by a matted curtain of black hair. Only one of the men was moving, and the motion was unmistakable.

Max stared. It came to him that he was watching the last throes of rape, but only the hands holding her wrists identified the act, for there was no struggle left in her, no resistance. His eyes took in the bloodstained thighs, the jerky rocking of her body as it was pushed back and forth. Even from so far away he could see that the thrusts were brutal. Her flesh seemed incredibly white against the grey marble of the altar, against the brown hands of the two Moroccan legionnaires and the black uniform of her assailant. She's dead, thought Max. She's dead, and they don't care. A wave of horror washed over him.

'The uniform.'

Max turned, surprised at the calmness of the voice, but Vinnie was still peering through the camera. Again Max looked into the church. The man had his back to them, but the uniform was recognisably German. There was another officer sitting only a few feet away, cap tilted back, Feldgrau tunic open, smoking a cigarette. The thrusting became faster, even more savage. A shoe fell from her foot. As it landed in the débris that surrounded the altar, it stirred a little cloud of dust that rose lazily through the shafts of light from the broken windows. All the faces inside the church were fixed on the woman's body. They don't know we're here, Max thought. Would it stop them?

Von Laer's whisper seemed unreal. 'The guns in the truck. Quietly.'

Max ran. By the time he and Jacky had returned to the church with their Schmeissers, Von Laer's Luger was in his hand. Jacky's kick took them quickly through the door, and the sudden clatter of their boots on the flagstones seemed unnaturally loud. The four men in the church stood motionless at the shock of their entry.

For a long instant they all watched each other. The rape was over, the victim lay still, one leg dangling obscenely over polished stone. But now they could hear the sounds she was making — low, fluttering moanings, halfway between sighs and sobs, eerie in the dusty silence. Slowly, her attacker began to turn. The profile was commanding, even noble, an aquiline nose over a jutting jaw. Then Max saw the death's-head insignia on the black lapels, the bars of rank at the shoulders, and he felt the machine-pistol tremble in his hands. It was only once the man stood fully facing him that he saw the eyepatch. The one good eye noted the weapons, the civilian clothes, but his face remained expressionless. Calmly, he began to button his tunic.

Von Laer's voice was curt. 'Your weapons.'

The Feldgrau officer's eyebrows rose at hearing German, and Max saw apprehension in his face, but none of the four men moved.

The shot from the Luger kicked up a spout of dust between the one-eyed man's boots. The gloved hands paused, then went on fastening the tunic. A cool one, thought Max.

'I want your weapons. *Now.*'

All of them looked towards the one-eyed man. He nodded slowly, then indicated the pistol that lay on the marble beside the sprawled woman. Max clambered over the altar rail and picked it up. He tried not to look at her, not to listen, but he could smell the musk of her body, and smell what had been done to her, even over the acrid odours of the church's destruction. While Jacky gathered the legionnaires' rifles, he checked the pistol's safety-catch and stuck it into his belt — and then, automatically, his eyes were drawn to her. Enough of the hair had fallen away to reveal her face. A Madonna, he thought, but then he saw the eyes. They gazed blankly upwards, past the jagged timbers of the roof, past the smoke-filled sky, beyond fear or pain. He looked down at the bloodstained body. Beneath all the grime she was beautiful, but suddenly he shuddered; there was an awful familiarity about the bloodied flesh on the marble slab. Quickly he picked his way through the débris to Von Laer's side. The Feldgrau officer came forward, unbuckling his holster. Indignation had replaced the fear in his bland face.

'This is outrageous! We are members of the Caudillo's personal staff! We . . .'

Both the speed and the power of Von Laer's blow were totally unexpected. The man gave a sharp cry as he fell to the floor. Max stared at him as he lay there, bent double in agony.

'I know exactly what you are. A disgrace to an honest uniform. You're no better than an animal.'

Crab-like, his eyes fixed on Von Laer's face, the man pushed himself away across the flagstones, one hand clutching his stomach.

Von Laer turned to the one-eyed man.

'There was a time in our country when the term "officer" was synonymous with "gentleman", but in your barracks I doubt if it does more than single out the better-paid scum from the rest. Regretfully I have neither the time nor the facilities to arrest you. The prospect of saving a military court's time by putting a bullet in each of your necks is tempting, but I find myself hampered by a concept called justice. I wouldn't expect a Gruppenführer of the S.S. to understand that, but it doesn't really matter.'

He paused. Max could see him fight to control his anger.

'So you may leave. Don't imagine, however, that this will be forgotten.'

He gestured upwards. Through the ruined window, Max saw Vinnie and the camera, still filming.

'We have evidence. I shall make it my personal business to have you brought to trial at the earliest opportunity. I want your names, then you may go. The woman stays.'

For the first time, the one-eyed man spoke. His voice was cultured, pleasant.

'Be my guest.'

Hessen, thought Max, feeling the panic rise in him — same accent as Bartsch. He watched the rage take over Von Laer's face. Was he going to shoot now? Would he kill . . .?

Max only just caught the glint of metal in time. He spun round, squeezing the trigger, and the kick of the weapon almost knocked it out of his hands. The first bullets found their target, and the rest of the burst raked the far wall, gouging splinters from the stone, decapitating a plaster saint. The echo was thunderous around the bare walls, and as it died away, Max stared stupidly at the legionnaire's body. There was no mistaking the finality of that misshapen huddle. The man was dead, the knife he had reached for still in his hand, a red stain spreading across the floor from the wounds in his chest. The S.S. man was the first to move. He went up to Von Laer.

'What *are* you?' he said, softly, 'S.D.? Propaganda? Abwehr?'

No one said anything. Dimly, Max was aware that the

woman's moaning had stopped. The one-eyed man picked up his cap and briskly wiped the dust from it.

'My name is Falkenheim. These are my people, but I am the only one who matters here.'

He made to pass, then paused and turned. The single eye carefully scanned first Max's face, then Jacky's, before coming to rest again on Von Laer.

'I shall remember you,' he said, quietly. '*All* of you.'

Still shaking, Max helped Jacky cover them all the way to the car on the other side of the church. As the big Hispano-Suiza revved away, Jacky gave him a cigarette and a troubled glance, for the insignia on the vehicle's side meant it was one of Franco's staff cars. They smoked, coughing on the red dust and the exhaust fumes, then walked back to the church in silence.

The first thing Max saw as they entered was Bartsch's medicine chest. Then he looked up towards the altar, and felt his heart sink. The woman's head hung limp in the crook of Von Laer's arm, and for the first time Max saw the jagged wound at her throat.

Bartsch's harsh voice came from behind them. 'Help me.'

He was pulling a long piece of blue cloth from the tangle of smashed pews. Max put down the Schmeisser and lifted a corner, glad of something physical to do. Finally the cloth came loose in their hands and the pile of wood collapsed on itself. They heard a thin scream of pain.

It took them a while to clear away the broken wood, and it was almost as long again before the child would let them lift her out. She cowered, whimpering, against the wall, cheek pressed hard against the plaster. Her right arm was bleeding. She was barefoot, but the brown cotton dress was almost clean, and Max could see a careful patchwork of darns across its collar. Her good arm clutched a long, thin leather bag to her chest. Vinnie brushed the black hair away from her face and wiped away her tears.

'Oh, God . . .'

They sat her down on one of the stools from the wrecked confessional, and Bartsch fetched dressings and began to clean the wounded arm. She gazed solemnly at their faces and bit her lip against the pain of the antiseptic, but there was no more crying now. Max listened to Vinnie's gentle murmur as he tried to soothe her, but somehow he knew she was beyond comforting, just as she was beyond tears. Nothing would persuade her to let go of the bag.

'Her child, you think?' Von Laer's voice was bitter with defeat, and Max saw the pain in his eyes.

Vinnie didn't look up. 'The same features. Unmistakable. It's her daughter.'

From behind them came the tearing of heavy fabric. They turned to see Jacky severing the blue altar cloth with one of the Moroccans' bayonets. One piece went over the bloody mess on the floor. Max saw a brown hand poking out from under the blue shroud, and the horror came back to him. Then he saw Jacky go up to the altar, gently lift the dangling leg on to the marble, and spread the other half of the cloth over her.

Later, Bartsch built his cooking fire in the lee of the church's south wall, and they left Max to tend it. Grimly he piled wood on the fire, peering into the flames, brooding, listening to the gunfire, the sounds of the graves being dug.

Just before midnight, a detachment of Italians marched through: Black Arrows, Fascist volunteers, wearily singing their 'Giovanezza' anthem. Behind them came the mule train, ammunition boxes packed two to a beast, then the radio truck. Through the crackle and whine of the static Max could hear the hectoring voice of Quiepo de Llano, the one they called the radio general, working himself into a fine rage.

Last in the column was a fat officer on a mare, ridiculous in jodhpurs and tasselled cap. Jacky gave him their papers. He inspected them, pretending to understand German, then saluted and left, legs flapping ineffectually against the animal's flanks as he tried to control it.

'What is it about a uniform that can make a man either a fool or a hero?'

Max looked at Jacky, surprised at such force.

'The same thing that can make him a beast.'

The unexpected voice was toneless. They turned to see Vinnie, holding the child's hand. Her eyes seemed huge in the reflected firelight.

'Fine lines, when you think about it. Between fool and hero and barbarian.'

Again the strains of Quiepo de Llano's voice reached them from the Italian truck, berating godless Communism and the international conspiracy of Jews. Max looked at the dark shadows of Vinnie's face and felt a sudden flush of anger. What are you, he thought, what are you *first*? A Jew? Or a homosexual? Or just a cold fish? You're even younger than I am, yet you have no anger. How could you stand there and film that filth today? *How could you do that*? He heard irregular footsteps. Schumacher stumbled into the ring of firelight.

'No accordion tonight, Max? Where's the accordion?'

He reeked of gin. Suddenly Max found the plaintive edge to his deep voice almost unbearable. He spun round, and saw the child carefully examining the haggard lines of Schumacher's grey, unshaven face. He fought back the tears.

'No accordion tonight,' he said, as evenly as he could.

Schumacher frowned. His voice slurred the next question. '. . . the hell are we?'

'Durango. Half-way back, Heinz.'

For a second the glazed eyes were confused, then they went back to their pain, and his shoulders slumped as he looked into the flames. A canvas bag landed at Max's side. Bartsch's voice was heavy with satisfaction.

'Meat. Fresh. Swapped it for gin with the Italians.' He nodded at Schumacher's dejected figure. 'He'll never miss it. Drunken bum.'

Suddenly Jacky's hands were on Bartsch's lapels, pulling, lifting.

Von Laer's voice came like a whiplash from the church door. 'None of that!' He came towards the flames. 'There's been enough blood here today.'

The child's eyes wandered round the ring of faces at the fire's edge. How old are you, Max wondered. Nine? Ten? Do you know the difference: between bad men and callous men, between sick men and hurt men? The smell from the bag reached him. Again his eyes saw the white body on the grey marble, the brown hand under the blue cloth.

A master butcher.

In the dim light he could just make out the shape of the dog, waiting as patiently as ever below the hanging corpse.

Meat, he thought.

Chapter 1
SECRETS

THE WIND GUSTED hard down the Freie Strasse, whipping the leaves into flat tornadoes that assaulted the ornate shop doorways. A sodden magazine page wrapped itself round the hot chestnut vendor's leg. He picked it up, examined it, then grinned as he held it up to me.

'*Bellissima!* Eh?'

The caption read 'The Look of the Nineties'. The damp of the gutters had wiped the gloss from the paper, but it was helpless against the sultry disdain of the model's face. He smacked his lips theatrically against it, then screwed it up and tossed it at me before going back to packing up his stall. I laughed as I snapped the locks of the fiddle case shut, shivering at the same time. The last shoppers went past me quickly, collars up, shoulders hunched, tightly buttoned and scarved against the chill. It was going to be the coldest night yet.

My left arm ached and my fingers were numb, but the weight of the hatful of money was pleasant, reassuring. I sat down on the bench and counted. Francs, Rappen, the occasional Deutschmark from the ones who worked in Basel but lived over the border; you could still spend them in Switzerland, you just paid a bit more. In Switzerland they knew all there was to know about making you pay a bit more, but I didn't mind. Nobody stopped me busking as long as I didn't break the rules laid down by the city fathers with their usual pompous benevolence, and there was enough in the hat most days to pay for the room, a hot meal and a few beers. I didn't want to think beyond that. I was nearer contentment than I'd been for a long time.

But it was getting really cold now; a swirl of leaves clung to my sleeve as I counted, and again I shivered.

Perhaps I wouldn't have noticed her so soon if it hadn't been for the perfume. It was rich and heavy and there was too much of it. I turned. Leather coat with a fur collar, high-heeled suede boots and an elaborately waved hairstyle that would have looked right on a thirty-five-year-old. The face wasn't quite the face of the nineties, but it wasn't for lack of trying; it was painstakingly made up, modishly divided into the flat planes of colour that the season had dictated. Despite myself, I felt uneasy; a girl on a page was one thing . . .

But calm came over me as I looked at her eyes, for beneath all the sophistication they were a waif's, not a woman's, and I remembered she was barely sixteen. Her expression told me nothing, but the pale hands showed her nerves. They fiddled with an expensive pair of black gloves, scarlet nails crimping the thin material.

'Helga wants you to come,' she said. 'It's Max . . .'

I waited for her to say more, because she obviously wanted to, but whatever it was died in her throat. I poured the money into the torn pocket of my jacket, suddenly conscious of how shabby it was against the perfection of her clothes. Each of us looked away from the other, but I saw the hot chestnut man's eyes glitter with appreciation as he dismantled his brazier. He gave us a low '*Va bene*' as we passed him. She gave him a bright, hard, professional smile in return. We walked off into the darkness.

Like the perfume, the smile was too old for her. I wondered how far it was on its way to becoming the oldest smile in the world. Was she actually practising her mother's trade, or merely grooming herself for it . . .?

Apart from the wind, the click of her heels was the only sound in the empty street.

'Alex.'

'Hello, Max.'

The sinews of his neck stood out as he tried to raise an arm in welcome, but before I was halfway across the room the gesture had died. His brow was heavy with sweat and the shirt collar hung from him as though it had been made for another man. I tried to hide my shock, for since I'd last been here the disease had wasted him dramatically, hollowing the face's flesh, hanging what was left of it like shrouds from the cheekbones. Only his eyes, deep in their dark sockets, retained their old vitality. There was a burst of loud music from downstairs, punctuated by the slamming of a heavy door. In the attic room there was silence.

'I do not have long, Alex.'

I didn't reply. His dignity deserved a better response than the conventions of grief or sorrow. There would be a proper time and place for sadness, but I knew it wasn't here or now, in this cramped room that was his home. I looked round it, trying to gather the strength I needed to be with him, the calmness, trying to hide how much the prospect of his death scared me, for before I met Max I'd been alone, and I knew I'd be alone again once he was gone.

There was nothing to connect the attic with the luxury of the brothel below. It was functional, spartan in its simplicity, but Helga said he was adamant that he had everything he needed. Books, the radio, a few sticks of furniture, a clean bed.

The accordion in its battered green leather case . . .

Until the disease had struck, it had been his sole source of income, for Max had lived his life on the street, a busker, content to offer his music to the passers-by and live from day to day on what landed in his tin cup. He had taught me how to survive.

He pointed at the bottle on the dresser and I poured out two glasses of the clear Schnapps. It was a raw, powerful drink that had become part of our evenings here, and I understood that he wanted me to treat this night as though it was no different from any other. The hand shook as it raised the glass, but he drank steadily enough. His voice was stronger now, the Berlin accent cutting through the vowels. It held no trace of self-pity.

'There is something I need you to do for me, if you are willing. But first there are things to explain,' he said. 'I must tell you that the story is not without violence.'

I swirled the Schnapps round the glass and carefully didn't look at him. Violence . . . Suddenly there was a desire in me to be gone from here, and I knew I had to conquer it. When I looked up I found Max's eyes upon me — and I knew that he knew it as well. His grizzled head nodded gently, taking my silence as acquiescence.

'Spain,' he said. 'The civil war, the Condor Legion. You know what that was?'

I nodded in my turn. It was the name of the air force Hitler had sent to fight along with Franco's nationalists. Max turned away and coughed long and painfully into a white handkerchief. Once the fit was over the face was even more gaunt, and I saw dark flecks of blood on the ancient suit's lapel. His trembling hand went to his pocket, and he put a photograph carefully down on the table between us. Its corrugated edges were limp and broken, the sepia tones faded. Five men, in German wartime uniform, grouped round a small statue of a knight on horseback. One man, an officer, was holding the hand of the little girl who'd been placed in the rider's lap. Everyone in the picture was smiling. Max pointed to the shadow that lay across the cobbles in the foreground.

'I took it,' he said, hoarsely.

One by one, the shaking finger counted them off.

'Bartsch. Orderly, not a bad bloke, just greedy — you know the type, always looking for the deal, the angle.

Jacky. He drove, like me. Wanted to be an engineer like me as well. Schumacher, took the stills. The three of us did everything together — drink, women, good times. Vinnie . . . He worked the movie camera. Just a kid, the youngest. A Jew. Not like the rest of us at all.' The finger stabbed decisively. 'Von Laer. The Colonel, C.O. Him and Vinnie . . . What's the English word? "*Queer*"?' He tried to laugh, but again the pain caught him, and again it became a horrible, gurgling cough. 'Ah . . . A good word for them.'

With agonising slowness the finger came to rest on the figure of the child.

'Maria.'

He slumped back in the chair, exhausted, a bloody bubble of spit at the side of his mouth. I watched him trying to gather concentration and wished I could give him strength.

'Rest awhile, Max.'

I leaned over and made to wipe away the blood but he stopped me, shaking his head.

'There's no time. They say I could go without warning, and that's a mercy, but I wasted too long deciding.'

He was weakening steadily now. The voice was a whisper, nearly drowned in the rasping of his breath, but his eyes gleamed with new urgency.

'Maria! And me . . . Listen!'

The shaking hand grabbed my wrist like a vice.

'I killed!'

His eyes bored into mine, defying me to look away, to hide.

'You learn! To live with it . . . Twice, I killed.'

I couldn't hide my panic. I would have given anything just to run, but I was held by the sheer force of his willpower. His eyes softened, but the iron grip lasted until he was sure of me. Shaking, I sat down and stared at him, a small, emaciated copy of the man I had known, dapper in the suit he would be buried in.

And then he told me the story.

Some people like to think Switzerland's a compromise between three cultures, but that's a lie — it's just the place where they confront each other. Basel's a German town in all but name, full of good German burghers who are perpetually annoyed at being Swiss. They tolerate the French and drink toasts to the fact that the Italians are far enough down the road to be safely ignored. The pedestrians along the Rheinufer all seemed to be wishing the river God-speed to the Fatherland — or perhaps Loden cloaks just keep the cold out better, for it's already a big river at Basel and a big river's wind comes off it. It cut me like a knife as we walked. We had buried Max an hour before.

'He was blackmailed, that's as much as I can tell you. Most of them were. He killed somebody in a fight in Berlin and they gave him the choice — army or jail. As far as I know it was the same for the others. He didn't like to talk about it.' She turned to me. 'Will you do it?'

She was big, statuesque, sexier in her fifties than most women are in their twenties. The question had been asked in one form or another at least five times now, and I still didn't know what to say. I looked at her. The mourning was perfect, the make-up immaculate. Any tears Helga shed would be in private. To the world she showed a facade as cold as the river beside us; a man might use her as long as the deal was mutually profitable, but her thoughts on the matter were her own. Yet I knew she had loved him. Max had brought us together in the hope that we might be friends, but the most we ever achieved was a recognition that both of us cared for him. She stopped abruptly and looked out across the water. I realised I still couldn't think of him as dead.

'He talked to me, Alex. Told me you'd been in trouble.'

I shifted uneasily.

'Don't worry. I don't know any of the details and I don't want to. You were a good man, he said. He used to talk a lot about good and evil, you know. Strange, really;

he wasn't religious.' She fixed me with a very intense look. 'He said that you needed to learn life over again. That you'd been badly hurt and you needed to learn to respond to things other than pain. He was a wise old man, and both of us know he was right. If you don't start soon, it'll be too late.'

She opened her bag, took out a cigarette and lit it with a swift, practised movement. The smoke blew itself out slowly.

'Let me be honest, Alex. I am hurt and angry that he did not come to me with this thing. I have money, I am thorough. I would have found this woman, if, as he believed, she is still alive. My business could have survived without me long enough for it to be taken care of. A Swiss whorehouse is no different from a Swiss cuckoo clock in the end — in, out and take the money.'

Neither of us smiled at the joke, but it showed me that she was nervous as well as determined. Spray splashed against the dressed stone of the embankment. How could I explain to her that I felt secure here? I watched her impatience give way to something stronger.

'I have to know if you are prepared to do it,' she said, brusquely. 'Now.'

'Helga,' I began, 'I don't even know if . . .'

She cut me off impatiently, throwing away the half-smoked cigarette. Her shoe ground it into the cobblestones as she took my arm and pulled me round to face our reflections in the shop window.

'*Look at yourself!*'

The sight of the figure I cut made me bow my head.

'You know what I see there, Alex? I see a tall man, fit and good-looking, a man who should be thinking about a future. Instead of that, he's given up on the present. He wants the world to believe he's worth nothing, that he can't do anything! You've a handsome enough face, Alex, but it's a loser's face, the face of a man who's stopped making decisions. Max was a busker because he wanted to be one. *You're a busker because you haven't the guts to be anything else!'*

She took a step back from me, embarrassed by her own anger.

'Don't you see he wanted you to do this for yourself as well as for him? If things had been different, he'd have liked children.' Her shoulders moved, eloquently. 'Too late for that, with us, and anyway, I have enough worries with Annette. But he looked after you like a son, Alex. When you first came here you couldn't have survived without him.'

The unspoken accusation hung in the cold air between us. I had no doubt she was right. I'd been unstable at first, paranoid. Drink would have inflamed bitterness, frustration would have fuelled anger to the point of no return — and I knew in my heart what the end of it would have been.

Violence, the Scot's answer to a world he couldn't understand and wouldn't accept.

A gentle old man had saved me from all that, had taught me that my talent could buy me back my life a day at a time. Now he was teaching me again. She was right, I had to do it. Even if it was nothing more than an old man's fantasy, I had to do it. But where to start? Even if the child Maria had survived, how was I to go about tracing the woman she had become? *Find her*, he'd said. *Find her and give her what's in the box.* But *how*?

Helga stared out across the brown, rain-swollen river, lost in memories, and once again I marvelled at the complexities people managed to deal with in their daily lives. Max had told me they'd been together for twenty years. A whore and a busker; they'd made it work. I put my arm round her shoulder and wondered what I'd do if such an unlikely chance of happiness came my way. She looked at me quizzically, a wan smile replacing her anger.

'It's already November, Alex. The weather's changing. Soon it'll be too cold to busk, anyway. Max never used to . . .'

She stopped. She was used to reading the look on a man's face.

'It's all right, Helga,' I said. 'I'll go.'

Later that night I sat alone in my cheap room in the suburb of Riehen, trying to make sense of it all. I could have gone back with Helga — she'd even hinted that her daughter would be pleased to see me — but I wanted to be alone. The contents of the old man's safe-deposit box lay spread out on the table in front of me, fragments of a secret life kept hidden for fifty years, the only witnesses to my quiet wake.

The documents were puzzling. I could read normal German script, but these were in the old Gothic print of the Third Reich, and they defeated me. All the papers bore two names, 'Erich Adalbert Von Laer' and 'Maria Von Laer', and on one I could make out the words 'Neustift' and 'Tirol'. Adoption papers? Bills of sale? Land deeds? I could only guess. They were all duly signed, witnessed, stamped and sealed with the full forbidding officialdom of Hitler's Germany. I knew I'd need help with them.

The first of the photographs was a studio portrait. The girl herself, aged perhaps eight or nine; a grave face, long and angular, with huge eyes. The kind of kid who would be unremarkable, until the day when adolescence replaced childhood and everyone saw the beauty. The background was a Chinese-patterned screen, the dress the ubiquitous sailor suit of the twenties and thirties, and she was holding a flower. The stencilled address on the back said the studio was in Schwerin. Schumacher, I thought, Max said Schumacher had come from Schwerin.

Then there was what was obviously a photograph of a painting. A woman in seventeenth-century dress, a sash across her full skirt. There was a heraldic device on the sash, almost hidden by a slender hand. She had a demure, almost saintly quality about her — until you came to her eyes. Even in the brownish tones of the old photograph they looked full of fire, and I wondered what colour they were and who she was. Again, the print was of professional quality, but this time there was no clue as to its history. I wondered if it was also the work of the photographer who'd done everything with Max and Jacky.

I picked up the third photo, the one Max had shown me himself. There was a caption in faded pencil letters on the back: '*In front of Vinnie's parents' house, 16/5/39.*'

The last thing I had wasn't from the box. It was a letter, written on the expensive stationery of an Interlaken hotel. Helga said it had come about ten days ago. She'd phoned the hotel, but they had neither a forwarding address nor a home one that corresponded to the name here. Once again I read it.

Dear Max,

To find you alive again after all these years was a shock, to hear of your problems naturally a sorrow, but I envy you the composure with which you seem able to face them. With my heart in its present condition, I must face the fact that my own time is not so far away. I wonder how I shall react.

As to the other matter, I know you want to do whatever is necessary yourself, but I repeat my offer. My help is there if you want it, and the situation may not be as simple as you think. Also, I want you to realise that you have absolutely no reason to blame yourself. At all. The same thing could have happened to any of the others. If there is to be blame (and what's the use of it after so many years?) then save it for the madmen who put us all in fear of our lives for so long.

The more I think about the situation, however, the more it confuses me. Why the circumstances have remained unchanged for so long is as much a mystery to me as to you, and I can only imagine that the solution lies deep in Burg Laer itself, but I don't really know. Memories have kept me from returning there.

I shall be home again soon if you decide you need me. I'm cutting this trip short because the weather has closed in so much. Don't refuse my offer out of stubbornness, old friend. It would give me pleasure to see a measure of justice done — if indeed justice is needed — and to help you ease your mind. Stay in touch.

It was signed 'Vincent Stein'. I turned it over again in my hands. Vincent. *Vinnie?* It had to be. But where was he and what could he tell me? I rubbed my eyes. The need for sleep was taking concentration from me, for I'd been awake over twenty-four hours now. Was it possible that Vinnie was still alive? What were the chances? What percentage of combatants had survived the war? Outside, the street was ominously silent. Even the Strassenbahn had stopped running. It was very late.

I made one last attempt at dragging my thoughts together. There were really only two pointers to act upon, and neither of them looked promising after half a century. A photograph studio in Schwerin had been the backdrop for a portrait, and a castle in Westphalia had been cited by the writer of a letter. Schwerin would be the more difficult, for it was in the East now, and I didn't know how long it would take to get there, or how to go about organising it. I stretched my legs under the rickety table.

Burg Laer. Castle Laer. The name was the only thing in the letter which positively connected it to this whole business. Max had told me that Von Laer's family had an estate near Münster. I put the documents together in a neat pile in the centre of the table, handling them carefully, perhaps because they were the physical evidence of what I had to do, a tangible proof that my life was again changing. I looked one last time at the faded brown snapshot and the girl's picture — and suddenly the silence around me lost its menace. It became a calm, born of the knowledge that I had decided to do something. Yes, I thought. Münster.

I would begin there.

Chapter 2
EYES

THE WIDE STAIRCASE swept upwards in an elegant curve. I followed the butler, the leather soles of my new shoes slipping on the marble steps. It was darker here than in the other part of the house, but there were no tourists clogging the stairs, no good German citizens hungry for the heirlooms of their betters. The only eyes that watched our silent progress belonged to the portraits. Generations of Von Laers looked down on me in mute disapproval, guarding their dignity from the safety of the shadows, secure in their gilded frames as they had once been in their gilded lives. *Ancestral gloom* . . . The phrase fixed itself in my mind.

With an absolute minimum of deference the butler opened the double doors, his gaze avoiding mine, his shaved head slightly bowed. He was certain I had no business here, but dumb insolence was as far as he would go until orders confirmed the fact. He didn't bother hiding his contempt; for the moment my presence would be tolerated — but should it become necessary, throwing me out would be a positive pleasure. His shoulders were broad, his voice hardly more than a growl. The accent was thick, foreign.

'Herr Fraser, *gnädige Frau.*'

She was seated by the fireplace. The high-backed leather armchair had been carefully placed to catch the bay window's light at an angle which would flatter her profile, and I was given ample time to study the effect, for she didn't move a muscle at the announcement. It was a fine enough profile for the artifice to be forgiven, I thought — until I realised the pose wasn't just vanity. Only when she could put off the moment no longer did she turn and face me.

I couldn't ignore the hideously skewed eye. No one could have. It searched a far corner of the ceiling while its twin surveyed me. I waited — for what, I didn't know, a greeting, a summons — but all that came was a shuffling noise from behind the chair. Four more eyes added themselves to the aristocratic appraisal, and I felt my mouth go dry. For a long moment the two Dobermanns stood like tense statues — and then, unafraid or unimpressed, they resumed their graceful stillness by the fire. They placed themselves artfully, in keeping with the room's elegance, like the paintings or the porcelain.

I tried not to look at them, for they were the only thing that could have made the ordeal worse. When I was seven I'd been bitten, badly, and the fear of large dogs had never left me. I forced myself to cross the huge expanse of polished floor, already uncomfortable in the suit Helga had bought me, the new briefcase awkward in the hand that for so long had carried nothing other than a fiddle. A well-manicured wave pointed me at the chair's twin. The gesture ruled out any formal greeting — one did not shake hands with the lower classes until the cleanliness of their pedigree was established. She was incredibly old.

'So, Herr Fraser. You wish to see me about' — she consulted a card on the table beside her — 'a matter concerning my late brother.'

I took a deep breath. How did one address a baroness? I found my voice.

'Yes,' I said.

Max's story took half an hour, its telling interrupted only by my occasional wary glances at the dogs. From time to time she shifted slightly in her chair, adjusting the pose without relinquishing it, keeping the awful eye from me as much as possible.

'. . . and so,' I finished lamely, 'I wondered if you could shed any light on the matter.'

In reply, she lifted a poker from the grate. Instead of a point, its end had been hammered into a stylised claw, three-taloned, Gothic. It looked skeletal, a blackened extension of her own bony hand. She thrust out for the fire's top log with it, but without enough strength to bite iron into wood. Instinct almost made me reach out to help, but I checked it; the frown told me it wouldn't be appreciated. Her next attempt took twice the effort, but it succeeded, and once the log had settled into the fire's heart she gazed at the flames for a long time. I watched, wondering what she was deliberating. Only once the last of the sparks had settled did her reverie break. Her hand abandoned the poker, its claw still in the fire, and found the bell-pull. The Dobermanns rose expectantly, tongues hanging, shaking themselves.

'*Sit*, Ritter! *Sit*, Prinz!'

Immediately they obeyed the authority in the voice and assumed their positions on the rug — and then the bigger one's head whipped round. The dark eyes fastened dangerously on me, as though it was all my fault. Nervously I moved in my chair; the other one turned and looked at me as well. The doors opened. The young dogs went to the butler immediately, silently, without command. The leashes locked with a metallic snap that seemed unnaturally loud.

'Half an hour. Make them work,' she said curtly.

He gave a brisk bow, and again I felt the disapproval as his eyes refused to see me. I heard the door shut behind me and tried not to show my relief.

'An interesting story, Herr Fraser.'

The voice was well-modulated now, even melodious. It was hard to believe that it came from the same person who had spoken to the dogs or the servant. It contained no hint of either belief or incredulity.

'If I might see the papers?' she said.

I gave her the photocopies, the pictures first, then the documents. She lingered a long while over the photograph of the child, then began to read, quickly. She had none of my difficulties with the script. I thought about the deeds as they passed through her hands, for Helga's lawyers had cautiously pronounced them genuine — and they'd also told me that the ensuing legal complications could be made to last for years. She read with the crazy eye closed, a monocle in the other. After a few moments she looked up, but she didn't speak.

'There is an indication that one of the others may be alive,' I said, to break her silence, 'but we . . .'

'It is my brother's signature.'

She nodded slowly, deliberately.

'Yes, it is Erich's signature.'

She let the monocle fall. It dangled on its golden chain, and once more her good eye found the fire. The poker's claw was red with heat, now. She lifted it from the flames and watched the glow die before speaking again.

'All of this is naturally a complete shock to me. Of course, if it is true and these documents are what they claim to be, the Austrian land belongs to the child.'

'Who owns it now?' I asked.

For a second she hesitated.

'The land in question was a separate bequest which was made specifically upon my brother by our uncle. When Erich died, it came to me.'

She gathered all the papers firmly in her lap, making no move to give me them back.

'It will all have to be verified, of course.'

The tone of voice left me in no doubt that I was going to be verified as well. I'd been expecting it, but I still felt my confidence begin to crumble. I musn't let it show, I thought, although I could already feel the red flush mounting in my face. Furiously I tried to concentrate on what she was saying.

'. . . of them. About the painting I have no idea at all. I would be delighted to help if I could, but as to what became of the child after he died, I cannot tell you. I have no idea whether she is still alive.'

'Herr Bauer was sure she was.'

I couldn't call him Max in front of this woman. There was silence. She rose, slowly. With the help of a silver-topped cane she began to move towards the window.

'Your brother. When did he die?'

The question seemed to take her by surprise. She spun round to face me, too fast. I saw the cane quiver, the bony knuckles tighten on the handle — and I just managed to reach her before she overbalanced. The stick clattered to the floor, and she fell against me. The tiny body was all but weightless. I heard a sharp intake of breath, like the prelude to a child's tears, and as I righted her I had an absurd, fleeting notion; I wasn't catching an old lady, I was teaching a two-year-old to walk.

'Are you all right?'

Her only answer was to take a pace back, out of my reach. She steadied herself against the chair's arm, avoiding my eyes. An embarrassed hand went to the heart-shaped diamond brooch at her throat, then fussed with the hem of her jacket, pulling at the tweed. I picked up the cane and held it out to her. For a second she stared at it, and then, slowly, the head came up. For the first time since I'd come into the room she forgot her deformity.

'You are very kind,' she said.

Now the voice was quiet, wistful. I found myself staring into the crazy eye. Had she spoken, or had it? Quickly she took the cane from me and turned away again.

'Excuse me, I was worried . . .'

'Very kind. Thank you.'

The repeat of the phrase was a rebuke. To herself or to me? Kindness . . . I watched her resume her progress towards the window, and wondered. She'd spoken as though it was a breach of some complex protocol. How much kindness, if any, she had known in her life?

'In answer to your question, Herr Fraser, the year of my elder brother's death was nineteen thirty-nine. He was one of the first.'

Again the voice changed, and I recognised the edge it had taken on. But which emotion was being suppressed? Bitterness? At the cruelty of old age, the indignity of stumbling into a total stranger's arms? For a few moments I was sure that was it — and then my eye caught the coat of arms on the far wall, and I thought again. A white unicorn, its horn almost piercing the breast of a black eagle . . . They were an ancient family. Most of the German aristocracy had despised Hitler as an upstart, followed him only in the hope of restoring their own former glories. The Baroness Von Laer had obviously loved her brother; how futile it must seem to her now, to have lost him to such a cause.

I joined her. Across the lake I could see the lithe black bodies of the dogs. They sprinted along the water's edge towards a wooden scarecrow, then set savagely about its padded limbs until the thin call of the butler's whistle brought them back to him. From time to time he glanced up at the window. Unseeing, she continued to look out, and again my eyes found the unicorn. The angle of its horn was exactly that of the hidden eye. An ancient family . . . With ancient values? Even at the beginning of this century, would such an eye have been deemed evil? Witch to the village, shame to the hall . . . Was that how it had been? And what had she been to herself? I wondered what it must have been like, to spend an entire life hiding one side of your face. She pointed to a small fountain, far away from us in the grounds. Through the trees I could see two baroque cherubs offering Cupid his bow and the long-broken ends of a handful of arrows.

'They played there. Him and the boy from Groningen, the Jewish boy. With the girl. They played there and I watched them from here. They splashed each other with water.'

The emotion in her voice was undisguised now.

'It was the summer before Poland. My brother and I were very close, Herr Fraser. That day was the last time I saw him, or indeed any of them. War changes everything.'

On the way out I paused at the last gilt frame: a teenage girl, slender, a heart-shaped cluster of diamonds fastening her blouse collar. The portrait was unfinished, a drab patch of darkness at its bottom right-hand corner, but whoever had painted it had caught the noble profile well, and the eye was safely hidden. It was hard, though, to connect such youthful bloom with the small figure I had left staring out of the window upstairs. I had sensed childhood in her, and old age, but little in between. I was glad the portrait told me I was wrong.

My scrutiny ended with the opening of the huge wooden door. The butler and the sweat-lathered dogs stood silhouetted in the harsh light. Pointedly, he opened the door wider. As I passed him I heard the rattle of a chain and a low growl. My grip tightened on the briefcase handle. Quickly I went down the flight of steps and joined the throng of Sunday tourists in the sunlit courtyard.

Like the dogs, none of them mistook me for an aristocrat.

'*Groningen?* In *Holland*?' The surprise in Helga's voice quickly became urgency. 'You have something?'

Explaining made it all sound so flimsy. The decision to follow the only lead I'd been given in Burg Laer had seemed logical at the time, but now the improbability of it was hitting me hard — and yet the old woman had talked of a Jewish boy from Groningen. Could it have been Vinnie? She'd talked of them playing together, him and her brother and the child, and Max had said that Vinnie was the youngest of them, as well as the closest to Von Laer. When I finished, there was silence at the other end, and as I waited for her to speak I realised I was surprised as well — with myself. I'd made a decision. Alone. Suddenly the doubts crowded in on me; it was hard to accept.

'Is it worth a try?' I asked.

'Why not? It's a long shot, but who knows? And we have nothing else. You sound tired, Alex. How long is it since you rested?'

An idea came to me. 'Helga, how good are your contacts in Interlaken? Can you find out if any of the people who stayed in the hotel that night were Dutch, or gave a Dutch address?'

She assured me she could, and we agreed I'd telephone again later. Suddenly her voice became softer.

'Alex, get some sleep, O.K.? Book into a hotel, a good one. Money's no object.'

The line went dead. I picked up the fiddle case and stepped out of the phone-box.

A *hotel* . . .

The thought of such a thing weighted my tiredness with fear and sank it in confusion. Suddenly it was all too complicated — people like me didn't stay in hotels! I peered round at the unfamiliar buildings. The statue in the photograph, the knight on horseback . . . Was it here? Last night I'd been certain, but surely it was all ridiculous. I should have stayed in Basel, never have got mixed up in this! A hotel . . . The wind caught at my collar as I fought back the panic. More strangers. More disapproval? Could I face that? I was ready to run from the decision — until I remembered I'd already made a bigger one. On my own, about something much more serious than a hotel. I leaned back against the phone-box. The decision to come here might have been wrong, but it hadn't been negligible, for I'd heard more than just concern in Helga's voice.

I'd heard respect as well, I was sure of it.

It was an odd realisation. My fears tried to negate it, to scoff it away, but I knew it was true. Drops of rain splashed at my feet. I stared at them as though they were evidence of a miracle.

I made for the town centre, slowly, glad of the relief from my panic, but still suspicious, still fearful that something or someone might rob me of it. Instinctively I avoided the main roads. It was nearly noon. In the side streets, pedestrians negotiated the puddles and each other, cursing the sudden rain, missing their footing on the wet cobbles. Cyclists dodged round them, avoiding the spokes of flowering umbrellas, their warning bells a harsh chorus to the throaty conversations. The shower became heavier, turned strolls into purposeful strides and, as always, being in the middle of such normality began to soothe me. The blankness of the passing faces was reassurance, therapy; I could never be *of* the crowd, I knew, but I could be in it. I walked on, taking refuge in being unremarkable, ignored. Within a few hundred yards I was back on an even keel, convinced once more of my anonymity. Clarity came with calm; Helga was right, I was tired.

But I was loath to give up such hard-won peace of mind. I walked on, beginning to enjoy the town, particularly the buildings. It seemed to me that a good bargain had been struck in Groningen, a realistic compromise between young and old. The place had preserved as much of its antiquity as any of Holland's better-known towns, but in a much less ostentatious way. The sixteenth-century houses that lined the street were well looked after, but they hadn't been neutered for the tourist cameras; they were alive, working. The sheen of renovation that began at the top of each gable only came so far down before prettiness gave way to utility — the bottom storeys were still warehouses, or florists, or Indonesian snack bars. I paused halfway over a canal bridge and looked along the bank. Here the bargain was a different one, between trade and domesticity. It was scruffier — débris in the water and dogshit on the quayside, barges full of coal, houseboats festooned with TV aerials. There was nothing orderly about it, nothing planned, but the down-at-heel air wasn't depressing. It was matter-of-fact, reassuring. Groningen still worked for its living; this was a town where heritage earned its keep. I crossed a busy road and found myself in the pedestrian precinct that was the town's centre.

The spirit of compromise hadn't worked as well here. There was something of the armed camp about it, a sense of uneasy truce waiting to end. Instead of dovetailing, old and new had staked their claims, ready to face each other out, ready for some final struggle for the town's heart. This was Groningen's commercial high ground; possession of it meant money, and money, as always, meant tension.

It was a confrontation that was mirrored in the faces as well as the buildings, and it had made its strongest camp outside the inevitable McDonald's. A gaggle of bored teenagers sat tribally on damp plastic seats, in silent judgment of the passing world. The only time animation touched the blank solidarity of their faces was when someone older came too near. The infringement would touch off a barely discernible exchange of secret grins, casual and contemptuous. The two middle-aged managers never saw it as the strolled past them. Cigars in hand, paunches cunningly disguised in dark pinstripe, they stared at the youngsters with as much contempt as they could spare — but the corporate lunch hour was nearly over, and they returned quickly to more executive pleasures, sneaking sly glances at the lingerie in the department-store windows, mentally fitting it over the hips of the young mothers as they passed with their prams. The women deftly steered their charges between the concrete flower-pots, pretending not to notice, coyly measuring them against the reality of their husbands.

I watched it all, trying to get a feel for this place that might hold the key to my search, but the more I walked, the more a single type began to personify the town for me. The lumpy housewives marched past, red-knuckled and string-bagged with the week's vegetables, stoic in their progress towards the bus stop. They were incongruous against the gaudy fronts of the supermarkets and the chain stores, but the freshly-painted wooden facades of the older shops made them seem timeless. I knew they'd long since learned to use the world of special offers and plastic signs, but there was a blunt peasant strength to them, a doggedness about their gait as they pushed through the throng. It spoke of something more durable than the twentieth century. I caught a silhouette in front of a neon-lit window; it was bowed with burden and slow in passage, but somehow I knew it would outlast its backdrop. I watched the figure until the town hall clock's chime cut short the train of thought. I heard music up ahead as I walked.

There were three of them, two boys and a girl, two guitars and a metal flute. She stood, they sat on camping stools. The music was German. I didn't know the piece, but they played it well enough, with that grave concentration and mannered style which only formal music schooling can impart. The two guitar cases held a sprinkling of coins, and someone had stuck a flower into the lattice of their music stand. Only the girl noticed me.

I hesitated before reaching for the wallet, but only for a second; Helga wouldn't mind. I put a ten-guilder note into one of the cases, and the girl nodded her thanks without breaking the melody. The desire to tell them I was a busker too surfaced briefly, only to drown in its own absurdity. I made to walk away — then stopped. Perhaps they could help. When the piece ended, I pulled the copy of Max's snapshot from my inside pocket. The crowds strolled around us, uninterested.

'Any of you know where this statue is?'

One by one they examined it, acknowledged the subject matter with puzzled frowns, then shook their heads. Only the girl's curiosity was stronger than her distaste at being shown a picture of a bunch of Nazis. She classified me immediately and returned my halting Dutch with perfect English.

'Important, is it?'

Her eyes quickly priced my clothes. I pulled another ten from the wallet and heard the two boys share a laugh as they started to put away their guitars.

'I'm trying to find out what happened to the child.'

Her expression softened. She was a maternal type, chubbily attractive, about eighteen. The money disappeared into the top pocket of her dungarees before she repeated the negative shake of the head.

'Sorry. But you could try my sister at the library, she knows a lot about the town. Ask for Elly. She'll be there after four.'

They dismantled their music stand and left, the boys teasing her about the ease with which she'd got twenty guilders out of a man. Watching them go, I felt lost, I didn't know why. I set the fiddle case down so that I could put the picture away again — and almost immediately a jovial-looking passer-by put a coin on top of it. At first I didn't understand, and then I shouted after him that it wasn't me who'd been playing, but he'd already gone. At the sight of the coin, Helga's words came back. *Money's no object* . . . My unease returned — and suddenly I knew the exact cause of it. I had *carte blanche* to spend a walletful of someone else's cash, but I'd rather have been like these three kids, earning my own, no matter how little. The coin lay on the case like a challenge. Why not . . .? Friday afternoon, always a good time . . . The fatigue dropped away from me with the decision; I'd busk — long enough to make up the twenty guilders I'd given away, at least. There was no more I could do for Max, not for the next few hours. Yes, I'd busk, but not here . . . This was wrong.

Now my walking took on a purpose, became a search. Busking's like any other trade, it has its do's and don'ts, its mechanics, its rules — and perhaps the most important single factor is the right pitch. It always exists; the place where geography and architecture combine psychologically to make people glad of an excuse to stop and listen. Bridges are good, and underpasses and entrances — or if it's just a street, a full one's usually better than an empty one, as long as it isn't too full. Passers-by mustn't feel in danger of being knocked over by the crush, and there has to be room for them to see each other give, to stand and enjoy. I'd been a busker long enough to have the feel, and the first place I found was perfect — a crossroads dominated by a round advertising pillar. It was occupied, though. The obligatory two drunks who inhabit every pedestrian precinct in Europe sat with their backs against a poster for *La Traviata*, messily swilling beer from litre bottles. But the next one I found was nearly as good — a square of wooden benches sandwiched between a butcher's shop and a café. The pavement was just the right width — enough space for people to pass in comfort, but not so much that they could ignore me. I took out my fiddle and left the open case on the pavement.

I began with waltzes — people everywhere love that rhythm — then just followed my inclinations and played whatever pleased me. Within half an hour I knew I'd chosen a good spot. The lunchtime drinkers in the café looked upon me with a benevolent eye, and when they left they showed their pleasure at the coming weekend by giving more than if they'd been sober. The mothers liked me as well. They stopped with their offspring and used me for a quick lesson in generosity. A guilder would be put in the child's hand, he'd be edged forward, and into my case the coin would go. Every time, people would stop and give, because everybody loves to help teach a child kindness. Then there were the courting couples, boys trying to impress their girl with a nonchalant toss of the coin, the professional types who liked to think of themselves as patrons of the arts — and best of all, the mid-afternoon coffee trade, older ladies in twos and threes, dressed up for their day out. They were the biggest catches, for the pressure among them to conform was tremendous; if one felt obliged to give, the others immediately reached for their handbags.

I gave in return, schottisches, airs, quadrilles, and watched and classified — and from time to time chided myself for analysing the people so much, for no matter how many generalisations I made, it wasn't types who were giving me money, it was individuals. One by one they made their contracts with me. An older man saw my grin at the way his wife brandished a newly-bought cucumber. It sealed a bond between us; he smiled back as he gave, glad of a chance to interrupt her grumble at the market's prices. After him came a punk girl with purple hair. She apologised for having no money — and gave me a bag of sweets instead. Two minutes later a small man stopped, blond and portly, an obvious anglophile. The cut of his tweed suit, the pocket watch and chain — the outfit was all so aggressively English that no Englishman would ever have worn it. He reached down with a five-guilder note, and almost overbalanced as a hurrying overcoat bumped into him. The case closed on his wrist. He tutted, then made a great fuss of reopening it.

'Is your hand all right?' I asked.

He assured me it was, then beamed at me.

'And how are you finding our late autumn weather?'

The archetypal English question! I grinned at him, but before I could answer I was accosted by an anxious lady with a dog. She wanted to give me fifty cents, but she only had a two-and-a half-guilder coin. Would I think her rude if she asked for change?

And so it went on — two music students, a priest, a merry old man who smelled of fish and beer, each of them different, each with their own reason to give. Only the housewives, carbon copies of the one I'd watched earlier, merged into one figure — never a big giver, but steady, faithful. She always seemed to be next in line, a couple of tiny copper coins in her hand. By the end of the afternoon she was my security, my assurance of a place in the scheme of things. I played for everyone, but for her most of all.

It was half-past four when I finished, and I decided to count the takings later. The library turned out to be near where I'd parked, and I put the fiddle case back in the boot before going across to it. As I pushed open the glass door, I felt a familiar stiffness in my arm from so much playing. The feeling was a pleasant reminder that I'd been working, and I smiled as I stretched.

'You seem content. Can I help you?'

I spun round to find a woman with fine brown hair watching me from behind a wide steel desk. For a confused moment I was tongue-tied. I felt myself blush; I was used to being heard, but not to being noticed. The only other people in sight were two old men reading newspapers at a table.

'Excuse me . . . I'm looking for someone called Elly.'

Her eyebrows made a question over the tops of her plain round glasses as she came round to the front of the desk. The handshake was light and firm. The brows furrowed as I told her how I knew her name, but sisterly disapproval disappeared immediately I explained what I wanted. She listened carefully, then held out a hand for the picture. She looked at it for a long time, then again at me over the spectacles, thoughtfully, before turning to a card index. Her hands selected two drawers, placed them on the desk, and began to sift through them.

'I have seen your statue, Mr Fraser, but you must excuse me, I cannot remember where, or whether it was the original I saw or merely a photograph. As I am supposed to be an expert on both the art and the history of this area, this naturally annoys me. Sit down, please.'

The voice was low and cultured, the smile brief and sardonic; one eyebrow lifted and a corner of the generous mouth curled. I could see the physical resemblance to her sister, but the features somehow added up differently. Except for the mouth, the face of this woman was more refined, thinner, paler, framed by high cheekbones and a delicate pointed chin. She wore a tailored, military-style khaki skirt and plain denim jeans. Lace-up ankle boots, no jewellery, no make-up.

I watched her work. Her movements were spare and efficient, born of long familiarity with her job, and nothing distracted her until the shoulder-length brown hair escaped the confines of its pin to fall heavily over her cheek. She shook it away with impatience, then carefully pinned it up again. The action was full of angular grace. She caught me looking at her and suppressed a smile. Again I felt the colour rise to my cheeks. I lowered my eyes. She stood up to cover the moment's embarrassment.

'You are English, Mr Fraser?'

'No. Scots.'

'*Ah.*'

She walked off between two stacks, saying something over her shoulder to the two old men. It sounded cheerful, but neither of them responded. When she returned, it was with an armful of oversized books. Without looking at me she bent over the desk again. I leaned back in the seat and saw the concentration gather in her brows.

I suppose I must have fallen asleep, for the next thing I remember was being shaken awake by her.

I looked at the clock, then round the room. The two old men were gone, and it was dark outside. She'd let me sleep for five hours. The night before, in Münster, there had been nightmares, familiar ones that had robbed me of all sleep. The strain of accepting any responsibility for my own life again had drained me. There was a sweet smell. *Coconut*, I thought absurdly. From her hair. *Why does she smell of that?* Her smile returned, but this time it was a gentle thing. Coconut oil, I thought, on her hair.

'It's in a museum,' she said.

We watched the traffic at the intersection where the statue had stood before the provincial museum decided to save it from the ravages of the weather. There was enough rain to make the windscreen wipers necessary, but not enough to keep them silent. They thudded, screamed, and thudded again. We sat in a silence filled only with their noise and my obvious disappointment. There was no sign of human habitation anywhere near us.

On the way she had explained that Groningen was a province as well as a town, then lapsed into silence for the rest of the drive. I had only told her the bare bones of the story.

'I am sorry. I wish I knew how to aid you further.'

Her English had a curiously formal ring to it, as though learned in a different century. I looked through the rain-streaked windows at the new village a mile away, a bleak, suburban ghetto of the town itself, with only a few old houses still standing. Would anyone remember Vinnie there? I doubted it. The exact reference she had so painstakingly searched out while I slept offered us nothing more than four gantries of traffic lights, swaying in the fierce November wind. Their crazy ballet lit up the windscreen and haloed her hair. Was she sorry for the false trail or just sorry for me, I wondered. Did I really look so vulnerable? And what was I supposed to do now — a house-to-house search of a dormitory town with an old photograph in my hand? The urge just to run from the disappointment was almost unbearable; if there had been a bar, I couldn't have resisted.

Thankfully she took control of the situation, turning the car round in a tight circle, accelerating back to the town centre. She didn't speak again until we drew up outside the library.

'I can offer you the spare bed at my house, Mr Fraser. Just the bed, of course . . . Nothing else.'

The attempt at wry humour couldn't quite mask the nervousness of the last words. I mumbled my thanks and said no, clumsily, for the thought of even scratching the surface of someone else's life was terrifying to me. Blank-faced, she watched me get out of the car, and suddenly I wanted to apologise, but before I could, she drove off. I walked across to Helga's BMW and leaned against the bonnet, exhausted. Max, I thought, what do I do now?

Later, in a cheap hotel, after I'd phoned again, I lay on the hard bed, angry at my own stupidity. The girl had taken me to the right place; he had returned there, to the new village. There *had* been a Dutch address among the guests in Interlaken that night, and Helga had managed to arrange an interview for me in the morning, with Leon Smulders, alias Vincent Stein.

With Vinnie, the Dutch Jew who had operated a German intelligence unit's movie camera fifty years ago.

It was a large, airy apartment, the top half of a two-storey building, well-hidden over a boutique and a hair-dressing salon. The man who had known Max so long ago sat opposite me, his eyes examining my face as we talked. The light from the big studio windows fell on a spacious, leafy room, its walls covered with cinema memorabilia. The noise of the traffic was a dull rumble behind the fluent precision of his English.

'. . . by the spring of thirty-seven, Berlin wasn't satisfied the aircraft were being used the right way. They wanted assessments: which squadrons were the most effective, which types of bomb did what kind of damage, that sort of thing. Horrific to think of now, of course, but it seemed normal enough at the time. It was just war, a *little* war, Mr Fraser, all of us thought of it that way, even then. It was no secret that Berlin was preparing for what was coming later, testing arms, training people. Everybody was; Germany, Italy, the Russians. Anyway, as soon as the bombers had done their stuff, we would go in. Most of the time it was easy enough to slip through their lines, and if there were problems, we were a newsreel crew with enough languages to make us sound international, and we had papers for both sides. We would film, take a lot of stills, drive like hell back to our own position. Process the stuff, give it a rough evaluation, and then back it went to Germany. Franco's people didn't even get a smell of it.'

He paused to light a cigarette, then gave me his full attention again, brushing an imaginary fleck from the perfect crease of his trousers. He was tiny, immaculately turned out — and impressive. Some small men dress meticulously because they see their size as an affront to their dignity, but he needed no such compensation. There was an assurance about him, a quiet stillness that spoke of absolute confidence in what he was and what he had done with his life. In the room there was only one object which could have identified him as Jewish, and the question that had hung over our entire conversation surfaced again in my mind as I looked at it; how could a Jew . . .

'It belonged to my father.'

He picked up the *Menorah* and contemplated it, choosing not to notice my confusion. I felt ashamed. Who was I, of all people, to judge?

'My father was a hard man, Mr Fraser, a fundamentalist of the Hasidic persuasion who had decided his only son would be a rabbi.'

For a second the seven-branched candelabrum turned in his hand, the light catching the ridges of its battered surface. Then it stopped abruptly.

'The loyalties of my generation are not always as simple as the historians and politicians would have your generation believe.'

The shame rose in me, but something in his tone quelled it; the rebuke was unmistakable, but neither angry nor unkind. When he began to talk again, I knew a privilege had been granted me. For Max's sake . . .? I wasn't sure, but this wasn't a man who would lightly explain himself to the world. As I listened, I remembered the old busker's description of him — difficult, withdrawn, caring about his job above all else.

'. . . Erich Von Laer was a genius, you see, as well as a man for whom I had much affection, Mr Fraser. An artist. A poet, a painter, and he would have been one of the most brilliant directors of the modern cinema had he lived, I am convinced of that. That was why I was prepared to continue working with him even after he found it to be his duty to join the Wehrmacht. The Abwehr came later.'

I opened my mouth to ask something, but my courage failed me. He gave me the sharp look of a man who didn't suffer fools. At all.

'If you have a question, ask it,' he said, curtly.

'Were you blackmailed, like Max?'

'No. Neither Erich nor I. Despite . . . what we were. We had our own reasons for going.'

He gave me another long look of assessment, then nodded, as though he had decided something. The precise voice went back to its tale.

'Erich had enough of his family in him to want to be a soldier, and he believed it wouldn't be long before Hitler and his people were ousted. Later —' he smiled ruefully — 'I discovered that to be a common enough fallacy. But at the time we thought we could use the situation; we were going to make a documentary of the war and be the German Eisensteins who told the *truth* about Spain.'

Once again the tone of voice was eloquent. A slow exhalation of cigarette smoke underlined the word's ambiguity. The smile disappeared.

'All great men have their blind spots, Mr Fraser. Erich Von Laer was naïve enough to think he could protect me; I was naïve enough not to care as long as I could still get behind a camera. And be with him,' he finished quietly.

He put the candlestick firmly down on the table, and somehow I knew that the subject of their relationship was closed.

'The problem was, of course, that taking on Falkenheim laid us wide open to attack in our turn. Information in the hands of a man like that is destructive power, and neither Erich nor I realised how much Falkenheim and the people around him loved that kind of power. A thug with intelligence is a potent combination, Mr Fraser. He was the most evil man I have ever met.'

He stubbed out the cigarette, half-smoked, and immediately lit another. The tobacco was Eastern, fragrant.

'So he was never charged with the rape?' I asked.

He shook his head.

'Of course not. When Erich tried the first time, we were still in Spain, and nobody in Berlin gave a damn how many Spanish women were raped as long as Franco was winning. There was nothing else we could do without completely exposing ourselves.'

Smoke spiralled upwards from the cigarette in his hand. The stumps of the two missing fingers were a patchwork of small white scars.

'After we got back, he sent in another report. I tried to persuade him against it, because by then I could see where it was leading us, but he could be stubborn as well as naïve. The incident had enraged him, and he still wanted to believe there was justice in the Third Reich. After the second time, Falkenheim simply decided we were becoming too much of a nuisance — the S.S. were great puritans, you know, and it would have done him no good at all if the affair had reached Himmler's ears. He was a rising star, his career was just beginning to take off, and we could have been a serious threat to him. Or perhaps it just pleased him to eliminate us; he was certainly cold-blooded enough for it. He simply came for us one night in Münster.'

'The girl. She was still with you then?'

Just the mention of the child seemed to relax him. He smiled as he sat back in the canvas chair.

'All of us were very attached to her, you know. She was a mascot, a symbol of our good luck. After all, we'd been in the thick of the whole business for over a year and not one of us had been so much as scratched. She was from Madrid, but we found that out only later. We could have taken her back there, but it would have been pointless — the rest of her people were either dead or scattered, everybody, the whole family. She and her mother had been with a group of refugees, but they'd got separated from the others. It seemed the only sensible thing to do, to take her home with us. Leaving her behind was unthinkable; we'd all seen enough dead children, and she'd just have been another one. So we decided — all of us, it wasn't any kind of order, Erich Von Laer wouldn't have given such an order. The idea was that eventually we would get her back to his family in Münster. It was understood that she was our responsibility. No one questioned that. Ever.'

'And she is still alive?'

His slow scrutiny reminded me that he knew nothing at all about me. A voice on the telephone had asked him to give me some of his time, but now he was being asked to give much more.

'Yes, she's still alive,' he said.

He picked up the documents, diffidently — and suddenly his voice changed again.

'I'm not at all sure she would want the complications of this, Mr Fraser.'

It was a challenge, an ultimatum to present my case. I found myself rising to it, wanting his respect.

'I haven't even begun to think about that,' I replied, 'but we both know Max wanted her to have them. It should be her choice, not yours or mine.'

Again the gentle smile played over his lips, and I knew I had passed the test. I waited for him to speak, but the silence didn't bother him at all — and once again the self-sufficiency of the man struck me. Apart from the dreadfully scarred hand, he had survived well, I thought. He looked affluent, prosperous and young for his years. The cream linen suit was beautifully cut and fashionable, the wavy silver hair indicated distinction rather than age, and although he must have been in his seventies, he could easily have passed for fifty-five. I knew just by looking at him that he had always been a loner, and as we sat there

I could see him recognising the same thing in me.

'Max,' he said, finally. 'Max played with that child day and night. She wouldn't talk at first, wouldn't tell us her name. He was the one who got it out of her in the end. We were near Burgos, trying to patch up the sump on the truck — it needed a new one, but parts were always a problem. We were camped on the banks of a dry stream, and on the second day he gave her the doll. Made it himself — nothing fancy, just wood and wire and a few scraps of cotton, but he was good at things like that. Anyway, the next morning we found her name spelled out in dust on the Merc's bonnet. 'Maria'. About a week later she started to talk.'

He shook his head.

'He was so worried when I met him that day. Worried that she thought he'd just deserted her.'

'You said you met him in Basel?'

'In the station. I was going through Switzerland to Italy, collecting locations for a documentary. He'd come from the doctor; he'd just been given the news. I recognised the accordion case before I recognised him. More patches than anything else, but still the same one he'd had in Spain — we used to listen to him playing in the evenings if things were quiet. We just sat in the station until it was time for my train. Hard to think of him as dead, now. I had only just accepted the idea of him being alive.'

'What was it that made him feel so guilty?'

The hesitation was brief, a formality; I had his trust now.

'You might as well hear the whole story, it can do no harm. We were at Laer, sorting out supplies and files and getting all our gear ready for Poland. At the time we weren't sure if the unit was to be kept intact, so we were putting our house in order. There was a phone call — one of Erich's contacts on the staff. An arrest warrant had been issued for both of us — me for being Jewish, Erich for concealing it. He'd been painting when the news came — his sister, I think. Falkenheim and a 'special detachment' were already on their way to arrest us, and we knew the others stood no chance either once they arrived. Not all S.S. were fanatics, by any means, but the types Falkenheim would pick wouldn't be likely to balk at killing off witnesses.'

His voice was unemotional, matter-of-fact.

'So Erich sent everybody off in the vehicles. Schumacher, Jacky, Max and the girl. I remember him kissing Maria, telling her to be good and do what her uncle Max told her. Max took the motorbike and they bundled everything else into the car — all the film we'd shot, all the files, the painting. Before they left, he gave Max these.' He indicated the documents. 'Told him to make for Switzerland and take care of the child. Said getting out wasn't desertion any more, just self-preservation from a bunch of lawless criminals. All Max told me was that there was some kind of road accident. After all we'd been through, a road accident! He crashed, and when he came to, the bike was in a ditch and the car was at the bottom of a ravine. Somewhere in the Taunus, I think. He was sure everyone was dead, and they were probably sure he was; I never found out. He just got back on the bike and headed south. Made it over the border and survived somehow. God knows how.'

'Why didn't you go with them?'

'I couldn't leave Erich to face them alone,' he said calmly. 'He refused to let them make him run.'

Again there was silence. What was more remarkable, the courage or the devotion? I passed the photograph across to him.

'You mentioned a painting,' I said.

He looked at it for a long time, the smile returning to his eyes.

'Yes,' he said, 'that's it. She had it with her when we pulled her out of the wreckage in the church. Rolled up in a leather bag.'

He gave it back to me.

'A Van Dyck,' he said.
'How do you know?'
'We proved it.'
The three-fingered hand stubbed out the cigarette.
'We proved it,' he repeated quietly. 'Erich and I.'

I sat in the café, watching the waitress scrub the tops of the pine tables, mulling over the story I was unravelling from the memories of these old men. Vinnie had asked me to come back later — a business appointment, he'd said, but I knew he wanted to be alone, to think things over. He'd told me that the orphaned Spanish child was now a Dutch citizen, living quietly on one of the coastal islands, but he still hadn't given me the exact address. The waitress came to refill my coffee-cup, and her wrist-watch said it was one-thirty. In twenty minutes I'd go back to the flat.

I thought about the end of Vinnie's tale. Even by the standards of those despair-filled years, it was extra-ordinary — what kind of courage did it take to survive a concentration camp and then start again? He'd told me that his own people had been the worst, but that it was understandable — a Jew who had been in the Wehrmacht, a homosexual who didn't care about being Jewish; to have expected anything other than persecution would have been unreal, he'd said. But somehow he'd managed to escape the road to the ovens, and neither hatred nor rancour had touched the way he thought of his fellow men.

The coffee was hot and strong, and I was content just to sit and sip and let my mind wander. For the first time since the start of this whole thing I felt pleased, with the world and with myself. I had been trusted to do something and I had at least begun it properly. Though my task had been born out of respect for Max, it had proved to be worth doing for myself as well. I'd been shown how a humane man could win against circumstances much worse than my own. A whole layer of self-pity had been stripped from me, and I felt deeply grateful.

The rain had started again by the time I left, but I barely noticed it as I walked. I wondered what the precise quality of this man Von Laer's magnetism had been, how it had manifested itself. They had been misfits, most of them, blackmailed by authority into a dangerous, dirty job. What was the power that had welded them into such a tight group of responsible men, ready to adopt a homeless child in a foreign land? Vinnie had made it sound as though there hadn't been the slightest hesitation about caring for the child, just as Max had told me there had been none about their determination to save her mother. They had stepped aside from their own role in a bloody civil war to save a child's life; it was as admirable as it was unexpected. The way both men had talked about this strange German aristocrat made me wish I'd known him.

I climbed the stairs to the apartment and walked in through the open door, then stopped in confusion. The once-orderly room was in chaos, the fine plants knocked over, the paintings and signed photographs lying broken and torn among them. Every drawer had been emptied, every cupboard gutted. Clothes lay everywhere, brightly-coloured shirts lying like carnival banners across the destruction. I felt something crunch into the carpet under my foot and recoiled instinctively. An earthenware pot. I reached down and freed the silver object that had been caught by its fall. It was twisted beyond repair now, one branch snapped off. Absurdly, I found myself thinking how angry his father would have been.

I stood with the ruined *Menorah* in my mind, paralysed, desperate to run but desperate to know as well. From the kitchen came the sound of percolating coffee, but the smell of it was tainted with something stronger. Somehow I found the courage to look further.

Vinnie was almost hidden by an overturned bookcase. Except for the trickle of blood at his mouth, he seemed as neat in death as he had been in life, despite the wreckage of the room. I freed the tiny body of its burden, then cleared away the volumes of cinema history that lay around him like a bizarre epitaph. There could be no doubt that he was dead, but I felt the pulse just the same. He was still warm; it couldn't have happened more than minutes before. The vision of another death claimed me as I touched him, and I felt wetness upon my cheeks. As gently as I could, I closed the eyes. When I stood up I was shaking. Who? *Why?*

Wildly I scanned the room for a clue, anything that would make sense of this barbarity, but all I could see was the violence that had robbed a civilised man of his life. My head reeled.

I heard a noise behind me, and spun round to find an elderly man dressed in blue overalls. The caretaker? His wide eyes stared slowly round the shattered room, and then he began to back away from me, looking in turn at the body, my face, the crooked claw of silver in my hand. Then suddenly he was gone, and I was left listening to the clatter of his boots on the stairs as he fled.

I looked again at the body which lay among the smashed mementoes of an extraordinary life — and then I turned and did the same.

Chapter 3
WIND

I CAUGHT A glimpse of a tear rolling down a pale cheek in soft focus, and then she stamped her foot and turned her back. Her lover had spurned her. The fringes of her dress were pointed with white lace; white for purity, white to give the lie to her scarlet heart, but I was her only witness. The only other person in the cinema was the usherette, the only noise apart from the screen the rasp of an emery board on her nails. I had to think.

I told myself logic was the best antidote, but it was hard to force down the panic. Who had killed Vinnie? And why? And what did it have to do with my search? Those were only the first questions, I knew, but they loomed before me like a mountain I didn't want to climb. The desire just to walk away, to decide it was a grisly coincidence, a malevolent trick of fate, was unbelievably strong. I shut the image of the body out of my mind and stared blankly at the screen. Vast mouths kissed each other in ecstatic slow motion. The ancient soundtrack swelled into a syrupy crescendo, metallically scratched with age. Atlanta burned. I had to *think*.

My gut-feeling told me it had to be connected to me somehow, it wasn't just a burglary I'd stumbled in on. I had gone to Vinnie searching for information, and whoever had killed him had been searching for something too, I was sure of that. But what? The painting? The woman's address? The unavoidable thought at last materialised in my mind. *Had I killed him?* I could have been followed. If someone was looking for the same thing I was . . . Had I led them to him? The bitter taste in my mouth was a compound of fear and guilt and anger.

I followed the train of thought as far as I could. If I was being watched, then someone wanted the woman; it could only be that.

Nobody other than Helga knew I had come as far as Groningen. Helga? Was there some reason why she should want this man dead? *Helga?* The thought was too fantastic for words, but the fantastic was already upon me. *Why*, I asked the screen. A flurry of unintelligible Dutch subtitles was my only answer.

I could go to the police . . . I considered the idea for all of ten seconds, then rejected it absolutely. By now they would have fingerprints from the flat and a description from the caretaker, and with my record I wouldn't stand a chance. I'd be the automatic choice for chief suspect, and I knew I couldn't stand prison again. Ever.

No, my only hope was to find the real killer or the motive for Vinnie's death, if I could stay free long enough to do either. I could see no one to help me but the woman herself — I was sure that she was still the key, that she could make sense of all this. I had to find her, quickly, and I also had to find her without leading anyone else to her, or there was a good chance of her ending up like Vinnie. Once again the memory of the dead man sliced through the armour I had tried to put up against it. I shuddered.

The death had only been a couple of hours ago, and it had produced a physical as well as a mental reaction in me every time I let myself visualise the scene; this time I couldn't fight it any more. I thrust myself deeper into the worn plush of the seat, trembling. Waves of giddiness washed over me and broke on my brow, and I was conscious of nothing but my fear and the sweat that poured from me. *Had I really killed him?* I do not know how long I sat there, stupid with fright.

The closing titles pulled me out of it. *Gone With The Wind.* Gone. That's what I had to be, what I had to do: get away. I couldn't move. The tight blue buttocks of a jeans commercial filled the screen, alluring, androgynous, a screaming rock and roll fantasy. The shrill voices grabbed at my fears and the speed of the sequence mocked my paralysis. I couldn't think as the hard sell continued. *Jenever! Tobacco! Boots! Perfume! Chocolate!* The commercials went on and on. Had Vinnie helped make any of them, I wondered helplessly. The slick American voices gave way to the guttural Dutch of the local ads. Restaurants, night clubs, buy your meat from Van den Helder, Hennie Beekman has the best selection of Italian shoes in Groningen. Holidays. Tape recorders. Bicycles.

Bicycles!

My brain began to work again. A bicycle was a good idea. I had to get out of this town without being tailed, and a bicycle was too fast for a man on foot to follow, too slow for a car. If either was tried, I had at least a chance of spotting it. Helga's car was out of the question. Holland might be full of BMWs, but not with Swiss plates; I'd be picked up within hours. I had to dump it somehow, or at least leave it behind. But a bicycle . . . In Holland everyone rode a bike, and I could just join the rush-hour traffic. I doubted if a policeman would even give me a second glance.

Shakily, I got to my feet and walked back up the aisle. To my relief the usherette didn't look at me as I made for the door. Outside, the rain was a steady downpour that washed the last leaves into the gutters.

Going back to the car was a risk, I knew, but I had to do it. I could leave everything else and still survive, but I couldn't leave the fiddle. So many times it had been meat and drink and solace to me, and though they hadn't let me play it when I was inside, they'd let me keep it near.

It was the only thing that had come through it all with me; I'd given everything else away. But it was a risk, just the same.

Two minutes took me to the multi-storey car park. I walked past the rows of vehicles, trying not to think of how easy it would be to keep watch from behind them, forcing myself to concentrate; the faster I did this, the less the danger. The BMW's boot opened silently. I grabbed the rucksack with my own clothes, emptied the briefcase and threw it in. I lifted out the fiddle, thinking furiously; the documents, where could I hide . . . Suddenly there were footsteps. I whirled round to see a middle-aged man getting into a Fiat, two cars away from mine. He gave me a polite nod. My heart hammering madly, I slammed the boot shut and strode past him, trying to look normal, waiting for the shout that would tell me it was all over, but it never came.

I searched each floor on the way down, looking for seclusion, and finally I swapped the suit for jeans and a polo-neck behind a clutch of rubbish-bins near the exit ramp. The documents went into the case-lining behind my bows, the photos into my coat pocket. Apprehension made me clumsy, but no one disturbed me, and once it was over I felt calmer; so far, so good. I slung the rucksack over one shoulder, the fiddle case on its strap over the other, and pushed open the service door. The side street was bleak, deserted because of the rain.

I walked. The cold and the movement were good therapy, and after about half an hour I had worked out what I needed. Most of my money was either in travellers' cheques or Swiss notes, and I couldn't afford to try changing any here. I'd been lucky in the cinema, but another face-to-face confrontation would be asking for trouble; they'd find the car quickly, I was sure of it, and a Swiss money transaction would be an obvious connection. So I couldn't buy a bike — and that left only one alternative; I'd have to steal one.

I had never stolen anything in my life.

Eventually, outside a café facing one of the canals, I found what I wanted. Two of the bikes on the rack by the front door were unchained.

On the street I could see only a few people, and the rain was heavy enough to keep their heads down. As casually as I could I lifted a bike from the rack. There was a loud clang of metal as I scraped it against the one beside it, but in the hubbub of noise from the café nobody noticed. I willed myself not to get on the thing, and walked it round the next corner. I mounted, cycled unsteadily down the bumpy street, then turned and joined the throng of bikes waiting at the main lights. They changed, and a small army of cyclists began to move through the gathering gloom. I bowed my head against the wind and pedalled out of Groningen.

'Thirteen guilders, please.'

I paid the woman quickly and headed back to the warmth of the VW bus, scanning the other customers as inconspicuously as I could. In the last ten days it had become second nature to look for suspicion in the faces around me, but there were only two old ladies in the shop, buying their husbands' supper. I felt calmer as I walked out, but then the mournful sound of a deep horn cut through the darkness and stabbed my fears awake again. The ferry that had brought me to Terschelling an hour ago was leaving, and once it was gone I would be stranded here, for it was the last one of the day. On each of the islands, so far, this had been the worst moment; a geographical constriction of my freedom, a tightening of the net. I got into the van.

The wind rocked the ancient vehicle and added a chorus of creaking springs to its banshee wail. I turned on the radio as I ate. The bread and cheese were still fresh, and salami spicy and delicious. Satisfied, I listened to the news, warmth seeping slowly back. The latest international crisis, famine in Ethiopia, a Hollywood star's third divorce — but no mention of the murder.

There hadn't been for five days now. Suddenly the adrenaline left me, taking the last of my strength with it, and I slumped back in the driver's seat, exhausted, relieved, wondering if I dared risk ringing Helga.

For the hundredth time I reviewed my reasoning. I had to assume they were out there somewhere, searching, but I could see no sign of anyone following me, neither police nor murderer. Hopefully I'd lost the killer back in Groningen, but the cops wouldn't give up so easily, and I knew I couldn't trust my luck yet. Helga was the car's owner. They'd have her address from the registration by now, and it followed that she would be under investigation or surveillance of some kind — and they could well be tapping her phone. If she was innocent, contacting her could only implicate her further, and it could also lead them straight to me. If she was guilty . . .

But at least I was no longer news. Neither press nor radio were interested any more. The newspaper reports had been both a worry and a blessing, for they'd talked about an Englishman, not a Scot, and the identikit picture had looked nothing at all like me. But the police would undoubtedly keep looking — all the papers had carried warnings not to approach me because I was potentially violent. There hadn't been the slightest speculation about motive, and no reports on progress with the case, but I knew in my heart they wouldn't stop.

I looked in the mirror, and a tired, thirty-two-year-old face stared back at me, the eyes red-rimmed, the skin unhealthy. I remembered Helga's description. What would she say if she could see me now? Fear and worry had etched a permanent line across my brow. Cutting the hair short had seemed an obvious thing to do, but perhaps I should have let the beard stay, for my face looked abnormally pale without it. But the story I'd decided on seemed to rule it out, and I couldn't come up with anything better. I wondered: were journalists who worked for the British forces in Germany allowed beards or not? I wasn't even sure whether they were soldiers or civilians — I was just praying no one else would know either.

The engine coughed bronchially when I pressed the starter, but it caught, and soon heat started coming through. Over the rattle I could hear the dull roar of the tide pounding the sea wall, although it was almost half a mile away. It was a bleak reminder; there was no escape from wind or sea on Terschelling.

The journalist idea had been the only thing I could think of that allowed me to be a stranger and ask the right questions. I was supposed to be writing an article on the effect of foreigners on the life of a small community. To compare, I told people, with the way British soldiers had affected places in Germany. Were there any foreign-born people in the area? The first few times I'd had to open my mouth had been terrifying, and on one occasion I'd nearly run — a village policeman had come in to buy a sandwich while I was talking to a café owner. But usually I just said my piece and waited. The response was mostly a bored negative, any suspicions allayed by the sight of my crabbed shorthand on a cheap pad. It seemed to legitimise things in peoples' eyes, and the skill wasn't on my record; in Barlinnie nobody had cared about shorthand. I switched off the engine again. I had to save fuel.

With the van I'd been lucky. As soon as I'd got out of Groningen I'd just ridden as hard as I could, oblivious of direction. The one idea in my mind had been to get as far away as possible, so I had just pedalled until I was worn out, stopping occasionally to check my back. I'd seen nothing and heard only the wind behind me as I followed the tortuous cycle paths. I'd ridden the whole night, spurred on by fear, taking relief in the physical exertion, and by morning I had aching muscles as well as the rudiments of a plan. In the town of Beilen I'd taken a southbound train with the last of my Dutch money, abandoning the bike with scores of others at the station. Again the rush-hour had concealed me.

It was only on the train that fatigue had finally

conquered fear enough to let me sleep. A watery midday sun had found me in the city of Tilburg, in the province of Brabant.

I'd banked on it being far enough away for the risk to be minimal – and I'd been right. It hadn't taken long to find a back-street hotel, and the old woman behind the desk couldn't have cared less who I was – she had eyes only for my Swiss money. Her shaking fingers had counted furtively, hidden the notes away behind her apron, and thrust a handful of greasy guilders at me in return. The rate had verged on robbery, but it had given me just enough.

The van had been the only half-decent vehicle in the seedy garage. I'd paid cash down, no questions asked, and driven off. One other stop, at a small printer's workshop in Breda, and then I'd headed back north. According to my calculations I had enough cash left for about twelve days of fuel, ferry fares and frugal eating. Twelve days to find a woman who had disappeared fifty years ago. It was the tenth day now, and the islands of Texel and Vlieland were behind me. It was the tenth day of sleeping in the van, the tenth day of no hot food, the tenth day of drawing an absolute blank, and I was down to my last fifty guilders. After that I had to take the chance of a traveller's cheque, or phone Helga, or steal. Once again I looked at the drawn face in the mirror. Or give myself up . . .

The idea wasn't new. I had discovered nothing, and I was finding it harder and harder to believe I was on the right track. When people did talk it was to curse the summer tourists or tell me how much they admired the British. I wrote everything down, even the sad diatribes about Indonesians who ate dog food, Moluccans who were just waiting for the signal to come for good honest folk in the night. The writing kept the disappointment from my face, for there were no Spanish ladies.

Resolutely, I put the thought of giving up anyway from me and climbed out of the van. It was dark now, and the wind had dropped slightly. I walked down the main street towards the Heineken sign, wondering if this was the biggest village on the island. The yellow brick houses were crammed against each other in an orderly huddle, each protecting its neighbour from the elements, like patient beasts grazing together. Every few seconds the beam from the lighthouse cast its cyclops eye over them, swelling the shadows, making battlements of the trim garden fences, monsters of the hardy shrubberies. Most of the shops had their shutters up tight against the oncoming winter, beginning the long wait for the brief frenzy of the next season. In the distance a church bell struck seven. The cold was bitter.

I pushed open the door and brushed aside the leather flaps that kept out the draught. It was like a thousand other Dutch pubs. A long bar of dark wood, a row of high wooden stools in front of it and a row of upturned bottles behind, glinting invitingly. The few tables were perched round the edges of the room, each with a flower and a plastic holder of beer-mats, but pride of place was reserved for the large pocketless billiard table. An overhead light proclaimed its importance and turned a merciless glare on the baize. The two players' faces were hidden in shadow, the brown of their overalls drab against the brilliance of the green cloth. The red-and-white shine of the balls was the room's only movement; the blue tips of the cues were motionless, frozen by my entrance. Behind the bar a radio pumped out football results, its monotonous drone challenged only by the drip of a beer tap and the ticking of the grandfather clock in the corner. One of the players called out 'Frans — custom, and they went back to their game. A door behind the bar opened, and the row of lights over the counter went on.

There is a face that is typical of the North Sea coast, from Flanders to Denmark, and the barman had it. Craggy, vulpine and furtive, the features of some long-forgotten Saxon tribe. He came forward. '*Goedenavond.*'

'A Pils, please.'

Waiting for the beer bought me time to size up my surroundings. He poured it, let it stand for a minute, took the head off with a plastic spatula, topped it up again. I felt his gaze upon me as I drank, and it wasn't hard to guess his thoughts. It was late in the year for visitors . . . I drained the small glass, passed it back to him, and watched him repeat the whole operation in silence. For a moment or two I made no attempt to break it. Behind me the billiard balls clacked. From my wallet I took out one of the cards I'd had made up in Breda and gave it to him. He held it under the light and perused it carefully.

'And what can I do for you, Mr Johnson?'

The English was thickly accented, the scepticism in the question evident. I went into my routine.

'As you can see, Mijnheer . . .?' I waited for him to tell me his name, but he said nothing. My spirits began to sink. I went on. 'I'm working on a story about . . .'

I gave him the whole spiel, careful to keep my accent as neutral as possible. As I went through it, I was aware of how contrived it all sounded. How many more times would I have to do this? I took out the pad.

'. . . and in particular I wondered if there was anyone here on the island who could tell me about the other side of it. A foreigner, maybe, or someone who didn't have Dutch as a first language. I'm sure you would know.'

There was no response. The small foxy face remained impassive. Carefully he put the card down and leaned his knuckles on the counter. The silence was total now; even the noise of the billiard balls had stopped. I began to feel uneasy. What was wrong here? The radio began blaring out inane music. The suddenness of it made me flinch, but the barman didn't seem to notice. He picked up a glass and began the automatic action of drying it with a towel. He didn't look at me.

'There are perhaps some people you could talk to, all right,' he said.

There was an inflection in his voice that I couldn't identify. He put down the glass and reached under the counter — and I knew suddenly that bad trouble was brewing here. Police? Had I been recognised? Whatever it was, I had to get out quickly. I got to my feet and reached into the pocket of my jeans for money. How far was it to the door?

The voice behind me was deep and lazy. 'Not so fast.'

I wheeled round. One of the billiard players was blocking the door, and the other took a step forward into the light by my side. The face was fleshy and strong, a broken, unlovely nose over several unshaven chins, a grim mouth. The hair was long since gone, but I still knew him. The billiard cue was clenched horizontally in his two fists, and the anger in the eyes was unmistakable.

'You're one of them!' I said.

Relief flooded through me. *At last!* Frantically I reached into the inside pocket of the coat for the photographs.

'I've been searching for you. I was a friend of . . .'

The world exploded into a brilliance of light, and I felt myself falling.

The child's face was long and grave as she looked at me, the expression the same as in the photograph. Three times I struggled up from the depths of unconsciousness, three times her serious gaze met mine, and the last time there was a middle-aged woman at her side. I recognised her as the woman the child had become. They stood above me, watching me go down for the third time. It only needed the woman from the painting to make them the perfect trio, the ghosts of the past I had inherited from Max. I no sooner willed it than it happened; for a brief second there were three versions of the face, but when I finally broke the surface into wakefulness I was alone.

Had Max and Vinnie sent a dream to haunt me? Would every awakening be like this? And why was the child wearing glasses? My feet scraped against the bottom board of the bed as I tried to stretch my legs. *Too short*, I thought. *The bed is too short for me.* Slowly I sat up. The door opened.

Her hair was the kind of silver grey which only comes from the deepest black, and it was all the more striking for still being long. Women of her age usually made practicality the excuse for cutting it short, but she had either resisted the impulse or had never felt it. It hung in straight, heavy folds, framing a face from which the beauty hadn't faded, although the world had certainly left its marks. Sadness and concern were written on it now as she looked at me. She stood for a long time in the doorway, as though unable to decide what should be done with me. She wore a leather apron over her dress, and there was a white porcelain coffee-pot in her hands. Her stillness seemed natural, the expression of a deep serenity; she was beautiful indeed, this woman Max had sent me to find.

Shyly a small figure peeked out from behind her skirts and scrutinised me. The spectacles were slightly lopsided. It hadn't all been a dream . . . Absent-mindedly, the woman reached down and stroked the child's hair. Daughter? Granddaughter? I felt myself smile.

She raised the coffee-pot and smiled back, but I shook my head. I wanted to say something but didn't seem able to, the words were somewhere else and I'd forgotten how to make my voice work. The child pushed past her and came up to the bed to continue her observation from a better vantage-point. Hesitantly, she tapped the bedcovers, then her chest — and then she smiled, too. I understood. I was in her bed. Her resemblance to the old photograph was uncanny.

'My daughter cannot speak to you. She is deaf and dumb.'

Deaf and dumb . . . Deaf . . . The words echoed round my brain. Suddenly I was very aware of the physical world around me, the warmth of the room, the crispness of the cotton sheets, the softness of the pillows. There was a pain in my head. Why? Again I tried to speak, and failed. I wanted to tell the child that being deaf and dumb didn't matter, I wanted to tell her mother how glad I was I'd found her, how important she had been to the old busker in Basel, but my head just lolled back against the pillows. I didn't seem to have any command over it. Once more sleep claimed me.

I came to with no idea of time or place, only the knowledge that something definite had woken me. Dressing was difficult; movement of any kind was torture, perception still at one remove from reality — but at least now I was sure it was genuine perception. At the bottom of the stairs I found a heavy door. I pushed it open. A courtyard . . .

The light was dazzling. I jerked my eyes away, and the sudden movement brought instant pain. Gingerly, I felt the lump behind my ear as I looked round. A byre, stables, greenhouses, a lean-to breeze-block building with a tin roof . . . The low concrete shed would be for pigs, I thought. The windswept silence was disturbing, and it took me a few seconds to work out why; the quiet of the farmyard was a less absolute thing, punctuated by the noise of beast or tractor. Whatever this place was now, it was no longer a working farm. I stepped back into the shadow of the doorway, out of the unbearably harsh light. Was there anyone else here? The loud banging that began was at once shock and relief; that was what had woken me, I remembered now. How far away was it? I tried to work it out, and couldn't.

I found a path that skirted the buildings and followed the hammering, realising how weak I was as I walked. How long had I slept? At first I seemed to be nearing the sound's source, and then it ceased altogether. I stopped at the corner of one of the sheds, confused, directionless, until it began again. It was directly above me. I saw the ladder. Slowly, my eyes climbed it.

She was perched on the top rung. At her waist was a joiner's apron, bulky with wooden handles, loosely tied over an old pair of men's overalls, much darned, irrevocably oil-stained. One leather-gloved hand held a nail-studded pine slat against the tattered tar paper of the roof, the other hammered. When she sensed me, she turned. The tool fell to her side.

She must have been nearly sixty, but the surprise of seeing me gave her the face of a twelve-year-old. The old felt hat that hid the grey hair was several sizes too big, like the overalls, and there was a smudge of dirt on her cheek. Together with the clothes, the dirty face made an urchin of her — a tomboy, I thought, one who'd never be too old to play on the roof. Seeing her like this I understood why they could never have abandoned her.

'You're Maria,' I said. 'You're Max's Maria.'

His name aged her immediately, made me regret that I'd said it. The surprised look was replaced by a smile that hovered between fondness and worry — and then she read my face, saw how much looking up at her was physically hurting me. She lifted the hammer briskly, drove home the last of the nails, then came down the ladder. I leaned back against the wall and shut my eyes.

She touched my arm gently. 'Are you all right?'

I nodded.

'Max sent you, didn't he?' The troubled look came back to her, but this time she couldn't manage the smile. 'Why?'

A tiny question, gently asked, but also the biggest question of all: where to begin? I felt my mind retreat from it, and again she reached out to steady me. The overall sleeve fell back, and I saw the crooked forearm. The breaks were old, and I wondered why the bones hadn't set straight. The flesh itself had been too badly mutilated ever to heal properly; six deep indentations, two parallel groups of three, behind each a long white scar. Chevrons, I thought, burnt into her arm, badges of rank in an army of pain. The memory of other scars came to me, the scars on the stumps of two missing fingers. Were they a higher rank? Vinnie was dead now, and Max too . . . Was death the highest rank of all? Why . . .? There was danger, urgency, I had things to ask, tell her . . . With an effort my mind pulled itself back from its wanderings.

Suddenly she let go of me and stepped back, hurriedly covering the scarred arm as though it still hurt — and for the first time I saw her clearly. The beauty I'd found by my bedside, the beauty I'd seen just a moment before on the roof — it was gone now, submerged in apprehension. I saw a face still individual, still striking, but it was a face lined with age, the face of a woman who'd obviously worked hard all her life. She was the girl in the photographs, but she was every housewife I'd seen in Groningen as well.

What had I expected?

I stood there, letting the wind press me against the rickety shed, numbed by the reality of her, the solidity. Explanation would have to wait, it was beyond me now. She understood my silence — instinctively, I knew it as I watched her — and instinct seemed to tell her what was best for both of us, now.

She picked up the makeshift wooden tool-box that lay at the foot of the ladder, held it out to me, then started back up towards the roof. When she reached the top, I gave her up the next slat and a handful of nails.

The effort made me dizzy, and again I closed my eyes. I could hear nothing except the wind whistling until the hammering cut through it and stopped my mind's drift. It was the most welcome sound in the world, an investment in hope, a belief in a sane future.

As I listened, I knew she was thinking the same.

The workshop smelled of oil, and the surface of the table was littered with bits of bicycle. Jacky swept them aside with his hand, placed the bottle of Jenever squarely between us on the battered wood and slid a glass across to me. I put down the cloth I'd been using to clean the fiddle and laid the instrument back in its case. He watched in silence, then sat down awkwardly, the smashed leg sticking out at an angle. Outside, a thunderstorm announced its approach, a low growl that broke through the wind's incessant moan.

'Frans says he's sorry he hit you so hard.'

He took a small black leather cosh from his pocket and handed it to me. It felt heavy, obscene; the lump behind my ear throbbed as I handled it. I gave it back to him in silence and watched him put it away. He took the stopper from the bottle.

'So am I, but how the hell were we to know you weren't the murderer?' One gulp emptied the glass. 'Even now, Willem's not too sure, but I never saw a killer yet who didn't carry some kind of weapon. Have a drink, Mr Alexander Fraser or whoever the hell you are, and tell me about these.'

He let my passport fall among the documents and photographs on the table, and refilled his glass. Carefully I lifted mine; the blow's ache was steady, insistent, but at least the dizziness was gone. Mechanically I began Max's story, wondering as I did so at my own stupidity; of course Vinnie had phoned them the minute I'd left him — and then the next news they'd had was his murder. My heart sank as I watched the heavy-set face across the table from me, for his expression told me they knew even less than I did about the killing. Why hadn't they gone to the police?

'So Max made it after all, eh?'

The voice and face was impassive, but his hands gave him away. They played with the empty glass, passing it between them like a juggler's ball — until he saw me watching. It went down on the wood with a loud crack.

'We thought he was dead. Schumacher found a gauntlet at the edge of the road, just by the drop. We were sure he'd gone over, bike and all, trying to miss the lorry.'

'What lorry?'

Again he filled the glass.

'It was standing in the middle of the damn road when we came round the bend. We only just missed it ourselves. Driver was dead — must've brained himself against the wheel when he tried to brake.'

'Vinnie told me your car was at the bottom of the ravine. What happened?'

'Who the hell cares?' he said, scowling. 'It was fifty damn years ago.'

The anger was a relief to him; he was the kind of man who would use it often, make a cloak of it to cover deeper feelings.

'We don't need this,' he went on, lifting the papers. 'Any of it. All we ever wanted was to be left in peace.'

He slapped them down again on the table. Then suddenly the belligerence vanished as quickly as it had come.

'I'm sorry,' he said. 'It's just . . .'

The wave of his hand was helpless, inarticulate. When he looked at me again the hard mask had vanished completely. It was a frightened, elderly face that showed behind it.

'Max was my best friend in the world, Fraser. I'd never have left him if I'd known.'

There was nothing I could say. Whatever else it had done, the information I had brought had reopened old wounds, stirred up old uncertainties. He stood up on his good leg, went over to the makeshift pulley which hung from the roof, and examined the bicycle that was suspended from it. In the skylight window above us I saw the flash of sheet lightning. A split second later the thunder came again, and I looked up. Only late afternoon, but the sky was almost black; it would come soon, now. Jacky spun the bike's rear wheel, then stopped it with his hand.

'We didn't know how far behind they were — Falkenheim's people, I mean. We had to make a quick decision, and I was for taking the chance. The dead boy was more or less the same size as me, so I took his papers and his clothes. The lorry was headed for Bremen — only bit of luck we had, that, because I'd family there. Anyway, it was loaded with files for the quartermaster's office, cabinets full of the bloody things. It took us about an hour to get our stuff into it, and then we pushed the car over the drop with the body in the driver's seat. I reckoned it would confuse them long enough to get us clear. Then when we got up north, my brother took Maria off to our parents' farm in Ostfriesland — middle of nowhere — and I took my chances and delivered the files. It was the safest thing I could think of. I became the dead driver. I became Heinrich Müller.'

The bitterness was back in his voice. He picked up a spanner and began adjusting the bicycle-chain mechanism with quick, deft strokes.

'Didn't anyone check?'

He gave a mirthless smile. 'You swallow that rubbish? German efficiency, the invincible war machine, all that?'

A rag appeared in his hands, and he began to wipe oil from the spanner. There was an aggressive edge to the action that warned me; his anger was rising again, fast.

'Everyone was so full of the news about Poland that nobody thought twice about me. When I delivered the stuff to that office they were all running around like blue-arsed flies trying to show how important they were, swearing loyalty to the Führer and shouting about *Lebensraum*. They had orders for me — join a new unit forming in Braunschweig. I took the chance that no one would know Corporal Heinrich —' savagely, he twisted a nut — 'Müller, and no one did. Nodody knew Corporal Müller, or Sergeant Müller, or Lieutenant bloody Müller either, all the way through Poland and France and Italy.'

He spun the back wheel of the bike again and went through all the gears of the complicated chain as it turned, testing them rapidly. The noise echoed through the big empty space of the workshop.

'I sweated for the first few months. There'd been a picture of a girl in his wallet, but nobody ever wrote, so I was in the clear. Then in forty-three I got this.'

He banged the spanner against his leg with a force that made me wince. It clanged against metal — a brace or calliper of some sort. Again he tried to go back to the therapy of the bicycle, but his anger finally overcame him. He threw the spanner down on the workbench and stood there, staring at the floor until he had himself under control. Then he went over and put the tool in its proper place in the rack on the wall.

I kept my voice as even as I could. 'Does it hurt a lot, the knee?'

He stumped back over to the table and sat down. It was hard to tell which was tiring him more, the pain or the worry. I realised he'd never come to terms with what the injury had done to his life.

'Sometimes, Fraser. Sometimes.'

His hand reached for the bottle again. Suddenly it was important for me to know all of it.

'What happened to Schumacher?'

The bald head shook.

'Don't know. My brother found him a car in Bremen; there were enough people there who owed us a favour. A car was easy, so was a ration book for Maria, later. Anyway, Schumacher said he was going home to Schwerin. Took all the files and stuff with him, God knows, I didn't want them. I tried to argue him out of it — told him he'd never make it that far without papers, but I couldn't budge him. I think he was over the edge by then, crazy. Maybe we both were. I never heard of him after that.'

'And Vinnie? How did you find Vinnie again?'

He looked at me so fiercely that I was afraid until I remembered his age, but before he could speak, there were footsteps. Maria walked between the rows of bikes, a tray in her hands. She put it down on the table and took the bottle firmly away from him. Her German was perfect, accentless.

'My husband met Vinnie again in Sachsenhausen concentration camp, Mr Fraser. After his injury, they sent him to the garrison there. He had no choice in the matter.'

The bowls of soup steamed untouched in front of us. I couldn't speak, couldn't take my eyes from him. I watched his face subside into despair, his gaze find the past — and suddenly I thought of Max. How sad Max would have been to see him like this . . . I looked up at his wife, and read the plea in her eyes. For *him.* She began to speak again, as much to calm him as to explain to me.

'There wasn't really much war for me. Learning German seemed a lot more important than the fighting, and so did the farm. I loved the farm.' Her hands went to his shoulders in a gesture of support. 'I stayed there right through the whole thing. All the neighbours thought I was a niece from the Sudetenland, and after Jacky's mother died I was more or less the farmer's wife. I kept house for his father and just waited for it all to end. I hardly knew Jacky when he came back for me.' Her fingers stroked the grey hair. 'When I was old enough, we were married. We were Dutch by then.'

Jacky's voice broke in, hoarse, low and tired, the Friesian accent harsh after the *Hochdeutsch.* She held him tighter.

'I tried to help, but what could I do? I couldn't get him out. All I could do was get him on the details that got extra rations, keep him away from the ovens, the burials. He understood, I know he did. After it was over, he helped us get the papers, the Dutch ones. He understood.'

He sat there, looking through me.

'He never came to see us. I couldn't expect that, even though we'd been friends. Not after the camp. But I know he understood.'

There was enough pain in the cracked voice to worry her. She cut in again, more anxious now.

‘Do *you* understand, Mr Fraser?’ she asked gently.

So that was why they’d hidden themselves on this lonely island, why they hadn’t gone to the police, why they’d never even gone as far as Münster in search of the threads of her past. She kept looking at me, wanting my acceptance for him.

‘Yes,’ I lied. ‘I understand.’

Never in a million years could I hope to understand what these people had been through. The thunder came again, right over us now, a rolling crash that rattled every piece of metal in the workshop. The first volley of drops was heavy enough to shake the row of pot plants behind the window — and hard enough to cut through the horror of the old man’s memories. A steady drumming began on the tin roof, and a different kind of worry showed in the tired face. He looked at her.

‘It’s all right,’ Maria said. ‘She has her yellow coat, and Mevrouw Bertelssen won’t let her out in this anyway. I’ll pick her up after we’ve eaten.’ She turned to me. ‘Lisa is very taken with you, Mr Fraser. There aren’t many treats for a deaf and dumb four-year-old on Terschelling. It would make my daughter’s day if you’d come with me to collect her from kindergarten. She has something to show you — a secret, she says. I know what it is, but I promised not to tell.’

The prospect of her daughter’s happiness lifted the years from her, showed me again a glimpse of the face I’d seen on the shed roof — and then she remembered her first duty; to him. Again the hands went to his shoulders.

‘Lisa is a great joy to us in our old age. Our first child died many years ago.’

This time it was Jacky’s turn to comfort her, and I knew she had told me in order that he would do so. Making him support her was the way she kept him in the present, I realised. How often did she have to do it? He caught me staring at him. Anger tautened his face again, but only for an instant; he didn’t have the strength, now.

'I know what you're thinking, Fraser. *The sins of the fathers . . .*'

She broke in quickly. 'Enough, now. Eat,' she commanded, 'and then I would like to know what this is all about.'

We ate in silence. I was a problem to them, I could see that. There was a sad irony to that fact. All my efforts, all Max's good intentions — they'd brought this family nothing but trouble. I wondered if there were still charges for Jacky to face, or whether in legal terms the whole thing was forgotten. I suspected the latter, but I understood why they were anxious to avoid the eyes of the world. The old man's last phrase seemed to hang over the table, and I knew that no matter how unfair it was, he was right. How could the sins of such a father fail to be visited upon the daughter? A concentration camp guard . . .? I remembered the reaction of the teenagers in Groningen to the photograph. Old hatreds died hard; a public airing of her father's past would dog Lisa all her life. As we finished the meal, Jacky began to explain the story. I was nowhere near as fluent in Dutch as in German, but even if I hadn't known a word, the changes of expression on Maria's face would have told me the stages of the tale. When she turned back to me, her voice was no longer steady.

'You are a good man, Mr Fraser. I'm proud to know you, and I'm glad my daughter likes you.'

A dam in my mind burst at her words, and feelings I'd been determined to forget flooded through the breach. What would it be like, to be part of a family, to have children . . .? Roughly I thrust the thought from me and let the cold reality of my situation take hold again. I was still a fugitive. What could I do now? Where could I run to next? *How could . . .*

The faultless German broke through the maudlin chain of thought, but now she was on the verge of breaking. 'Lisa would have liked Max, too, I think.' Suddenly her face was shiny with tears, and the fine head of silver hair buried itself in her husband's shoulder. She leaned against him for a moment, then straightened herself and brushed them away. It was a long time before she spoke.

'This land, in Austria,' she began, determined to keep the tears at bay. 'We don't need it, Mr Fraser, but Lisa . . .'

The rest didn't need to be said. It was obvious how hard their little business drove them, and it was equally obvious that there would never be more than a bare living in it. The rental bikes for the summer tourist trade might bring in more than the repair work, but there certainly wasn't the kind of money it would take to give a deaf and dumb child a decent start in life. Money, I thought, always money. I looked at Jacky.

'What happened to the painting?' I asked. I had to begin probing, or I'd never find out why Vinnie had died.

It took a long time for the question to penetrate the blackness of his thoughts. The thunder came again, swelling the rain's attack on the roof like a drum roll. The big head lifted slowly.

'Schumach —'

The door opened again noisily, and a brown-overalled figure burst in. Willem, the other billiard player.

'Mijnheer, there's a car! I think it's the police!'

There was a moment of frozen indecision. She was the first to react. The fiddle case was thrust into my hands.

'The back way, through the garage.'

She bundled me through a side door. I heard a brief clamour of voices, and then the key turned in the lock behind me and cut off sound and light. An icy finger of fear touched my spine. Keep your head, I told myself. *Think!* I felt in front of me — something massive, a truck or a van. Which way? I could hear the pounding of my heart above the storm as I began to move. Inch by inch I edged my way round the vehicle. It seemed an age before I reached the other door.

The full blast of the rain was a shock. It came at me almost horizontally, a thousand needles in my face. I fought it, trying to get my bearings — house and workshop to my right, the two big greenhouses on my left, sloping down from the main buildings. There was a cacophony of noise from them; a creaking of wood, a whirring of torn polythene as the cheap replacement panes gave way to the wind. I stood there, numbed by the violence of the downpour, trying to think. Open country, it had to be . . .

The other side of the garage looked the most likely route, but I held back just in time. The ground was already a quagmire; I'd leave footprints a blind man could follow. I took the paved path I'd taken earlier instead, trying to remember if it circled all the buildings. There was nothing round the first corner, but I saw I'd have to pass the workshop window. I crept along, got down on all fours and crawled under the shaft of light. At the far side I pressed myself back against the sodden breeze block. Should I risk the next one? I heard Jacky's voice from inside, shouting — and before I could stop myself, I looked.

A leather-jacketed back blocked the window. Behind it I saw another figure, a small blond man in a grey-green tweed suit. The man at the window moved. I pulled back, fearful of discovery — and as the rain battered me against the wall, I knew I'd seen the second man before. The anglophile! The one who'd given me money in Groningen! My mind raced. The busking had been before Vinnie's death . . . That meant . . . Suddenly I *knew*. These men weren't the Dutch police, *they were Vinnie's killers!* I had to get help, and fast. If . . .

I froze. A torch-beam scanned the sheds in front of me. Someone was coming round the corner.

The greenhouses were my only chance. Two steps took me to the nearest one. I shoved the fiddle case down behind a pile of sand and flung myself flat, praying the squeak of the door would be buried in the storm's roar. I crawled along the cinder bed between the rows of plants until I was hidden by a stack of seed-trays at the far end. How many of them were there? I could hear nothing except the frenzied flapping of the polythene, but there was enough light from the workshop window to let me see the path outside. I could make out a figure. He was coming along the side of the greenhouse now, very slowly — and the torch-beam had gone off. Fear stabbed at me. He'd heard! Was there a door at this end? Would he come in? I squirmed round in the darkness, trying to keep silent. A weapon, anything! A brick, a stone . . . My hand touched wood. A handle. It was a garden spade. He was at the top end of the greenhouse now, less than a yard away from me through the glass.

He pushed the door open — and then the torch-beam flicked on and showed me the gun. There was no time to be afraid. I lunged, ramming the spade upwards at his head as hard as I could. I heard a horrible crack as it caught bone, then he grunted and fell backwards through the plants. There was a dull thud, then nothing except the noise of the storm attacking the greenhouse. I scrambled up, the shovel in my hands, ready to hit him again — but there was no need.

It was the stillness of him that made me panic. Within seconds I was shaking with it, helpless. God help me, was he dead? Suddenly every nerve in my body was telling me the same thing. *Run! Get the fiddle. Get away from here!* I dropped the shovel, ran back through the greenhouse and grabbed the instrument case. I couldn't have killed him! It was impossible! The rain lashed at me as I stumbled back out into the open. I slipped and fell. When I picked myself up, I found myself again looking through the workshop window — and what I saw inside was even more impossible.

Near the main door, a brown cuff stuck out from a pile of overturned bikes. *Willem* . . . An awful coldness seized me; I knew what it meant, I *knew*. I wanted to look away, but I couldn't. Instead I drew nearer. Jacky was slumped over, completely still, the table in front of him covered with blood. I came right up to the glass.

The first I saw of her was the mutilated arm. The sleeve of her blouse had been torn back, and it shone white against the oil-covered concrete floor. I felt reality slipping away from me. Beside her body, the man in the grey leather jacket was unscrewing a round cylinder from the barrel of a gun. He turned, laughing at something, and I saw a livid red scar down one side of his face. The anglophile came into view. I saw him take a pair of yellow gloves from his pocket and walk over to the table. His forefinger began to trace a pattern through the blood beside Jacky's head. It was like watching someone else's nightmare.

I scrambled away from the window, back down the hill, splashing through the mud, heedless of noise in my desperation. Her voice came to me through the teeming rain . . . *You're a good man* . . . I stopped, fighting for breath . . . *I'm proud to know you* . . . I slumped back against a wooden wall, then recoiled instinctively; it was the shed, the one we'd repaired that morning! The future . . . Max, I whispered, there's no future, she's *dead*! Why did you bring me here? Again I heard her voice . . . *I'm glad my daughter* . . .

Lisa!

The thought of the child cut through my terror. As soon as they searched the house, they'd know there was a child . . . With horrifying clarity I saw what they would do. Killing Jacky and Maria had been more important to them than catching me. There could only be one reason for that . . . They'd shoot the child without a second thought, I knew it. Anger roared through me. *I had to find Lisa and get her away!* I leaned against the rotting wood, nursing the rage, the wind tearing at the roots of my hair. Suddenly everything was plain: I knew exactly what had to be done. I hated it, but I had no choice. The man I'd killed had a gun.

I fought my way back, cursing myself for panicking, watching the workshop lights for changes, steeling my nerves — but when I reached the greenhouse my courage almost failed me. The way he lay meant the weapon was under him. The thought of touching him was terrifying. I put down the fiddle case, rolled the heavy body over, and felt a warm stickiness. I jumped back in fright. Eyes closed, I forced myself down again for the pistol. I prised the thing from his fingers and thrust it into my pocket, and saw something else gleaming in the darkness. I reached down. Keys, a wallet. His pockets had emptied themselves when I rolled him over.

The wallet was open. I found money, German and Dutch, credit cards — and an I.D. card that identified him as Heinrich Gutterman of the Deutsche Bundeskriminalpolizei. I stood in the greenhouse, shivering, unable to comprehend. A *policeman . . . I'd killed a German policeman!*

Only the thought of the child kept panic at bay. There was no time to think about this; he'd be missed soon. I looked at the keys. *Car* keys . . . It was worth a try.

I only had the vaguest idea of the place's geography, but I'd seen enough of the outbuildings to know that they'd give me cover, at least as far as the open courtyard. It all depended on the vehicles, where they were parked, how many there were . . .

Two minutes took me to the corner of the barn. I looked; two cars, both empty, Maria's Renault and a grey Mercedes. There was twenty yards of open ground to cross, but apart from the porch light, this side of the house was in darkness. I sorted through the bunch of keys till I found what looked like the right one, took the gun from my pocket, and ran hell for leather across the yard.

I was sure I wouldn't make it, that the front door would open and they'd come running out. Twice I nearly fell, and once I almost dropped the gun, but my luck was in. The Mercedes wasn't locked. I threw the fiddle case on to the back seat and tried the key in the ignition. The wrong one! Heart in mouth, I worked through the bunch. If it wasn't here, I was finished! Finally I found it, made to start the car, then got out again, damning my own stupidity.

The first of the Renault's tyres was easy. The valve came away in my hand and air hissed out, but the trick didn't work twice. On the second tyre the perished rubber ripped, but the seal refused to give. I had no blade, nothing sharp, so only one thing for it. I ran for the Mercedes again, got in and turned the ignition. The starter whirred endlessly. I could have wept for frustration — a *Mercedes*, for God's sake! It caught. I wound down the window, aimed the gun, and pulled the trigger. The shot was thunderous. I saw the tyre collapse as I let out the clutch, and then I was halfway to the main gate, skidding wildly on the yard's mud. Once I reached the main road I looked back. There were lights, figures. I jammed my foot down hard on the accelerator and made it over the first hill.

The car was simplicity itself to drive, but my nerves were so far gone that I almost went off the road at the first bend. I tried to concentrate: a couple of miles to the village. The kindergarten; find the kindergarten! I swerved to miss an old man on a level crossing. The outskirts already . . . How much of a start did I have? When was the last ferry? I screeched to a halt in the main square and struggled out; no point in even thinking of concealing the car. A girl passed me, pushing a pram. I yelled after her.

'The kindergarten, where is it?'

She stared at me as though I was from Mars, and I realised I'd shouted in English. Adrenaline gave me the Dutch, and desperation gave me the lie.

'There's been an accident, I'm a doctor. It's urgent!'

It flustered her even more.

'Oh! Oh dear! which one? There are two.'

What the hell was the woman's name?

'The Swedish lady!'

'Mevrouw Bertelssen? Her husband's Danish, not . . .'

'Quickly, please. It's important!'

Her jaw dropped in confusion. 'I don't know which one it is . . .'

By now I was speechless with fear. Someone tapped me on the shoulder. I whirled round, my hand on the gun in my pocket — and found a middle-aged woman opening her front door.

'Behind the church, up the steps.' She chuckled. 'Mind you keep off the rug, though, the state you're in! She'll skin you alive if you make a mess.'

I looked down at my clothes, wet through, covered in mud. There was an overcoat on the car's back seat; it would have to do. The two women watched me struggle into it, then sprint across the square.

I reached the church before common sense prevailed. Calm, I told myself. Calm down. Nobody's going to give a child into your care if you act like a maniac. I took a deep breath, then forced myself to walk instead of running. My composure lasted till I rounded the corner. A handful of adults and a gaggle of children were gathered round a flight of steps, buttoning coats, laughing, shaking rain from umbrellas. Suddenly it struck me — the rain! Dear God, the rain had almost stopped. Was she still here? I ran across the street. What was she wearing? I saw a yellow PVC coat on the steps, and whirled the child round.

'Lisa!' I began, but it was a little Indonesian face that stared at me in alarm. I stood there, helpless as it crumpled into tears.

'Leave that child alone!'

A formidable woman in horn-rimmed glasses was frowning at me from the top of the steps. 'Who are you? What do you want?'

'I'm here to collect Lisa . . .' I ran out of breath and words at the same time. I closed my eyes, trying to remember the child's surname.

'I don't let my children go off with strangers, young man! Kindly tell Mevrouw Goosens that in future I'd be obliged if she'd inform me . . .'

'I have to take Lisa *now*. It's *urgent*!'

Interrupting her was the worst possible thing I could have done. I watched the scowl deepen to outrage — and suddenly the urge to take out the gun and just push her aside was overwhelming. But I knew I was lost if I gave in to it; a hue and cry here in the village would finish everything. She opened her mouth again, ready for a withering blast, but it was the child herself who broke the deadlock. She appeared on the steps, her face radiant at the sight of me, and before anyone could stop her she was at my side. I lifted the tiny wicker basket she was carrying and scooped her up on to my shoulder.

'Wait! You . . .'

The woman's indignation died away as we rounded the corner. Lisa hugged me as we went, grabbing the lapels of my coat in tiny handfuls. I half-ran, half-walked, giddy with relief at holding her, and before we'd gone twenty yards I was talking to her, whispering, even though I knew she couldn't hear a word.

'. . . It's all right, Lisa. Everything's all right . . .'

We reached the car in seconds. I put down child and basket on the passenger seat and reached for the starter. The ferry . . . Could we make it? I spoke my thoughts out loud, more for my own comfort than anything else. 'Still a chance, Lisa. All we need is —'

Her hand on my arm stopped me. She still had a smile on her face, but it was doubtful now, shy, for she'd caught my sense of alarm. Both of her hands were holding the wicker basket on her lap — and suddenly my pulse was racing, the blood was roaring in my ears. The surprise! The memory of her mother almost broke me, but I managed to keep it from my face. Anxious now, Lisa slid the basket across the seat to me. I tilted it up to inspect it, and a claw raked my finger. I pulled back my hand — and she laughed. Before I knew it, I was laughing too, stroking her hair, hugging her close so that she wouldn't see the tears.

There was no time to settle her properly. I jammed the

seat-belt into its clasp and gave her back the kitten. It was a simple equation now, between the speed of my pursuers and the last ferry's departure. Every second counted. As we approached the quay, I saw the boat. It was already loading, the queue of cars snaking forward a few yards at a time. I held back on the impulse simply to join it, and parked in the side street opposite. Were these people desperate enough to try killing me and the child in public? I didn't know, but if they were, the queue would make sitting ducks of us. But they couldn't have reached the village this fast, surely . . . I got out, peered along the quayside — and immediately saw the gap in my logic. A glimpse of grey leather jacket settled the matter beyond doubt. I sprinted for the car again, damning my own stupidity. Bikes! Of course! A workshop full of them!

It took us less than five minutes to reach the other side of the island, and I tried to hide my mounting desperation as we drove. That ferry had been our only link with the mainland, and being cut off from it gave us no choice but to hide . . . But *where*? The headlights showed me nothing except long stretches of dune — useless. A few miles further up I swung back across the island again in the hope of finding better cover. The road came out at a lone house beside a gate in the dyke. There was a ramshackle collection of sheds and a crumbling concrete slipway down to the water.

The house was in darkness. I pulled over; just driving was pointless. A map? I tried the glove compartment but all I found was a radio. Lisa glanced up at it, then went back to her pet, and the prosaic sight of her at play with the kitten triggered all my doubts. Where the hell could we go? The island was tiny; the most cursory of searches would turn up this car. We had to ditch it. And how long . . .? Smiling, Lisa read my thoughts. Her hand went to her stomach and patted it in the universal gesture: *Feed me.* Then it stroked the basket; *and my kitten.* I remembered the sweets I'd been given in Groningen. The fiddle case. I undid the catches and felt around in the top compartment. Strings, two boxes of rosin, spare . . . *Two* boxes of rosin? I gave Lisa a handful of sweets, and brought out the rosin.

Since leaving Basel, I'd never had more than one box, I knew. I opened the one I didn't recognise — and found a flat black cylinder about the size of an acorn. With sinking heart it dawned on me what it was. I looked again in the glove compartment.

The square box wasn't a radio; there was no longer any mystery about how they'd traced me as far as Terschelling.

But when? How? The little man . . . I remembered him stumbling over my case in Groningen. I laid the bug in the glove compartment beside the receiver and smiled, determined to keep my fury from the child. What did it matter now? Once again, anger cleared my mind. The best option was obvious; I'd been given it only a few hours ago. Again I scanned the house, but there was still no light.

'Come on, up you get,' I muttered. I lifted Lisa and her kitten out, thinking, this was your father's idea first. I sat her down on the kerb.

The slipway curved to the left before it reached the water, and it was just wide enough for the car. I drove the Mercedes down until the foam was almost up to the wheels, opened both front doors and put her into neutral. Once the handbrake was off, she began to move. I jumped out and watched her roll as far as the curve, tip gracefully over, then hang for a long moment until the waves began to drag at her. Bitterly, as she went into the water, I remembered Jacky's words: *It would confuse them long enough . . .*

'*Ik heb nog nooit iemand zoits zien doen!*'

I spun round and made out a man's figure in the dark. I could see Lisa's yellow coat by his side. He held her hand, she held her basket. My fingers curled round the handle of the gun.

'I don't understand.'

His English was rusty, heavy with accent. 'Ah, British . . . I say I never before have seen anyone throw away a Mercedes! I cannot blame you, I think, not after what they do in the war. Your daughter?'

The question almost threw me, but he didn't notice my confusion. When he let go of her hand, she ran to me. I could make him out now. He was small and old, his face lined with age. One sleeve of his jacket was empty, pinned up at the shoulder.

'I see you from the window. A lot of money, I say it to myself, a man has to have a lot of money to do this.' I could hear the irony in his voice. 'Or maybe a lot of problems. You have problems?'

I nodded. The wind threw spray at us. I didn't trust myself to speak.

'Police?'

'Yes.' A ray of hope came into my mind. 'German police.'

He spat.

'Policemen are . . .' he snapped his fingers, searching for the word, '*bastards*! German policemen will most of all be bastards.' His ability to muster the profanity delighted him. He looked down at Lisa. 'Something bad, is it? What your daddy does?'

The wizened face frightened her. She turned away from him and clung to the leg of my trousers. He laughed.

'You love him so much, it cannot be so bad.'

I found my voice. 'We need help, a place to hide.'

He stroked his chin. 'German policemen! I enjoy, I think. Hurt them back some.'

The empty sleeve flapped loosely. He kneeled down, still trying to woo the child. There was a noise of breaking glass and tortured metal as the waves began to pull the Mercedes across the shingle. He looked at the car, then me, considering, calculating. Again he tried to chuck the child under the chin.

'Well . . . we must not let your daddy's sins come on your head, eh, my pretty? But better we do not hide here. Better . . .'

Hearing the phrase again took me to the edge of madness, squared the circle of desperation in my brain. Five people were dead. Why? *The sins of which father* . . . Jacky or Max? Max had been father to me . . . Had his sins led me here to watch them die? I held on to the child's hand, fighting for sanity as the spray drenched us.

'. . . the cutter.'

My silence alarmed him.

'I said I take you to Ameland in the cutter. German *bastards*,' he repeated nervously.

Ameland was the next island up. I stared at him. It was the last link on the chain of insane logic. A concentration camp guard's daughter, saved because an old man hated Germans . . .

Suddenly his face split into a sly grin that evaporated my madness. Something much more mundane than hate was written on it. 'In the cutter. For five hundred guilders.'

For the tenth time in an hour I tried to stretch my limbs quietly enough not to disturb her. Enough grey daylight was seeping in through the narrow windows for me to make out the interior of the church, now. It was simple and bare.

As slowly as I could I got up from the stone floor and stepped over the kitten's box. Lisa's feet were lodged tightly in the waistband of my jeans, and I'd taken her inside my sweater in an attempt to keep her warm. She hadn't slept until we'd left the old man's boat, and I knew the depth of her slumber now was a measure of her exhaustion. With heavy limbs I walked towards the altar and levered myself gently down on the front pew. I was as tired as she was; the trek along Ameland's sea wall had taken my last reserves of strength. Every bone in my body ached.

The metal of the cross, whatever it was, gleamed like gold in the darkness. It brought back childhood memories. Of God . . . Of an eight-year-old who wondered who God was, and why his mother talked of him so much and so sadly; a small boy who felt the mute force of his father's anger at both God and her, who knew all these things were woven together, who knew somehow it was all his fault.

The images crowded in on me as I sat cradling the child in the cold church. *Six days shall ye labour* . . . School assembly, the draughty, overcrowded hall, prayer somehow part of discipline. Our Father help us pass 4B science and may the second eleven beat St Modan's . . . Let us show our love for our neighbour by not vandalising the school buses . . . Who else opened their eyes? Who else looked across the sea of bowed heads and saw the fervent clasp of the headmaster's hands, the disappointment on his earnest face? *On the seventh day* . . .

The Sunday-school teacher was the first man I ever feared — the stinging hand across my cheek for giggling, the stern words with my mother — but the minister was the first man I ever knew to be a liar; the smooth, oily voice, ingratiating, assuring his well-heeled parishioners that the eye of the needle would, of course, be big enough for them . . . It all crystallised into the figure of a fifteen-year-old boy holding a cheap copy of the New Testament, given for Christmas by an ageing Aberdonian aunt who made him promise never to dance with Catholic girls because they were immoral.

But even then I'd known it was the Old Testament, not the New, which ruled Scotland. There were no prodigal sons, only winds and whirlwinds: you reaped what you had sown, and that was the end of it.

I stared at the cross as Lisa slept on in my arms. The gun dug into my thigh, a bulky thorn in the flesh of my conscience, and in spite of everything I believed I found myself muttering what I could remember of the twenty-third psalm. The child's head stirred on my shoulder.

And for Christ's sake help me take care of her, I added, almost aloud, *if you exist . . .*

The light was stronger now. I turned and began to walk towards the door, the half-dry jeans stiff against my legs. We were safer here than we'd been on Terschelling, but it still wouldn't do to tarry. We'd best be gone from this place.

Yea, though I walk through the valley of the shadow of death . . . The line repeated itself over and over in my head. I was in the same position now that Max and the others had been in fifty years ago. In a church with an orphaned child, surrounded by danger. *Yea, though I walk through the valley, I will fear no evil . . .*

Evil. These men were certainly that, but I put away the guilt I felt. I could have no true remorse at the fact that I'd killed a man. He had hunted me with a gun, and if I'd turned the other cheek, the child in my arms would have died. Evil was the right word.

I had to involve someone else, now. All these years ago there had been friends to help Max, and I knew I could do nothing more alone. I had to trust another person; *trust* them, not just buy them like I'd done with the old boatman. It gambled everything, a simple throw of the dice, with nothing more to back it than my own judgment, but I could see no other way. It was no longer just a question of my staying free, there was the child's life now; to bring her safely through the valley, I had to have help.

I pushed open the door. The wood had splintered easily when I'd forced it. It was a small enough crime in comparison with what I'd already done, but I felt guilty about it just the same. Guilt over a torn piece of wood, but not over a death? Hurriedly I went out into the wind, carrying my fourfold burden of child and fiddle, beast and gun. The next few hours would tell if I was right or wrong.

Chapter 4
HOUSES

I LISTENED TO the footfalls on the creaking wooden staircase, sure it was her, but the knife tightened in my hand just the same. The key turned; I sat down again and tried to go back to preparing the meal, but relief made my reach too eager. The bag of groceries slipped from my grasp, its contents tumbling out over the linoleum. Quickly I thrust my hands out of sight under the table so that she wouldn't see them shaking.

She sat down opposite me without taking off her coat and began to pick things up. I watched the lithe grace of her, stretching, gathering, an armful of packets, a handful of vegetables. The ginger kitten sidled round her hands, hissing, spitting, pouncing on the paper bags. She laughed as she shooed it away. Once the last of the potatoes had been rescued, she lifted a damp cloth from the sink behind her and sat back, wiping her hands. I waited for her to toss the hair out of her eyes, but when she did so it was still somehow a surprise, a beautiful one, and it began to relax me. Through the door of the living-room I could see Lisa playing with the doll's house, serious and silent.

'I brought these,' Elly said, taking two large books from her shopping bag. They were stamped with the crest of the public library on the spine. 'One of us has to begin to learn, Alex.'

I agreed. We'd been here a week now, and our worries about the child were increasing. She could make sounds with her throat which were meaningless to us except as proof that she needed something, but the best we could do was guess or draw pictures until either we established what she wanted or gave up in defeat. When we failed, the frustration was the worst thing I'd ever known; to be unable to help made me feel worthless as a human being. Through the doorway I watched her. Mouth set with concentration, she placed a tiny bed in a tiny attic with exaggerated care. Every day we'd been here, I realised, she'd smiled a little less.

But she wasn't unhappy, either, and she seemed to accept me. Once, she had cried. To watch it without doing the same had taken every last ounce of my self-control, and I knew it had affected Elly just as deeply, but all we could offer was the comfort of our arms. I watched the precision of her play and wondered what she made of us. What filled the soundless world she lived in? Was she merely waiting with infinite patience for her parents to come and take her home? I picked up one of the books: the prospect of any kind of progress was a relief. Elly took the knife and a bowl and made space. The pile of sprouts grew steadily, fresh and green, a small cross cut into the base of each of them.

'Well?'

I tried to keep my voice neutral. The book was filled with diagrams of hands. To my uninitiated eyes they were halfway between supplication and semaphore. She didn't look up from the vegetables.

'They are *almost* certain you are dead, and Lisa as well. It was the gossipy one who always comes in for the books about fishing, the one who brought it in the first place. He said I could take it down because the inspector was certain you had drowned.' She blushed. 'He . . . *admires* me.'

The odd choice of words was typical of her, the embarrassment wasn't. I tried not to think about what it meant, or what I wanted it to mean.

It had been her idea to phone the police on the pretext of wanting to take down the reward poster they'd put up in the library. The bodies in the workshop had been found the morning after the killings — and for the week since, the papers had been full of little else. I lifted the *Groningse Courant* from Elly's bag. The 'Star of David murders' they were calling it — for that was the design that had been painted in blood beside the head of Jacky Goosens, now known to be Heinrich Müller, former concentration camp guard. The lead story speculated on the connection between these deaths and that of Leon Smulders the week before in Groningen, and the middle pages held a sober editorial on anti-semitism and its backlash. I remembered Vinnie, and grimaced; never had I seen a man so unconcerned with his own race or religion. It was all a smokescreen, I was sure of it.

I'd been trying to work it out for a week now, here in this tiny flat above the warehouse, listening to the Groningen traffic, trying to amuse the child as best I could. Elly pulled a bundle of carrots from the shopping bag and cut through the string with her knife. She began to clean them, and I felt a long sigh escape me; the bluff with the car had worked. It was more than I had dared hope for.

As I watched her slim hands pare the carrots, I wondered at the changes in her. It had been hard to persuade her on the phone. My call from Ameland had been confused, cryptic — and her first response to it had lain between scepticism and outright hostility. But when the boat had docked the next day, she'd met us, and we'd thrashed the thing out for hours in a wet lay-by. At first she had been convinced that I was dangerous, that the presence of a kidnapped child was proof of my madness, but when I told her I'd be willing to take my own chances if she'd just look after Lisa, she'd begun to believe me. Her only condition had been that I surrender the gun, and I had been glad to give it to her, to be rid of the thing. It lay hidden behind the bookcase in her bedroom.

'Do you still think we should go on with the rest of it?' I asked.

'Yes.' Her voice was emphatic. The hands never faltered with the knife. 'Anything which reinforces what they want to believe helps us. They're already halfway convinced. I don't think it's too much of a risk.'

The stubbornness in her voice was a challenge, but I chose to ignore it. We'd argued for hours the night before, because we both knew how real the risk was, but in the end I knew I had no choice in the matter. She had more or less told me that she'd go ahead and do it, with or without my approval, and if it came off, she was right, it could help a lot. Tomorrow she'd take the ferry to Terschelling, as a foot passenger. At some point on the crossing, a bundle containing my fiddle case, my passport, and one of Lisa's shoes would be dropped over the side. Elly would wear gloves, and she'd touched none of these things, we'd reasoned, so fingerprints wouldn't be a problem. Then she would spend the rest of the day making the reason for the trip, sketching on the island like the amateur artist she really was.

With luck, at least some of the things would be washed up in a logical place, and then we could only hope the last doubts of the police would be stilled — or at least further muted. I knew it was as hard for her as for me to put faith in such amateur criminal expertise, but there wasn't the slightest hesitation on her part, for she knew as well as I did that one thing was necessary above all else.

Alexander Fraser had to die before someone else could be born in his place.

To sit here beneath the sloping roof of this cramped kitchen and plan my own death was strange indeed, but I knew that was the easy part; my rebirth would be both riskier and more complicated. I took a second knife from the table drawer, and she pushed a handful of carrots over to me. She watched the clumsiness of my efforts, but the mocking smile was banished after a second, for she took great pains to curb her scorn at my lack of domestic skill. We sat in the weak light, each of us alone with our thoughts, until she broke the silence.

'On Friday I can borrow a vehicle that will suit us better, and tomorrow I'll find someone to take the cat. It would be stupid to wait any longer, Alex. Sooner or later one of my friends is going to turn up and find you here. And I bought these today.'

Again she reached into the bag. She passed the packages across to me with a nonchalance that was entirely false.

The intimacy between myself and this strange, courageous girl had been growing daily, although not once had we touched each other. It had begun with her acceptance of my story, grown with her decision to involve herself, and now it was expressing itself in all sorts of ways, subtle and unsubtle. I examined the packages of children's clothing in their bright wrappings. Jeans, tee-shirts, socks, underwear, a dainty pair of shoes. I looked at her. Her gaze held mine for a second and then she looked away. Again she blushed. We both spoke at once.

'She'll miss the kitt —'

'She'll need the clothes. I . . .'

Suddenly both of us were watching the child. Playing house, I thought. Lisa wasn't the only one . . . Sooner or later we were going to have to stop, but neither of us had the courage to say so out loud. It was a fragile edifice we'd built around the little girl, and it had already outgrown its initial purpose; neither of us was using the game just to keep our fears at bay any more. Why had she never married? Had the intelligence frightened them all away? She put down the knife.

'Alex,' she began.

The tone of voice warned me. She was a fighter, I'd known it since the first day — and I knew what was coming now. I'd been waiting for it, dreading it.

'I have to know.'

The tension in me flared into anger.

'Know *what*? I've told you everything! I've given you the gun! What more . . .?'

'Giving me the gun means nothing if you won't give me your *trust*,' she said quietly.

'I've trusted you with Lisa's life and mine.'

'No, you haven't, Alex. You've trusted me with your future, but you won't trust me with your past.'

I saw the determination in her eyes and knew the truth of what she said.

'Why do the posters say you're violent?'

Her face was taut with strain. I looked at it for a long time, trying to fix it in my memory. Each separate feature of the face that was trying to help a fugitive and take care of a handicapped child at the same time. She had one thing in common with the woman who had died so brutally on the island: a beauty which would not wither with age, no matter how much it changed.

'Alex, you're the most gentle man I've ever met. Tell me.'

She wasn't afraid, I could see it as I watched her, and it was only that which gave me the strength. I felt the sharp blade of the forgotten knife cut into my trembling hand. Drops of blood began to fall on the white tablecloth. I tried to wipe them away, but they became a red smear that stared at me in familiar accusation. The bitterness rose in me.

'My wife died,' I said. 'I caused it.' I closed my eyes and heard my voice rise to a shout. 'It was an *accident*!'

She looked past me at the doorway. I turned to see Lisa, holding her kitten, staring at us, sensing the trouble. I held out my arms. Hesitantly the child came to me, let me comfort her.

'It was an accident,' I whispered, but even as I did so, I knew I didn't believe it myself.

The throb of the ship's engines was a steady brown noise,

rhythmless and strangely comforting. Lisa lay in my arms in the back of the converted ambulance. We'd deliberately kept her awake as long as we could on the drive between Groningen and Ostend, and we'd chosen the shortest possible crossing. I lay comfortably, drowsy and warm on the foam rubber, the ship's motion rocking me gently towards the edge of sleep. We were underneath one of the back bunks, and there was plenty of room in our snug, motorised womb. Another hour to Dover, I thought, but reality seemed remote, and for a rare moment I was free of worry and doubt and fear. The child's breath on my cheek was innocence, trust.

I wondered where Elly was, above us. As we'd waited in the queue of cars she'd been tense and silent, the strain evident in her face. In the last two days she had filled the vacuum of speech between us with action and determination. Not once had she tried to make me elaborate on what I'd told her, not once had she trespassed on the forbidden ground which had sprung up between us. Somehow we'd become closer, but our closeness was a window that we could look through only as long as neither of us touched the glass.

Would it work? She had the nerve, the guts, I knew that. She said it would only be marginally more difficult than the border between Holland and Belgium, and we'd sailed through that without even being stopped. She was sure she could charm her way out of any difficulties with customs or immigration, and only a direct search would reveal the two of us in the back. I hadn't wanted to think about the consequences of failure, but she'd told me how precisely she was aware of them; aiding and abetting both suspected murder and certain kidnapping would not carry light sentences.

But, in spite of the risks, hope stirred in me. Once again I let myself think about the previous night, for there was no one here to see my optimism or ridicule my feelings.

I'd woken in the small hours. The small room where I

slept was still strange to me, and it had taken a moment to recognise the shelves of art books, the pale water-colours of her student years. I'd admitted to myself that sleep had become impossible with the excitement of anticipation and taken a slim volume on expressionism from the shelf, determined to plough my way through the Dutch as a penance for the pleasure of the pictures.

She was seated at the table, modestly clad in a thin robe. In front of her lay cloths, my bow, small bottles of cleansing oils. In the corner stood a violin case, newly bought, expensive.

The battered wood of my fiddle looked completely right in her hands. I stared at it while she stared at the book I held. For a long time we sat in the stillness of the cold Groningen night, knowing that each of us was trying to penetrate the other's world.

I lay in my dark hiding-place in the ship's belly, hugging the memory and the child to me.

To walk across the pale frosted grass of the Downs was exhilaration after the cramp of the crossing, to move freely after the days of confinement made me almost giddy. I stumbled, laughing, and she caught my arm and didn't let go again. The child ran ahead in the fading sunlight, scything the clumps of gorse with the stick I'd cut for her, and then a slight breath of wind cleared the mist. Lisa pointed down at the ambulance sitting on the road below us like a brightly-painted toy, and I felt my face break into an idiot's grin. The cold sun smiled back at me. I caught her up in my arms, yelling like a maniac. Her laugh was a silent reward.

'You have a new man's smile. Are you one?' Elly asked.

'No, but I soon will be, won't I, Lisa?'

I rubbed my nose against hers and felt her tiny fingers tug at my hair. When I put her down, she went immediately to retrieve her stick, and I sat down beside Elly, breathless, dizzy with happiness. As we looked across the valley from the vantage-point of the cold white rock, her hand found mine in the pocket of the cheap anorak. Her hair blew across my face, and the pungent smells of tired travel hadn't quite obliterated the scent of coconut oil. My joy was complete; for the briefest of moments, I'd won against the system, and the girl by my side was determined to help me savour victory to the full. We'd been waved into England by a bored immigration officer who hadn't even wanted to see her passport, she said, and the customs men had been more interested in her looks than in her van. We'd laughed over her blushes for miles. Never had I imagined myself capable of such celebration.

Lisa found the stick and began her game again, whirling like a dervish until a big hare bounded over the field in front of her. About twenty yards away it stopped, and child and beast looked at each other, transfixed. She stood completely still, her breath coming in fast white puffs, almost solid in the cold air. Then she chased wildly after the hare until it disappeared. When she could no longer see it, she stopped and marched back, staff in hand, a determined little pilgrim on a long road, glasses askew on her nose.

'We'd better go, Alex. She'll catch cold.'

We trudged back down the hill to the bus, both of us loath to leave this lonely place where we'd been so happy, swinging the child between us. She clambered up on to the front seat and began pretending she was the driver. I took her in my lap as I climbed in behind the wheel, and she continued the game with the determination she brought to all her play. Then she turned, and there was a bout of sign language between her and Elly, fast and practised on the one side, hesitant on the other. I hadn't been able to learn as fast as Elly, but even I knew the sign Lisa was repeating to her. I handed her across and started the motor.

'She's telling me she can drive like her . . .'

'. . . daddy,' I finished. Both of us paused. I pulled the

old ambulance out on to the road.

Her voice was concerned as she went on. 'You shouldn't let it worry you too much.' Once more she paused. 'I mean . . .' She stopped again, trying to choose the right words, and kissed the top of Lisa's head. The dark interior of the vehicle hid her face from me. 'What I'm trying to say is that if you have to lose a father, then it must be reassuring to find such a nice uncle so quickly.'

'Is that what you told her I am?'

She shook her head. 'I didn't tell her anything. I'm not good enough at all that . . .' she gestured at the sign-language book which lay on the dashboard . . . 'yet. She told me. She said you are her new uncle and you're nicer than her Uncle Willem.'

My heart lurched as I remembered how he had died, but I said nothing. After a moment she continued. Her voice held a different note now.

'I can barely remember my own father. I must have been about two years older than Lisa is now when he died. My mother brought the two of us up, me and Jutta. It would be nice if you could meet her. She's a fine, upright old gossip these days, but she never lets the village forget she was the doctor's wife.'

The nostalgia in her voice had acquired its usual sharp edge. Sometimes it irritated me, but I recognised it for what it was: a disguise for an excess of love.

'We didn't have any handsome Scotch uncles when we were girls, Alexander Fraser,' she said, mockingly, 'and we didn't have Lisa's courage either, when I think about it. Jutta used to say that all the other children had daddies, so we used to pretend, take turns. I was a better daddy than she was.' Her voice softened again. 'Children are adaptable, Alex. Lisa's a very tough four-year-old. Aren't you, *kleine engeltje*?'

She tickled the child under the arm. Lisa squirmed with delight and wriggled her way round into her favourite cuddling position, head pressed tight against Elly's chest. When I saw her together with the child, I kept wondering why she wasn't married with a brood of healthy kids of her own. I wanted to ask her all sorts of questions, but I didn't know how to begin. Again she spoke.

'I'm more worried about you than I am about her.'

Still I didn't answer.

'I have no psychology, but it's obvious that what you're about to do could hurt you a lot, Alex. Perhaps I don't have the right to be, but I am worried.'

I kept my eyes on the road, but she leaned over and let her hand find mine on the gearstick.

'What other way is there, Elly? I can't do anything without a new start. And anyway, I've done enough running. I can't live the rest of my life like that.'

A week ago a conversation like this would have been impossible for me, but the confession I'd made to her had been some sort of turning-point. For the first time the whole story had been told; not even Max had known all of it. The knowledge that I could still mean something to someone, in spite of what I'd done — that was incredibly important to me. It couldn't take the guilt away — nothing would ever do that — but it could put it in a different place. Also I knew we were taking on the task of being the child's unofficial guardians, at least until we could be sure of her safety, and to play my part in that I had to face the challenge of sorting out this whole business. That meant I had to have a new identity, one which could travel in reasonable safety, operate without fear of harassment.

There was no way to that new identity without settling a score, claiming payment for a debt that was owed to the old one, to Alexander Fraser. As we parked the van in Oxford, I knew that my new-found fortitude had brought a more dangerous thing in its wake; I wanted the satisfaction of seeing this through.

We walked through the old town towards the station, looking for a telephone, icy puddles cracking beneath our feet. The fabled dreaming spires were discreetly hidden, cloistered off by yellowing walls which separated Town and Gown as surely as if they had been Brahmin and Untouchable — thick walls which kept the power of the college groves safe, anonymous. The darkness which clung to them was a second line of defence, the freezing fog a third. Its might thus armoured, academia brooded and watched, content to let the neon bluster of the commercial streets pretend to be the town's heart.

The shops were gearing up for the frenzy of Christmas. A banner blew in the wind, strung out over the main street, grimy with the soot of countless student coal fires. *Only twenty-two days left*, it said. The number was replaceable. Beneath it, garish lights shone down on the frozen knuckles of the Salvation Army band at the corner. No matter how manfully they blew, the carols seemed tainted by sadness . . . *O Come All Ye Faithful — And Spend.* Determined faces went about the task in the shadow of the fake holly and plastic ivy. I stiffened, holding the sleeping child momentarily tighter as two policemen, in their comic-opera bobbies' helmets, walked past the phone-booth, but Lisa slept on, tired after so much fresh air. The carol changed, and I sang softly along with the tune, watching Elly through the glass. *Let Nothing You Dismay*, I thought, surprised at my own calm.

But still I felt uneasy here. I was much more of a stranger in this southern England of theirs than I'd ever been in Basel or Groningen, or any of the European towns I knew from my days as a language student. It was the air of privilege, the ripeness of the bourgeois accents that threatened me, made me feel so conspicuous.

I was Scottish, working class, and theirs was a world in which I could participate only as an outsider — not even as a rebel, just as someone who had been successfully excluded. But if I were honest, there was a part of their secure existence which I envied . . .

When she came out again, her smile was uncertain. 'Everything is all right. We're expected. All three of us.'

She looked anxiously at my frown. This wasn't the way it had been planned. 'Alex, please don't be angry. I told her I have a friend with me as well as my niece, but it's up to you. If you want to go tonight, you still can. She'll be so pleased to see me it won't matter. But what harm can it do?'

It was the first time she'd asked me for anything, and she wasn't good at disguising how much she wanted it. She'd cared for me, planned for me, broken laws for me. Most of all, in the face of common sense, she had trusted me. She'd given me everything she could. Her hair flew back in the familiar gesture as she waited for my reply. Big flakes of snow began to fall round us.

I tried to work out what difference one night would make, but my objectivity was a sham; I wanted it as much as she did. I let her take my arm and begin to lead me. Slowly our little surrogate family started to move through the crowds, back towards the van. We'd been thrown together by a bizarre mixture of history and circumstance, the three of us wedded to each other by rites of violence; surely we had the right to steal a few hours' peace, a respite . . . I offered up a silent prayer for it as we passed the musicians. They were waiting for their conductor to begin the next carol, blowing for warmth into their freezing hands. I put a coin in their tin as we walked by, and received a cheery 'Goodnight to you' as my benediction.

I played the Bach clumsily, forgetting the end several times before the right phrases came to my fingers, but the harpsichord sounded so wonderful it didn't matter. Even my flurries of wrong note were transformed. The instrument's voice made them into graceful things which echoed round the room's panelled walls, and the perfect balance of the ivory keys made playing effortless. I had never touched such a fine instrument before, and the very act of laying hands on it was a pleasure. I tried to remember when last I'd spent an hour at a keyboard.

'Bravo, young man.'

Elly and her Miss Mary stood framed in the doorway. The apology which sprang to my lips died, dismissed imperiously before it could be uttered.

'Play. Nobody's touched the thing for years.'

She gave me a wry smile as she marched towards the fire, and I smiled back, a fellow conspirator. Harpsichords which had lain untouched for years were rarely in perfect tune. I played a single chord, let it resonate round the room, and thought about everything Mary Wellbeck had said to me since I'd entered her house; a subtle series of intelligence tests, all to one end: to find out if I was good enough for her precious Elly. I felt myself smile, for it had all been so sincerely done that it was impossible to resent. Elly put the tray down by the fire, and as I watched her and the old woman together, I knew I'd found the source of many of her mannerisms, as well as the stylistic vagaries of her English. The two of them were very close. I bent over the keyboard again and played a chord sequence which I remembered as something by Scarlatti, but I could get no further than the opening bars. What was missing? An F minor? I tried, but it still didn't fit. The women watched me from the fireside, one frankly proud, the other frankly curious. I tried a C minor, and this time it worked, but it was only another few bars before I faltered again. Suddenly a bony hand, gnarled and spotted with age, was holding a glass in front of me.

She watched me drink, nodding with approval, then stood beside the harpsichord, not bothering to hide the closeness of her scrutiny. The eyes were dark and bright with intelligence, the sharp contours of her face unsoftened by the salt-and-pepper hair in its unfussy knot. How much had Elly told her? She stroked the satinwood of the instrument in a thoughtful way and nodded again, satisfied she had catalogued me correctly. She turned to Elly. The look was a mother's, something between warning and congratulation.

'Mind he takes care of you, now. Goodnight.'

Her footsteps receded against the snap of the fire's pine logs. That was all we needed to make our crazy family complete, I thought, a patrician art historian for a granny. Elly gazed into the flames and I looked round the walls again, slowly, letting the good malt whisky warm me thoroughly before my eyes came back to her. This place was where she had studied, and she fitted it well — better than the tiny flat in Groningen. She was at ease in this house, and it wasn't hard to imagine long evenings spent in earnest study here, quiet discussions dominated by the sardonic smile. Somewhere above us a door closed. I shut the lid of the harpsichord and went over to her by the fireside. A mild version of the smile was there when she looked at me.

'I thought you only played the violin.'

'I thought you only worked in the library.'

The smile became a laugh.

'What do you think of my Miss Mary?' she asked.

'I like her.'

It was true. I felt none of the alienation I'd expected when we first arrived. Mary Wellbeck was the youngest daughter of a wealthy landowning family from the Midlands, an upper-class intellectual whose name was familiar to me from my university days. She had a formidable reputation across several widely-differing academic fields, and from what Elly had told me about her time here, I gathered she was a born teacher. That was a gift I would always respect, because there had been a time when I had wanted it so badly for myself.

'She says there's some sort of playgroup in the village where I can take Lisa.'

She looked at me anxiously, knowing that most of my fears had been stilled, but not quite all of them.

'She hasn't asked any questions yet, but she's bound to notice everything's a bit strange. It's the first time she's heard anything about my having a niece, for instance, but I'll tell her the rest only if I have to, Alex, even though I trust her. One lie is enough. She'd know.'

I was sure she was right about that, at least. I couldn't imagine much getting past that canny, quick mind.

'Is Lisa in bed?' I asked.

In answer, she rose and held out her hand to me. As quietly as we could we went up the Georgian staircase to the room where the child lay. Elly opened the door silently. Lisa was fast asleep, huddled in a corner of the huge bed. From somewhere one of the two women had found a teddy bear, and it lay between the white sheets at her side, a solemn brown sentinel with a chewed ear. We stood in the doorway, absorbing the peace of the sleeping figure.

'Goodnight,' I whispered, laying my hands on her shoulders.

I felt her body stiffen as I leaned over to kiss her cheek. It only took a second for the tension to conquer me as well — and then she spun round to face me. The movement wound us into a fierce hug, a protective, sexless embrace that crushed our bodies together for the first time. It was an electric moment. Her shoulders trembled, and I could feel wetness against my cheek as she fought for control. Suddenly she twisted round in my arms, and again both of us were looking at the serene face on the pillow, as though it was for Lisa to decide, to sanction. The child slept on, undisturbed by our gaze. Finally, Elly closed the door and laid her head slowly against my shoulder. We stood like two halves of a tired sculpture, supporting each other in silence, waiting . . . When she began to tremble again, I knew she was losing her battle against the tears. The certainty of purpose that had got us here had evaporated, its adrenaline dissipated by the reaching of our goal — and it had taken her strength with it. Our physical safety had been an overwhelming imperative that had used all her courage, and the only thing it had given her in return was a refuge from her feelings — a false refuge; planning and action had smothered what was growing in her, but they hadn't killed it, or even diminished it, they had merely allowed it to grow in the dark. It filled the air around us now, and without the imperative she had no armour against it, and neither did I. I knew it as I held her, but I was frightened. Of the words. Of what they were supposed to mean. Of the gap between that and the reality they had brought me, before. She looked up at me, and I saw her find the courage. She blurted out a beginning for us.

'Alex, I . . . Don't leave me now. *Please.*'

The last words were a breathless, whispered rush. I held her tighter to me in reply. For a second more she tried to fight it, but then the tears of relief pulled themselves out of her in great, racking sobs.

Only once we were in the big double bed did she stop crying. We lay, arms round each other, each of us trying to give as much comfort as we could, both of us glad of the covering mask of darkness. It took a long time for exhaustion to sweep our fears into sleep.

Dawn was beginning to break when we stirred. It was a drowsy consciousness of her nearness which woke me, a softness of skin against my own, a gentle rhythm of breathing. Instinctively I pulled back, and felt her waken as well — and for a moment each of us seemed surprised to find the other there. I watched inhibition and anxiety grow in her eyes, just as I knew they were growing in mine, but then, just as quickly, I saw wonder and wanting replace them.

We were not gentle lovers. With the touching of hands and bodies, an animal urgency overtook us. It woke a wildness in me, and to feel it flow through her body as well as my own made me want her even more. A pale winter moon shone down through the window, fighting the daylight, making half-shadows of the white neck and the slim hips as she clung to me. Every so often one of us would draw back, but now that the dam had burst, hunger was greater than timidity. Her body was firm and strong, demanding — and when she climaxed it was a big, juddering, gasping thing, arch-backed and open-mouthed, which left both of us trembling in its wake. Once it was over, she pushed me from her and rolled away, her back to me. For a few seconds I didn't understand, but when I held her to me her face was once more wet with tears, and all of the panic returned to me tenfold.

'I didn't mean to hurt you.'

Neither of us could stop shaking.

'*Elly* . . .'

She shook her head and put a finger to my lips. For a long time we just lay on the old creaking bed, cradling each other, holding as close as we could — and then the excitement wrapped itself round us again. Once more we began, slowly, deliberately. Her small, hard breasts rubbed themselves against me, brown nipples big with desire. As we closed with each other I could feel the beating of her heart, and it filled me with joy; I had imagined that love and lust were dead things to me, that the cruelties and disappointments of my marriage had left me without heat or passion to give, but as her body moved with mine I knew it was no longer true. I wanted this woman. I was lost in her.

When we were calm again, she spoke. 'I'm afraid of your going away, Alex. And I'm afraid *for* you as well.'

'So am I. Perhaps that's why we're here.'

For a long second the smile ruled the wide mouth.

'The maiden giving the warrior strength before the battle, you mean?'

I said nothing. She turned away, angry with herself for the joke, fearful of the admission she had just made. When she spoke again, it was in a tiny, lost voice that should have belonged to Lisa. 'I'm glad I made love to the Alexander Fraser I know. I'm frightened of him becoming someone else.'

Outside, the moon was gone. Snow began to fall again, heavily.

Chapter 5
ROOTS

THE PIPED MUSIC was polished and featureless, and the clatter of glasses being none too gently washed broke through it defiantly, a child's rattle thrown on the aural linoleum. I could feel the barmaid's eyes on me as I moved back to the window. It was no wonder; this was the third day, she was bound to be getting curious. I took another sip of the flat beer and wondered how much longer I could nurse the half pint, for the last of Elly's money was almost gone. Would he come? Again I looked out across the street; if he ran true to form, it'd be soon now. I felt the weight of the gun in my inside pocket. The tension rose like a coiled snake in the pit of my stomach.

There was a draught as the swing doors of the lounge bar opened. The old man's rheumy eyes fastened briefly upon me, then lost interest. He shuffled determinedly towards the bar. I'd been eliminated as a potential touch two days ago.

'Ah'll huv a pint o' heavy, hen. And a wee sensayshun.'

She went sullenly to the taps as his voice raised itself in pitch to a declamatory, hectoring note, cracked and wavering.

'Ah eywys huv *exackly* the same. 'M a man o' habit.'

She ignored him. Obstinately he went on.

'Whit hairm dis it dae? Bettur tae meddle wi' the deil ye ken, hen. Eh?'

'*Haud yer wheesht, ye styipit auld bugger!*'

The slap of glass and coin on wood and the noisy downing of the cheap whisky terminated the mutual offending of sensibilities. It was their daily ritual, and on its completion they were both content enough to let the muzak once more hold sway.

I looked out at the lunchtime bustle of Falkirk's Newmarket Street and permitted myself a smile at the old man's reworking of the ancient burgh's motto: '*Better meddle wi' the deil than wi' the bairns o' Falkirk.*' Once it might have been an incitement to valour, but now it held good in a grim sense that was a mockery of civic pride, for this was a pitiless town, relentless in its pursuit of profit. They'd rob you blind here with all the douce, two-faced piety they could muster, wringing their hands as they did so, crying over how poor they were.

It was a place that had been born in error and raised without shame. East and west, north and south, they'd reached out to each other over the fertile loam of the Scottish lowlands, and Falkirk was the misbegotten result. It was like a child drunkenly conceived in the back seat of a rusty car — unwanted, unloved and left behind. Like everyone else, its parents had just been passing through, and like many another cheerful bastard, it shrugged its shoulders at life's joke and prospered well enough. Half market town, half decaying industrial monument, wholly uncertain about its future, Falkirk called the hard cash of the present its only God, made its own way in the world — and spat in the eye of anyone who dared criticise. But it was a town that always made me uneasy. I could deal with the hardness, the grabbing hands behind the traders' glib smiles, but there was a forbidding clannishness about Falkirk that made me glad I didn't come from here.

And then I thought of my own home town — the prim snobbery-ridden burgh of Stirling. Maybe Falkirk wasn't so bad after all; at least they looked after their own.

Suddenly it was on me. I saw the figure I was waiting for emerge from the double doors of the register office. Now or never. Quickly I zipped up my anorak and slipped out of the side entrance. I was just in time to see him disappear round the corner, but I wasn't worried; from my two-day vigil I knew his destination. It had been worth the wait.

He was quite badly overweight, and he waddled. The double-breasted blue blazer hid the paunch from front and side as he searched for a sight of himself in the shop windows, but from behind, the flapping of the jacket's vents and the flat-footed gait made the roll of the buttocks almost comical. From time to time one hand brushed the thinning hair back into place, while the other tapped the rolled-up newspaper against a grey flannel leg, beating time to the tune I could see him whistling. Memories came back: he'd been a good musician in his day . . . Like the two previous lunchtimes I was worried in case he spotted me, but he was far too preoccupied with himself to notice anything other than his own reflection — and the women. He ogled the typists as they clutched their skirts against the damp wind, and waved to the bored girl in the doorway of the second-hand shop. She ignored him. I followed him past the car park and saw him go into the Burns Bar. I gave him a few minutes, then pushed open the ancient door.

There's a smell to a good pub in Scotland, a smell that can overcome all the sourness, the squalor that lives with the drink — thick, yeasty and warm as the beer itself, overlaid with the sharp tang of the last drops of the dram wrung lovingly into the pint. Between the dark doorway and the partitioned horseshoe of the bar it enveloped me like a fog, and in the distance of four or five paces, I'd stepped back in time to a place where generation upon generation of Scottish manhood had held both its liquor and its tongue. The white-jacketed barman served me a pint and went back to his paper with a civil nod. I looked round the room. No garrulous winos or sullen barmaids here, just hard, steady drinkers. This was the place where John Knox's conscience drank on his night off. Silent as the most Presbyterian of kirks, and ten times more pious.

He was standing a little way from me, one foot up on the bar rail, eyes on the racing page. I took my pint and walked slowly round to him.

'Hello, Geordie.'

I had the satisfaction of watching the colour drain from his flabby cheeks. His first instinct was to run, but I was between him and either of the doors. He backed away as far as he could, up to the next partition, but his eyes never left mine.

'You're supposed to be *dead*! The cops were round at your father's place askin' questions last week.'

The aggrieved tone of his voice tugged at my anger, but I resisted it and didn't reply. Automatically he smoothed the hair and straightened the rugby club tie. All the time his eyes scanned my clothes and face, searching for the clue that would tell him whether I'd come for revenge — and in its absence they retreated into fear, real fear. What had become of the friend I used to know? He raised a nervous hand.

'Alex, please, man. No trouble, eh? What's by is by, and there's no help for it now. What good would it . . .?'

I cut him off. 'I've debts to call in right enough, Geordie, but not that kind. There's something I need done. It won't take long to explain. We can talk in there.'

I nodded at the semi-private cubicle behind him at the far end of the bar. Anxiously, he looked round for help, but there was none.

'Alex, I've got to get back to . . .

'Now, Geordie.'

He shrugged his shoulders and carried pint and dram over to the booth. The walls were covered in notices for the local steam railway preservation society. He peered at each of them in turn as though they held some message for him, then sat down abruptly, avoiding my eyes. Talking to me was reality, and he would have done anything to avoid it. Wearily, the stomach sagged towards the iron table.

I closed the door, and took a piece of paper from my jacket pocket. 'That's what I need.'

He read through it quickly, then looked up, amazement written across his face. 'You're *mad*! I couldnae do any o' this, man! For starters, I'd lose the job! It's not even my bloody *department*!' He slapped the paper down on the table. Genuine surprise had given him enough courage for the moment's bluster. 'And if they found out, you know where I'd end up! In the bloody . . . *Oh, Jesus,*' he finished softly.

There was silence. Fright took hold of him at what he'd nearly said, and the smell of it was strong enough to fill the small room. Sweat, alcohol and aftershave compounded his fear into an aphrodisiac cocktail for the cheapest of sadists. His hand shook as he drained the whisky, and then he looked away in genuine shame.

'I'm sorry, Alex.'

I searched his face for traces of the boy I'd grown up with. We'd been inseparable. Somewhere, in his mother's house or mine, there was a hoard of old photographs. Two freckled-faced kids wearing Rangers strips, me holding the ball . . . The unsmiling sixties pose of two teenagers against a peeling council-house wall, cheap electric guitars, hair as long as either of their fathers would allow . . . St Andrews beach, the four of us, all mildly drunk, Isobel and Moira in matching swimsuits . . . Him being best man at my wedding, me being best man at his a year later. The joke he'd made then should have told me. I'd got the sexy twin, he said, he'd got the one that could cook. But as I looked at him, I couldn't connect the memories with the figure before me. Who was this small, mean man, this balding, middle-aged drunk, dressed like a bad parody of a young executive? He'd married a cheerful, pretty woman, as much saint as her sister had been devil. In the space of six years, his philandering had transformed her into a feckless ruin, a Valium-shrouded ghost who stared away her days in front of a television set, the occasional nervous breakdown her only claim to life. Geordie's response had been predictable: more of the same. More girls, more bets, less success with either. The horses galloped him from one debt to the next, and the women . . . He chased them doggedly, with cold determination, a lonely, dutiful lecher. What could they see in him except sadness? I tried to wash the bitterness from my mouth with the beer. Why did I care?

'Listen to me, Geordie. Very carefully. If you don't, I'll make bloody sure you *do* go to jail. You see, Geordie, you're my last chance. I'm running now, but if they get me I won't keep my mouth shut any more. I only did it the last time for Isobel's sake, but she's past saving now, poor bitch. This time, I'll make damn sure they know all of it. I've nothing to lose.'

'It was *you* that bashed her brains out, no' me,' he said.

This time I let the anger have its way. Three years of bitterness drove it furiously into the open. I grabbed him by the collar and heaved. The slam of his head against the wood reverberated through the whole pub. There was a crash of glass as the table overturned.

'It was you that made sure she bled to death, though. Wasn't it, Geordie?'

The memory gripped me as tightly as I gripped him. The half-renovated cottage, pristine in the snow under the moonlight, testament to my doomed determination to save the marriage with a fresh start. The pair of them, sprawled on the big brass bed — him drunk, her excited at the thought of us fighting over her. The unbearable sound of her laughter as she lay there, naked and beautiful, taunting, playing with the danger, sneering the words at me: '. . . *not the first, and he won't be the last* . . .'

But he was the last. I remembered the scream as I hit

her, the sickening noise of her head meeting the brass fender — and then the terrible chill as her blonde hair became the brilliant centre of a widening dark pool. I looked into Geordie's eyes. We might still have been there. The terrified expression on his face now was exactly the same as it had been then, as he watched me lift her back on to the bed. It had taken the ambulance an hour to get there, and I could still hear the grim sympathy in the doctor's voice as he told me what I'd already known.

'You bastard,' I said. 'If you hadn't taken the car and run, I could have saved her.'

'Alex,' he whimpered. 'Alex, I didnae . . . NO!'

He screamed as I raised my fist, but before I could hit him, a hand gripped my arm. I turned to find a middle-aged man with a kindly face, brows furrowed with concern.

'Hey, jist a minute, son, eh? Mibby ye's could settle up yer differences withoot the rough stuff. Seasonigoodwull an' a' that, ye know whit ah mean. Eh, boys?'

In the confusion, Geordie took his chance. Before I'd gathered my wits, he was out of the booth and running. I grabbed the slip of paper, shouldered the philanthropist aside with a roughness he didn't deserve, and made it to the door — just in time to see a grey leg vanish into a close across the street. I sprinted after him, but I could have taken my time, for all it mattered.

Except for one flat on the ground floor, the whole tenement had been condemned, and both stairs and back entrance had been bricked off. Once again, Geordie Murray had run into a hopeless dead end.

It stank of spilt wine and urine. I took the gun from my inside pocket. As I walked down the close I could hear him crying; it was a high keening noise, the call of a desperately wounded animal, punctuated by the snivelling of a kid who'd never grown up. I forced his chin up with the barrel and stuffed the sheet of paper into the top pocket of the blazer. Suddenly there was a familiar childhood smell which almost killed my determination; he'd pissed himself in fright.

'Okay, Alex,' he whimpered, 'I'll get what you want. I'll do it, honest, I will. *Please*, Alex, don't, oh don't, *for Chrissakes I never meant it*! It was *her*, Alex, she wanted it.' He was trembling uncontrollably.

'By tomorrow, Geordie.'

I lowered the gun and let him collapse against the wall. He took a deep breath, then stared at the ground in front of me.

'Only thing's the money, Alex. There's nane there, man. Isobel's . . .'

Anger saved my resolve. I dragged him up the rough brick surface and pressed the barrel of the gun against his head.

'*Don't lie to me!*'

He shut his eyes and sobbed. His voice squeezed itself out between tightly clenched teeth.

'*Honest!* There's nae money. The bookies . . .'

Somehow I knew it was true. I forced myself to think. 'Forget the money,' I said, although I knew how much of a complication it meant. 'But the rest of it by tonight. At my father's house.' I moved closer to him. 'And, Geordie, remember to get *all* of it right. Because if I think you've screwed it up, or gone to the cops, or breathed a word of this to another living soul, I swear to God I'll be back to kill you.'

I let go of him. He fell to his knees among the litter of broken glass and used condoms. When he finally picked himself up, he made no attempt to recover the shards of his shattered dignity.

'Alex,' he began, but he stopped as soon as he saw the contempt in my eyes. Without another word, he turned on his heel and walked quickly out of the close.

I slumped against the wall and put the gun in my pocket, giddy, weak from so much anger. I tried to take a deep breath, and couldn't. The stench of the place joined forces with my own self-disgust at what I'd been forced to do. I bent over and retched violently.

The road up to the castle was steep, and I took my time. I was earlier than I'd expected and the climb held memories for me, calm ones. I needed calmness. Even now, a day later, I could still taste the sourness the encounter with Geordie had left in my mouth. Elly and the child had become my antidotes to violence, but in their absence the wet shine of the cobbles was the best of substitutes. I could almost hear the ring of my mother's heels on them as she led me up the street, a six-year-old boy anxious to see the soldiers on parade. We'd stood in the sleet and she'd sung quietly along with the tunes the bands played. There was no sleet on the esplanade now, just a faint haze of mist that would later freeze into dank fog.

Stirling Castle. A grey watchdog perched on a black rock, no longer sure if there was anything left to guard, dreaming of strife and the blood of past feuds . . .

But it was a guardian too old to have eyes or teeth, now. The town below fed it a meagre diet of tourist pap and forgot about its existence. Stirling lay under its shadow like a drowsy woman, the snowy hills a rumpled coverlet tossed away to the north, the tortuous windings of the Forth her discarded ribbons — naked except for a southerly necklace of sad pit villages, her string of grimy pearls. Below me I could see a stocky, duffel-coated figure making his way up the hill. I turned towards the castle gate. Better if the attendant didn't see us go in together.

He caught up with me just by the Great Hall, and for a few seconds we looked at each other in candid appraisal. He was smaller than me by a few inches, but the overall impression he gave was of bigness — a big, heavy man who wore his harsh outlook on life where everyone could see it. His body was bulky, densely-packed and still powerful, and his mind hadn't slowed at all with age. The handsome head was square, broad and massive, built for battering down the walls of other peoples' opinion. The face it wore had a ruddy complexion that might have been a drinker's, but anyone who'd ever crossed swords with my father knew better. It was a face shaped by anger, a face that had long ago become convinced that wrath was the best way to force the world's hand. The natural redness of it had been accentuated by the climb, but I could read the love in it, and the relief. And the uncertainty . . .

'So you *are* alive! When you phoned, I thought it was somebody's idea of a joke. I didn't tell your mother for fear of it. But she'll believe me now. Alex! I . . .'

His voice faltered as he gripped my arm. Alarm rose in me at the implications of what he'd said.

'Dad, you can't tell her.' I watched the hurt grow in his eyes, and inwardly cursed myself for being so stupid. 'Not yet, Dad. Nobody here except you and Geordie Murray knows I'm still alive. Mother couldn't hide it. You know that as well as I do.'

'Geordie Murray. *Aye*.'

He walked away from me, over towards the battlements. The contempt in the last syllable confirmed a long-held suspicion — that he'd marked Geordie down as a waster long before I had. How much had he guessed about the circumstances of my marriage? I wasn't sure, but he was no fool, for all the stubbornness of his faults. I tried to remember a time when we had been at peace with each other, but as I followed the broad back along the parapet, I admitted to myself that it had never existed. He stopped at a corner to stare at the patterns of the headlights on the road below, and when he spoke he didn't look at me.

'Three years. She's not seen you or even heard from you. You wouldn't even see her when you were in *Barlinnie*! Now she's not a mile away and you won't even let her know you're still alive! What kind of son d'you call yourself?'

It dawned on me that, despite my phone call, he had no real inkling of the danger I was in. My confusion rose even further, but it couldn't keep pace with his temper.

'*Three bloody years!* As if it wasn't bad enough already that you've . . .'

I broke in as quickly as I could. The longer his anger lasted, the longer it would take to convince him of the seriousness of my situation. I should have known: we'd never been able to speak to each other without fighting first.

'Dad, what did the police tell you?'

It was the red rag the bull in him needed. '*Never mind what the bloody police told me! Is there no respect left in you?*'

'*Dad! For Christ's sake!*'

We were shouting now. I looked round anxiously, but there was no one else in sight. We were alone in the gathering mist with only our rage for company. I forced myself to calm down.

'*Listen* to me. Father, *listen*! *Please*! I have to know what they told you. *It doesn't concern just me*! I have to *know*!'

Something in my voice got through to him. His eyes measured me again, as though I was one of the colliery engines he'd spent his working life inspecting. For a long time he stood, taut, letting the anger simmer, and then the shoulders slackened and it evaporated in a sigh of defeat.

'They asked about two men. One called Smulders. I don't remember the other name. Gough, or Gower, or something.'

'Goosens?'

'Aye, that was it, I think.'

'And what did they say about them?'

'That they'd both been killed, that it was to do wi' you. No more than that.' He ran his hand over his brow and turned towards me, trying to keep the emotion from his voice. 'And they said you were most likely drowned. What's all this about, Alex? How bad is it this time?'

'Dad, I can't tell you. It's better you don't know.'

Again the frustration translated itself into movement.

He glanced from side to side as we walked, restless, avoiding my eyes, unsure of what to say to this son who had become so much of a stranger, unsure of his anger because it hadn't brought the responses he expected. The massive stone buildings of the castle offered neither of us comfort as we passed. I thought of the courtyard which was hidden deep in their grey centre, where a medieval Scottish king was said to have kept his lion. That was what I was reminded of, looking at him; there was a power in him which rebelled at the thought of confinement, restriction. I knew his mind was already trying to jump the walls my problem had put round it. We paced on in silence for a long time.

When we stopped again, it was on the outer fortification which overlooked the slum they called the Raploch. The rising rags of grey smoke from the chimneys made it eerie, as though it was hanging from the mist. From the heights of the castle the dirt and the sadness were plain to see, but distance was kind to it. Close up, the reality of it was savage: a bitter, pockmarked ghetto that seemed to have been expressly designed for a single purpose — to barbarise its inhabitants by removing the last of their dignity. By day it was merely ugly, but by night it was science fiction, a hellish moonscape populated by wary tribes, the grim territory of a separate society guarded by its own warrior caste of dour weans and angry dogs.

My father looked longingly down upon it, a freed beast remembering the security of the cage. 'It's not easy with your mother,' he said, almost to himself. 'Since it started. Your trouble, I mean . . . The minister's hooks are deeper in her every day — she nearly *lives* in yon bloody church.'

He looked me squarely in the eye. The anger was gone, now, all of it.

'I'm frightened for her sanity, Alex. Since they told us you were dead, she's hardly looked up from that damn Bible. Useless bloody book . . . When we lived down there, it was better.' Again he gazed down at the Raploch. 'But it's never been easy,' he added softly.

It was as near complaint as I'd ever heard him come. They had married for love. His family had looked on in hard disapproval because she wasn't from their class; hers had banished her with terrible swiftness for marrying below her station. For a while the pair of them had defied the prophecies of doom by building a tight, closed world on the triple foundations of love, mutual respect and bright dreams. The goals had been a measure of respectability for him, safety from poverty for her. He'd worked all the hours the pit could give him, fighting to better himself — and winning — but the cold reality of the daily struggle had slowly eroded the joy from her heart, and without it, her ability to hope had died. She had none of the cheerful acceptance of poverty that the Scottish working class used as balm on its wounds. A middle-class childhood had left her with frugal, educated tastes; she was content to save every penny, but terrified of not knowing where the next meal was coming from. She searched the Raploch for colours, and her eye met only sordid shades of grey. Her response was to turn to God, to seek a higher authority to explain, to justify. My father never became bitter, but the rational man in him was outraged by it. They had furious arguments. His reason would hammer uselessly at her piety until both of them remembered their love, and then there would be exhausted calm. I remembered the morning after one such storm, in the old house down there in the Raploch, when a small boy climbed into the big double bed between his parents. Beside his father's head was a book called *Science for the Citizen*; on her side, nearly covered by thick auburn curls, lay a leather-bound Bible.

Now, standing beside him, I felt an old, familiar pain, for I knew I'd never given him as much love as I'd given her. The depths of my consciousness threw up memories for my guilt to catch. His disappointment at my lack of interest in the mechanical things which were his world had been obvious. He'd wanted a son to share the delights of stripping down a motorbike engine on a Saturday morning, and instead he'd watched me follow her path instead of his, spending my Saturdays learning to play the violin and piano with strangers. He'd accepted it quietly, without rancour or comprehension, burying the hurt. I'd been the tip of the wedge that Scotland's granite-faced God had driven between them — I knew it as I looked at him. Now I had to force him to withhold the small comfort he longed to give her, and I hated myself for it. But I had no choice.

'Dad, please try to understand. There's something I have to do. I'm not dead, but there are people who'd like me to be. I promise you I've done nothing wrong, but somehow I've landed in the middle of other peoples' business. I haven't killed anybody. I've saved a life — a child's life — but she's still in as much danger as I am. I need *time*. Don't take it away from me.'

He searched my face again, then the huge head bowed in resignation, and once more his eyes found the mean streets of the Raploch. I knew that he was thinking of her, that in spite of everything he loved her so much, and suddenly I found myself thinking of Max. They shared two bonds, my first and second fathers: both had loved rare women, and neither had been given the son he wanted. He stared on, fascinated by the grey and red roofs that held so much of his past. When he spoke, it was with weary certainty.

'It's time you stopped blamin' yourself for the death, son. I never did, nor anyone else who knew her, either. I don't like to speak ill o' the dead, but she was rotten right through, Moira was. But I saw it too late to help you. I blame myself for that.'

The shock of his words created a silent vacuum of unreality; it was quickly filled by my tremendous shame. I thought of the years of battles we'd had. How much I'd underestimated him, how much I'd failed to learn . . . Before I could speak, he put his hand on my arm.

'It's all right, son. It's enough that you're not dead.'

He reached into his pocket and brought out two envelopes, one buff and official, the other cheap and bulky. Briskly he thrust them towards me. 'If you need more help . . .'

I shook my head.

'Good-bye, Alex.'

'Good-bye, Dad.'

He marched off down the hill without looking back, and I watched until the mist swallowed the heavy figure. I opened the buff envelope. There was a duplicate birth certificate in the name of Alexander Lawless, born 8/10/57 in the parish of Bothkennar, and another in the name of Elinor Lapsley, born 23/4/60 in the burgh of Falkirk. There was a duplicate of marriage between Alexander McLean and Elinor Hunter, dated May 1983, and duplicate birth certificates for Elizabeth McLean and Elizabeth Lawless, both dated June 1985. I felt a surge of satisfaction. They would provide the necessary basis, the passports, driving licences, etc., that I needed for our new identities. The ones for Lisa and Elly were insurance, but Elly had insisted on them in case anything happened to me and she had to carry on alone. I hoped fervently we'd never need them. I tore open the other envelope.

There were fifty brown Royal Bank of Scotland ten-pound notes in it. It was two hundred more than I'd asked for. I looked again at the houses below me. Suddenly the street lights switched themselves on, harsh spotlights highlighting a monument to bleakness. The Raploch faced me, unabashed and defiant, its poverty bathed in their sickly yellow glow.

I stood in the mist, wondering how many sons ever understood their fathers.

'So I can tell her?'

'Yes. Tell her and show her the photograph. Ask her if she can help identify it, or if she knows anyone else who can. But make sure she understands how important it is to be discreet.'

There was the customary pause that I'd grown used to as we tried to say good-bye to each other.

'She'll help, Alex, I know she will. Good luck.'

I put the phone down and walked away from the open line of booths, hoping Elly's assessment of her old tutor was right, feeling strange in the new clothes. The black overcoat's astrakhan collar rubbed uncomfortably against the back of my neck. I stopped to adjust it, and as I caught sight of my reflection in the windows of the waiting taxis, there was a moment of non-recognition. But the doubt only lasted a second, for the image was right: from fur hat to polished brogues I was the picture of the well-to-do orchestral musician, and I had a brand-new passport, issued the day before, to prove my identity to anyone who might query it. Even if Elly's judgment of Mary Wellbeck was wrong and she went to the police, she knew nothing of Alexander Lawless or his destination. The reassuring weight of the fiddle, snug in its new case, was my only link with the past. I stopped in front of the big departures board and looked around.

Half past six in the evening at Central Station was a ballet school gone wild. Glaswegians walked, ran, leapt and staggered past each other, punctilious in their avoidance of bodily contact, for in this town you could never tell what an accidental shunt might bring in its wake. Politeness and aggression were both recognised norms, and respect for the city's volatility had made Glasgow a breeding-ground for generations of dancers. Even those who were merely waiting jigged about a little, warming up for their performance, one eye on the knots of silent policemen who were spread around the place, the other on the board above them.

Only the old woman was absolutely still, as she'd been when I passed her on my way to the phone; still and silent, a disconnected counterpoint to the mad minuet which surrounded her.

She stared at the five-sided glass cubicle from the tunnel of her head-scarf, her eyes tiny pinpoints of light, all but invisible beneath lids that were swollen red pelmets. It was a structure which stood out from the rest of the station fittings, a futuristic litter-bin which people threw their beer-cans at instead of into. A scrum of them garnished it now, as though the thing had its own gravitational pull. Occasionally one of the passers-by would stare at the old woman in her turn — in appreciation, for Glaswegians have a ready eye for paradox. Her brown wreck of a coat might have been fashionable in the forties, the blue ankle-socks and cracked polythene children's sandals in the sixties, but it was the plastic shopping bag which caught the attention. Her worldly goods poked through the surface, but the yellow-on-purple legend was still readable: *What Every Woman Wants* . . . The bag stirred in the feeble wind, slapped against a bare, blue-veined leg. The sign on the cubicle which held her eyes said *Meeting Point* in red and white. She stood rock-still, a parable caught between two ironies.

I watched her as I waited for my train to come up on the board. The newness of the clothes was enough of an irritant to make me fidget. Unconsciously, I joined the station's restless dance, moving about, tapping my feet. I was impatient to be away from here, to take the next steps towards solving the puzzle surrounding myself and the child. Around me the conversations drifted, the chorus of the Greek play Glasgow likes to make of its Saturday night; a continuous performance that oscillates between extremes of comedy and tragedy, a drama which depends on reaction to drunken boredom for its theatrical staple, a spectacle dangerously careless of the distinction between actor and audience.

'. . . 'n iffy hadnae, ah'd a been black affrontit, Mary, ah'm tellin' ye. He tellt me no' tae be sae . . .'

'Mason's honour, ah says, we nivver *touched* the boy!'

'So anyway. If you get the tickets, I'll get the drinks, and we'll split the taxi, eh? Ach, don't be . . .'

'. . . says tae her, whit's the gemm, hen? Gonny stoap throwin' up ower the guid suit! Ah ask ye, Harry! A bran' new bloody suit! *Piyerre fucking Cardang! A hunner'n'twenty smackers*, an' she's . . .'

'Ah'll gie yizza song, so ah wull!'

Heads turned. A small, bald man lurched out of the main entrance and embarked upon his crossing, swaying dangerously, blown by haphazard, personal winds. Everything about him was brown, from the suit to the flat half bottle held aloft, the loser's trophy. His voice echoed above the crowd.

'*When yeeooooouuuuuuuww aand aaaaaaaaayyyyyeuh* . . .'

Good-naturedly the crowd took him in its stride, moving aside to broaden his channel.

'. . . *weeeerrrr youuuuuuuunngg, uh, Maggieeeeey.*'

He stopped abruptly, feet apart, swaying, unsure whether to vomit, and then suddenly no one was looking at him any more.

It began like the distant roar of surf, as though the sea had reached as far as the end of the station platforms. People recognised it. Courses changed subtly, and there was a sudden bustle among the policemen as the roar became a familiar chant.

'*Herewego, herewego, herewego!*
Herewego, Herewego, Herewego-oh!'

They surged across the station floor, a red-and-blue mass slogan, glassy-eyed, happy because Rangers had won. Only the old woman and the drunk stood their stubborn ground and made them break ranks. She stayed as silent as before, but he chose the moment to resume his song.

'*Whehennnuhh, youououuuuuwand haaaay, weeee-errr* . . .'

'Gie's peace, faither!'

'Kinye whustle, auld yin?'

His lack of succcess infuriated him. The eyes focused, saw the motifs, the colours, the tattoos. *No Surrender! 1690. Remember the Boyne! U.V.F. and the Red Hand.*

He spat, and raised the bottle like a liberty torch. 'Prodestint basturts!' he bellowed.

Only a few of them turned, but it was enough. He'd found his audience now. His alliterative gifts asserted themselves.

'*Yizzurra Bunchy Bluenose BASTURTS!!*'

Almost wearily, as though violence was the one chore too many in a long day, half a dozen of them began to move towards him. He was only saved by the intervention of authority. A big sergeant strode quickly across the station floor, gripped the brown figure by the scruff of the neck, and shook him like a terrier shaking a rat. The bottle smashed on the ground, and a thin stream of greenish bile ran from the old man's mouth. The policeman waved a threatening hand at the supporters.

'Awa' hame. The lot o' ye!'

They whistled and jeered their derision, but within a few minutes the chanting was almost out of earshot, the bulk of the mob gone. The sergeant dumped the old man down on a scruffy red plastic seat, and my train came up on the board. The singer stayed upright for a second, then slumped over into slumber — and suddenly the old woman's glassy stare turned itself on his brown figure. I picked up my fiddle case and made to move, but a hand on my shoulder stopped me. I wheeled round to see the big policeman, and the panic rose so fast I was incapable of speech. He was holding something out to me.

'Must've fallen from your pocket, sir.'

I took the glove, tried to force a smile, and couldn't, but he was so pleased with himself he didn't notice. When he saluted me, grinning, it was all I could do to move my legs in the direction of the train without breaking into a run, but I finally managed it. As I passed them, the old woman's scrawny hand was beating jerkily against the drunk's suit in a futile attempt to wipe off the vomit.

My heart thumping madly, I headed for the train that would take me away from Scotland.

Chapter 6
REVELATIONS

IT WAS EARLY MORNING by the time the train reached Basel, and I was grateful for the illusion of cover the darkness gave as I hailed a taxi from the station rank. I'd slept all the way from Ostend and I felt rested, but excited at the same time, for I knew the coming confrontation would be decisive. Whatever happened, I was about to take a step towards the truth.

'*Wohin?*'

I gave the driver street and number. He scrutinised my face in the mirror, noted the dark glasses, then concentrated on his driving. The men, and occasional women, who patronised that address were not anxious to have their privacy invaded, and it was better business to be discreet; under the circumstances, the glasses were logical.

As we drove through familiar streets I took stock, nursing my confidence. The passport had received only the most cursory of glances at each border, my fiddle and bag lay in the station's left luggage office, and there was nothing to connect me with the Scottish busker of a month ago. I stood a reasonable chance of preserving my anonymity – at least in front of relative strangers. Only one thing nagged at me: had it been wise to leave the gun? From one point of view I was glad I had, for the thing made me uneasy, but there was no denying the potential danger I was courting. Everything would depend on how long it took to get through the preliminaries, how well I could read the situation. Once again I wondered how much she was involved, whether she had set the whole affair up for some reason of her own, but as we turned into the familiar wide street I found myself hoping my suspicions were unfounded, for to me she was still Max's woman. In the end, though, I knew there was only one certainty; I would end up with either a friend or an enemy tonight — there could be no middle ground.

The taxi followed the accepted practice, coming to a smooth halt under the chestnut tree fifty metres from the house. I tipped the driver accordingly, and he pulled away quickly, leaving me alone in the street, breathing clean, cold, Swiss air. Snow crunched under my feet as I walked up to the heavy door and rang the bell.

An eye appeared at the spy-hole, and I heard bolts being drawn back. The door opened to reveal a huge man who was a stranger to me.

'You have an appointment, sir?'

'No,' I said, 'the house was recommended to me.'

I was ushered into a small hallway which smelled of fresh wood and paint, and before I could object, he frisked me. As his hands made their deft investigation I congratulated myself on not bringing the weapon and registered the fact of the changes; something serious had happened here, for all of this was hardly an incitement to custom. He muttered an apology, then shifted his enormous bulk to reveal a second spy-hole in the plywood wall between us and the house's interior. Evidently I was being further inspected. Then the door swung open, and I stepped on to plush carpet and into perfumed air.

The atmosphere was old-fashioned, luxurious, like a turn-of-the-century hotel, redolent of money and service. The antique desk that dominated the spacious hallway was worth a fortune — and the girl beside it looked every inch as expensive. She wore a simple dark grey skirt and a pink-and-white candy-striped blouse, its collar elegantly fastened by a small cameo brooch which matched the ring on the little finger of her left hand. The hand hovered uncertainly in the air, and even though I hadn't taken off the glasses, she saw me staring at it. The cool receptionist's smile faltered enough to show the childish confusion beneath; I'd caught her doing her nails, and she couldn't take my coat as her mother had trained her. But she recovered quickly enough.

'Alfred, the gentleman's coat.'

The big bodyguard's murmur was deferential as he slipped the garment from my shoulders. 'No appointment, Fräulein Annette.'

I let him take hat and gloves as well, but I kept the glasses, for I was still fearful of recognition. Then she spoke again, in that formal third person which the German language reserves for its most delicate transactions, and I breathed a sigh of relief. She didn't know me.

'Perhaps the gentleman has a preference for one particular young lady?'

'My friend advised me to ask for the services of Madame herself.'

Her voice took on a tinge of professional regret as she sat down again behind the desk. The wet scarlet nails held themselves carefully above the green leather of the top. 'I'm afraid Madame sees callers only by appointment.'

Before I could say anything, she pressed a button on the desk and gave me the bright, hard smile that made it impossible to believe her age. Here in the ornate hallway the innocence of its certainty was oppressive. It married a child's confidence to an adult's worldliness; I would be persuaded to an acceptable alternative, it said, she would see to it . . . The routine tripped smoothly into action.

'A drink while you choose? Cognac?'

With clockwork precision the big bodyguard appeared at my side with a tray. I let the warmth of the liquor seep through, and waited, for it was important not to rush this

— a customer in my supposed position wouldn't refuse the free show that came with the pretence of choice. One by one they came out of their rooms to take their places at the banister above me. A note of pride crept into her voice as she introduced them; a ringmaster was showing the crowd her thoroughbred stable.

'Fräulein Sophie and Fräulein Andrea.'

A tall brunette with a Lauren Bacall hairstyle leaned languorously over and gave me a long, heavy-lidded look, shapely breasts pressing through the red angora of her dress with measured coquetry. A second later she was joined by a dark-complexioned girl, ample and contented-looking, obviously Spanish or Italian. She waved coyly and hitched up her skirt to pull a stocking to the top of a plump thigh. Further down the corridor I heard a door open. Peals of feminine laughter reached me as a third girl, grinning hugely, strode up to join the other two. She wore only a tiny pair of pink briefs and black high heels. She combed out her blonde curls as she stood by the rail, big breasts dancing gently with the movement.

'Fräulein Caro.'

Caro shared a dazzling smile between me and Annette.

'Hannelore is still busy.'

I used the time to try and collect my thoughts. Should I insist, or was there a better way . . .? The bodyguard refilled my glass as the three prostitutes patiently waited. Occasionally one of them would shift her stance a little, not ostentatiously, but with calculated knowledge of effect, gently competing for my custom with a slight undulation of hip or bosom, a graceful trailer for the excitement of the main feature. But there was nothing brazen about this market-place, and I knew I would be allowed to make my choice in peace, however long it took. In the Cantons, old traditions die hard; no matter what the establishment, the customer is still king. I drained my glass and turned to the desk.

'The ladies are all very lovely, Fräulein, but I would really rather spend some time with Madame. Perhaps she would be available later?'

All of them looked at me with interest. I was a curiosity to be filed away, for Madame's speciality was no secret, and I was undoubtedly young for that particular addiction. Again Annette's training asserted itself. She walked purposefully to the desk, ready to show me the other side of Switzerland's traditional coin; if the customer wants something badly enough, then he can be made to pay through the nose for it. Young or not, she was making the decisions here.

'Very well. I will ask if she will see you.'

She lifted the telephone, spoke a few words, then began to climb the stairs. The three girls, professional curiosity sated, turned away from me towards their rooms, haunches swaying insolently, making sure I knew what I was missing. Caro looked over her shoulder with a glance that seemed to say it might be a pity, but it only lasted a second. There was always the next client.

I heard voices from above, and then Annette came back down the stairs. Her smile was fixed firmly back in place, and she raised an admonitory finger when she reached me. From a sixteen-year-old, the gesture was just too fantastic, and as the finger wagged I struggled to keep my face under control. We were back in the nursery; a child was wearing mother's high heels.

'Madame will see you in ten minutes. But it's always better to make an appointment.'

The card she handed me had a telephone number embossed in gold, but neither name nor address. For all the emotion in her voice, she could have been announcing that the dining-room was still prepared to serve me a hot meal — instead of informing me that her mother was ready to accept my money for some highly bizarre sexual services. She sat down again, very businesslike, completely uninterested in me, poise restored by a successful transaction and dry nails — and then her attention switched itself back on as she remembered the last detail.

'Madame will fix the fee personally, and you may pay me on your way out.'

One of the doors above us opened, and an elderly grey-haired man appeared. A giggling girl, completely naked, gave him a friendly kiss, carefully wiped the lipstick from his cheek, and straightened his tie. He came jauntily down the stairs, taking a handful of notes from his wallet. The money was fresh, crisp and new, and Annette took it with as much pleasure as he gave it. I watched him eyeing her as she made out an ornate receipt, but if she was aware of the scrutiny, she gave no sign. How many of the patrons of this place were waiting for the day when she had a room of her own instead of merely a desk? He took the receipt and left in silence, another good Swiss burgher politely and punctiliously serviced.

The telephone on the desk rang, its modern burr jarringly at odds with the Edwardian opulence around it. She listened briefly, then stood up.

'If you'd care to follow me.'

I climbed the two flights of stairs behind her, my mouth dry with anticipation, and as she held the heavy door open I felt her eyes once more upon me. Was there a flicker of recognition? I went quickly past her into the room and heard the hiss of the door closing behind me. *Soundproof* . . . The fact clicked into place in the back of my mind. One swift glance round the walls made the reason for it crystal clear.

I'd known what to expect, but it was still weird. The room was L-shaped. One wall was completely taken up with complex fitments — shackles, collars and chains, restraints of all sorts, the complicated paraphernalia the masochist demands. Polished wood and gleaming brass, their extremities covered in leather and black rubber, reached out from its surface. The facing wall held a series of racks. Whips of all shapes and sizes hung from the topmost one, their handles sticking up in a phallic row, their ends dangling over the gags and masks which hung below. The wall ahead of me was a series of interlocking mirrors in which I didn't recognise myself. Reflected in them I could see the room's hidden alcoves — specialised bowers of exact, arcane fantasy, rigidly precise settings for brutal ritual. In the first of them, a heavy harness hung from the ceiling above a riding saddle, in the next stood a set of medieval stocks. The third held a small cage. There was no bed.

'Take your clothes of. *All* of them.'

Helga's voice seemed to come from nowhere. Then the mirrors slid off to one side, and behind them I saw a walk-in wardrobe, big enough to be a room in its own right. It was lined with racks of costumes, male and female. Smells of leather and rubber and perfume wafted out to me. Helga stood in the middle of it all, a small riding-crop in her hands.

The tightness of the garment that encased her amazing body showed every contour of it, thrusting her sexuality out in a way that was much more explicit than nakedness. The suit held her from neck to thigh in leather, hermetically sealing her torso between the extremities of high boots and flaming red hair. Zippers around breasts and between legs were the only sign that the armour was penetrable, but they were formidably guarded by rows of buckles and studs. The shining boots had fantastically high heels and intricate lacing. She slapped the crop lightly against them as she moved towards me, smiling coldly through the severe mask of make-up. About two feet away she stopped, a predator confronting its prey. The leather creaked. I didn't move. She was like a distillation of sex.

'Come now, don't be foolish. Or shy. Everything you want to . . .'

When I removed the dark glasses, she took a step back. Her face, long accustomed to the crazy, the unexpected, the sordid, didn't register the shock, but the deep intake of breath betrayed her. I tried to read her expression and failed completely. She didn't acknowledge my presence at all, she merely accepted that she no longer had a customer by turning and hanging the riding-crop in the rack. I couldn't keep the question from my mind. Was she somehow behind this whole thing? Had I ended my search in failure by coming here? She walked quickly back into the other part of the room and disappeared behind the last mirror.

'So you're not dead. How did you fool them?' Her voice was calm, conversational. Too calm.

'It's a long story,' I said, guardedly. 'We have to talk, Helga.'

I heard the heavy rustle of leather, then a metallic sound that I recognised — too late. She came quickly back into view. I stared stupidly at the gun in her hand. It was small, but I had no doubt it would make a very effective hole in me, and I also had no doubt that she was capable of pulling the trigger.

'The truth, Alex. What happened in Holland?'

'I was followed and set up to look like some sort of crazy Jewish murderer. Who by and what for I don't know. I found the woman, but she's dead now.'

'Did you kill her? And Smulders? And the others they talked about?'

'I was going to ask you the same question.'

There was a long silence as each of us measured our suspicion of the other.

'Helga, if I killed them and got away with it, why am I here? What do I have to gain? I'm not armed. I've no hold over you — I'm either crazy or innocent. Either way, you could kill me now and nobody would be any the wiser. Everybody thinks I'm dead already.'

'Max used to say you'd been near madness,' she said softly. 'I will take no chances with you.'

Involuntarily I raised my hand in protest, but she misread the gesture. The sound of the gunshot was like a thunderclap in the small room. The impact slammed me backwards, but I managed to stay on my feet, and when I looked at her again, the telephone was in her hand. I clutched at my arm as the pain began to bite. She went pale under the make-up, and then without warning the door crashed open. The big bodyguard checked his natural instincts and turned to Helga for permission to finish the job. I felt my anger burst open at her betrayal.

'*Max was right not to trust you!*' I shouted.

Her face went from pallor to icy whiteness, and for a moment I thought she was going to finish me off. She pointed the gun at my head, her mouth compressed itself into a thin crimson line, and then suddenly her eyes filled with uncertainty as the implications of what I'd said hit her. I saw the gun falter in her hands and felt blood trickle over my wrist. It seeped down between my fingers and began to drip on to the carpet. She fell back against the glass, staring at the red flow. Her shoulders slackened. The big man and I automatically waited for her to decide what was to come next.

'It's all right, Alfred,' she said. 'Would you please bring the first aid box? And ask Fräulein Annette to come up here.'

She was shaking. I opened my mouth to protest at bringing the girl, but the sternness of her look silenced me; for some reason it was important. I watched her conquer her body by sheer willpower, clenching the fist of her free hand until the trembling stopped. The gun dropped to her side. We waited.

'I'm sorry, Alex.'

I nodded. There wasn't anything sensible to say. I looked at my right arm. The bullet had hit just above the elbow, and I could feel the flesh numbing except for the nucleus of pain around the wound. But the relief I felt banished any other sensations. Each of us waited for the other to speak, in a silence made awkward by the realisation that we were allies.

'Will you help me?' I asked, finally.

'If I can.'

The door opened soundlessly and Annette came in. She went quickly to Helga's side, then glanced at me. Recognition made her eyes wide, and the sight of the blood made them wider. She looked at her mother in complete bewilderment. I felt the big man's hands on my collar. He slipped my jacket off and tore at the fabric of my shirt. For a second I worried — the fiddle . . . Would I still be able to play?

His voice gruffly reassured me. 'Nothing serious. Went straight through.'

He pointed at the splintered wood in the middle alcove; Helga's custom-built boudoir would need a new pair of stocks. Quickly he finished the improvised tourniquet and pulled tight. I winced.

'Thank you, Alfred, that's all. No word of this to the girls, though. The gentleman slipped and required assistance.'

As the heavy door hissed shut behind him, I looked at the two women. They made a surreal tableau against the mad backdrop of the room, the leather-clad whore and her teenage businesswoman daughter, both older in the ways of the world than I'd ever be. Helga put a protective arm round her daughter's shoulder. Her voice was tender as she spoke to the staring girl. 'You see, *Liebchen*, Alex has come back to us.'

I lay in the familiar attic room and waited for sleep, but the pain of the wound nagged me back into wakefulness every time I reached the brink. Light was beginning to seep through the mask of snow on the windows now, enough to let me examine the changes there had been since Max had lived here. The room felt smaller, somehow.

It had already begun to achieve the kind of storeroom status that eventually overtakes all unoccupied space. Some of the girls' trunks were piled in the corner, covered by heaps of brocade curtains, and there were other odds and ends. Candlesticks. A carton of cocktail glasses. A long mirror, cracked at the top right-hand corner. The left-over junk of a brothel looked just as forlorn as the unwanted lumber of any other big house, just as impermanent. I poured myself another brandy and thought again about what Helga had told me.

I'd been right about the phone being tapped. It must have been easy for them to trace the number from the BMW's registration, and from what she'd said they'd moved with incredible speed, for they'd even known the content of the two calls I'd made from Groningen while we were still trying to trace Vinnie. It confirmed what I'd already guessed — that the surveillance must have begun at Burg Laer. But I put that problem to one side for the moment; there was too much to think about at once.

It was the same man, the small fat one, the anglophile who'd put five guilders and a radio-controlled bug in my case. From Helga's description, I was sure of it. She said he'd come at first with one other German and a couple of detectives she already knew from the Basel police. The Swiss had been hard. There had been none of the humorous politeness which they usually reserved for their dealings with the city's prostitutes, and they'd made it plain that not even Helga's extensive network of contacts could save her. If she didn't co-operate, they had the power to close her down.

The Germans had looked on as the Baselers questioned. Had she known that I already had one manslaughter conviction? Was she aware of any reason why I should want to kill people in Holland? And how had I come to know Max Bauer in the first place? She'd lied, told them I'd merely asked for the use of the car for a few days, that beyond that she knew nothing. She'd heard I was in some kind of trouble in Holland, but no, she hadn't been worried, the car was well insured. I was a friend of Max's from the street, and she was prepared to be charitable out of respect for his memory . . . They'd left without telling her anything.

Later the two Germans had come back, alone, and this time they'd grilled her for hours, but the questions had been completely different. What did she know about the painting? Had Max known what had happened to his old unit's records? Had he kept any film? Any files? She'd told them nothing, since she knew nothing, but it didn't stop them. The other man had knocked her about, she said, and enjoyed it. A thin man in a grey leather jacket, with a long scar on his face . . . Annette had been due to come home soon, and she'd offered them everything — money, the girls, herself, to get them out of the house before her daughter returned. They'd gone only when it was obvious they already knew more than she did.

The next day she'd paid the girls off and closed the place down. It had been two weeks before she'd deemed it safe to open again — and then only with protection. Alfred's role was a dual one, technician as well as bodyguard. The phones were clean now, but he checked them regularly, and his presence at the front door would intimidate and delay even the most persistent of policemen. No one would get past him before Helga was warned and away.

There was a knock, and before I could tell anyone to come in, the door opened. Annette stood, barefoot, wearing a black silk robe, its hem fringed with expensive lace. Although the make-up was gone, she still looked impeccably groomed. Her scarlet-nailed hands held a tray with wine, bread, cheeses.

'I thought you might be hungry.' She put the tray carefully down on the bed and began to open the wine with a horn-handled corkscrew. The heavy silk parted to expose a long, perfect thigh. She made no attempt to cover it. 'How bad is your arm?'

'It'll heal quickly enough.'

She handed me a glass and a napkin, and tried to smile a hostess's smile.

'You used the front door today. That's why I didn't

recognise you. And you look different without the beard. Younger, I mean.'

A warning bell began to ring in the back of my mind. What had begun as cool small-talk had already acquired a layer of adolescent admiration. I felt myself redden. Gingerly I sipped at the dry white wine and avoided her eyes, suddenly very conscious of my nakedness beneath the sheets.

She tried again. 'Do you like wine?'

'Sometimes.'

'Red or white?'

'Both.'

'At school we used to drink red wine at night in the dormitory. My friend Rosa used to get the gardener to smuggle it in for us. That was before I was expelled.'

'Why were you expelled? Because of the wine?'

She shook her head gravely. 'One of the girls' fathers used to come here. He was frightened I'd tell her I'd seen him, so he told the Direktor what Helga did for a living. He said he didn't want his daughter mixing with people like us.'

She shrugged her shoulders, accepting the double standard. Why didn't she call Helga mother?

'I didn't mind. I wasn't good at school. Max told me you were a teacher once. Is it true?'

The question surprised me out of the comfortable effects of the wine and the cognac. I wasn't sure what to tell her. What did she understand a teacher to be? It was hard to imagine her sharing a common definition of the word with the kids whose days I'd tried to fill. The sour stink of wet Glasgow weans on a Monday morning banished her perfume as my memories paraded themselves. Kids . . . Endless lines of them, waiting for school buses, school dinners, most of them just waiting for the day when the endless line stretched only to the counter of the dole office. How far had I come from all that? The distance between a Glasgow classroom and a Basel brothel, between welders' weans and whores' daughters

. . . It wasn't something I could measure in miles.

But as she sat there, this harlot's child who was such a curious mixture of innocence and worldliness, I knew the differences were only in the veneer — her situation wasn't unique, just more extreme. I remembered a winter morning, a cheeky thirteen-year-old excusing herself for being late. Her mother was in bed with the lodger, she'd said, and she had to make her father's breakfast. I remembered sturdy weans who looked after wee brothers and sisters with rough affection while Maw went off to the dancing with the latest in a long line of 'uncles.' The girl in front of me was removed from them only in the outer things that an expensive Swiss boarding-school could finish. Underneath she was kin to the kids I'd known; she got on with living in the world she'd landed in and took a bizarre pride in doing her strange job well. Suddenly I found myself thinking of Lisa and Elly. I wanted to be with them very badly.

'Were you a *good* teacher?'

The question was so earnestly put that I had to smile. I shook my head. 'No. But I wanted to be.'

Clumsily I shifted position in the bed. The tray tilted — and without thinking I grabbed for the wine bottle with my right hand. I was only dimly aware of the crash as everything hit the floor. The pain from my wound was excruciating. I shut my eyes tightly and waited for it to subside — and suddenly her arms were round my neck.

There was a moment's indecision as her mouth searched for mine, but it ended in a naïve parody of a seductive kiss, and it died as soon as she knew I didn't want it. For a second she clung to me, unsure of what to do next, and then, slowly, she sat back, eyes downcast, hands demurely in her lap. Through the curtain of waved hair I could see the deepening blush of her cheeks. Without looking at me she bent down and began to pick up the food and the broken glass from the floor. I had no idea what to say to her. Convention of any sort was meaningless in this situation, in this of all houses. Only the truth would do.

'Annette, I'm sorry. Since I left here I've . . . met someone.'

She stood up. Her confusion lasted until she looked at herself in the cracked mirror, and then the metamorphosis took place. I watched confidence come back to her at the sight of her own body. Her head rose, and then she spun round quickly. The black silk ballooned out, floated down, then clung to her once more.

The sudden turn was graceful enough to be dance, but the look she gave me ended all thought of music. It was as though the girl was seeing me for the very first time, seeing me as a male animal, judging me physically. A scarlet forefinger found the edge of the black silk, pulled it away from her skin, slowly, erotically, revealing a woman's full breasts and a russet tangle of pubic curls. My penis began to stir beneath the sheet, and I knew she could see the effect she was having on me. I couldn't pretend to be immune to her; Elly had changed all of that.

'Wanting is different from loving,' I said hoarsely, aware of how ridiculous it sounded. 'It would be wrong.'

She made no attempt to answer or to move, and I didn't trust myself to say more as I looked at her. Desire welled up in me. Men would pay a fortune for her some day, if that was the road she chose. She picked up the tray and walked to the door in silence.

After she'd gone, I lay there, awake and alone, my arm hurting. I knew the whore's daughter in her could deal with it, but I was angry with myself just the same; it was the sixteen-year-old kid I'd hurt.

I was still trying to digest Elly's news when the elderly black Mercedes came to a halt beside the pile of bricks. Alfred let it roll back on the slope until the gear caught, just as he'd done every day for the last week, and Helga got out of the passenger door and came up the newly-laid path to the house. As I heard the front door slam I folded away the letter; it was the fifth time I'd read it since its arrival that morning.

She threw coat and gloves down on the sofa and went into the bedroom. When she came up the steps that divided the big split-level room, the crisp linen dress had been exchanged for a bright yellow track suit that took twenty years off her age. She unzipped a slim black document case as she came.

'How is his arm?'

The doctor appeared in the kitchen doorway, drying his hands on the dishcloth. It was the same man I'd seen coming down the stairs, my predecessor at the brothel. His grave bedside manner had contained no allusion to the meeting.

'As long as there's no strain, it will be all right. No lifting, no carrying, no punching . . .'

He went back into the kitchen, carefully rolling down his sleeves. His voice rose, the *Schweitzerdeutsch* accent making a comic song out of the words. '. . . and no violin. Teach him patience.'

Helga and I smiled at each other across the big table. She handed me a large manilla envelope.

'Read.'

The private detective's report was thorough and logically laid out, and the first thing it showed me was the extent of the problem, for the sheer volume of information was vast. But the detail brought me no nearer a solution, for it magnified all aspects of the puzzle to the same degree. I could see why the Tirolean land was important now, though. There was a lot of it, or rather there had been, before it had been sold off in bits and pieces over the years.

It wasn't an untypical story. The Sixties tourist boom had turned any bit of Austria which was half-way picturesque into a gold mine for those with the foresight and the capital to build, and the pastures which had once covered almost all of the small valley had quickly been surrounded by hotels and luxury real estate, once someone had seen their potential as ski slopes. In the last ten years the place had become fashionable, attracting the rich, and what had once been a sleepy alpine village now even boasted a casino. I read through the impressive list of firms with a stake in the place and began to understand why the appearance of an unknown heiress would cause consternation — but what still didn't fit was the violence of the reaction, if reaction it was, the brutality with which someone had tried to suppress the claim. At least half a dozen of the firms on the list were highly respectable international concerns, household names. Surely their first reaction would be to bring out batteries of lawyers to negotiate? Only if and when that failed could I see them resorting to anything more extreme.

The doctor reappeared, bag in hand. 'Alfred will run you to the station,' Helga said.

'Thank you, I prefer the exercise. Until next week. The usual time.'

His smile was at once sly and timid, and Helga returned it with a frank grin as she rose from the table to see him out. We watched him wave to Alfred and march off down the hill. When Helga spoke again, her voice had taken on the bored, flat tone she used for professional judgments.

'He's a good doctor, checks the girls for me every week. You can't be too careful these days. He likes to pretend Hannelore is in love with him. If you met his wife, you'd understand why.' She indicated the papers. 'Interesting?'

'Very,' I said. 'I see some of it now, I think. And the other?'

She swivelled her chair round to look across the grey river towards the small town. The *Fachwerk* houses of Baden clustered together at crazy angles, their walls stacked drunkenly against each other like the sides of a card house in danger of falling. The sun came out from behind the clouds, and the bright light gave the grey roofs a momentary spectrum of colour.

'Not so easy, Alex. You don't ask a private detective to investigate a policeman, not unless you are prepared to give him power over you. The ones I know are all either highly respectable or cheap and seedy, and I trust neither type on principle. So I took a risk, a calculated one.'

Hearing her talk of trust reminded me of Elly. Somehow it had become a key word for Helga, one she used often, and I had the feeling that this whole business, coming as it did on top of Max's death, had caused a reappraisal of her private values, for there was a determined anger about the way she had espoused the cause of Lisa's inheritance. She had gone about collecting the information with a relentless energy which I had never suspected in her, marshalling her contacts with a tenacious efficiency more appropriate to a corporation executive than a brothel madam. At times, the gap which divided the two extremes seemed wide enough to be called schizophrenia. She continued, talking as much to herself as to me, measuring possibilities in the light of factors I couldn't see.

'There is an official — a high-ranking official — of the Berne police who is, to say the least, very fond of the services I provide. I tell you this so you can see why the information is not as complete as it might be. I can only press him so far.'

There was a delicate silence as I realised that we were talking about blackmail. She pulled a photograph and a single sheet of paper from the case.

'That's him, yes?'

'Yes.'

It was the same man, in the same grey-green tweed suit. The features were set in a fleshy frown as he looked somewhere into the middle distance, but there was no mistaking him. She donned a pair of horn-rimmed glasses and began to read from the sheet.

'Weidemann, Hans. Detective-Inspector, Münster

police. Forty-two. Several years' service with specialist tax and finance sections in Bonn and Berlin, superiors surprised when he opted for a straight provincial police force, but it was put down to marriage. Otherwise nothing unusual about him except that he seems to have been quickly promoted. Four years ago brought off a spectacular series of arrests in London, to do with a forgery ring.'

The English, I thought, he was so damn smug about his English.

'Nothing very much known about his private life except that it's very private. Lives well. Married rich, invested clever.' For a moment she carefully avoided my eyes. 'The other man, Gutterman, worked for him.'

I said nothing. She went on.

'The only connection I can make for you could be coincidence. Weidemann made a killing on the market several years ago. Obviously party to inside information. One of the firms in the other report made the same killing. Wertheimer Holdings.'

I looked again at the list of companies involved in the Austrian land. Wertheimer seemed one of the smallest — a hotel, a piece of the casino. Was it a connection? I didn't know. I stood up, careful not to put any weight on my arm, and slid open the balcony's glass door. Below me Alfred was singing softly to himself as he worked. The tuneless drone was soothing and the cold air freshened me, but neither did anything to organise my thoughts. Behind me I heard Helga's brisk stride as she went across to the rowing machine in the far corner.

'You're sure they never asked you about the land or the ownership?' I asked.

She took off her glasses, settled on the seat and regulated the levers of the apparatus. She shook her head as she gripped the oars.

'That means . . .'

'. . . that they think it's secure,' she finished impatiently.

We'd gone through this time and time again. I watched thigh and arm muscles tense as she began to pull.

'What would happen if I went to the big firms on the list with the story?' I said, although I already knew the answer.

The oars settled into a steady rhythm as I looked out again. The doctor was almost at the bridge now. Her voice gave no sign of effort as she replied.

'At best you'd warn them, at worst you'd lead them straight to you and the child. They'd know there was still an interest, that the inheritance issue is still alive. Stupid.'

She began to pull faster, the metal oars scudding through the artificial current of the pistons with mechanical ease, hydraulic grace.

'I see no reason to think that these people will stop short of killing you and the child if they can. That is the premise we have to work on. You know it as well as I do.'

I walked over to the machine, and held Elly's letter out to her. She read it in her usual quick, thorough manner, hunched over the oars, dark patches of sweat spreading under arms and between breasts, then nodded in agreement.

'The painting. It makes sense. A million, maybe even more. A lot of money to anyone, Alex. A fraction of it would buy your death and mine many times over.'

I went back out to the balcony. The house Helga was building here on the hillside was still unfinished, and Alfred was working methodically at the wall of what would soon be a garage, brick and trowel tiny in his gargantuan hands. I envied him. A simple job of work to do, a trowel or a fiddle to hold; it would have been so much comfort . . . Suddenly the vision of Maria, hammer in hand on the shed roof, came back to me. The memory had haunted me for days. I pulled myself back from it, forced myself to concentrate on Elly's news. *As much as one and a half million dollars*, the letter said. It was unbelievable. I turned again, hearing the rhythm of the machine stop. Helga came back to the table and pulled the passport that called me Alexander Lawless from the bag, laying it down on the polished wood like a challenge.

'The decision we came to four days ago, Alex . . .' she waved at the papers on the table . . . 'none of this changes it. There is still only one avenue we have not explored. We have to try it first, and you are the only one who can go. It's a risk, but I see no one else we can trust. If it turns out to be worthless, we have to consider other ways, more dangerous ones. But not until this has been tried.'

Trust again . . . But I knew she was right, just as she had known it days ago. I opened the passport and saw the visa. It was the kind that would allow me a long stay. How had she managed to get it without the obligatory month they demanded? She handed me a slip of paper with an address and a longer number on it. The address was different, but it was at least evidence that there was still a Herr Schumacher in the town of Schwerin. Our eyes met.

'You're sure this is the right one? It's a common enough name.

'My contact tells me it's the right one. The studio is long gone, though.'

'How?' I asked, holding up the passport.

Her shoulders moved in a shrug of indifference, and the tone of voice shifted back again to boredom. The predictability of human behaviour was her stock in trade.

'You seldom need to blackmail communists. Bribery is easier and quicker. They like hard Western currency. It's worth remembering.'

She delved once more into the bag and brought out a thick wad of German money and a set of keys. The notes were new, high denomination.

'This time I can afford no chances, Alex. I've bought you a car in Lübeck. Nobody can trace it to me. The number's a bank account, Deutsche Bank, Kiel, name of Lawless. If you have to run this time, there's nothing more I can do to help you.'

She handed me an envelope. It felt stiff. 'From Annette,' she said calmly.

I put it in my pocket and decided to ask the question I'd been thinking about for days. 'Did you send her to me, that first night?'

'No. But I knew she would go to you. She cried for a week when she thought you were dead.'

She walked away from me, towards the bathroom, unzipping the top of the suit as she went.

'Why didn't you *stop* her?' I said angrily.

She turned and faced me. Her hands rose above her head, pushing out her breasts as she tied the flaming red hair back into an efficient ponytail. The task didn't distract her; she had the ability to separate mind and body. She measured the words exactly before she spoke.

'You don't know much about women, do you? When you left here the last time, you were only one step away from being a broken man. That's a normal part of a young girl's myth, a man waiting to be saved, but you added a lot to it in her eyes. You were the man who was above prostitutes, the puritan. I decided to let her try to win you in spite of that.'

'Why?'

She took off the yellow top and flung it impatiently into the corner. She crossed her arms over her breasts, their swell still shiny with sweat, and stared out of the window at Alfred and the mixer. When she looked at me again, it was with the whore's eye.

'Maybe it was the Dutch girl, maybe the responsibility. Or maybe just the violence, I don't know.'

She walked into the bathroom, and I heard the note of satisfaction that crept into her voice as she raised it. 'Whatever it was, you came back *strong*.'

Chapter 7
LIES

THE TRAFFIC WAS SLOW as I came into the ancient Hanseatic city of Lübeck from its southern suburb of St Jürgen, where I'd picked up the car. I felt calm, rested, even though the wound from Helga's gun was still hurting. The night before, on the train, it had opened again, and although I'd bandaged it as tightly as I could, the bleeding hadn't completely stopped. I'd have to be more careful, I told myself; a fresh dressing as soon as possible, then change it regularly.

I eased the big Volkswagen estate on to the ring road that followed the line of the Trave river and watched the national monument Germany calls the Holstentor become smaller in the rear-view mirror. In a less frenetic age the Holstein Gate had guarded the town's access from the West, but now it was honorably retired as a museum. On the lithography of the brown fifty-mark notes that nestled in my briefcase, its massive twin towers stood bolt upright, but in reality they leaned towards each other a little. It was a fittingly ironic picture to carry eastward with me; West Germany's economic miracle might be sagging, but they'd be damned if they'd let their money admit it . . . The big car was a pleasure to drive, and I found my mind once more coming back to the information Elly had sent me.

Mary Wellbeck had set aside her initial scepticism

about the painting's history, and had discreetly circulated the photograph in the expert circles to which she had access. Enough guarded interest had been expressed to whet her own curiosity, and after many hours spent in the Witt Library, London's premier art archive, her considered opinion was that the portrait could well be a Van Dyck — a very early one. There were immaturities of both style and composition, she said, but it was impossible to be exact from a photograph. Also there were curious anomalies about the painting. Although the style of the woman's dress was English, the heraldic device on the sash was either Spanish or Italian; she couldn't be sure which without more information. But one awesome fact remained. The estimates of an undiscovered Van Dyck's worth on the open market ranged between the figures of a half to one and a half *million* dollars.

I drove, following the signs through the leafy suburb of Schlutup, manoeuvring past noisy roadworks to the West German checkpoint. What were the chances of its having survived, or of my finding it? The odds were impressive enough, anyway; a fortune to a busker's life. And if I returned empty-handed, as I probably would? The depressing train of thought was interrupted by the young policeman who took my passport. He examined it with enough care to remind me that this wasn't just another polite European pretence of a border. I took it back in silence and drove past the tri-coloured concrete poles that separate Germany from itself.

There were changes in the scenery, man-made ones. The pleasant wooded thickets stopped short at the end of Schleswig-Holstein, cropped by the militarists of Mecklenburg in the interests of a clear field of fire. It was a hundred yards to the first of the barriers, and automatically I slowed down. Eyes were upon me; I felt it, and then the glint of binoculars confirmed it. My progress was monitored from flat-roofed concrete observation towers, shabbily-built things that had a mean air about them, an air of wartime austerity, as though their drabness would be replaced one day, but only after final victory. But whose victory, I wondered, and how long would the waiting last? Their cramped confines were in sharp contrast to the modernity of the fences, the arc lights, the guns on the shoulders. My wheels clattered across the metal plates of a vehicle trap, then back on to the bumpy road surface that led to a different society — one with no confusion about its priorities; this was a land where technology would build better fences before it worried about the comfort of its soldiers.

I joined the queue of cars in front of the numbered lanes of the huge customs shed. It was the only new building, and it straddled the road like a malevolent metal spider, its functional lines unsoftened by anything remotely aesthetic. Behind its drab facade, braced by a pair of rusting cement mixers, stood a makeshift wooden hut. The words 'Welcome to the German Democratic Republic' were painted on it in flaking letters, and the clusters of black, red and gold flags which flanked the message on either side were steadily losing the battle to keep their colours against the grey of a thousand uncaring exhausts. As I switched off the motor I was aware once more of the eyes, this time from the dark depths of the shed's interior — and the feeling which had nagged at my subconscious for the last few minutes surfaced.

There was a familiarity about the air of selective authoritarian neglect; if there was ever again a border between Scotland and England, this was how it would be . . . Too poor to be impressive, too scared to be human, barbaric by default.

In front of me a uniformed figure rapped on a car window, and I heard a loud, aggressive voice, demanding impatiently, '*Autopapiere! Autopapiere!*'

A knock at my side startled me out of reflection. A skeletal brown hand was splayed out over the glass, an elderly face grinning beside it. I wound down the window.

'Pardon me, sir, but do you know how long this is liable to take?'

Both the accent, and the politeness were pure American.

'I have no idea.'

His smile widened a notch or two at finding a native English speaker. 'Say, you're British!' he said. He noticed the fiddle case on the back seat. 'You playin' over there?'

I smiled back and didn't answer, but I didn't want to be ruder than necessary to discourage him. 'Perhaps one of the other drivers would know,' I said.

He beamed at me and stalked off, apparently unperturbed by the snub, but before he could find anyone else to talk to the queue of cars moved, and his long spindly frame scuttled back to the big Plymouth beside my VW. American forces, I thought automatically, then discarded the notion — he was someone's father or grandfather, over for the ancestral visit or the grand tour. The line began to move, but the battered old Saab in front of me stalled and wouldn't restart. A pretty girl in jeans got out and tried to open the bonnet without success. The old American and I reached it at the same time, and we both saw quickly that it was beyond first aid, for when the bonnet finally rose it revealed a sticky black mess of oil.

The old man seemed to know where to look. After a few moments he straightened up and said apologetically, 'I'm sorry, miss, but I'm afraid your car isn't going anywhere for quite a while. Crankshaft, I think.'

She muttered a brace of pithy Swedish expletives which the American politely declined to understand, and we began to push the car out of the line, leaving a trail of oil as we went. Ahead of us I could still hear the shouted demands: '*Autopapiere! Einreiseerlaubnis!*'

Then they saw us, and the metallic voice of the tannoy system spoke. '*Halten Sie sofort!*'

There was an empty lane under the big gantry ahead of us to the left. The American pulled himself up to his full height, waved his hands and pointed theatrically towards it so there could be no doubt about our intentions. Once again we put our hands to the grimy body and shoved. The loudspeaker howled at us, '*Sofort anhalten!*'

A lumpy woman in the uniform of the border police emerged from the customs shed and marched towards us. She was followed by three unsmiling boys in blue shirts, their hair shorn with military ruthlessness. They pushed the car into the empty lane in our stead and waited for orders, but the woman ignored them. She barked out '*Kommen Sie mit!*', and the girl just shrugged and walked after her. The three boys stood, faces expressionless, determined not to see us.

The American frowned at the woven badges on the blue sleeves; the insignia read '*Freie Deutsche Jugend*'. He turned to me. 'What's it mean?'

'Free German Youth,' I replied.

He peered at me sorrowfully, as though it couldn't possibly be true, then shook his head. 'Do you think we should wait?' he asked, finally.

The tannoy answered him before I could. '*Wieder einsteigen! Sofort!*'

We went back to the cars and drew up together to present our documents. Black-gloved hands conveyed them to unseen inspection somewhere inside the shed as the Swedish girl came out again, utterly crestfallen, a sheaf of official grey forms in her hand.

The American pressed a button. His window rolled down with a sibilant hiss. 'Bad luck, miss,' he said. 'Typical communists.'

Anger robbed the face of its pertness. She shook her head furiously and answered him in an accent as American as his own. 'No. Typical fucking Germans.'

I watched him blush, and felt sorry for him. Again the tannoy shouted.

'Lawless! Herr Lawless! *Visa Abteilung!*'

With a start, I realised it was the name I was supposed to answer to. I drove through and parked carefully. The wooden hut smelled of strong tobacco and beer, its only furniture a rickety bench seat with the stuffing ripped out. I went up to the small hatch in the wall. It opened, and a thin face slid into view.

'Visa.'

I handed him my passport.

'There is a surcharge of five marks.'

I fumbled in my pocket until I found a note. It was a crisp new picture of the Holstentor. He silently counted out forty-five East German marks, four greasy ten-mark notes and a handful of unnaturally light coins. I put them in my pocket without protest.

'Destination?'

'Schwerin.'

'Purpose of visit?'

To locate and smuggle out a priceless painting, I thought. To try and discover the truth behind a series of violent deaths. To try and secure a future for myself, a Dutch librarian and a deaf and dumb child. To . . .

'Purpose of visit?' he repeated, patiently.

'A holiday.'

The face jerked its features into the semblance of a smile. 'Enjoy your stay in the German Democratic Republic.'

It had once been a large, spacious villa, back to back with its twin, its view of the lake front unimpeded by anything more than a cluster of pines, but at some point the house behind had been clumsily demolished, leaving a multi-coloured scar of pockmarked plaster at the back of the remaining one. The faded pinks and blues were the street's only colour, caught between the gunmetal grey of the water and the rain-streaked concrete of the new flats. I opened the rusty gate and walked up to the front door.

The brass bell-pull was ringed by a border of pasted-on paper names, and the large garden confirmed that the villa no longer housed only one family, for it was now a neat patchwork of allotments, each cared for with parsimonious pride. I glanced round nervously as I waited. This villa was luxury accommodation as far as Schwerin was concerned, I realised, for massive tower blocks surrounded the street on three sides. My imagination militarised them – they were sentries, immobile, uncompromising, ready to check the growth of any beauty not sanctified by political orthodoxy, featureless . . . As the footsteps came, I pulled my collar tighter and shrugged away the conceit; they were just places for people to live, their ugliness no worse here than in Glasgow or Dortmund – or anywhere else the planners of the fifties and sixties had been given a free hand. There was an impressive rattle of keys and bolts, and then the door opened to reveal an elderly woman, tiny, dressed in sombre black except for a white lace shawl across her shoulders. She saw the violin case in my hand and smiled.

'Herr Schumacher is busy at the moment, but if it is urgent . . .'

It took me a moment to comprehend the coincidence, for I'd brought the fiddle with me from the hotel merely as a comforter, a psychological prop against my nerves. One look at the kindness in her face made me reject the possibilities the situation offered. I decided on honesty.

'It's not about the violin, Frau Schumacher, but I would like to speak with him if it is possible.'

'Fräulein Schumacher.'

The correction was brisk, almost curt, but before I could apologise she had started back down the corridor. I followed her past a rusting row of letter-boxes, through an obstacle course of bicycles and litter-bins. The walls were brown-edged, peeling, what was left of their paper stained with damp, the plaster behind pitted and crumbling, but the door at the bottom was solid enough. Its massive oak panels dwarfed the birdlike figure as the keys jangled again. The handle turned. I was aware of a familiar smell, but I couldn't place it.

The interior was a shock after the dark neglect of the

passage. Once it had been part of a kitchen, a grand one — the size of the black iron range was testimony to that — but now . . . I stopped, unable to conceal my surprise. What was the room before me? A miniature of what the house had been? Behind me I heard the keys again. Or a bastion against what it had become?

Half-museum, half-fortress . . . I took a few steps forward, then hesitated again at the carpet's edge. Stepping on it seemed like sacrilege, for though it was almost threadbare, age hadn't entirely destroyed its Persian grandeur. Beside me a sofa faced two high-backed chairs, their wooden frames polished, their upholstery painstakingly mended. The backs and arms were covered with the same intricate lacework that was upon her shoulders, and it peeped out from below the brass-potted aspidistra on the table as well. Two shelved walls, intended for pots and pans, now held her treasures — a rosewood musical box, two silver candlesticks, the last of her crystal and porcelain. Her bed, a heavy brocade counterpane between mahogany ends, nestled below them. Everywhere there were mirrors, hanging, standing, the grandest of them a full-length cheval glass in the far corner. We caught sight of each other in it. The smile told me she was pleased with her room's effect on me, but it disappeared so quickly that I knew I hadn't been meant to see it. She turned, embarrassed, and for a moment every glass in the room concentrated its reflection behind her figure, framing it in lace. The vision was at once Victorian and surreal: a genteel lady, inside her own sewing-box.

But my surprise was quickly superseded by excitement. The kitchen's one drabness was the cheap plasterboard partition which divided it, and she had done her best to hide its roughness with memories. At least fifty photographs stared down at me, sepia-toned and solemn, carefully arranged in clusters of three and four. I examined them as she knocked on the connecting door; shooting parties, garden fêtes, a Christening, a First

Communion . . . The sharp detail of the prints and the rigid formality of the compositions spoke of an old-fashioned professional hand. I resisted the temptation to lift one down and look for the stencilled address I'd first seen in Max's safe-deposit box. She ushered me in.

The smell intensified, and the fiddler in me recognised it before I found its source. He was a bowmaker. His figure was bent over the spirit flame, a long stem of unvarnished wood in his hands. He didn't look up as I entered, nor did I expect him to; one wrong turn, one split second too long over the flame, and many hours of work would be wasted, the bow's capacity for even tension ruined. I surveyed my surroundings as I waited. The workbench, two chairs . . . The couch would be where he slept, I thought; I could see blankets below the litter of tools. The room had only one other furniture: violins.

He had as many of them as she had photographs. They hung from walls and ceiling, backless, pegless, some cracked, some in need of varnish, most beyond repair. There were a few fine instruments among the wrecks, I could see, but as I watched him work I knew they were just camouflage; bowmaking is the most all-embracing of passions, meticulous and exact, jealous of its sister crafts, a discipline that demands acolytes rather than apprentices. This man had taken its vows . . . A long minute passed before he indicated his satisfaction by taking the slim wand from the burner's reach and putting it down on the bench. The blue flame made ghostly shadows on the wall and on his face, the only brightness in the brown, utilitarian room.

Even after he turned to me, it was a few minutes before the absorption in his eyes died, and I used them to search his features, to look for an older version of the grinning face I remembered from Max's snapshot. His hair was thick, black and oily, cut in a style which hadn't been seen in the West for years; long locks brushed back from the widow's peak, falling into untidy black wings over the ears, the fashionable hairstyle of the German intelligentsia of the twenties. Both body and face were squat and fleshy, the latter bearing the permanent blue jowls of the heavy shaver and the double chin of a plentiful but unhealthy diet. His suit was baggy, ill-kept, square-cut with high buttons and a small collar, modelled on the rostrum dress of countless communist leaders. It was shapeless from constant wear, patched with perspiration at the armpits. On his feet he wore open sandals, lovingly mended at the straps with electrical tape.

I fought to keep down the chagrin as I searched for the resemblance I'd hoped to find, but I couldn't fool myself. My eyes took in the small enamelled badge that told me he was a Party member. He dissected me from behind the almost opaque lenses of his plastic-framed spectacles, and when he took them off to rub the redness from his eyes I knew with absolute certainty he wasn't the man I wanted. Helga's contact had been wrong.

'What can I do for you, Mr . . .?'

'Lawless. Alexander Lawless, Herr Schumacher. I come from Scotland.'

'Ah, Scotland. The land of Robert Burns.'

His voice was quizzical as he waited for me to explain my presence, and I realised I was staring at the badge. My spontaneous reaction to the old lady's honesty was echoed here as well, but something in his manner held me back, made me shy away from the truth; I was by no means certain of my own judgment, particularly here — and I had better be careful, for I could sense this man's intelligence. Quickly I improvised.

'Excuse me, Herr Schumacher, but I already see I have made a mistake in disturbing you. I was looking for a gentleman who photographed some of my relatives before the war. I wasn't sure if he was still alive, but from my mother's description he must have been much older than you. As I'm on holiday here, I thought I would try. I hope you'll forgive the intrusion.'

He put on the thick glasses and scrutinised me

carefully. 'My half-brother was the photographer, Mr Lawless, but I'm afraid he died many years ago. You will excuse me in my turn if I ask how you found us.'

'The address on the back of the photograph I have was here in the same street,' I said. It was true enough. 'I asked in your post office. They were able to trace you.'

It seemed to me I'd been lucky enough to strike the right lie. He rose from the chair and walked to the door with the stiff gait of a man who takes too little exercise.

'Ah, the post office. They are certainly very efficient. Gretl, we have a guest. From Scotland.'

He waved me to the only chair. I sat down. The room was stuffy and overheated, and I was glad to unbutton the heavy coat.

'My poor misguided brother was killed in the war, Mr Lawless, the stupid war none of us wanted. Perhaps we can be of help to you in his place?'

Suddenly I knew I had to go gently here. The woman gave me respite by appearing with a tray bearing glasses, bottles of pale spirits. I leaned forward. 'I wondered if there were perhaps any pictures still in existence. Of my family, I mean. Or even negatives.'

It was weak, I knew it, but if the painting was here I had to begin some sort of dialogue that could lead up to it. His reply was to hand me a large glass, filled to the brim with heavy yellow liquid.

'To Robert Burns,' he said, solemnly.

Burns . . . I'd forgotten he was an officially approved poet behind the iron curtain.

'To Stefan Zweig,' I replied.

He smiled in genuine pleasure and emptied his glass in a single draught, but by the time I had done the same his eyes had lost their joviality and gone back to their quiet analysis of me. The liquor was home-made, delicious and fierce. It burned in my throat as I waited for his answer.

'I'm afraid nothing of my brother's survived the war. Everything was destroyed except for the photographs Gretl has on her wall next door.'

Somehow I'd known it since I entered the room, but to hear it actually said was like a physical blow. He refilled both our glasses and watched me trying to hide my disappointment, and for what must have been a long time nothing was said. I stared at the flickering blue flame and listened to the woman going about her household tasks through the thin wall. It fell to him to break the silence. He began to probe.

'And are you a communist, Mr Lawless, that you take your holidays here?'

'A socialist.'

'Ah, a *socialist.*' He turned away from me and gave his attention to the bow for a second, comparing it with another which lay on the bench. His voice changed abruptly in tone. 'A difficult word. A word with many meanings. What does it mean in Scotland?'

'The definition is very broad.'

He smiled again. 'I see. You are what is called, I believe, a "fellow traveller".'

Both of us drank again, if only to cover the hiatus the insult had brought into the dialogue. Lenin had called fellow travellers 'useful fools'. I looked at him, suddenly recognising the type, familiar enough from the smoke-filled pubs of my Glasgow student years; the intellectual to whom all facets of learning — art, science, philosophy — are merely extensions of one discipline: politics. Nothing, not even a bowmaker's fanaticism, would ever challenge its place in this man's life.

The realisation made sense of the bare, functional cell of a room. They were usually Marxists, monks of the dialectic to whom the mental life was all and physical comfort somehow sinful. I watched the smile take on a satisfied edge as he reached again for the bottle, and understood; now that the reason for my visit had been dealt with, he was warming to his chosen task; for if my glass was laced with the after-taste of failure, his had given him an appetite for rhetoric. He was hungry for debate, for disagreement, he wanted to provoke. He sat back in his chair and baited the trap that would give him the excuse.

'And what do you think of our country, Mr Lawless?'

The first wave of the alcohol reached me, and my disappointment almost made the bait irresistible. It was many years since I'd met a man who wanted a political argument and didn't care about winning it. But prudence held me. I stalled. 'It's very interesting.'

He laughed. 'No comparisons with the West, Mr Lawless? No limited admiration for our system, qualified by liberal scruples?'

'I don't know enough, Herr Schumacher.'

Again I drank, and again he laughed, but this time there was a sadistic edge to it.

'I approve of a cautious man. The real hero of our revolution was the mole, and the mole comes to the surface only after many tunnels.'

His eyes alighted on the fiddle case and then came back to mine.

'You play, Mr Lawless?'

'I try, Herr Schumacher.'

'Full orchestra or chamber?'

Once again I retreated into the disguise I had adopted, but through the increasing fug of the alcohol I knew this man would find me out if I lied to him about music. I drank again.

'I am an amateur in the classics. The music I play is the traditional music of Scotland. Music collected from the people. By Robert Burns, among others.'

'You give concerts of this music?'

Concerts . . .

I thought of my old pitch in Basel; the casual toss of the coin that had to be scrambled for before it rolled out of reach . . . The puzzled smiles of the well-meaning passers-by who enquired what my real job was, their incomprehension when I told them I was dependent on dry weather and their charity to eat . . .

I remembered the first time I'd ever busked. My first

money had come from an old lady, barely able to walk, leaning on a stick. To change direction and move towards me had taken her an age, and I could still see the blue veins in her shaking hand as she held out fifty Rappen. I'd had to stop playing to take the coins, but the dignity with which they had been given had completely banished my humiliation. It was a lesson in kindness which I had never forgotten. As he picked up the bow again, I pulled myself back from the memory. I had to leave here. There was nothing further to be gained by staying. I rose.

'Yes, Herr Schumacher, I give concerts of a sort. However, I've already taken up too . . .'

He broke in as though I hadn't spoken at all. 'Of a sort. I see. A most *mysterious* man. You become more enigmatic by the minute, Mr Lawless. Not quite a communist, not quite a performer, not quite an ordinary visitor. Perhaps I should explain to you that the making of violin bows is merely the occupation of my later years. It pleases me, you understand, to retain a useful function in this democratic republic of ours. But before I retired —' he squinted along the bow's length, examining the angle of its curve — 'I held a position of some responsibility in our post office. They did not give a private citizen's address to you.'

The effects of the drink were clawed back by pure fright. His eyes examined me, intelligent, interested.

'I do not know who you are, or what it is you want, Mr Lawless — if that is indeed your name. Perhaps you will tell me in due course, but in the meantime, an old communist offers you the hospitality of his home. Would you share an evening with me, or are you not quite a drinker in addition to the rest of your incompletions?'

He walked over and filled my glass once more. Whatever he thought I was, he was completely unafraid, and though I couldn't see beneath the surface of his intentions I knew I had no choice other than to do as he bade me. The first of the bottles was two-thirds empty now, but there was no hesitation in his hand as he poured. I took off my coat and sat down again in silence.

It began slowly. For the first two hours we measured each other, glass for glass, circling each other's knowledge like dogs ready either to fight or to run together. Politics, music, scraps of philosophy, more politics, the tail-ends of our prejudices and the ragged remains of our unfinished experiences. The more I drank, the more the disappointment of the dead end burned in me, and it quickly became obvious that his communism was a much-scarred edifice, battered by the compromises and contradictions of his homeland's progress. But a communist he was, and a fine example of the breed, as immovable in his faith as an Ulster Orangeman or a white South African. Our differences became louder, echoing round the bare walls, resonating through the bodies of the violins — until by dusk the drink had made a decision for us; we were friends enough to fight with each other. The purpose of my visit seemed small now in comparison with the necessity of defeating him. Our contest of wills was almost tangible, a third presence in the room. He railed at me, bottle in hand.

'Your West! What is it? A monster that feeds on everything else in the world! The only comfort is that in the end it will feed on itself. It justifies only its profits, it eats its talented children instead of educating them. Nothing has changed since Burns. *Nothing!* There is still no appreciation of the ordinary man. "*The rank is but the* . . ."' He searched for the word . . . '"*guinea stamp, a man's a man for* . . ."'

'Don't quote Burns at me. You know you're right, it's the oldest trick in the book. Talk in truisms, and no one can contradict you.'

I got to my feet, shaking and sweaty from the alcohol and the heat, and went to the window. In the weak light of the street lamps the remains of the demolished house's summer arbour made slim chequered shadows on the ground, and I caught a glimpse of the old woman, wicker vegetable basket in hand, disappearing round the corner. I pointed to the blocks of flats that towered over the old villa.

'That's your alternative, is it, your socialist dignity? What you Party members salve your consciences with when you can't sleep at night? Stalinist cages as rewards for docility. At least where we come from we admit our mistakes, but not here! Even the Russians have begun to change, now, but not you! To your party that monstrosity will always have to be a victory. *That's* your reality! Burns said, "*Facts are chiels ye winna ding.*" It's a failure, all of it.'

I'd finally succeeded in goading his anger, but he had learned his debating well. He frowned, drunkenly.

'*Chiels?* What is *chiels?*'

'A chiel is a creature. It means a man — no, not a man, a *Mensch.*' I picked up the bottle and drained the last drops from its neck. He opened another and threw away the cork. 'It means that facts are things that can't be ignored. It means your communism is a sham. Learn your Burns!'

The last taunt enraged him. He pulled himself up with an effort, but he couldn't stand. His body crashed down on the seat again, and he looked angrily round the walls of the room, as though its confines were to blame. Then he focused on me once more.

'*What do you want here?*' he shouted.

I slumped back against the partition wall and felt it give under my weight. There didn't seem any point in lying any more.

'I'm looking for a painting that was either stolen or lost during the war. Your half-brother knew about it. I thought he was still alive and I wanted to ask his help. I wanted to give it back to its rightful owner.'

The sweep of his arm took in the whole room, but I knew it was meant to take in much more. 'That's what we wanted to do as well, what we still want to do. What we *shall* do! There is no painting here. If there was, I would give it to the authorities. The people are the rightful owners of all art.' He gestured at the violin case. 'You are a fool, but you are not a bad man. Play!'

It never occurred to me to refuse. It took a fumbling minute to free the fiddle from its case and an age to rosin the bow, but the instrument felt firm and good in my hands. Hesitantly, I drew the first notes from it. At first I was aware of his interest, his approval, but gradually that drifted to the edges of my consciousness and I played, as always, for myself. I played song tunes and marches. I played jigs, reels and hornpipes, attacking the melodies, slurring the grace notes, mixing up the parts. Only when I began to play the strathspeys did it change. The familiar snap of the bow cut through the fog of drunkenness and brought me confidence. The tunes came to life. They began to play themselves, and time existed for me only in their irregular, elliptical measures — and when I began to play the airs, it ceased to exist for me at all. I saw Elly's face before me, and Lisa's. I played Marshall's 'Farewell', and all the Gow tunes I knew. I played 'Though I Go To Bed, Little Does Sleep Come to Me'. I played every slow, sentimental tune I could think of, until the alternating images of the two faces took the last vestiges of my concentration. Then I sat in the dark and felt disappointment come back with the first flimsy threads of sobriety. What could I tell her? What could I do now? The old woman's voice broke my reverie, coming from the far corner, only just loud enough to hear. I looked at my adversary. The blue flame was low now. His head lay beside it, his breath blowing the oily forelock as he snored. I had no memory of her coming into the room.

'You play well. It has been a long time since anyone played music in this house. Would you come with me now, please.'

I packed the fiddle into its case and followed her out of the apartment, up the stairs. On the top landing she opened a low door which led to a rough wooden ladder.

'Be careful of the floor.'

I edged my way up into the cold darkness behind her, smelling the sweetness of the rotting wood as I entered the attic. I heard a match strike and saw the room take shape in the candlelight. She was standing beside an old wooden chest, its rounded lid fastened by ragged leather straps.

'Help me,' she said.

The first of the straps unfastened easily, the second fell to pieces in my hands, and the chest creaked open in a cloud of evil-smelling dust. She put the candle down on the rotten boards and began to lift out the piles of clothing she had worn as a girl — dresses and suits, blouses, shoes, all of them fighting a losing battle against the ravages of the damp. I stood and watched, feeling myself tremble slightly, fighting the twin unrealities of the situation and the alcohol. Eventually she came to what she wanted: a brown oilskin packet, efficiently sealed. It took me a long time to open it and make the mouth wide enough to insert a hand. Inside I felt leather. I drew out another, smaller, bag and pulled its draw-strings open.

The canvas was about thirty inches by twenty, and it rolled stiffly open to show the features I already knew from the photograph. I shifted my gaze from the woman with the sash to the photographer's sister, my unlikely saviour. At first the dim light showed me only the lace of her collar, the cotton blouse in her hands — and then I made out her face. The kindly eyes had found a faraway place in the darkness.

'They brought her here, once, the child. When we were in the other house. I brushed her hair the day Heinz photographed her. They all took such good care of her.'

Delicately her fingers brushed the painting's surface. I thought of a Dutch island, a white, scarred arm on a damp concrete floor.

'The last time Heinz came he was alone, and he knew they weren't far behind. They got here just after we'd burned his uniform. We had barely enough time to hide everything in the summer-house before the search started.' Again the thin hand reached for the canvas. 'He said it belonged to Maria and he hoped she would come for it some day, but he didn't know when. Then they took him away, the one-eyed man and the others. We never saw him again. He didn't seem to care very much any more.'

The candlelight made it easy to imagine her as she must have been in nineteen thirty-nine, young and fresh, courageous enough to take on the S.S. for the sake of someone she loved. She went on.

'Heinz was always good to me. We used to have parties here, before the war. With music. He used to tease the Berlin boy about bringing me flowers. The girl is no longer alive, is she?'

'No, but her daughter is. I'd like to take this to her, if I may.'

She nodded gravely and put down the old blouse. 'He was very handsome, the Berlin boy.'

She began to fold the clothes back into the chest. I stared at her, trying to connect the tiny figure with my memories of Max. I was only dimly aware of the chest shutting again. She put her hand on my arm, and the calm touch made me aware once more of my own trembling.

'Willi is a good man, Mr Lawless, but he will feel it his duty to report you in the morning.'

Her words brought back reality. My wounded arm ached from playing, and I felt my head beginning to throb. I thrust the canvas into its bag and stood, at a loss for words, for this was beyond recompense or thanks. Quickly I bent over and kissed her on the cheek. For a moment she held herself very still — and then she handed me the oilskin packet, a faint blush on her lined face. There was something else at the bottom of the bag, but I didn't look, for I knew she was right; I had to get out of the country, and I didn't have much time. She blew out the candle at the top of the stairs.

'Go now,' she said. 'Go quickly.'

The officer looked at his Russian watch, and I fought the urge to look at mine.

'Indeed, Mr Lawless.'

He was very young, and his fresh, healthy face was no longer as politely expressionless as it had been half an hour before. I'd just given my story for the third time. Each time it had been received with guarded scepticism, each time I had been referred to a higher official, but I couldn't read the situation, and I had no idea if a decision was near. What powers did they have? Could they just keep me here, arrest me on speculation? I kept my hands out of sight in my pockets; I could keep my face immobile, but the hands would give me away, I was sure.

They were suspicious — firstly because I hadn't used even a tenth of the time my visa allowed, secondly because of the money. Through the flimsy walls of the draughty hut I could hear the sounds of my car being thoroughly searched. I looked again at the pile of notes on the table, then at the young, unsmiling face.

'I wasn't aware there were restrictions on the amount of Western currency I could bring into the GDR. If I have broken some regulation, I can only apologise.'

My palms were sweating. The reappearance of the corporal who had originally taken my passport prevented the officer from answering. A slip of paper was handed over, and then the corporal just waited beside the desk, his shapeless wreck of a uniform in sharp contrast to the captain's sleek, fitted tailoring. They'd checked with my hotel in Schwerin to see whether I'd done anything out of the ordinary, whether I'd left under questionable circumstances — the captain had told me so, quite openly, watching for reaction. As I waited in the dour silence, I wondered yet again how I could have been so naïve. A large sum of hard currency, carried openly in a briefcase

. . . How long did I have before the bowmaker reported me to the city police?

Again the young man looked at his watch, unaware of sharing my preoccupation. He rose. 'Follow me.'

There was a convoy of Polish trucks drawn up in front of the first barrier. Two of the drivers looked on impassively while a third argued with the brown-overalled official who was inspecting his cargo. His harsh Slav voice rose in excitement as he pointed at the side of his articulated trailer. The whole length of the corrugated metal was smeared with the slogans of the Solidarity union, and the smoky smell of cured meat came from its open back doors, despite wind and rain. The other two vehicles shone with the prudent cleanliness of recent washing. The captain ignored the whole scene and made straight for my car.

Two overalled Grenzpolizisten had the rear end raised on a big jack, and a third was under it, feeling about inside the wheel arches. Drugs, I thought, that's what's worrying them, why the money interests them so much . . . Freezing rain lashed at us in heavy gusts, stinging our faces as we walked across the tarmac. The wind was nearly gale force, strong enough to sway the metal boom of the border barrier like a giant conductor's baton. Moodily the young officer began to poke around the car's interior, sticking his hands at random down the backs of seats, lifting carpets, but after five minutes he seemed convinced of the futility of the exercise. Eyes fixed on my face for signs of guilt or panic, he pointed imperiously at the spare wheel, and suddenly I wasn't sure how much longer I could keep up the bluff. The guard twisted the valve, and air left the tyre in an almost human sigh, resigned and weary.

'The goods to be declared?' asked the captain.

One of the guards jerked a lazy thumb towards the hut, and then stiffened to attention at the annoyance in the young man's eyes. He saluted smartly.

'Inside, Captain.'

The Solidarity driver was waving his hands around now, his voice raising itself to a pitch of pure rage, but still the captain ignored it. I followed his slim back as he marched towards the other room of the low hut, grateful for a moment's relaxation from the hard stare. Inside I saw everything I'd bought lying beside my fiddle case on the trestle table, but our sudden appearance caught the old corporal unawares, and he wasn't quite quick enough to mask his expression. I recognised the wistful look — I had seen it in the shop in Schwerin where I'd hurriedly bought the toys. It was a look full of innocent longing; for one man, it said, to be able to buy so much, so many presents, one man.

The officer scowled at him, then turned to me.

'Open the packages.'

The two of them watched me unwrap them. Swiftly they went through the big doll's house and the set of building blocks, examining them with professional ease, sure in their knowledge of what was capable of concealment. I willed my heart to beat steadily, masking my nerves with a frown. They took the classical records from their sleeves and went through the illustrated story-books page by page — and then suddenly the officer stalked out of the room, unable any longer to conceal his anger at finding nothing. The corporal watched him go, holding the large stuffed elephant in his hands, his eyes amused at the juvenile display, his fingers running absent-mindedly over the seams of the toy, checking for tell-tale breaks in the stitching. He put it down and lifted the big refracting telescope from its leather case. The pleasure of handing it shone in his eyes.

I tried to keep my voice even, casual. 'It's for my oldest boy.'

'He is the one who is ill?'

The sympathy in his voice made it obvious that he was a father, and I felt a pang of shame at having to lie to him. He touched the metal nameplate that said 'Carl Zeiss, Jena' almost reverently. 'A fine thing,' he said. 'As good as any in the West.'

'Better,' I replied. 'They make the best in the world. That's why I bought it here.'

He didn't reply. The rough hands turned the telescope slowly, assessing, weighing.

For a moment I was sure my nerve was going to break, but then he beamed at me in honest pride, and I realised he just didn't want to put it down. The smile became apologetic. He shrugged, embarrassed, then gave a perfunctory glance at each end and laid it back in its case with exaggerated care. I wondered what he would have said if he'd seen me smashing all the precision of the interior glass to make room for the oilskin packet that was now taped inside. I'd replaced the top lenses as exactly as I could, and their opacity hid the painting totally. He lifted the screw-on eyepiece from its compartment — and as he looked through it I felt my heart beating like a drum. *I was going to get away with it!* From outside I heard the sound of another car drawing up, and a familiar voice answer the guard's blunt demand for a passport. Through the open door I saw the tall, stooping frame of the American I'd met on the way in. The officer came back into the room, pulling on immaculate leather gloves, looking enquiringly at the corporal. The old man's shake of the head made his brows knit together in annoyance. He turned to me.

'Empty your pockets, please.'

I saw the corporal's face register distaste behind his superior's back, and decided to say something. To show no annoyance would be out of character. 'Is this really necessary?'

'Empty your pockets!'

The corporal avoided my eyes as he took the items from me — the car keys, some small change, the snub-nosed key of the left-luggage locker in Lübeck station, where I'd left the gun and a spare bag. I handed over the hastily-written receipts for the morning's purchases, Elly's letter, the envelope Helga had given me from

Annette. It was still unopened. The captain picked it up from the table.

'What is this?'

'It's private.'

'Open it.'

He saw me begin to protest, and ripped the envelope open. He drew out a photograph: Annette, posed against the mirrors of her mother's room. She wore a black corset, stockings and heels. I caught the end of the inscription as the gloved hands turned it over: '. . . *from Caro. She thought you might prefer me like this. I still love you, Annette.*'

Both of their faces changed. The old corporal looked at me in disappointment, and the captain, after a lingering look at the picture, couldn't keep the smirk of triumph from his features. I watched the tension leave his thin shoulders; it was only a small victory, but it was enough.

'Pornography is forbidden in the German Democratic Republic,' he said happily.

For an instant he was just a boy, delighted that his side had won — and then a different look, more appreciative, crossed his face as he examined the picture again. He banished it quickly, aware of the corporal's gaze.

'It is a capitalist disease which we will not tolerate!' he snapped, thrusting the photograph back into its torn envelope. 'You may go now.'

He put the envelope firmly away in the top pocket of his jacket and laid my passport and the pile of Deutschmarks down on the table. I was about to protest, when a hand touched my sleeve.

'Why, hello there, sir!'

The warm friendliness of the American's voice took us all by surprise — and before anyone could speak, he'd spotted the telescope. In one quick movement he was at the table, the big cylinder in his hands.

'Say, what a beauty! Must've cost a fortune! Why, back in the States, this . . .'

I snatched it from him before his examination could reveal anything, shovelling keys and papers and money into the briefcase with my free hand. 'Excuse me, I have to hurry. I've been kept here a long time.'

He gave me the beginnings of a vague, disappointed smile. It lasted until the corporal held out a hand for his papers.

Silently I blessed the photograph as I rewrapped the parcels. A telephone rang somewhere near, and I could almost taste my own fear. Had Schumacher reported me yet? The young captain looked on, rocking contentedly on the heels of his boots, smiling, attributing the fumblings of my shaking hands to shame. He gave the American's passport a perfunctory examination as he watched me. I made two trips to the car with the toys, the fiddle, the briefcase and the telescope, and once everything was packed away I leaned against the Volkswagen, dizzy and sweating in spite of the freezing rain. Still I could hear the phone's insistent ring.

The old American passed me as I got into the driver's seat. 'Nice to meet you again,' he said, determined to ignore my rudeness.

I smiled at him nervously, trying not to look back at the door of the wooden hut. As I got into the VW, I heard the creak of the barrier opening, the damp roar of the truck engines starting up. I moved forward into the line. Without looking, I was sure the young officer's gaze was still upon me; it wouldn't stop until I was in the West, I knew.

The Solidarity truck followed the American's Plymouth past the red-and-white striped pole, and I squeezed myself between it and the next of the lorries. My eyes stared, unseeing, fixed on the slogans of the dirty back doors. I willed myself not to measure the distance to the West German side. We passed a guard, an observation tower, another barrier, all at funereal speed, and then our convoy began to accelerate. The final fence loomed. Only yards to go. *Come on!* The seconds stretched. *Come on . . .* My fear stood poised, ready for the jump that would turn it to elation. *Come —*

'*HALT!*'

My reflexes obeyed, almost made me hit the brake. I caught sight of the officer's accusatory figure in the wing mirror.

'*SOFORT!*'

He broke into a clumsy run, shouting. I heard a shrill whistle, then a curious sound, half-whine, half-thump. Only when the captain's reflection starred did I realise it was a shot. I pulled the wheel wildly to the left and rammed my foot down. I could hear the Polish driver's terrified shouts as I skidded past his articulated cab, through the final double fence — and then I almost lost control.

There was a guard directly in front of me, firing bursts from his automatic rifle. They went over the car's roof, but he stood his ground — until he saw that I wasn't stopping, and then he wasn't fast enough. Time seemed to break down into a series of slow, connected segments as the inevitable happened. I was aware of the bonnet hitting him, his gun spitting fire, the repeated dull thud of his bullets punching into the big vehicle behind me, all in slow motion. Reality came back to speed when he hit the windscreen. The impact shattered one side of it and knocked me from the steering wheel. His gun and one polished jackboot came through the broken glass, and for an awful second he hung there, a limp, bloody mess of leather and metal and flesh. I regained the spinning wheel with one hand, trying to keep the flying glass from my eyes with the other. Just in time, I pulled the car back from a course that would have sent me crashing off the roadway, and then I stamped on the brake and felt her slide away from me.

The Plymouth had stopped. My back wheels screeched to a halt inches away from it, and the soldier slid bloodily off the bonnet. I grabbed the telescope and stumbled out of the car, to see the old American, half out of the driver's seat, staring backwards in horror. Then I heard the crash, and whirled round as well.

The anti-vehicle ditch had opened just too late to trap me — but it had caught the Solidarity lorry in my stead. The cab was half in it, facing downwards at a crazy, broken angle. I watched the dirty grey box of the trailer jackknife across both lanes of the road, thin black snakes of rubber flying up from the burst tyres of its back wheels.

The whole truck would have overturned if it hadn't been for the mesh fence. Steel smashed into steel with a horrible, grinding crash, and the stanchions keeled over at an impossible angle, but they didn't give way. The lorry's back doors flew open, disgorging the load in a dark red mass that slithered across the bent wire. I saw the driver clamber out of the twisted remains of the cab and run wildly for cover — and then there was only the tortured squeal of metal as the last of the collision's impact dissipated itself. I stared, until I saw the uniformed figures trying to get round the still-moving mass of the spilled red cargo.

I yelled at the old man as I yanked the Plymouth's door open. 'DRIVE!'

It was less than a hundred yards to the West. The old man shook with terror as we picked up speed, his jaw working soundlessly. A hail of bullets smashed into the big car, tearing off the radiator grille, sending us yawing off to one side. A column of steam spouted upwards, then streamed along the sides of the bonnet, but, miraculously, none of the shots hit us or the tyres. I tasted blood, spat glass from my mouth. Ahead of us I could see waving figures dressed in the familiar olive uniforms of the West German police. The old man clutched the wheel tightly. I shut my eyes, sure we'd never make it.

Then, after an age, another sound superimposed itself on my consciousness.

They were *cheering*. As we came round the bend,

safely back into the West, they were yelling, applauding wildly. The people from the waiting cars, the lorry drivers, the passengers of the big coach — they were shouting, clapping their hands. *They thought we were escaping refugees!* Even the policemen . . .

The police!

The thought pulled me back sharply from the craziness of the situation. What should I do? The old American turned to me, deathly pale.

'Why did they *do* that?' he said testily.

I stared at him like an idiot, listening to the cheering, unable to comprehend what he was talking about, but then the uniforms claimed my attention again. *What should I do?* My dilemma grew as we rolled towards the first of the smiling policemen. Could I give myself up now? Now that I had the evidence, the painting? The man waved us eagerly through to a parking space, and another two of them converged on us, running. Shaking like a leaf, the old American got out of the car.

'Why did they . . .?'

Instinct or gut reaction, something at any rate deeper than logic, sent me sliding across the wide front seat. I gave an imbecile smile at the face bending down towards the window — and again my foot went down as hard as it could. The car roared away from the border post. Once more I heard shouts behind me, this time as much of puzzlement as of anger, but the end result was the same; within seconds they were sprinting for their cars. Over my shoulder I caught a last glimpse of the old man's dazed, wondering expression as my blood-smeared hands fought to keep hold of the wheel.

But my problems were multiplying fast. The big car was ailing now, and I knew I didn't have much longer before the engine seized. The steam was gone, and the agonised, high-pitched whine that was building up told me she wouldn't go much further without water. I passed neat rows of houses at breakneck speed, but she began to falter and miss as I slalomed my way through the roadworks on the next hill's crest — and then the engine finally cut out, leaving me slowing down in unnatural silence. It was only the last of her momentum that rolled us off the main road into a sloping alley. The steering locked, and she crunched gently to a halt against a low garden wall. Clutching the telescope, I got out and stumbled down through a thicket of pines until I found cover. The sirens got louder. I hid behind a wooden fence, listening to their angry wail as they passed the Plymouth by.

I waited, crouched on my knees in the mud, rain dripping from the collar of the once-smart coat. I knew I couldn't afford the luxury of rest; once they discovered they'd lost me, they'd double back, and it would take them no time at all to find the car. I fought my way back up the slippery slope to the main road, crossed it, and then sprinted for dear life up the lane opposite.

For five minutes I just ran, zigzagging my way through the side streets, expecting a policeman at every intersection, but none came. I made it to the next main road without hindrance, and paused, fighting for breath. I was on a pleasant, tree-lined suburban avenue, prosaic enough to make me doubt my own sanity. Had I really just escaped from East Germany? The whole episode couldn't have taken more than fifteen minutes from start to finish. My arm ached as I tried to wipe the blood from the cuts on my face. What now?

My salvation came in the form of a dumpy, slow-moving city bus. It came out of a side street about thirty yards off and turned away from me, towards Lübeck. I ran after it stiffly, my legs leaden, and just managed to jump on before the concertina of the back doors closed. I grabbed hold of the rail with my left hand, the telescope clutched in my right. How much time did I have? How soon would they find the car? The shock of the whole incident suddenly distilled itself into one awful fact. *My fiddle!* I'd left my fiddle behind in the Volkswagen. In East Germany! The bus gave a lurch as it went round a corner. My fiddle. *And everything else.* The passport! *The key* . . . I closed my eyes, wondering if I was going to faint. A sharp tap on the arm made me open them again. An elderly gentleman was staring at me in disapproval.

'You should pay,' he said.

I went through the pockets of the coat, then those of the suit. There was nothing except broken glass.

'I have no money,' I said, in as level a voice as I could find.

He shook his head in sorrow and disgust, reached over and put a *Deutschmark* into the automatic dispenser, and handed me a ticket. I mumbled my thanks. The bus began to fight its way through the rain towards Lübeck.

Chapter 8
STRENGTH

'THE LORD LOVES a sinner who repents, my friend. What is your problem? Is it alcohol?'

I took the tract from the muscular young man with my free hand, and saw how badly it was shaking. My eyes met his, read the crazy, righteous concern in them, and instinctively my other hand clutched the telescope tighter under the wet cloth of the coat. Then the drinker at the next table hawked and spat noisily, breaking the spell, and the young Christian passed on through the freshly-painted *Glühwein* stand, offering his salvation to the makeshift decorations and the customers' indifference. The two identically-dressed skinheads at the far end jeered at him, and one of them threw a half-full paper cup as he passed. It splashed against the wall, but he didn't break his stride or even take notice of the red stain. The foreman of the squad of painters saw it and started cursing, but he stopped abruptly when he saw the invitation in the two adolescent faces. They wanted violence.

How much longer? The lights of the wooden *Weihnachtsmarkt* booths shone wetly, and appetising smells of *Wurst* and *Reibekuchen* reached out to me as I waited for enough darkness to move in safety. Rain scudded across the crowded street, whipping at the striped awnings, rattling the town hall windows as the storm blew itself out, and I noticed that the shivering was no longer something I could control. The evangelist marched on into the crowd. I heard the fervour in his voice, undismayed by failure.

'Repent and ye shall be saved, for the Lord Jesus is merciful! Come to Him and repent!'

I went after him down the street, scanning the throng for uniforms. It was dark enough now, and I knew I could put off action no longer. I had to get out of Lübeck, and *fast*, but not before I'd somehow got to the money and the spare passport that lay in the station locker. But how, without a key? And what was I to do with the painting? The crowds parted to let the tall young man through, ignoring him except for the occasional muttered 'Amen' of the older people. I followed in his wake until I came to the side street where I'd seen the waste-glass container.

It was only four hours since I'd escaped from the East, and the police search was closing in with frightening speed. The odds, already bad, had been worsened by circumstance. I'd descended from the bus in Lübeck's old town, where the crowds were thickest, only to find myself in the most effective of traps — a city surrounded by water. The loop of river that had made it a natural defensive site in the middle ages had also made it the easiest of cities to besiege, and that was exactly what the authorities had done. From the abandoned car, they knew I was on foot, and the bus passengers would have confirmed that I was penniless. The next step was logical: as well as the squads who were actually searching for me, there were men at every gate and bridge, and the railway station was on the other side of the river. For the moment I could at least avoid anything that looked like a green uniform, but sooner or later I knew I would have to brave the cordon.

But one problem at a time. I took the oilskin packet from the metal tube of the telescope, and looked round. The crowd in the main street was oblivious of my existence, intent on their missions of purchase, and I could see no one in the other direction. The carnival lights twinkled from across the river, a quarter of a mile away, but there was no one to see me push the telescope through the hole. It landed with a heavy, satisfying crunch among the bottles and jars, and I breathed a sigh of relief — with any luck it wouldn't be found until the container was emptied. I'd thrown its case into a rubbish skip on the back of a lorry, hoping the Hamburg address on the side meant it would soon be gone. The leather bag which held the painting — and the round metal tin I'd found below it — slid easily out of the oilskin packet. I pushed that in as well. I dropped the tin through the hole I'd ripped in the coat's lining, but the bag was more awkward. My shaking hands made the task twice as difficult as it should have been. Why couldn't I . . .?

Suddenly I was on all fours, the wet pavement spinning beneath me.

Even after it was over, it took a while to work out that I'd fainted, for the disorientation lasted long after the end of the fit. I pulled myself up, hand over hand, grateful for the solidity of the glass container. Again my head swam, but this time I was ready for it. What had I been doing . . .? I held on to the cold metal, trying to remember. It had been *important* . . . It had . . .

A few yards away, two policemen turned the corner.

There was a doorway behind me, up a small flight of steps. I sank into its shadows as they came almost level with me, and when they stopped, I held my breath. Had I been seen? I heard a muttered comment and an answering laugh — and then the painting rolled into my sight, kicked contemptuously out of the way. They moved on towards the intersection, then stopped again. I pressed myself as far back as possible. All I could do was wait; all I could see was the painting. An old master . . . How much was the thing worth? One million? One and a half? I watched it getting wet in the gutter. A gust of wind tore spray from the puddles, caught the street's litter. An ice-cream wrapper whirled up, floated down, fastened itself to a corner of the canvas.

Firmer steps approached from the main street, and I heard an exchange of banalities about the weather. The tract distributor came into view, and when he turned, he saw me. His eyes followed my line of vision to the painting on the ground, and then he looked again towards the policemen. I shook my head at him and shut my eyes. Would he understand? I could only hope he wouldn't give me away.

'Goodnight, gentlemen,' he said.

Their slow walk died away until it was indistinguishable from the background murmur of the crowd's noise, and a spasm of shivering made me fear again for my balance. I gripped the fluting of the stone arch behind me. The evangelist picked up the canvas, shook water and débris from it, and came up the steps. He opened one of the doors to reveal a dimly-lit interior. A small church . . . The unexpected light made strange shadows across his face.

'*It is better to be a doorkeeper in the house of the Lord than to dwell in the tents of sin,*' he said. 'This is yours, I believe.'

He unfurled the canvas at arm's length, like a prophet with a scroll. Blankly, he stared at it. Then he thrust it back into my hands and made to pass by.

I grabbed at his sleeve. 'I need money!' The desperation in my own voice surprised me. 'Please help me! I can pay you back. Just a few marks.'

I had to have the price of a seat in a café or a bar, anything that would get me off the street. He shook his head deliberately, with the air of a man well used to both request and refusal.

'I never give money to the likes of yourself. The soul's salvation is more than the body's need, my friend.' He looked again at the painting. 'But if you are desperate, there are places in this town where they would give you a few marks for your picture. Goodnight.'

As the grey door closed, it dawned on me that he thought I'd painted it myself. I wiped water from the canvas and examined it as best I could in the darkness. Had it been damaged? I didn't know enough to do more than hope not. Angry with myself, I went down the steps to retrieve the leather bag. What the hell had made me faint? I rolled up the painting, put it back inside its familiar home, then stuffed the bundle back into the torn coat lining, on top of the tin. The wet Baltic wind tore at my hair as I mentally thanked my strange benefactor for the idea. I had perhaps an hour before the shops shut.

Enough time to find a pawnbroker.

If the elderly waitress hadn't caught my arm, I'd have fallen over the chair instead of sitting down on it, for I was barely capable of staying upright. She took the two carrier bags from me and I held on to the edge of the table like a drowning man clutching a raft, watching the menu swim before my eyes, hoping the drinkers wouldn't notice. Apart from the tropical brightness of the juke-box in the corner, the room was just a blur, and once more I asked myself the question: how much of this could I take? The dizziness wasn't permanent yet, and I was pretty sure I could stop myself from fainting again, but the spells were becoming longer, and my head had settled into a steady ache. I was ill. Seriously. I forced myself into acceptance of the fact; trying to ignore it was a stupidity that could only add to my predicament.

And that was grim enough already. The search had now intensified enough to make the streets hazardous in the extreme, and every time the giddiness came over me, the chance of a blunder doubled. Twice now I had misjudged, nearly walked straight into the cordon. How long could I keep dodging them? How many . . . The metallic clatter of coins in a slot startled me. I looked up. I could just make out the waitress's lumpy black-and-white silhouette against the juke-box's neon backdrop. Suddenly the room filled with a boy's clear soprano, soaring effortlessly over the plastic sentiment of a thousand artificial strings.

'*Silent Night . . .*'

In the circumstances, it was ironic. Christmas, of all things, had saved me; if it hadn't been for the crowds the cops would have had me by now, I knew it.

When she came back, I managed to order *Goulaschsuppe* and *Bratwurst*, and then I just waited, feeling the haze begin to clear. Maybe hot food would help, but I couldn't spend much, for the sixty marks I'd squeezed out of the pawnbroker was all but gone already. He'd have given more if I hadn't insisted that he take the tin as well, but I'd followed my instinct, and now I wondered if I'd been right. Was the thing important? Again I wished I'd had a chance to examine it, but in the pawn shop there had been no time to press the bargain.

But at least the picture was reasonably safe. The envelope that contained the pawn-ticket was in my trouser pocket. I touched it for reassurance as the meal came, then ate, slowly, concentrating on the food, trying to keep my shaking hands from spilling soup over the table. Total clarity returned without warning, sooner than I'd expected. The abruptness of it made me sit back in relief, until I saw the abandoned newspaper on the next seat. The headline drew my eyes like a magnet: 'Police comb Lübeck for mystery refugee', it said.

The conversations around me confirmed how completely the town had been sealed off, for the Gasthaus's regulars were more than a little disgruntled at yet another disruption of their routine. Bad enough, the Christmas madness, but this crazy damn refugee! Show your papers at every bloody corner . . . bastard wants sending back, bloody town's full of them . . . I listened to several graphically sadistic suggestions as to my eventual fate when taken, until the waitress objected to the language. For a second, 'Silent Night' found a different irony, and then, chastened, they steered the talk into safer waters. What about Borussia's chances, eh? Get a hiding from Leverkusen tonight, high time too . . . I sat there, wishing I could drop the issue as easily, trying to gauge the odds against me. I couldn't fool myself: my chances of escape, already slim, were dwindling by the minute.

The article could have been worse, though. It gave the facts of the escape, but without details, and that at least gave me some hope. I was banking on the probability that whatever co-operation there was between East and West hadn't yet yielded results, crossing my fingers that the Lübeck police didn't know about my locker at the station. If I was right, it was still worth the gamble of trying to get to the money and the passport, but on the debit side, the facts were starker.

They would have my fingerprints from the Plymouth by now. That was a certainty, and a chilling one — it meant that Alexander Fraser was no longer safely dead, that Weidemann and his scarfaced thug were only a phone call or a computer readout away. I shuddered again. The fates being planned for me around this comfortable German room would be mild compared with the reality of falling into their hands, I was sure of that. Weidemann would have no scruples about disposing of me — and no difficulty either. My record called me both unstable and violent; it would be easy enough to fake an attempted escape or a suicidal assault, whatever the situation demanded. The fiction would end with the sad necessity of my death, but there would be no tears shed by the authorities, either here or in Britain; I would be just another statistic of failure, a hard case beyond rehabilitation, propaganda fodder for the next capital punishment manifesto. When the waitress came back, I paid, tipped enough not to be remembered, and carried out my two bags. The toilet was in the yard at the back.

I discarded tie, jacket and overcoat, leaving them on the peg behind the cubicle door, and took the overalls from their wrappings. I trampled out their newness on the dirty floor, put them on, then prised the lids from the paint tins with the big screwdriver I'd bought. It only took seconds to daub white emulsion all over myself, and when I looked in the mirror, I was pleased with what I saw; I'd pass reasonably close scrutiny, and the obvious freshness of the paint would discourage physical contact. I gave the two brushes a liberal coating of both paint and turpentine, stuck one in my top pocket, and slid the screwdriver and hammer into the leg-slots provided for tools. The other brush I would carry in my hand. I smeared some paint on my face to cover the cuts and bruises of the windshield glass. It stung, and in the confined space of the toilet the combination of the pain and the smells made me giddy again. I almost gagged, but I went out into the yard, and the damp freshness helped me hold back. I splattered paint on my shoes and rubbed more dirt on the overalls with a filthy wet rag that I found in the corner. I wrung the thing out and put it into my pocket, then went out into the street. It was still raining heavily.

It was the hour when the streets change hands in any big city, when the last of the late shoppers mingle with the vanguard of the entertainment-seekers, like the scouts of opposing armies on neutral ground. I made my way down the hill towards the footbridge that was my target, paint dripping from the tins, and overtook the first of the carnival customers, four serious-looking punks with multi-coloured hair, gravely bent on revelry despite the weather. The black waters of the Trave reflected the ferris wheel lights as I approached the two policemen who guarded the slim bridge. I slowed down deliberately, letting the punks catch me up, and felt the adrenaline surge; everything depended on how well I could carry the bluff.

'*Ausweis*,' said the first one, sticking out a gloved hand.

'Why?' I asked.

'Never mind, just show us your papers,' he said impatiently.

I gestured with the brush towards the funfair, and a few drops of paint flew from its tip. He swerved to avoid them hitting the green leather of his coat.

'*Hoi!* Be careful, damn you!'

I took out the evil-smelling rag and began to clean the brush. 'They're over there, mate, where I'm working. What's it all about, anyway?'

They ignored the question and looked at each other. The punks arrived at my back.

'You should carry them, always,' the other one said, half-heartedly.

His nose was blue with cold and he looked miserable. The punks shuffled their feet behind me, and I could see the two policemen eyeing them with ill-disguised impatience; they were a more interesting argument than I was.

'Don't be bloody stupid, mate. In *this*?' I said.

I rubbed my hand on the overall leg and yanked at the tins to indicate what I meant. More paint dripped, as I'd intended. Both of them shied away again, paranoid about getting it on their uniforms, and behind me I could hear the teenagers feeling obliged to get noisy in such close proximity to the cops. A voice muttered something about Nazis — and the two policemen stiffened perceptibly. One of the girls made to move past, but an authoritarian hand stopped her.

'All right, go on then,' the first one grumbled at me. 'But don't get caught without it again.'

His partner sneezed wetly.

'*Gesundheit*,' I said, giving them the cheekiest grin I could manage.

I stuffed the rag back into my pocket. As I headed out over the bridge, I heard their voices become aggressive, rising confidently to the lure of the punks.

My euphoria at having pulled it off lasted about halfway across, and then the fever shook me again, this time in real earnest. I set the tins down and pretended to be putting the second brush away in my top pocket as I leaned against the railing for support. It slipped from my hands and I looked back in panic, but they were too preoccupied with their argument to hear the splash. For a moment I held on to the railing, watching the slow swirl of the dirty water, then I forced myself to pick up the tins. Very slowly, I headed for the unfocused blotches of light in front of me. Sweat was pouring from me now, and my head was thumping with pain. To reach the other side took an age. As soon as I made it, I disappeared out of sight behind one of the big carousels and sat down on a crate in the darkness, fighting the desire to lay myself out flat and just close my eyes, for I knew if I gave in to it I wouldn't get up again. Pink and white toy horses bobbed crazily up and down at the edge of my vision as I waited for the fit to pass.

How much strength did I have, and for how long? Even though the dizziness wasn't completely over, I struggled to my feet. I had to get to the locker quickly, for there was still a very real chance of my being recognised. The prints from the Plymouth would have brought a photograph from my record by now, and at least two of the border cops had seen my face. Money and I.D. were imperative. They'd get me a hotel and a doctor, keep me off the streets till the search was called off. I felt again in my pocket for the envelope with the pawn-ticket; if I managed to find safety, I'd redeem it myself and fly to England; if not, I'd post it. It was already addressed to Elly. I began my walk to the station.

It took ten, slow, painful minutes, two stops, and more strength than I knew I had. The main booking hall was above the platforms, and the echo of my footsteps was loud between the thunderous rumblings of the passing trains. I went to the lockers at the far end, thankful now that I'd chosen one out of sight of the main ticket counter. The corner was deserted except for a young soldier and his girlfriend, and when she saw me over his shoulder she broke off their passionate embrace. Blushing, they pushed silently past me.

The heavy screwdriver was best quality Solingen steel,

but so was the barrel of the lock that was protecting my goods. Sweat ran from me as I tried to force it, but I couldn't — there was no angle at which I could apply enough pressure without either the door or the tool bending. I heard footsteps, and hid the screwdriver under my coat, turning my back until they were safely past. I waited till the roar of the next train was at its peak.

I had to use the screwdriver as a chisel. I placed the blade against the locker's hasp and hit it once with the hammer, as hard as I could. The plastic handle of the tool sheared in two — but so did the lock, and with a great reverberating clang, the door sprang open. I grabbed the bag, threw it down, unzipped it, and reached inside to feel cold steel. The gun was still there.

Only then did I see the street cleaner.

He was still in his teens. The faded blue denims and round cap had once been the uniform of the German manual labourer, but now they were the badge of the Federal Republic's new poor, the immigrant workers from the Balkans and further east. His knuckles tightened on the handles of his dustcart, and the lids of the two bins rattled like cymbals as he stopped and stared at the gun in my hand. His eyes widened with fear, the whites pale against the swarthy skin and the jet black of his dirty hair.

'*Ich Türke! Nicht schiessen!*' he shouted.

I heard the echo of other voices, footsteps, and felt the trembling begin again, violently, reaching its peak much faster than before. I wanted to tell him I meant him no harm, but I couldn't speak. I threw the gun back at the bag and leaned against the broken locker as the weapon bounced and skidded across the tiles.

Through the haze, I saw a hand pick it up. I struggled to focus, and saw two grinning faces, two badly-shaven heads. Where had I seen them before? One of them spat at the Turkish boy, and his partner's sneering laugh identified them — the two kids from the *Glühwein* stall . . . The one holding the gun sauntered over to me, hooked a foot through the handle of my bag and drew it to him. When he saw the cash inside, he whistled in appreciation.

'Well, well . . .' He nodded at the young Turk. 'Going to shoot him, were you? Can't blame you for that, Dad. Can't blame you at all.'

His friend's laughter egged him on. He walked over to the street cleaner, pointing the gun. The Turkish boy backed away as far as he could, rigid with terror, his whimpering so loud I could barely hear the skinhead's whisper. The finger tightened on the trigger.

'. . . *pig*, aren't you? *All* Turks are pigs . . . and pigs should be *slaughtered*.'

Below us, a train rumbled to a halt. My legs began to give under me. I heard the guard's whistle, felt the coldness of the metal on my back as I slid downwards. Why couldn't I stop myself falling? I stumbled over the paint-pots to land heavily on my knees. It took the last of my strength to look up. Where were the skinheads? I heard running feet, laughter. The bag! It was gone . . .

The street cleaner was slumped against the tiled wall, sobbing with relief. When he saw me staring at him, he pointed towards the ticket counter. '*Warte. Ich bringe Polizei. Zwei minuten. Iss gut. Nur warte.*'

I shook my head, and tasted a sour, bitter bile in my mouth as his image blurred before me. Desperately I tore the envelope and the last of the pawnbroker's money from my pocket. I held the crumpled handful out to him. There was a roaring in my ears. '*Kein Polizei*,' I said. 'No police. Post this. Please post it.' I realised I was speaking in English. Why couldn't I speak German?

Hesitantly, he came forward. '*Iss gut. Nix Polizei. Polizei nix gut für Türke. Nix gut, nix Polizei. Iss gut.*'

I tried hard to nod, and felt the money and the envelope slip from my grasp. The spilled paint felt pleasant and cool as I fell forward into it. Blackness covered me.

It was the music that woke me, a wailing confusion of notes. Every so often a wave of arhythmic drumming would surge through it, shaking the floor beside my mattress. My brain struggled to understand, but my ear couldn't impose order on it. What was the scale? Eastern . . .? I heard voices approaching. Again I tried to concentrate, again my mind failed me. I could hear anger and appeasement, a feminine voice and a masculine one. What was the language? My hands felt round on the lumpy mattress. Where was I?

The curtain that divided the room was pushed aside. The woman was middle-aged and fat, her black dress covered by a fraying purple cardigan, her dark hair trapped beneath a floral headscarf. He was young, blond, lightly bearded, dressed in jeans and leather jacket, and when he turned to look at me, I saw the priest's collar at the neck of his check shirt. Behind the two of them I saw the source of the drumming: three female children, replicas of their mother, peering at me from behind ancient treadle sewing-machines. At the sight of me, the woman burst into another torrent of speech, fierce enough to drown the radio's music and bow the children's heads again over their work. It took him a long time to calm her. Finally he drew the curtain shut and perused me gravely. The noise of the machines swelled to a crescendo, then died away.

'Excuse me, I know who you are, I think.' The English was halting, the accent Eastern European, the tone apologetic. 'It is not hard to guess, Mr Lawless.' He pronounced it with the accent on the second syllable. He shrugged. 'They give your name in the last paper last night. And your picture.'

When I said nothing, he sat down at the table.

'We do not have much time, I am afraid. A barge leaves Lübeck in an hour. It takes a cargo of sand to Dortmund. The captain will leave you anywhere you please.'

'Where am I?'

'You do not remember?' A frown creased the pale brow. Nervously his hand worried at the wisps of beard. 'Perhaps it is not surprising. The wound from your arm. It is why you fell in the station, I think. In English, 'septic shock'; I look it up last night.'

'Who brought me here?'

'Mehmet. Mehmet Atasayar. The Turkish boy.'

The street cleaner . . . I looked down at the fresh bandage. 'Did you do this?'

'It is perhaps not so good,' he apologised. 'I was medical student once, in Budapest, but I forget, maybe.'

Suddenly I remembered the ticket, the painting. 'There was an envelope . . .'

'Mehmet . . .' The motion of his hand indicated it had been posted. 'He says you sleep easier if you know it is safe. But now hurry, we have not much time. The barge waits. Please, we go. The woman, his mother, she is frightened.'

Dortmund . . . From Lübeck to Dortmund, on a barge. That meant it would pass . . . His urgency broke in on the confusion of my thoughts.

'Please, Mr Lawless, we go *now*. We . . .'

'Why are you doing this?'

He blushed. 'I live here in this building with the Turkish people. They are good people, work hard, is not easy for them here in Deutschland, much trouble with the police. I hope some day to make them Christian, maybe one, two, maybe Mehmet, but it is hard, you know, to win *Vertrauen*. You understand *Vertrauen*?'

'Trust.'

Speaking the word brought back my confusion; it was a word that belonged to Elly, or Helga — not to this boy priest.

'. . . are not used to trust. Last night after he brings you here, he is frightened, he comes to me, he thinks you are dying, maybe. He asks my help. Is important I help. If I get you away, he will trust me more, perhaps. You understand? You are a Christian?'

On the other side of the curtain, someone turned the radio up. The weird music swirled round the dingy room, making nonsense of the question. Again I didn't answer.

'It does not matter. My father, he help you.'

He saw the doubt in my eyes. For the first time, a smile touched his pale face. 'No, not My Father . . .' He crossed himself. 'My *father*.'

Chapter 9
BEASTS

EVEN THOUGH I knew they were gone, my fear of the dogs still held me. I tried to conquer it as I waited behind the thick wall of rhododendrons, but it was a thing I'd never been able to control. I listened. I could hear the mill-wheel, the distant roar of traffic from Münster's ring road — and the throbbing. It was faint, steady, its centre deep in the castle itself. I pushed through, snapping the branches, and looked both ways on the main drive. This time there was nothing but darkness stretching in either direction. They're *gone*, I told myself, but the terror was persistent — it was as though my mind was working on two levels, the deeper of them immune to logic. But through the fear I was sure now; Burg Laer and its grounds were deserted.

I was certain the inhabitants had left, for watching them go had nearly finished my chances. I'd seen the first two vehicles in time, the lorry and the long dark limousine, but the jeep that had come after had all but caught me in its lights. First the frenzied barking had nearly paralysed me, and then I'd panicked and flung myself into the shallow ditch between hedge and drive. Only once the vehicle had roared past had I realised that the animals weren't loose, hunting me, but in the jeep, being taken away. Now I stood on the rutted gravel, feeling the fear well up once more. Again I tried to confront it. Dogs and darkness had triggered it, I knew, but it was more than just that — over the last few hours a dread had grown inside me, something I couldn't name.

You came back strong . . . I kept hearing Helga's words. Was that my fear? Losing my new-found strength? Or was I afraid of where it might lead me?

I sat down on an ornate stone bench, shivering in my shirt-sleeves, contemplating my bleeding hands, ruefully remembering the leather gauntlets I'd been offered. The place being shut up had made nonsense of what little planning I'd been able to do. On my last visit, Burg Laer had been thronged with visitors, and that was why I'd come on foot rather than find a car. The cheap raincoat, the dark glasses; it would have been enough to keep me inconspicuous among them, but now . . . I looked down at my clothes. The coat had been abandoned as soon as it was dark enough to scale the gates in safety, for its whiteness had made me almost luminous, and the undergrowth had torn the trousers and shirt in half a dozen places. I stood up again. I'd been right round the place now, twice, and had seen no signs of humanity since the cars had gone. There was no point in waiting any longer.

The moon was full, and walking towards the castle in its light did nothing to ease my foreboding. Once again I wished I'd been able to talk to Elly, for if ever I needed level-headed advice, it was now. Where was she? Every call to Mary Wellbeck's number had brought only the maddening politeness of the answering machine. Why? Where *were* they? What would she make of this; what did I hope to gain? I tried to reason it out as I drew nearer the huge mass. On the barge the logic of coming here had been unassailable: this place was the root of the conspiracy, this was where I'd find out what had made it grow. It had seemed like the hand of fate that the vessel's route to Dortmund should bring me within a few miles of here . . .

But the barge was like a dream, now. The noise grew

louder as I neared Burg Laer, and again my mind split. A pump? Something to control the water level? A beast . . .? The sound was menacing enough to be alive, and in the frosty darkness there was nothing absurd about the fantasy. Could the castle have a life of its own, the throbbing its heart, the roar of the mill-wheel its voice? My courage faltered as I came to the edge of the leaf-covered lawn. Again I listened. It had begun suddenly, just as I'd neared the place for the first time. Had my presence brought it to life? The silhouette seemed to swell before me in the moonlight. Night had trimmed every vestige of baroque prettiness from it, and what was left was medieval, brutal. Again I willed myself forward; it was either take the risk or turn back.

It was what the Germans call a *Wasserburg*, a castle built on piles driven into the water, and the main gate was the only way in that didn't involve swimming the lake and scaling the wall. My reconnaissance had shown me a rowing-boat drawn up on a jetty at the other side — a way out, perhaps, if I needed one, but no help to me now. I hesitated at the narrow drawbridge, then made for the wicket gate of the huge door, my footfalls loud on the ancient wood. It would be locked, it was sure to be . . . Half of me wanted it to be, wanted the excuse that would take the decision from me, force me to turn back.

But it wasn't. I went through the gate and the deep archway behind.

Standing in the castle's courtyard was like being inside a rotten tooth. It was oval, bounded by high towers on three sides and a lower wall on the fourth. The short flight of steps that led to the main door was on my right, and apart from that I saw only a stairway up to the top of the wall and another down to what had to be the cellars. A tattoo of tyre-tracks marked the frost in front of the descending one. I went down the worn steps. The iron door at the bottom creaked open.

There was some light, but it was dim, the source far off in front of me. I groped my way down more stairs and saw the discoloured streak along the roughly-plastered wall. Below the water-line . . . The air got warmer the deeper I went, but it was stagnant, dank with smells of decay. The throbbing was much louder now. I followed its echoes along the narrow corridor, and with the warmth and the dampness the sensation of being inside a living thing intensified. Again the fantasy gripped me. What kind of beast was this? Hand over hand I groped my way along its umbilical cord, wondering what I would find in its womb. I wound my way along the twisting passageway until I came to the source of the light, a thin sliver of brightness under another door. I stopped; no weapon, no plan, no armour against what might be inside . . . It wasn't too late to turn back . . . I pushed the door open and heard the clankings, the thudding, and my fears vanished. My hand found a light switch.

I'd been wrong. It wasn't a pump, it was a generator, a massive one, and most of the noise coming from it could have been avoided if they hadn't been in such a hurry to leave, for whatever machinery had been here had been ripped out rather than dismantled. The empty housings rattled, the rows of loose bolts along the walls jingled and sang. Thick tendrils of cut-off electric cable sprouted as far as the floor, vibrating the débris that covered it. Machines? What kind? There was a chemical smell, acidic, pungent . . . I picked my way through the rubbish to the complex chart on the far wall. The dates along the bottom went well into next year, but they were the only thing that made sense to me.

I got down on my knees and tried to sift through the mess. Plaster, shards of brick, paper, mountains of it, shreddings, clippings. What had this place been? And why had the exodus had been so sudden? My fingers found something solid, a rubber stamp, about an inch square. I tested it on the blood on the back of my hand. 'Spielbank Neustift' . . . I sat down abruptly on the nearest pile of rubble and looked at the thing.

The casino.

A connection. I'd known it, I'd been sure, but the excitement rose in me just the same. I went back to the generator and examined the board of switches above it. *Time* switches . . . From the dials I could see it was set to run every night for varying periods. Why? Surely the castle was near enough to Münster to take electricity from the city grid . . .? What was this all about? What was . . .

Behind me, the timing device switched off the generator — and I heard footsteps.

They were directly above me, slow, slightly irregular. I switched off the light and listened. They got louder, then faded away, and the generator roared into life again, its cacophony masking everything. I fought back the urge simply to run. Desperately I looked round; I had to get out of here, for the cellar was a natural trap. I stuck the rubber stamp into my pocket and began to retrace my steps along the dank corridor, hoping the generator would cover my noise as well. Warily, I peered round the door that led out into the main courtyard. I could see a glimmer of light, now, from the main part of the house, and the doors at the top of the steps were open. Who? How many? There was no one in sight. I nerved myself up to try for the main gate; there was still a chance.

Half-way across the courtyard I realised I was no longer alone. I didn't see it, or smell it; my fear *sensed* it.

Only one of the Dobermanns had gone in the jeep. The other stood in trained silence under the archway. I looked into the obscene grin of the hanging jaws and knew that even if I found the courage, I had no chance of getting out; one more step would have him at my throat. I backed off slowly until I saw the muscles in his hind legs tense, and then he leaped in trained silence — and I sprinted up the steps to the open double doors faster than I'd ever moved in my life. I only just made it through. The ferocious snap caught my left shoe as I tried to kick and shut him out at the same time. The heel disappeared into the jaws, but I won. The door slammed shut, and I stumbled back as the silence of the attack erupted into a wild fury of barking. The forelegs pounded the wood, the door moved alarmingly. Panic touched me again. How strong was it?

Sudden bright light and an authoritarian voice ended my speculation. '*Was ist los? Wer ist da?*'

It was the old woman, the baroness. She was wearing a white cotton nightdress, leaning on her stick at the top of the stairs. *The limousine . . . Who had . . .*? I saw the good eye take in the scene. She turned quickly. I heard the slam of a door, the rattle of a key. The telephone, I thought, taking the stairs three at a time; *I have to stop her using the telephone!*

The drawing-room door that I'd once been ushered through with such cold deference gave at the first charge of my shoulder. I ran across the room, tore the phone from her grasp, and yanked the cable from its socket by the fireplace. Outside, the dog was still going crazy. I found my voice.

'I wont' hurt you. I just . . .'

How *dare* you!' she said, drawing her tiny figure erect. 'How dare you enter my private apartments! *Leave!* Now, at *once*!'

The command in her voice mesmerised me. It was absolute, unwavering; it didn't encompass even the thought of disobedience. I was helpless before it, unable to make the next decision, whatever it might be. She glared at me, rigid with outrage, trembling with the intensity of her anger, and then, slowly, the haughty facade began to crack. The hand that held the stick shook. A muscle in her scrawny cheek started to twitch. Wetly, the mouth opened.

'*Dirt*,' she hissed. '*Vermin!* A beggar from the streets!'

The sound of another furious onslaught on the doors spun me round.

'Afraid of the *dogs* of his betters!'

Could the Dobermann come through? *Could . . .*?

It was the shadow on the wall that saved me. I

swerved — just in time, for the downward swing was as accurate as it was determined. The poker whistled past my cheek and dug its talon deep into the parquet. She lost her grip, staggered, and fell. I stood, shocked, watching the metal wand quiver, hearing its vibration sing out over the dog's fury. The blow would have killed me, I knew it; where had she found such murderous strength? I looked down at the crumpled heap on the floor, and remembered the last time she had fallen in my presence. We were a far cry from that now, from polite talk of kindness . . . Slowly I reached down to help her.

She pulled herself up on my arm — and spat in my face.

For a moment I held her, stunned, but then I let her fall. I wiped the foulness away, waiting for the rage to pass, my eyes tightly shut. I opened them to see her perched on hands and knees like a squat, deformed version of the dog outside, the wild eye staring upwards. Disgust swept through me; she had been the first of the liars, the sender of my tormentors, the beginning of the corruption.

'Why did you lie to me?' I asked, quietly.

She said nothing — but the head began to turn, jerking itself round until the eye found the poker once more. I gripped the iron, and she scrambled hurriedly away on all fours. It took all my strength to dislodge the thing, but finally the wood gave, leaving a tight triangle of gouges, scarring the surface behind with long splinters. The pattern . . . I stared. It was something I'd seen before . . . Suddenly I was cold, suddenly I wished I'd never come back to this place.

A badly-set arm, lying on a concrete floor . . .

I held up the talon, slowly, forcing my mind to accept it, not wanting to believe in such cruelty. It would have been hot from the fire — two blows, smashing the arm, raking across the flesh . . .The pain must have been incredible. My grip tightened as the despair mounted in me. The iron throbbed in my hand, became warm, unbearably heavy. Its mass seemed to grow, shutting out everything else in the room until the horror of its sharpness was the only reality. As I turned it, the darkness of the metal deepened before my eyes. I felt the sinews of my own arm tense, as though the thing was part of me, as though I could make the three points move, curl in, clutch at the air.

My eyes found the crest on the wall, then came back to the Baroness Von Laer, bedraggled, cowering in fright against the wainscoting. I had found my beast now, many times more savage than eagle or unicorn; I held its claw, I knew its name.

Madness . . .

She retreated even further, mistaking my silence, wedging herself into the corner, the eye fearful of retribution. I let the poker drop to my side.

'Maria . . . Why?'

My voice was barely a whisper, but it was a scream that answered.

'I *hate* her! Erich gave her our name, our *land*! I hate him, I hate them all! I . . .'

'*Why did you kill Maria?*' I shouted.

The generator's note changed. The lamps flickered and almost died, but the near-dark was no mercy. Within the four walls there was a silence, false, illusory, waiting to be filled, bounded by the noises of machine and dog. A girlish chuckling began, low and happy, its coquettish edge chilling in the dim light. Quickly it rose, became louder and faster, until the electricity recovered and she saw me again. For a confused second, time and space were lost to her, and then her insanity reclaimed them. She threw back her head and bayed laughter at me. Her hysteria rang round the walls, desperate for release, chasing the other sounds, the wild barking, the menacing throb from the cellar. The dissonant maelstrom was torture to hear. I listened to it until once more the word came, unbidden, to my lips.

'Why . . .?'

Even as I repeated it, I knew the question was senseless — but I got an answer just the same.

'It wasn't *me.* It wasn't *Ilse.* Ilse's not bad. She's *not.*'

The calm childishness of the voice was obscene, worse than the laughter. She cocked her head to one side and put a finger against her jaw. The smile was awful, a glazed parody of fond remembrance. When she spoke again, I heard the lilting sing-song of the nursery, the musical drone of childhood's fairy tales.

'Lit-tle Ma-ria,' she said, '*so* pretty. Everybody loves her *so* much. All the big men. She's so, so pretty. Erich says she's my new sister. Lit-tle Ma-ria.'

Cheek pressed against the wall, she began to rock to and fro, like a priestess in the grip of some private rite. The words took on her rhythm, the voice rose, just as the laughter had done. A dribble of saliva ran from the side of her mouth. I stepped back, repelled.

'Ilse's *bad,* Erich *says,* Maria's *never* bad! Ilse's *bad,* Erich *says,* Maria's . . .' The chant stopped as abruptly as it had begun. The voice came back to the nursery. 'Ilse's bad, but Erich's bad, too. With the Jew-boy. I saw them, Jews . . .' The face left the wall, fixed itself into a ferocious frown. '. . . are *very* bad.' She scuttled forward again, till she was at my feet. The eye looked up at me. 'Everybody knows that.'

The last three words were delivered in a voice utterly reasonable. The dishevelled head nodded earnestly in confirmation, and then her face became sly.

'But I stopped it.'

Her expression didn't change, but I saw the tear form in the crazy eye. I watched it escape, run down to join the line of drool from the half-open mouth, and tried to take in the fact she had just given me. *She* had been the informer, the one who brought the S.S. For her own brother. I remembered the emotion in her voice that first day. It had been love, I was sure, but sorrow filled me as I recognised what it had become. I gazed down at her. Love lost was bad enough, but love supplanted . . . She'd told me herself how close she had been to her brother. To lose her place in his affections, to see it taken by a child, a total stranger — on top of her deformity, that rejection must have been the deepest hurt of all, impossible to bear. Such pain, unchecked; there was a pitiful inevitability to its progress. Hurt to hatred, hatred to revenge, revenge to guilt, the wounds reopened every day until they festered into — this. I watched her silent weeping, fighting the pity in me, forcing myself to remember what she had been, what she had done, trying to ignore what she had become. I could do nothing about this woman's misery, and other things were more important than its fifty-year-old wellsprings. Her craziness made one fact plain: she could not have planned any of the deeds that had hunted me across Europe like an animal.

'Why did Maria have to die, now? She was no real danger to you,' I said. 'Who gave the order?'

She looked at me again. Through the tears, cunning contorted the lined face back into its idiot smile.

'In the country of the blind . . .' she began, but then her head began to nod again. She resumed her insane cackling, the laughter rising and falling like the wail of some fractured siren. Wisps of grey hair, wet at the ends from tears and spittle, stuck to her cheek. I pulled her to her feet and slapped her as softly as I could. The awful noise stopped.

I waited for more tears, but they didn't come, and as I sat her down on the low table, I saw the blankness in her eyes. Desperation touched me; she was retreating even further from reality. I shook her. 'What was happening here?'

The good eye fixed itself on me in a catatonic stare.

'In the cellar. What were they doing?'

There was no response. Through the barking, I heard the generator stop. This time the lights died completely, and in the sudden dark the white nightdress made a ghost of her. Again my anger tried to become pity, again

I tried to fight it, but I couldn't, no matter how terrible her sins. Her crimes had made her a prisoner of her past. What did she live for, now? Had she just been left here to die? The thought pulled me sharply back to the present. There was nothing more to be learned here, and I didn't know if they'd return for her; to stay any longer was stupid, dangerous. But how was I to get out? I felt the weight of the poker in my hand. By now the fury outside had subsided into low growling, but I doubted whether even such a vicious weapon could stop the dog. The boat . . . I went to the balcony and opened the doors — and saw what had been hidden from across the lake. The rowing-boat was up on the jetty because its timbers had rotted through. I came back into the room and saw her head turn towards me in that queer way that meant she was trying to hide the crooked eye.

'Erich?' The voice stopped me dead. It was pleasant now, adult. 'Erich? Why is the dog barking?'

The tiny figure became a white blur, and suddenly I saw my own face instead of hers in the darkness. The fear rushed up, filling me, engulfing me. Once more Helga's words came out of nowhere, finally putting a name to the dread this place had laid upon me.

Max said you'd been near madness, once.

Madness . . . I remembered how it had stalked my own life. For more than a year — every action, every thought, mined with bitter memories, innocently concealed, sharply sprung . . . Every day a battle, with a beast as strong as it was cunning; pain its heart, rage and jealousy its horns . . . Had it lured me to this place? Had I come here to be destroyed? I struggled against the thought. I was *strong*! She was a pathetic old woman. Madness was the mirror of her own soul, not mine! As I fought the fear, my mind hung in the balance, and then the rational part of it seized the chance she was giving me.

'I don't know, Ilse,' I said, trying to keep my voice even. 'Go and see.'

I crossed the dark room and found her cane.

She took the steps at a snail's pace. I followed a few yards behind, trying to move soundlessly despite my shoe's missing heel, anxious lest I disturb her trance. I watched the bare feet on the marble, listening to the stick's tapping, the panic rising in me as we neared the dog. Outside, the animal quietened at the sound of her approach. I couldn't stop myself from stepping back as she opened the door.

The Dobermann let her take it by the collar, but it never took its eyes from me. Her voice was an innocent whisper.

'Good, Ritter, good dog. *Schönes Ritterschen. Schönes* . . .'

I watched, terrified. She stood, patting the sleek coat, staring past me. Was I still her brother? Was she still seeing . . .

'When will it be finished?'

What did she mean? My struggle or hers? For an awful second I was sure that she was sane, that it was all an act, that she would lift her hand from the quivering neck.

'When, Erich? When will it be finished?'

I realised she was staring at her own portrait. She began to pat the Dobermann again, but I could see it was barely under control. Was she crazy? Was I? I forced myself to act. My eyes tightly shut, I edged past the terrifying smell of dog, feeling for the door, hearing the throaty growl, the low whispering.

The cold air told me I was outside. I opened my eyes and saw the full moon, and realised I was still holding the poker. Silently I put it down on the top step. Then, without looking back, I limped out of Burg Laer.

Chapter 10
TRUST

I SAT ON the winch and pulled the collar of the old donkey jacket tight, for the wind which blew in from the North Sea had lost none of its force in the passage across Holland. It attacked the damp fields relentlessly, whipping at the grass, almost flattening the bushes with every gust. Only the church spires and the artificially straight rows of poplars on the canal banks defied it, but it skirted all such man-made outposts with a guerrilla's ease and claimed their hinterland for its own. I thrust my hands deeper into the jacket pockets as I looked over the bleak landscape, wondering how long it would take for a deal to be reached back in the wheelhouse, feeling the barge's course alter subtly as Janos steered for the highest point of the bridge's arch. As always, I scanned the rail for onlookers. No one . . . Could it really be true that they weren't searching for me? We'd watched every bridge, patiently observed every stretch of bank, but there was no sign of them. *Why?* She must have told them I'd returned to Burg Laer, surely . . . Through the arch I could see the grey-and-black mouth of the next lock.

Janos shouted. I walked back, skirting the red mountains of sand, balancing my way along the narrow walkway. It was fifty yards to the wheelhouse, but knowing the two strangers' eyes were upon me made it longer.

Inside it was warm, the smell the typical cigars-and-good-coffee aroma of Germany. Janos was the first to speak.

'Mr Dinculianu is willing to carry you, Alexander, provided you can give him certain assurances. He does not want to pry into your business, but he wishes to be certain there is nothing difficult about your problem, nothing ...' He paused ... 'political.'

They were father and son, the older man a smaller, unhealthier version of the younger, baggy-eyed and sad. Some illness had robbed the dark face of all vitality, and the heat of the wheelhouse had left droplets of sweat at the greasy hairline. He looked doubtfully at me, then removed the cigar from his mouth with a ring-laden hand. He muttered an unhappy sentence of Romanian into his son's ear. The boy translated it into English.

'You no terroris', mister, eh? No R.A.F., no crazy Arab here to kill Jews, blow up politician?'

The gun-chewing defiance of the stance belonged on a New York street corner, but the Balkan accent compromised it for ever. He couldn't have been more than seventeen.

'Terroris' bad for business. Much trouble, cops. What happen you, eh? Why you need such hurry?'

Janos broke in angrily, and the three of them had a long, heated exchange, of which only the tension was comprehensible to me. When it was over, the father stuck the cigar back in his mouth and the boy's jaw automatically went back to its chewing. Janos turned to me.

'Mr Dinculianu says it is worth two thousand marks, but as a special favour to me he will take you for fifteen hundred.'

I read the warning in his eyes. Don't agree to anything immediately, he'd said, don't let them smell bigger money, it's dangerous. I let the silence stand for a second, pretending to decide.

'All right. Tell him fifteen hundred — but half now, half later.'

Again they argued, but the father and Janos were both pressing the boy now, and I could see him losing. He was too young to accept the defeat gracefully. His eyes began a restless search of the cabin, avoiding mine, glowering at each wall in turn – until they found the icon. Madonna and Child triggered his frustration into a final snort of disgust. The older Dinculianu regarded his son sadly, then shrugged his shoulders in resignation and scowled at me. The stub of the old cigar arced precisely out of the open door and over the stern. A new one appeared from the inside pocket of the shiny suit. As soon as it was lit, the nicotine-stained forefinger stabbed at my chest.

'*Aber keine Waffen.*'

I don't carry ...' I began, but Janos broke in again.

'I guarantee it,' he said quietly.

There was silence, and then Dinculianu nodded sourly and went down the stairs towards the main cabin without another word. The boy followed. I heard his nasal voice, bitterly remonstrating, until the door closed behind them.

'Businessmen,' Janos said.

I knew it was a euphemism for smugglers.

'One must deal with such people occasionally. They work the Danube – radios mostly, pop records and jeans for the black market, buy in Hamburg, sell anywhere between the Czech border and Constanta. Maybe drugs, too; I don't know. There's some risk, of course, but they are more professional than they look.' He jerked a thumb at the cabin below. 'They'll stay out of sight – they don't want the lock-keepers to see them this far out of their normal schedule. I told them you're British army, a deserter.' He saw my eyes cover the bank again. 'Still worried?'

I shook my head, but the noise of a diesel engine showed him the lie. A builder's lorry on the left bank – could it be them?

He tried to allay my fears. 'Relax, Alexander. It is not the way they would do it.'

There was no uncertainty in the voice. The wheel turned in his steady hands. 'And stop worrying about the boy. He will be there.'

He hesitated, aware that he was only adding to my nerves, and we both looked at the lock ahead. It was still too far off to make out figures, but I knew that if Sandor wasn't there, the police probably would be. If my host was afraid of the possibility, though, he hid it well. His face was untroubled as he spoke again.

'You have the modern gullibility, Alexander. You believe too much in computers. Computers are like women, they believe what you tell them if your first moves are correct. They are easy to lie to because they have only one interpretation of the truth. Be calm. Nothing will go wrong.'

I sat down at the table, wanting to share his optimism, but still wary of anything that smacked of hope. But as I watched him alter the barge's course again the tension began to leave me, and suddenly I felt ashamed at my lack of confidence. He'd been right so far, in everything he'd promised or predicted.

It was a week now since we'd left Lübeck, and for the first four days we'd hardly talked. The mixture of frustration and relief I'd felt at my double escape had left me unsure of who or what to trust, and he had been content to let me brood, bury the burden of my troubles in the physical work of the barge. He'd spent the time letting me know I was safe, politely asking the occasional question, but always in such a way that I knew explanation wasn't obligatory. We'd been within fifty miles of Münster before I'd felt ready to take him into my confidence.

I smiled at the memory, for it seemed inconceivable now that I'd ever doubted the man. He was forthright, honest, the fiercest of allies and, more important, one with exactly the experience I needed, for no man knew more than Janos Dabasi about evading the eyes of authority. We were as different from each other as two human beings could be, but once I'd heard his own story it was easy to understand his immediate acceptance of mine.

I watched him steer. He was a stockier version of his son, the pale priest who'd brought me to the barge in Lübeck, and he shared both the boy's faith and his quiet determination — but there the similarities ended. A dissident who'd been forced to leave his native Hungary, Janos was a curious mixture, part cheerful fanatic, part reasoned idealist, the kind of man who always thinks of himself as a rebel — and always makes an effective one because he has both the vision to see a better future and the skills to fight for it. But it was obvious to me that he was also the kind of man for whom the act of rebellion itself was more than the cause it served. In Budapest he'd fought the communists tooth and nail for the right to worship his Catholic God with dignity, but I had no doubt that seventy years ago he'd have been just as happy fighting the church for the right to be a communist. As I watched him, I wondered if the breed would ever die, that percentage of men in every generation who can only function as outlaws.

He had served his chosen cause well, though. He'd battled long and hard, skilfully, obstinately — only to be forced out in the end by the very success of his own intransigence. He'd become too visible, a focus for too much protest, and the reactionary elements in the Kadar regime, ever fearful of a repeat of the fifty-six rebellion, had begun openly gunning for him. They'd made it obvious that his next spell of imprisonment wouldn't be short, and when that threat failed, the persecution of his family began. Police harassment, jobs lost, permission to study refused . . . For his children's sake, he told me, he'd left. Now he captained the *Ursula*, and said he much preferred the Dortmund–Ems canal to any of the university desks he'd known. I didn't doubt it. I watched him reach down to the crate under the table, and found myself thinking, not for the first time, about his homeland's new freedoms. It was all so much easier in Hungary now, no longer impossible to leave . . . Would that tempt him back?

The builder's lorry reappeared. Uneasily, my eyes followed it along the bank. Janos brought out two beers with one hand.

'Drink and forget your fears, Alexander. Everything is under control.'

I took a long pull at the dark beer and tried again to relax. It was hard to believe that things could simply go right, although I'd had proof enough of his expertise as a fixer, for his decision to help had already borne ample fruit. When I'd returned to the barge in Münster, he'd simply asked what I needed, and when I'd said a passport and an immediate passage to Austria, he'd told me bluntly the first was impossible in less than ten days, but the second was easy, passport or no passport. When we docked that night, he'd gone out in search of a telephone.

The two Romanians had been the result, but long before their arrival, Janos had examined my problems and proposed a solution to the thorniest of them. Patiently he'd made me go over everything that had happened since Max's death, and when he'd heard about the bank account Helga had opened in Kiel, his smile had broadened with satisfaction. Did I know the number? Yes, I did, but wasn't it too dangerous? My protests had been waved aside, and Sandor, the young refugee who was the vessel's mate, had been sent to get the cash. There was a fellow Hungarian in one of the banks in Gronau, Janos said, a friend who would gladly induce a little computer error in a good cause. He seemed certain — but I was still more than half-way convinced the boy would be arrested the minute he tried to lay hands on the money, for I had to assume that Weidemann knew who Alexander Lawless was by now, and the account was in that name. Soon, we'd know . . .

'You are still sure? Of what you intend to do?' Janos

asked, without taking his eyes from the canal ahead. 'I only ask because Dinculianu must be told if there are changes.'

Again I brought out the stamp I'd found in the cellar. Spielbank Neustift; it was the only place left to look.

'Yes, Janos, I'm still sure.'

A contented grin split the lines of the weathered face. 'I had a feeling you would be. I think you're wise — to move quickly, I mean.' He shrugged. 'But they may be waiting for you, Alexander. You must remember that.'

He was right, of course — but he knew as well as I did that I had to try. He wiped his hands on an oily rag, then reached over to cut back the engine revs, and as I saw the smile linger at the edges of his mouth I felt again the delight the man was taking in helping me, and I knew, suddenly, why he'd never go back.

The plotting, the underground meetings, the urgency of the secret life he'd left behind in Hungary — more than any physical place, these things were the heart of his memories, the star around which his exile would always orbit. Conspiracy . . . The less Budapest required it, the more barren it would be for him, and it was the promise of that which was animating him now. There was a unique logic to the situation; his return for helping me was a taste of the clandestine, one which could be savoured on either side of the Iron Curtain, for a natural rebel like him had no need to discriminate between nations or ideologies. The German state would do just as well as the Hungarian one for a test of strength and intelligence. Everyone's policeman was Janos Dabasi's enemy; what mattered was being *against* . . .

As he steered the *Ursula* along the canal my thoughts turned once more to the phone call I'd made the night before. Elly and the child were still safe. My relief had been tremendous — they'd all been in London, checking details of the painting — but it had been short lived, for the disapproval in Mary Wellbeck's voice had been undiluted by distance. It was obviously harder on the older woman now that Elly had gone, and I could only hope that the journey to Lübeck and back wouldn't take long, for there wasn't much patience left in Elly's Miss Mary; when I'd told her of my plans, the silence at the other end had been deafening. I put away the rubber stamp as we entered the confines of the lock, and heard the engine note change with the echo of the walls. Once more I silently blessed the young Turk for sending the envelope with the pawn-ticket. Janos stopped the motor.

The big hydraulic arms pushed the gates shut behind us, and the massive structures were slowly revealed as the water level fell. A thin stream trickled through the minuscule gap between them, until the rising pressure pushed it into a jagged spout that almost reached our stern. Then the water's weight closed the doors completely, the spout died — and I wondered if my crazy run across Europe was going to end the same way. I'd managed to squeeze through every time they'd closed in on me so far, but how much longer could I keep it up? Janos was right, my luck had been incredible, but surely it must run out soon . . . Darkness came over the cabin as we sank into a world whose boundaries were grey stone and black iron. I closed my eyes to shut out the vision. It reminded me too much of a cell.

The big Magyar mistook fear for prayer. 'It is good to believe,' he said seriously.

I stared at him. It was hard to credit that this was the same man whose wits had outmanoeuvred a government for years, who pronounced so urbanely about women and computers, for when he talked about religion, his utterances were almost simplistic. What did his son make of the paradox? As if to underline the question, the gates at the other end of the lock opened, and a shaft of miraculous light found his face. Absolute certainty was written across it, and for an instant I was bitterly envious. Of his conviction, his faith. I couldn't conceive of anything as unshakable ever touching my own life, much less ruling it, but the comfort it gave him was obvious.

What did I believe in? The barge answered me with a lurch as Janos moved her forward; for a fugitive, motion was a more than adequate god.

'Look to your right,' he said.

We came slowly out of the lock on to the next stretch of open water, and on the right bank I saw the grimy yellow car and a scrawny denim-clad figure leaning against it, smoking. Janos shouted from the door and Sandor replied, but the exchange was in rapid-fire Hungarian and the boy's long, mournful face gave nothing away. I waited anxiously. The barge came alongside the mooring, the two of them quickly made her fast, and then Sandor went back to the car and brought out a large white paper packet. One-handed, he swung himself on board, and I could hold back no longer.

'Well?'

'He has brought food. From the *Imbiss.*'

Neither of them paid me any heed as Sandor unwrapped Schnitzels, fried chicken, potato salad, setting them down on the chart table. Then the boy reached into the pocket of his dirty denim jacket and casually put down a large wad of banknotes in the midst of the cartons. Both of them grinned at my expression, for they knew I hadn't really believed they could do it. I turned to Janos, searching for the right words. His hand upon my wrist stopped me.

'I will give your thanks to the boy,' he said. 'He has never done anything like this before.'

'Tell him I admire his courage.'

Sandor and I had no language in common. The translation was one low, soft phrase, and when the boy looked at me again his features held a polite, composed smile that belied the flush of pleasure on his cheek. I guessed the smile was the formal way a compliment was received in his Carpathian homeland.

Janos reached out for the food, but suddenly there were footsteps from below. He managed to scoop up the bundle of notes and thrust it into the pocket of his overalls before the two Romanians appeared. They paused on the top step and looked warily round — and for a wild moment I caught myself believing they could smell the money. Then the son looked at the half-opened packets of food on the table and his face settled back into its normal contemptuous sneer, until his father snapped out an unmistakable sentence of command. The boy scowled, and slouched sullenly past me, out on to the deck. The father simply waited, his sallow face expressionless. Janos opened the locker above the wheel, brought out a battered tin cash-box, took a pile of notes from it, and counted seven hundred and fifty marks into the Romanian's hand. I watched Dinculianu's eyes carefully follow the box's path back to the locker. The son stuck his head in through the wheelhouse door.

'Okay.'

There was a brief handshake between Dinculianu and Janos, a sealing of the bargain, but the Romanian made no move to repeat the politeness with me. I got a last, suspicious stare; I was merchandise, and dubious merchandise at that.

The three of us waited until they were off the barge and walking down the road towards the corner *Gasthaus* before sitting down again. Janos opened more beers.

'Right,' he said, 'this is what you do.' He pointed at the yellow car. 'You can drive that?' I nodded.

'As soon as it's dark, you go. To Passau. You know Passau, on the Danube? Good. There's a little town a few kilometres upstream called Vilshofen. Drive straight through if you can, but if you have to sleep, use the car. For hotels you need documents. Once you get there, find a bar down on the river called the Schwarze Ritter. Just go in and wait. The Romanian's people will pick you up. They'll take care of you and the car. If anything goes wrong, you stole the car, you never heard of me or Sandor or the Dinculianus.'

He pulled the thick bundle of banknotes from his pocket and handed it to me. There had been no time to count it, but now I could see the sum was huge. I divided the cash into two roughly equal piles; half would be more than enough for now, whether my plan succeeded or failed.

'Take the fifteen hundred and keep the rest for me. If I need it, I'll have you send it somewhere when I get back.'

It took him by surprise. The beer bottle came slowly back down to the table.

'And if you don't get back? I do not want your money, Alexander.'

I'd anticipated this. I put the notes in his hand and closed his fingers round them. 'If I don't make it, or I don't need it, then I'm sure there are others. If not in Hungary, then somewhere else, East Germany maybe, Romania . . . who need help. To get out.'

He picked up the pile of money and riffed through it, slowly, considering. Then without saying anything, he reached again for the tin box, and I knew the decision was made. Sandor pushed the key-ring across the table to me.

I sat in silence as they ate, staring at the car keys. It seemed strange, wrong somehow, to go south, with Elly probably less than a few hours' drive away from where I now was, but it had to be done. Evidence against Weidemann was the only way forward, and logic told me I had to try for it. But I knew that wasn't the only reason . . . The boy's voice broke in on my thoughts. Janos gave me a shrewd look, nodding his head in assent as he listened.

'What is he saying?'

'That he would not like to have you as an adversary. He says no matter how much you try to hide it, you always look angry. He says you are tired of being hunted.'

It was true. I knew inside myself that going back to Burg Laer had changed things. I looked at Sandor's dark, thin face, so serious above the trim edge of black beard, and for an instant we understood each other perfectly. The boy knew what it meant to be hunted. I wondered if my slowly-kindling wrath would be as obvious to someone who'd never had to run for his life. Before I could say anything, Janos picked up the car keys and thrust them into my hand. I felt something else along with them.

'As soon as it gets dark,' he said.

I opened my hand to find the keys, and a small wooden crucifix.

It was early the next morning before tiredness made me pull off the *Autobahn* to sleep, and I already had more than three-quarters of the journey behind me. A chorus of birdsong woke me from a fitful doze in the car's cramped back seat, and I was grateful to get out and stretch in the cold air. The narrow side road I'd chosen was deserted, its silver layer of frost undisturbed by either man or vehicle. A pale winter sun forced its way up into the clear sky, and the fairytale landscape of Bavaria built itself slowly round me. The clock in the onion-domed steeple struck eight, clearly audible across the valley.

I decided there was no greater risk in getting food and fuel in the town than on the motorway, and got back into the car. The road wound and twisted back on itself, making a long journey out of two kilometres before letting me reach the first of the houses. I parked in the pleasant square and went in search of provisions. There were only a few people about, heavily clad against the winter cold.

A regional election was due in the New Year, but here, at any rate, the contest had already been all but won. Every lamp-post, every tree, every shop window I passed bore the same face. It followed me the length of the street, watching me buy sausage and cheese, promising me fairer deals, new brooms, a better Germany for my children. It was old, but still full of energy. As I waited in the queue at the baker's, it gave me a multiple smile from the wooden fence of the building site opposite, twenty feet of hearty insincerity, sanctified by the necessary credentials of politicians everywhere, regardless of party or philosophy: perfect teeth and smartly-cut hair. The hair in particular was just right, a friendly grey that hovered on the edge of white, ambiguous enough to denote wisdom without denying vigour. The face wasn't one I would have trusted.

The baker's face made a fat and jovial contrast. He selected the *Brötchen* for me, commenting on the weather, scratching his pink, bald dome as he rang the till. Was I on holiday here, or just passing through? I was on my way to Austria for the skiing, I said. *Ah*, the skiing. His daughters skied, but it was so expensive! The cost of it all! The boots, the special clothes! Where did it all end? It would be one mark twenty for the bread, he said. I looked again at the posters as the broad rustic accent continued with its happy catechism of complaint. The smile seemed to widen, as though it was listening as well . . .

A bespectacled boy, young and earnest, came into view. The red ban-the-bomb symbol on the back of his green army jacket had been sprayed on hurriedly, and something had smudged it before it was properly dry. He carried a bundle of white papers over one arm, a brush and can in his other hand. He began carefully at one end of the row, sticking his posters diagonally across the others; the design was a crudely-drawn dove above the word '*Friedensliste*'.

'*Verdammt!*'

The baker was out from behind his counter, striding towards the boy with surprising speed. He grabbed him by the sleeve, spun him round. The slap was staccato, loud in the empty street. Brush, can and posters fell to the ground as the blow knocked the boy back against the fence. There was no retaliation. The boy's head bowed. Slowly he raised a hand and rubbed his reddening jaw.

One by one, the flimsy white posters of the Peace Party came away from the fence in the baker's fat hands. He crumpled each one into a ball and threw it at the youngster. Once they were all down, he marched past him, back into the shop, wiping his hands briskly on his white apron.

'Will there be anything else?'

His eyes bored into me, daring me to disapprove. I shook my head and went outside. The boy had vanished; victory had been conceded.

The sun glinted on the golden hands of the church clock, and the snow-capped hills behind the houses were still as perfect as they had been five minutes before, but somehow the beauty of the place seemed awful to me now, tainted by something old and sad, like a tree whose wood is cankered deep inside. My eyes found the face on the wall. The bottom of the last poster had been ripped away by the baker's zeal. The smiling mouth was gone, and without it the blue eyes told a different story, far removed from goodwill and promises of fresh prosperity. I hurried away to the car with my bag of groceries, trying to escape their gaze.

Chapter 11
TRICKS

WATCHING THE SNOW, I was glad of the sunglasses. The uniformed chauffeur two tables away wore the identical style, and whenever either of us looked round the *Imbiss* we made reflections in each other's mirror lenses. His big Mercedes limousine stood outside, shiny and black, the surrounding brilliance of the snow's glare and the darkened window glass making it even blacker. It dwarfed everything else in the car park except for the beer lorry, and its engine purred with conspicuous contempt for economy. Every few minutes the chauffeur would give it a cursory glance, then go back to his intent inspection of the female skiers. The smile he gave me belonged to a garrulous man, starved of conversation.

'Good skier,' he said, as a yellow-clad figure sat itself on the chair of the ski-lift. 'Nice ass, too.'

The way he pronounced the word showed he thought I was American. I smiled my agreement. The trim figure moved skyward, and he followed it until his attention was pulled, automatically, to the next girl in the line. I watched the yellow suit until it was no more than a dot, three-quarters of the way up the mountain.

'Francesca!' the chauffeur called. The kitchen door opened, and a dark Italian head appeared. I caught a whiff of garlic. '*Noch 'mal.*'

The yellow girl began her run. The gentle arabesques she made on the smooth piste were magnified ballet, the curved graph of a more graceful mathematics against the straight line of the cable car's descent. She glided past the *Imbiss* window towards her young man, happy and blonde, carefree and healthy, smiling at the prospect of the waiting embrace. I took off the sunglasses and rubbed my tired eyes. In the wake of my clandestine journey I was weary, and the depression I'd been fighting was crystallised suddenly into loneliness by the sight of the laughing couple.

Unbidden, the little boy brought me another *Glühwein,* walking slowly, concentrating all his attention on the glass. The woman watched him from the kitchen door, the Christmas candles forgotten in her hands, her smile a struggle between maternal feeling and swift arithmetic. She would be the instigator of the trick, I guessed; nobody would mind paying for the unwanted second drink when it was served with such earnest innocence. Glass and saucer touched the green tablecloth unspilled, and motherly pride won out immediately over commerce in her voice. A voluble stream of Italian addressed itself to an unseen figure in the depths of the kitchen, momentarily drowning the noisy delivery of beer crates at the back door.

I drank the hot wine gratefully enough, though, for the ride in the postbus had been cold as well as bumpy. Once again I wished I had a vehicle, but how did one rent a car without either passport or driving licence? Gravely, the boy examined me from the safety of the bar counter, adding me to his knowledge of the mysterious world of adults, until my *Danke schön* sent him scuttling back to his mother in the kitchen. I went back to my perusal of skiers and landscape, trying to fix the place's geography in my mind as the cable car slid down the wire towards us, its progress monitored by the chauffeur in between sips of coffee.

The monastery which had given the town its name some four hundred years before stood high above on the peak, defying gravity as it clung to the grey rock, ingeniously engineered by men as cunning in protecting their privacy as they were tenacious in propagating their faith. The mountain which had once separated them from the town was now the biggest and best of the slopes, a parade-ground dotted with the bright uniforms of the latest ski fashions, and the monks were no longer alone on their peak, for the twentieth century had brought them a new role; cancer now ranked alongside faith as a credential for entry into their formerly exclusive world. The monastery had become a sanatorium for those whose condition was deemed inoperable.

I wondered what the monks made of their mountain now. Did they approve of the snobbish democracy of the slopes, the downhill chic that was the price of upward mobility? Were the invalids envious of all the rude health, the peacock brightness? Below them the sons of industrialists and Bavarian bakers' daughters dreamed of each other and rubbed shoulders in safe anonymity, demonstrating grace and style in stance and movement. The boy's mother brought the chauffeur more coffee, and for the few seconds of her walk back to the kitchen, he watched her stout behind.

Barely fifty yards away from the monastery walls, on an outcrop of rock too steep to hold snow, stood the temple of a different god, secured by a different cunning, as impressive in its own way as the older building. The casino which was the object of all my illegal activities had been ingeniously built, cut half-way into the face of the rock, a monument to technology rather than tenacity, perched on huge concrete legs that arched back into the stone. Below us, the town of Neustift nestled in the twin security of a sheltered valley and a never-fail cash crop. Business was steady in the winter sports trade; the well-off could afford to insulate themselves from boredom as well as cold, and the bars and restaurants were fat on the prosperity of *après-ski*. The snow had been exceptional this season, they'd told me on the bus. The *Imbiss* where the chauffeur and I sat was midway between religion and comfort, at the foot of the ski-lift that fed the slopes, beside the terminus of the cable car that served the casino. The view in every direction was breathtaking. I sat and wondered how much of it belonged to a Dutch child who'd never be able to tell anyone how beautiful it was, and the realisation came to me slowly: my planning stopped here. I had no idea what to do next. All I knew was that I had to get into the casino and find out what was going on there.

Stiffly, I rose, and as I reached into my pocket for money, my hand found the crucifix. I fingered the polished wood gently, thinking of the big Magyar and how much I owed him, wishing I had the benefit of his methodical mind now, wondering if he'd paid the Romanians the other half of their fee . . .

For his faith in the efficiency of the Dinculianus hadn't been misplaced. I'd been collected, delivered, and carried down the Danube in the empty hold of a Black Sea oil barge, well out of sight of prying eyes, without a word I could understand being spoken. I'd left the vessel warily at Linz, to emerge one surreal afternoon later at the town's station, fully kitted out for skiing, and as I looked at the figures on the lift I was satisfied, for I was totally unremarkable among them. The obvious newness of my outfit marked me down as a beginner, but I felt that Helga's money had been well spent; from red woolly hat to fur-lined boots I was the most typical of low-budget skiers. There was only one problem — I'd never been on skis in my life.

I got up and put a handful of Schillings on the table, and the chauffeur rose at the same time. He held the door open for me and we both went out into the freezing alpine air as the cable car came into its concrete dock. A pneumatic hiss of doors was the prelude to the appearance of a woman in her forties, well-preserved, immaculately dressed. She wore brown leather trousers and a fashionably-cut fur jacket that had been carefully chosen to match her straw-coloured hair. As she stepped from the gleaming red pod, the chauffeur turned to me. His confidential whisper betrayed the brandy in the coffee.

'Burgermeister's wife,' he said. 'Not bad for her age, really. Likes the tables as well as the other, if you get me. His third one. He owns most of the town, but it's her that has the fun of it — you wouldn't believe what she gets up to! Still, I don't suppose she gets much at home, when you think of his age. Got to admire him for the thought, though, eh? Randy old bastard.'

She waved to him as she walked to the Mercedes. ''*Tag*, Johann!' she shouted gaily.

'*Grüss Gott*, Frau Bartsch!' he shouted back, running down the wooden steps with an alacrity that spoke of good wages.

I hesitated, but then the long black rear window descended with push-button ease, and I knew the name was no coincidence. The face was the right age. It hadn't changed much in forty-odd years, except to get fatter. It was still strong. The jowls of his cheeks were solid slabs of red, the neck bulged over the collar, sleek and fleshy, pink with health. I thought of a tiny figure in an attic room in Basel, so thin as he neared his death, so calm in his acceptance of a life that had excluded all but the barest of necessities. A large signet ring flashed in the sunlight as the figure before me waved to the woman. Excitement stripped away fatigue and made me quick again.

I called to the chauffeur. 'Where would a man go to get a good drink around here?'

He shouted over his shoulder as he hurried to open the door for her, 'Hotel Neue Post!'

It was the right name, the name from the detective's report, the hotel owned by Wertheimer Holdings. I watched the big car roll off down the hill, mesmerised, until the Italian woman's voice surprised me. She was standing behind me in the doorway, one hand holding a wreath of pine branches, the other running stubby fingers through her son's hair.

She crooned gently to the boy. 'Eh, Paulo, maybe one

day you buy your mama a fur jacket for Christmas, eh? Maybe you even marry a beautiful girl with blonde hair, eh, *bambino*, eh?'

The child nuzzled his face into her apron, and an overalled man, young and fair, as Germanic as they were Latin, came out and joined them. Handling the heavy crates had left a fine film of sweat on his brow. 'And I'll be Burgermeister, eh, Francesca?' He put a brawny arm round her.

'That'll be the day!'

'Why not!' he protested, laughing. 'I'm mean enough. Here.' He held out a pink invoice. She snatched it away from him, laughing as well, and made to fold it away in the pocket of her apron.

'No, that's not the way. You've got to do it like this.' He grabbed it back from her and began to check off the items in a gruff voice, heavy with parody.

'Twelve cases Pils, ten cases Weizen. Are you sure, Herr Ott? I only counted eight. Two . . .'

She slapped his wrist in mock indignation. 'Away with you, he's never like that!'

'He bloody well is! That's how you get rich, darling! If you don't believe me, come out on the round in the morning.'

'Enough of your nonsense, Michael Ott!'

They danced around in giggling pantomime, her grabbing for the flimsy pink slip, him keeping it out of her reach, both oblivious of my presence. The child circled them excitedly, catching the infection of their mirth without understanding the cause of it. Finally she caught the paper, and his handsome face took on a resigned look.

'That's how you get rich, all right,' he said wistfully.

Their laughter subsided. She said nothing, and rumpled the child's hair again. I thought of the little swindle with the *Glühwein*, and wondered . . . About being rich. How far would a man go to be really rich? He wasn't a bad man, Max had said, just greedy . . .

'Paulo will be Burgermeister,' she said lovingly. 'Marry a rich lady and buy his mama a big black car, eh, *bambino*?'

I turned and looked at the boy, and the movement made them all aware of me. Adrenaline and fatigue built fantastic thoughts; he was the right age, all right — to marry Lisa, some day . . . The delivery man shooed the child away from my disturbing gaze, back into the warmth. Needles dropped from the wreath as she held it, awkwardly, waiting for me to go. I went down the steps.

Paulo was the right age, but the man from the beer lorry was the right *size*, I thought. Overalls and a cap . . . I was no longer without a plan.

The preparations had been easy enough. It was only a few kilometres' bus ride to Innsbruck, and an hour's shopping had bought the clothes. The last item had been more difficult, but eventually I'd found a hunting shop that had one, and I was back in Neustift before dark. A phone call to Mary Wellbeck had been the only other precaution. Once more I'd spoken, frustratingly, to the answering machine, but at least I'd left a record of what I was about to try.

It was almost dawn now. I leaned against the concrete wall at the back of the Hotel Neue Post, hidden behind the big garbage skip, listening to the chink of glass as the beer crates were taken from the lorry. It was bitterly cold. Snow fell in feathery flakes around me.

I took the revolver from my pocket. For a second my index finger hesitated, but then it curled round the trigger. It was just as heavy as the German automatic had been, its balance felt the same, and to me it was indistinguishable from a real gun. I could only hope my adversary would think the same, for everything depended on it.

But I had learned about guns and their power, now. Until the shot was fired, until the bullet left the barrel, a gun's only effectiveness lay in the amount of menace with which it was wielded. The deciding factor wouldn't be my opponent's fear, but my own confidence — *I* was the one who knew it was only a replica, albeit a perfect one; I was the one who knew how naked I really was. But there had been no other choice; to buy a real one required a licence. The noise of the crates stopped, and I stood up and stretched my aching limbs. Any second now.

I heard voices. The cheerful tenor of the delivery man made a quick duet with a disgruntled bass. A door slammed, then the motor started and the lorry pulled away from the hotel's back door. I moved quickly. There was no way of checking how many people were around, but I was banking on nobody expecting trouble through the back entrance at seven-thirty in the morning. I crossed the car park, went cautiously in, and the sounds and smells of a big hotel beginning its day met me in the hallway. The kitchen door flew open and a young waitress in black came out, tying on an apron as she walked. Her tired eyes regarded me without interest, red-rimmed and listless.

'Where the hell is he?' I asked irritably.

She jerked her head backwards at the kitchen, stifling a yawn as she went by me. I went up to the door as she passed into the *Gastzimmer.*

'Herr Bartsch,' I called out, 'there's a mistake with the order.'

I was pretty sure I had the accent and the voice's register more or less right, and I was counting on the door to mask any differences. I heard the scrape of a chair being pushed back from a table and pressed myself back against the wall, praying no one else would appear. The massive body came through and stopped in confusion.

'Herr Ott, I've told you a thousand . . .'

I put the pistol to his ear. 'Turn round.'

He did so, slowly. The eyes took in me, then the weapon, trying to calculate the danger.

'The cellar,' I said.

We went down stone steps into a musty room, and he sat down heavily on a pile of crates and watched me lock the door. For a second each of us appraised the other, then his eyes went back to the fake gun, then to the clock. I fought to keep the elation from showing in my face; if I could keep cool, the bluff had worked.

'Herr Bartsch, I need to know now if you will be missed in the next few hours. Don't think of lying to me. If someone comes down these steps unexpectedly, I'll kill you.'

The voice was as big and sturdy as the frame which housed it. 'In this country, nobody worries about the boss till they see him. I know who you are. Tell me exactly what you want.'

I was taken aback by the promptness of the invitation to deal. I hadn't expected capitulation to be this easy, but as I looked at him I understood: he was the kind of man who would always bargain rather than fight. Or was there more to it than that . . .

'What I want is very simple, Herr Bartsch. I want to know it all – every detail, every single thing there is to know about what is happening here. From the beginning. Talk. *Now.*'

He hesitated a second, weighing the situation before he answered. Was I wrong, I wondered? Had I misread him somehow? Was there some kind of elaborate trap here? Then the big grey head nodded, and as he watched me I knew he had seen it, the look, the same look the boy Sandor had seen on the barge.

I had stopped running.

The cellar was warm, and even though the old man was stripped to shirt and braces, he was sweating. His voice droned on, by turns sardonic and scathing, interrupted only by the wine. I'd listened for almost two hours now, fascinated.

'. . . don't much care about it, do you, Fraser? Money?'

It wasn't a question, it was a barb, tossed out to see

what it could hook. It wasn't the first one. Bartsch waited, but I'd learned the game by now. When no reaction came, he snorted in derision. As he reached for the glass, the word echoed round my brain.

Money . . .

Profit, pure and simple; the machines run by the generator at Burg Laer had been old-fashioned printing presses, used to counterfeit the banknotes of a dozen different countries. My eyes went from the wine glass to the big head, shaking in disgust at me. As he poured, I contemplated the scale of what they had done and wondered how much of his exasperation was real.

It was a clever scheme, a perfect marriage of audacity and thoroughness and, like all such schemes, its mechanics were simple and bold. Spielbank Neustift offered a service to those of its customers who beat the odds and won. It was logical as well as attractive to the clientèle, good psychology — the sort of small, flattering convenience that let the average man feel he had joined the ranks of the rich. It was simplicity itself: the winner could cash in his chips in a selection of different currencies.

Most of the gamblers used the facility only if their stay in Neustift was at or near its end, and anyone who asked for the service was discreetly screened. If their circumstances fitted, a certain percentage of the winnings they took home would be counterfeit. Never too much; a steady trade was the aim, unnoticed by either banks or governments as more than a nuisance.

The brilliance of it lay in the concept, Bartsch said, the layers of risk automatically eradicated. False money went straight on to the streets of a dozen countries, with only the slightest chance of its ever being traced back to Neustift. The operation was a total success, and had been for more than five years, with only a few hiccups at the start. They never picked really big winners, because large sums would be banked, and they'd quickly learned to pitch the casino's odds in favour of the man who liked to gamble modestly, a few hundred here or there. It didn't sound like big money until you added it up over the year, the old man explained, then you realised how steady it was. As long as they were careful never to foul their own nest by faking German or Austrian notes, or overloading any one currency, it could go on for ever.

As he drained the wine glass I prayed for him to keep talking, for there were other swindles and I wanted the details, but so far he'd let only fragments slip. Sometimes the money would be laundered through another gambling operation, but they got a lower price on the faked notes that way, and for some reason they could only use it occasionally. He'd mentioned a racetrack as well, but he hadn't said where it was or how that angle worked. The deep voice continued — and as I listened I understood why my initial appearance had caused such consternation; I had disturbed the workings of a quiet gold-mine. He paused. The big hand pulled another bottle of wine from the rack and brandished it at me, half in offering, half in defiance. This time I didn't even bother to cock the weapon; both of us knew there wasn't going to be any physical resistance. He poured another glass and drank half of it.

'So you see, Fraser, it doesn't really matter to me. If they kill you, everything goes on as before. If you win, there isn't a shred of hard evidence to connect me to any of it, and anyway, there's not a court in Europe that would send me to jail at my age. They should have told me about you right from the start — either that, or Weidemann should have put you in the ground in Holland. Pure incompetence, that, cocky little bastard . . . Too late to worry about it now, though. All I want to see is the matter settled one way or the other. Uncertainty's bad for business.'

'Why did they clear out of Laer?'

'You, mostly.' He sat back, appraising me. 'You're a wild card, Fraser. After the carry-on at the border, nobody knew what the fuck you'd do next.'

'How does the money get here?' I asked.

'Sometimes Weidemann brings it, sometimes Lemke, sometimes both of them.'

'Lemke's the one with the scar?'

He nodded. 'Gutterman used to do the run as well.'

Another barb, this time well baited; the name of the man I had killed. Again he searched my face, again I let myself show nothing, for the less he knew about my feelings the better. The probing had been as constant as the information; though I had the upper hand for the moment, Bartsch was old and wise in trickery, and this was a corner he had been in before.

'Details.'

'I don't have any. They come once a month, stay here overnight, take a phone call early the next morning, then go up there. Sometimes they come back here, sometimes they don't.'

'If you don't have the details, how do you know so much about the rest of it?'

'I make it my business to know. What are you going to do with me?'

I didn't speak. His cynicism couldn't hide all the voice's bitterness — and I was sure now of what had only been a guess earlier: they hadn't cut him in on the big money. There had to be a way I could use that . . .

But how? It was a lever, but I didn't know where to apply it. I could only wait, just as he was doing. The flow of facts was steady, but slow . . . Deliberately slow? Behind the bravado he was working up to an offer of some kind, I could feel it — for in Bartsch's world everything had a price, and he was trying to gauge mine as we talked. Again I remembered Max's description of him. It had been correct as far as it went, but it had missed out one vital thing: the kernel of ruthlessness at the man's centre. It was a tough, solid core that had served him well over the years, helping him barter and blackmail his way to prosperity, letting nothing stand in his way. For Bartsch, obstacles were things to bargain with, and if that failed, he would balk at nothing to remove them. But I believed him when he said he couldn't be touched, for along the way he'd perfected the rogue's first skill. None of the skeletons in the closet would bear Bartsch's fingerprints; the man was a survivor.

'You're like *him*,' he said, looking up at the clock again as he refilled his glass.

'Who?'

'Von Laer. Same kind of pig head. Right up to the last minute, when Falkenheim had him shot. Roaring about Germany and justice. Fucking *justice*! Christ, Fraser, if I'd had half the stubbornness of either of you, I'd have made *real* money instead of settling for this.' He dismissed everything around him with a vague wave.

'Why did Falkenheim shoot him that night?' I asked. 'He could have had him sent to the camps, like Vinnie.'

The look he gave me was a mixture of black humour and total contempt for such innocence. 'Plenty of reasons, Fraser — but mostly because he *hated* him. Can't understand good old-fashioned hate, can you? Lots of people hated him. Falkenheim hated him for interfering, his sister hated him for being queer, for giving the land away, and I wasn't sorry to see him go, either. Nearly had *me* shot once, sanctimonious prick! I'd've shot him myself, if I'd ever had the chance.' He took another mouthful of wine. 'Or the guts,' he added, reflectively. He spat out a piece of cork. 'But I wasn't really that bothered. I was too busy trying to stay alive. You going to tell me that was wrong?'

Again I said nothing, but he read my face, and he knew I couldn't condemn him for it. It was enough to make the hard persona slip, and suddenly I was confessor as well as interrogator. It seemed genuine.

'Hell, Fraser, what else was there to do? It was a madhouse. They'd just shot Von Laer, Vinnie was gone, and I was next for it, so I bought time, told them about the others, about the kid and the painting. They didn't believe me at first, but the sister backed me up, she'd seen the thing. She was insane, even then. Crazy, totally — watched them shoot her brother without turning a hair. Anyway, I told them. Max and Jacky had it, I said, and I was the only one who knew where they were headed. Falkenheim went wild, but I told him if he shot me he'd never set eyes on it. You have to understand what it was *worth* to him! If he'd taken it to Goering or Himmler, his career was made. I told them the whole damn story and it only just saved my neck. You'd've done the same.'

I wondered if he was right. Would I have been a Bartsch or a Von Laer, or something in between? I didn't know, but I found myself in grudging admiration of the old man, despite what he was; it must have taken a cool head and a lot of guts to bargain in that situation. He went on, losing himself in the memories and the wine.

'You've no idea what it was like. The S.S. ruled the whole damn country — not even the Gestapo argued with them. They locked me away for three weeks, a barracks up near Oldenburg. Never charged me. Falkenheim didn't need to, his word was law, then. Not like later. It wasn't so bad, but I was going out of my mind with fear, I didn't know what the fuck was going on. Then one of the guards told me they'd bungled it — found the car in a ravine near Taunusstein, but there was only one body, and no painting. Couldn't trace Max or Jacky, and when they finally caught that fool Schumacher in Schwerin, they found damn all. Idiots! You've got it, haven't you?'

I stopped myself from answering, but not fast enough; this time he'd won his reaction. He waved it away as unimportant; he'd known anyway. His hand wiped the top of the bottle, the glass forgotten now.

'Falkenheim came to see me in Oldenburg. It was funny, really — I was shit scared and trying to hide it, but I needn't have bothered. We both came from the same patch, up in the Westerwald, the back of beyond, and he recognised the dialect. Swung the balance for me, that.

He'd seen how useful I could be to him by then, but he'd still have shot me on principle because I'd been one of Von Laer's people. He was hard as nails. Young, ambitious, poor as a church mouse — didn't have as much as a pot to piss in, then. Not a Nazi — precious few of *them*, when all was said and done — or even much of a soldier. Just along for the pickings, and he saw I was as well; we both had the right weather eye for money and opportunities.' His mouth curled into a vicious grin. 'Made for each other, we were. Rare old time we had of it, too, up till Russia. Sergeant Bartsch found the loot, *Obergruppenführer* Falkenheim "requisitioned" it. War's just business, really . . . All changed after Stalingrad, of course. Lucky to get out of that.'

'And the land? Here? How did you get the title to it?'

He frowned at me. When he spoke again, all trace of softness was gone from his voice. 'What the hell do you care, Fraser? Let's just say I knew where enough bodies were buried to get my share.'

I decided not to press it, despite my frustration, for there were more important things. But his reluctance on the subject was a reminder just the same; I was still a long way from the truth of what had happened here. There was silence. He took it, used it like a wrestler taking a fall, turning the momentum to his own advantage.

'You'll never get rid of it. Alone. The painting.' He fingered the neck of the wine bottle. I waited for the pitch. He leaned towards me. 'I could organise it.'

Again he pressed the advantage the silence gave him.

'Look, Fraser, I don't give a shit what you think of me, even with a gun in your hand, but don't you see the *chance* you've got here? D'you think you can smash the whole thing wide open with a pistol? Put everybody in jail and be a hero? Where's the percentage in that? You're in a position to deal, now. *I know how to do that.* All my life I've had to do it for myself, and I can do it for both of us now. This is a beautiful set-up, and I could get us a big slice of it. It would take a long time to explain why, but they're in the shit right now, and we'd have them over a barrel. *Think*, man! Think of the money that's being made up there!' He leaned back against the wall, eyeing me as he raised the wine bottle to his lips.

'When do they bring the money next?'

He exploded in anger at me. 'Damn it, man, it's the chance of a *lifetime*! The sweetest con! Nobody gets hurt except the banks! *Why the hell not?*'

I felt his frustration touch my own, tempt me to explain, but as I looked at him, the impulse died. Reasons, principles, love . . . What could these things be to Bartsch except more power to bargain with?

'Just tell me when the cash comes next.'

Again he looked at me, but now I felt his manner change. The massive head nodded slowly, as though in confirmation; this time, the appraisal was final. He shrugged his shoulders and laughed. As I lifted the gun, his eyes found the clock again.

'You're too late,' he said.

'What do you mean?'

'They're not *complete* fools, Fraser. No home-made stuff's gone out since you paid your little nocturnal visit to the baroness.'

'What have they done with it?'

This time it was his turn to keep silent. His eyes went between my face and the gun, measuring again, trying to assess just how far he could go in his defiance. I felt rage rise within me, and fear — for if they escaped me now, I was finished. The pistol grip was slick with sweat in my hand, reminding me of my impotence. How could I force him further? Hit him? Could I hit an old man? I lowered my eyes for an instant; I knew I couldn't cold-bloodedly do such a thing, but it was vital that Bartsch didn't see it. My anger came to the rescue.

'So help me God, Bartsch, if you don't tell me, I'll burn this whole damn place down round your ears. Tell me. *Now*.'

The threat to his property worked where a threat to

his person would have failed. I saw the alarm in his eyes.

'Okay, okay, if it gets you out of here.'

He raised a placatory hand — and suddenly my assessment of him was as complete as his of me. I had all the man's character now; Bartsch was a hard, pitiless centre surrounded by the sum of his worldly goods, no more, no less.

'They're here, now. They came last night. The phone call came about ten minutes before you did. They're still in the town, somewhere.'

Now I understood why he'd talked so readily: to buy time, not for them, but for himself. Bartsch didn't want a confrontation, he wanted a deal. For that he needed us apart, so that he could play middleman.

'How many of them?'

'Four.'

'They brought more money?'

'God, you're as big an idiot as they are. They're here to take the rest of it *away*.'

'How do they carry it?'

'Lemke has a black briefcase.'

'Time. How much do I have?'

He hesitated again, but this time only for a fraction of a second. 'Maybe a couple of hours.' He emptied the wine and read my thoughts. I watched his lip curl in contempt. 'Don't worry, Fraser, I'd be the last one to go running to the cops.'

I stood up. Even though he was ten years older than Max had been, there was no weakness in him, no frailty, and suddenly his robust health was an affront to me, an advert for the triumph of corruption. He met my gaze steadily, and I knew he was weighing my chances against them, just as he'd weighed his own against me. I couldn't read the outcome in his eyes, but somehow it angered him that I kept standing there, after I'd won, after the transaction had been completed.

'Get out of here! You're wasting time!'

He was right. I unlocked the door. His voice rose to a

shout as I ran up the stairs.

'I don't give a shit who wins! I pay my percentage to you, to Wertheimer, it doesn't matter a damn!'

I found myself at the reception desk, with the handsome, tanned face of the woman I'd seen coming out of the cable car staring at me in bewilderment. I hardly noticed her as I went through the front door. The heavy fall of snow wasn't over, and big flakes were still swirling down. *The casino*, I thought desperately. If I could reach the casino, there was still a chance.

A pair of headlights flashed from a snow-covered car in the street opposite. I wheeled round, expecting attack or challenge, ready to run, but there was no one. Again the lights flashed, repeatedly — and this time I understood: the signal wasn't *because* of me, it was *for* me. Warily I put my hand on the fake gun in my pocket and began to cross the narrow street, but then I halted. I recognised the vehicle's outline under the covering of snow. When the driver's door opened I saw brown hair, spectacles, a pale face. A smile of relief banished the worry from it, but only for a brief moment.

Elly.

The mid-day crowds manoeuvred their way good-naturedly through the freshly fallen snow, laughing as they slipped on the paving-stones, and angelic choirs sang carols from the tape players of the fashionable boutiques that lined the main square. As we sat silently in the warmth of the car, watching, I realised it was Christmas Eve. The fact belonged to a different world, a world far removed from my reality or Elly's. Once more I tried to digest the news she'd brought, to sift through all of the fantastic implications, but it was impossible to bring my mind to bear on it; my fear of what would happen to her left no room for other feelings. *I had to get her away.*

'You can't stay here, Elly.'

She turned away, staring out of the window as though she was seeing the town and its inhabitants properly for the first time. Her gaze came to rest on the casino, high up on its mountain. I had never seen her so tired, so drawn.

'How did you find me?' I asked.

'It wasn't hard. Mary got the message you left last night, and it had to be the hotel or the casino. I had to come, Alex — I just didn't know what to do after Lübeck. Was it wrong of me?'

'No, but it's dangerous for you to stay.'

She pushed the hair back from her brow in a tired copy of the gesture I knew so well, and as I waited for her to speak I sensed what was coming.

'Alex, do you have to go through with this? I'm afraid for you. Couldn't we just go to the police, with what we know? Or just go away, the three of us? Perhaps they'd leave us alone, now.'

The longing in her voice was infectious. It made me want to find her a refuge, a peaceful place somewhere — anywhere, as long as it was far from guns and violence, fear and greed. But the bitter truth was that her news pulled us even further away from the chance of such a thing, for the one piece of evidence I'd been so sure of had turned into illusion.

'Are you certain?' I asked quietly.

The question lifted some of the weariness from her, and her voice took on the tones of professional competence I'd first heard so long ago in a Dutch library.

'There's no possible doubt. I've not had much training in that side of things, but this is obvious.' She leaned over and brought it out from under the rug on the back seat, unrolled it, and held it against the wheel. 'Two things. The varnish is wrong, and so are the brush-strokes. Brush-strokes are as individual as handwriting, Alex. Mary and I looked at a lot of Van Dycks in London; it's a fake, a copy.'

She rubbed her brow with the back of her hand, and I saw it shaking. She was exhausted; she'd driven all the way from the north of Germany to tell me this, to ask me what to do. I only wished I had an answer to give her.

She went on.

'It's not a forgery, just a very good copy that was never meant to be sold. Any competent forger would at least have tried to do the varnish the right way. But it's not a real Van Dyck.'

I stared at the painting for a long time, bitterly remembering the trail of death that had led to it, the hopes I'd built on its recovery. Suddenly a police car accelerated past us, and Elly started like a frightened animal. The driver braked hard as he left the square, oblivious of our presence, and anger surged in me as I looked at her face. It was pale with fright and shock. I couldn't let her live in such fear any longer; this thing had to be finished, and soon. The painting didn't alter what had to be done — we still needed evidence, and every minute I sat with her might well be taking it further out of our reach. I had to convince her. I put my arms round her.

'Elly, listen to me carefully. I need you to go. *Now.* If they get both of us, everything we've been through has been for nothing. If you stay clear of me till this is over, we have at least a chance.'

'I've only just found you again, Alex. Let me help. Don't send me away.'

I put the canvas on the seat behind us and lifted the round tin. She'd told me there were letters in it, but the German was beyond her. She leaned her head against the window wearily.

'I love you,' she said. I could hear the determination in her voice. 'I don't want you to do this thing, but if you have to, then I don't want you to have to do it alone. I've learned what it's like to be really alone, now. The way you think about things changes. You don't . . .'

I broke in with the argument I knew I'd have to use.

'Have you thought about Lisa? What happens to her if they get both of us, Elly? Who looks after the child then?'

She made no reply, and I knew I had won my hollow victory.

'Leave me the car. Rent another one and go to

Innsbruck airport. If I'm not there by tomorrow morning, go to the police. One way or another it'll be over by then.'

'Alex, there's one more thing you should know. About Lisa. The woman in the . . .'

I pulled her round to face me and gripped her by the shoulders.

'*Elly, not now!* Go now, I haven't much time.'

I didn't know the harsh voice as my own. I closed my eyes tightly, forcing myself to stay calm. The thought of what could happen to her held me like a vice, and I knew I was helpless until I was free of it. When I opened my eyes again, she was staring at me.

'You *want* to do this, don't you?'

'*For God's sake!* It's not a question of that. If I run now, there's no security, no peace, ever again. I . . .'

I stopped. Both of us knew it was true, but we both knew she was right as well. The dark, weary circles under her eyes spoke of the strain, the weeks of uncertainty, constant fear; I owed her all of the truth, not just the acceptable part of it.

'No. You're right. I want to do it as well.'

'Revenge, Alex?'

How could I tell her? They'd hunted me with guns, killed without compunction. I thought of Max; they'd built a nightmare on the foundations of my loyalty to an old man. I thought of the battered, bloody torso of an East German border guard, of Geordie Murray's obscene fear; they had forced me to be as ruthless as they themselves were, to use the anger I'd sworn was buried forever. I could tolerate no more of it, and the only freedom was to beat them completely, to bring them to book. But there was no time, now, to explain it all. I shook my head.

'Not revenge, Elly. I'm neither judge nor jury. I will use no more violence than I have to. Go. Now.'

'Alex . . .'

'Elly, if you love me, *go!*'

She bowed her head in pure misery, then looked at

me, but I couldn't meet her eyes. She opened the door and got out without another word. I moved across to the driver's seat and put the car into gear, and as I drove off, I could see her slim figure in the mirror, watching me go. The jolly Christmas crowds instinctively avoided her, as though they knew how sad she was, how alone.

I read the letter again.

Herr Von Laer,

Please excuse the fact that I write in English, but neither my Spanish nor my German is precise — and while there are friends enough in London who would translate for me, it would be madness for a political refugee in this country to advertise contact with a member of Hitler's Wehrmacht. To be frank, were it not for the esteem in which both my parents held you, I would not dream of taking such a risk.

The past tense with regard to my family is, sadly, forced upon me, for it is with great regret that I inform you of my father's death, ten days ago. His demise was sudden, and, I am assured, painless — the official cause was given as heart failure, but my own belief is that the shock of enforced exile from his homeland, coming so soon after my mother's passing, was simply too much for him. I have yet to come to terms with either the fact of his dying, or my own anger at it. I shall mourn him greatly.

This letter fulfils one of his last wishes, and its substance is simple: he wanted you to know — urgently — that the evidence he had sought on your behalf exists. In the last days before they forced him to flee, he found it among the Gondomar papers, but it was impossible for him to bring the documents with him to England. That he was able to escape at all was a miracle, for the Falangists were determined to have him, even though he had taken no part in his country's politics since the fall of the Azaña government. My only comfort is that he did not die surrounded by

Franco's thugs, but with the last remaining member of his family by his side.

I return the photograph. England is the land of my mother, but it is also the land of Chamberlain, and anyone who fought in Spain for the Republican side is regarded here more as an object of suspicion than of sympathy — and certainly would not be trusted with access to historical archives, no matter how old or how irrelevant to the struggles of today. There is nothing practical I can do with it, and perhaps you have other avenues open to you. I hope so.

I know how much he approved of your intentions, and, incidentally, of your plan. He admired you greatly — he was adamant that the example of men such as yourself was proof of the futility of crude nationalism and its meaningless racial labels. I can only say how much I agree with that sentiment, for I believe it applies to him as well.

I wish it was in my power to offer you a support which was other than purely moral.

It was dated the fourth of May, nineteen thirty-nine, and signed Peter Alvarez. The photograph was of the Van Dyck, a battered copy of the print I'd taken from Max's box at the start of the whole affair. As I put the envelope back in the round tin with the other letters, I heard the mournful toll of the monastery bell, and wished that my own grasp of Spanish was better, for Elly had been wrong: only the first four letters were in German. Apart from this one — the only one in English — there were two in an elegant Castilian longhand. I hadn't been able to decipher all the German, but pieces of the puzzle were beginning to fall into place.

I looked down to gauge the cable-car's progress, blowing on my hands, for with the engine off the car's heat had soon gone, and the cold was intense. The red gondola swayed up towards me through the strong wind, the late afternoon sunlight glinting on its windows, casting strange, fluid shadows on the snow below, blue and ghostly, as though some changeling beast was stalking its metallic prey up the mountain. A count of the pylons between the red cylinder and its terminus told me it was still at least five minutes off.

Once it stopped, I had to be ready to move quickly, though, for I knew the routine by now, and the turn-around was fast. It would dock, disgorge its well-dressed cargo of sightseers and casino-goers, then collect those making the return trip and move off again, all in under ten minutes. Only while it was actually in its bay would there be any human activity around the casino's ornate bronze doors. The rest of the time they remained firmly shut, leaving the mountain to the winds and my tired eyes.

I checked my watch against the bells, fighting fatigue and the growing certainty within me that I was too late. My fears for Elly's safety had been stilled, but it was a cold helplessness which had replaced them, for time had not been on my side. The ascent of the winding service road that was the alternative to the cable car had cost me a precious hour — three hours ago. Had Weidemann come and gone? In his place, I'd have used the morning, taken care to avoid the customers, but perhaps there were other considerations. Speculation was useless, anyway; I would wait till there was absolutely no chance left, and what would happen then was something I was determined not to contemplate yet. I lifted the fragile roll of celluloid.

It had been at the very bottom of the round tin, below all the letters. I held it up to the light, and the first few frames were enough to tell me I had the beginnings of the whole affair in my hands. The material was scratched and buckled, so stiff I was afraid it would tear as I unrolled it. The faces were too small to be recognisable, but there could be no doubt about the event recorded on the old film: even in miniature, the brutality was obscene. I rolled it away again as the cable car docked, and felt the tension rise as I scanned the faces of the emerging passengers — a plump middle-aged man, jovial with drink, flanked by two women, obviously wife and daughter, both expensively wrapped against the wind in sleek furs. All three of them were laughing. The wife turned, jerking at a long leash, and I saw the object of their mirth, a dachshund, yapping at their ankles in excitement. I stared at the dog's garish red-and-white tartan coat in frustration; it was obvious that the laughing family group had nothing to do with me.

My disappointment was so intense that I almost missed him as he passed. He must have come from the other end of the car park, a side door somewhere behind me. I willed myself to hold back for a few seconds more, blessing the snow for giving the vehicle such perfect anonymity as I let him get further away. The thin wisps of his brown hair blew in the wind as the leather-jacketed back marched towards the concrete platform, the heavy bag in his right hand. He never heard me get out of the car, never saw the fake pistol come up. A surge of satisfaction went through me; this time *I* had the upper hand.

'*Lemke!*'

He spun round.

'If you move, you're dead!'

Whatever he felt, he masked it well. The eyes above the long scar showed no emotion at all, and through my elation I took the warning; the laughing face I'd seen beside Maria Goosens's body on Terschelling . . . This man enjoyed killing; I mustn't underestimate him. I came forward. He didn't move.

'Put the briefcase down and back away. Slowly.'

The big square leather bag crunched down into the snow, but I didn't let myself look at it. I kept the gun on him and shouted over his shoulder to the fat man as I lifted it.

'Don't be frightened! You're not involved in this. Get back in —'

The shriek was high and piercing. Shock ruled out thought as I recoiled from the briefcase and the noise, and then I realised it was an alarm. Slipping, I grabbed for the case again. As I fell to my knees, I saw Lemke's hand reaching inside his jacket. Automatically I jerked up the fake gun.

'No!'

The one terrified word was all that came out. The high sound swirled round it, a tortured animal cry, burning into my mind, raking across the threshold of pain. Behind Lemke the dog was going crazy, churning the snow in its desperation to pull away from it. I saw the two women, mouths open, but the alarm's endless screaming swallowed theirs. The note began to change, rising in pitch, merciless — it was unbearable! I wanted to run, cover my ears, but somehow the arm that held the replica stayed rigid, pointing.

Again I shouted. '*Stop it!*'

It had to finish! It *had* to! My eyes were fixed on him. He seemed immune to the terrible wailing, a rigid silhouette against the snow's glare. The last of my rationality fastened on his stillness. His hand was no longer moving . . . Why? I fought the sound's omnipotence, desperate for reason. *Why was Lemke's hand important?* I scrambled to my feet, the urge to panic mounting inexorably with the noise. His hand! It was vital! *Why?*

It was only the consciousness of other sounds that told me the alarm had stopped — a babble of voices from the casino steps, a whining that was pure pain. The dog . . . The wind gusted, throwing the piteous whimpering at me with the powdery snow, and the enormity of it all rushed in. A toy gun! I was defenceless. All my hand held was a useless lump of metal, he would kill me! I forced myself to speak.

'Slowly, now. Barrel first. Throw it to me. Then put your hands up.'

My voice was hoarse with fear. My whole body began to tremble — with the intensity of the bluff, with the plain absurdity of what I was doing. Keeping hold of the toy pistol was an act of faith, sustained only by my desperation. He would know, he *had* to, his instinct would tell him, see the fake for what it was. The pale face never lost its blankness. Why didn't he . . .?

His automatic landed in the dirty snow at my feet.

I stared stupidly at the thing. It was the gun that had killed Maria, I knew it . . . As I picked it up, I felt a thrill of revulsion that almost made me lose control. The replica dropped from my other hand. I let it lie, and saw understanding come to the scarred face. The red line twisted as he lost control. The look of hatred lasted only a second, but its savagery was an instant awakening, a cold douche that doused the last of my panic. Again I forced myself to heed the warning; *this man is a professional killer.*

'Down on the ground. Face down.'

He did it. Still covering him, I went over and lifted the briefcase, and then a familiar voice came from the crowd on the steps behind.

'Police. Drop the weapon, Fraser.'

'*Him!* Groningen! The tweed suit! *And how are you finding our late autumn weather* . . . The gun seemed to pull me round. I heard my own voice yelling his name. Shouts of warning answered. Through the dizziness I saw the crowd scramble for cover, and then focus came — and my finger faltered on the trigger.

This time the shock was bewildering. Weidemann . . . The butler from Laer . . .

And *her.*

She was pinned between them, only kept upright by their arms, barely conscious. I took in the half-closed eyes, the head swaying against the butler's shoulder. What had they done to her? Lemke's automatic shook in my hand, but Weidemann stood his ground, unconcerned. He held no gun, but the bulge inside the butler's jacket was obvious. It was pressed hard against her side. Bitterness welled up in me, then fear — for her.

'No more nonsense, Fraser. Just drop it.'

Fake money and a fake gun, a fake victory as well . . . Weidemann's voice was calm, sure. He had me, and he knew it; I couldn't just walk away. Even before the automatic had dropped to my side, Lemke was back on his feet. He pounced for his weapon. I heard a final scream from the fat man's wife, saw the beginning of her faint, and then metal smashed against my jaw. I fell back in the snow, tasting blood, and saw the replica in Lemke's hand. He tested the useless trigger, then threw the thing away. The real gun came up. I stared into its obscene black snout. Weidemann's voice sounded like the echo of my own, but its shouted urgency seemed miles away.

'*No!*'

But Lemke was beyond control now. He and I were in our own world, cut off from the others — and the power in it was his. He kept his back to the steps, deliberately, I knew; only I was to see his face, only I was to be shown the intensity of his pleasure. Slowly, the gaunt features took on life. The grin was feral, a predator's anticipation. The sigh that accompanied it was soft, release as well as triumph. There was no doubt: he was going to kill me.

'Lemke, *no*! I forbid it!'

I gripped the handle of the briefcase. Suddenly the dachshund was on top of it, besoide my face, yelping. Instinctively I flinched, hit out at the loathsome smell. I saw the pistol jerk in Lemke's hand, but somehow I never heard the shot. The case was torn from my grasp.

I closed my eyes. What came now? Pain? Or oblivion? Release ... Lemke's release would bring mine ... Wasn't that the deal in our world, the only deal between executioner and victim? I wanted it, longed for it, I was ready for the suffering. I waited.

Nothing.

Death ... Could death really be this easy?

When I opened my eyes again, I saw the smashed briefcase, and then the headless dog, a few feet away. The blood had streaked the snow into red-and-white ribbons, a bizarre extension of the coat's tartan. The forged note fluttered gently down round the little corpse. I looked up at the dejected figure on the steps.

How had they found Annette?

Chapter 12
BARBARITIES

EITHER THE NOISES or the pain woke me, but when my eyes found only darkness, the memory of both was lost instantly. I stumbled round the small, airless room until I fell over the mop and bucket in the corner, and then I picked myself up and felt the shelves on the wall. The relief was overwhelming; it wasn't a cell after all. Dizzy, sweating, I slumped down on the bench and examined the clothes that felt so strange. Overalls, a jacket . . . Why was I wearing these things? How long had I been here? There had been an injection, I could remember that — but everything else was hazy. For a second I listened to the strange whirrings and bangings. They grew, surrounded the space I was in, then receded, and as they died away it all came back to me: Bartsch's hotel, the delivery man's disguise, the dog . . . Bitterness cut into me like acid; I'd lost it, everything. I rubbed my aching jaw and wondered what they'd done with Annette.

I heard heavy footsteps. A key probed the lock, and once more the bizarre noises approached. My fears swelled with them as the handle turned. When they fell away again, I was left with a dark bulk in the doorway.

'Weidemann wants you.'

The snub nose of a pistol ushered me into a dimly-lit passageway, and a fresh wave of metallic shuddering passed over my head. I looked up to see a shiver of vibration surge along the big central heating duct, jarring its stanchions one by one, rattling the thick clusters of electric wiring that bunched along its sides. The butler's gun nudged me forward, and the corrugated steel added the echo of our footsteps to its repertoire. As we wound through a concrete warren of service corridors I could hear the wind's moan over the disjointed clanging. Where was I? A final turn brought us to another door. My custodian flung it open and pushed me through — and then I hung back, suddenly giddy, the light hurting my eyes. I was on a minuscule landing at the top of a spiral staircase, very high up. I gripped the iron rail. The space before me loomed, threatening in its silence.

It was big enough to house a large aircraft or a small ship, lavishly appointed in a frenzied parody of eighteenth-century opulence. No expense had been spared, no extravagance neglected. The concrete walls hid behind embossed wallpaper, stucco cornicing, curtains of silk and damask. The roulette wheels glittered, the light dazzled. It fell from crystal chandeliers across lush expanses of baize and velvet, and then ornate mirrors caught it, multiplying the vastness into an endless landscape of red, green and gold. I stood on the tiny platform, listening to the sound of my own breathing as I took it all in; this was the heart of it, this was what I had come to find.

Gradually the craziness of the detail forced itself upon me. The tables themselves were bulky and businesslike, but the confusion of styles around them was frenetic. Everything jarred — baroque balconies hovered over Regency screens, Palladian statues nestled in alcoves behind Moorish divans. There were fountains in every corner, the biggest of them a gilded nymph who might have been stolen from Versailles. The waters streamed from her hands into a pool of garish green light, sending rippling shadows across the ceiling's golden dome. I waited, listening to the door being locked behind me, wondering . . . What did the people who came here see? The wealth? The vulgarity? Or did winning transform this into elegance? My eyes wandered the length of the incredible room, and then they fastened on the one artifact that rendered the whole attempt at gentility futile.

No filigree of vine leaves, however finely silvered, could disguise the bars of the cashier's cage. It was the room's shrine, the bestower of riches, the taker of tribute. It sat in the far wall, its ugliness visible from every side, a squat trap, a greedy, ever-open mouth. Again the gun prompted me.

We descended. The reek of stale cigar smoke and perfumed sweat rose to meet us, the sour residue of the gamblers' excitement, and the last of the illusion drowned in it. The reality of the surface was tawdry, stale-aired, littered with the flotsam of modern revelry. We went through the bar, a plush wasteland — abandoned cocktail-shakers, jagged reefs of broken glass, a row of fruit machines, handles at half-mast, an open electronic till, blinking defiance at the Christmas tree's fairy lights. The blue banner above the counter was torn, one end of its seasonal greeting lying wearily in a sodden mess of cigarette-ends, its cataracts of tinsel sagging over an army of spent champagne bottles. We picked our way past islands of abandoned chairs and chipped marble tables, making for the screened-off section at the far end. That would be where the big money played, I thought. I could hear a low muttering of voices from it. A half-drawn curtain showed me it was still dark outside.

I passed through the screens — and stopped in surprise at the first person I saw. Bartsch's wife glanced up from her make-up mirror. She gave my face and body a quick, hard, female appraisal, then went back to her eyebrows. I made to go on, then stopped again. Behind her, Lemke leaned against a mirror. The sallow face stayed carefully expressionless at the sight of me, but I could feel the hate. The eyes gave it away, shining with expectation, like a dog waiting for a bone.

Annette sat between the two of them, slumped against the wall. There was no neat business suit now. She was clad in denim skirt, soiled yellow tee-shirt and filthy white training shoes, and the perfect hair I remembered was a mess of dirty, dishevelled curls. She lifted her head. The tear-stained face stared at me blankly, as if she couldn't work out who I was or why I was there. From the state of her pupils I could tell she'd been drugged, and it took a long time for recognition to come to her. When it did, it brought other knowledge with it. Fright showed in her eyes. She glanced over her shoulder at Lemke, then hurriedly hid her face again. His thin lips broadened into an obscene smile as he looked at me. My eyes took in the dark bruises on her arms and at her wrists, the torn skirt, then found his pitiless face once more. The smile broadened even further; whatever he'd done to her, he'd done it because he thought she was mine.

I turned to Weidemann. 'You bastard!'

He was bent over an old-fashioned projector, frowning as he tried to thread the film through its complicated system of wheels and sprockets. The canvas was spread out on the table beside him, held down by ashtrays and empty beer glasses, the letters in a neat pile beside it. Anger stripped the correct English away from him, leaving a soft Rhineland accent in its place.

'Shut your mouth, Fraser. You are in no position to argue. Over there.'

The gun prodded me towards a high-sided gaming table by the far wall. My fiddle . . . Beside it lay a pile of banknotes — the money I'd abandoned at the East German border. And there was no longer any mystery about why they'd taken Annette. I stared at the photograph I'd last seen in the young border officer's hands; she had snared herself with it instead of me. Its innocent coquettishness seemed pathetic now.

I turned to the instrument. It was without strings or

bridge, and as I lifted it I felt the wood sag. The top was almost torn off, and the urgency of their search had badly split the purfling and the back's central seam. A few hours before I would have been enraged, but now it was just another fact, another weight to be counted in the sum of my defeat. Again the burden crushed down upon me: frustration and guilt, revulsion. *What had they done to the girl?*

Weidemann's voice broke in on the chaos of my thoughts. 'I hate unexplained things, Fraser. They bother me. Large sums in *Deutschmarks*, for instance. German cars, Dutch cars. Quite a coincidence that a man who makes his living begging in the gutter never seems to lack for funds. You have a backer somewhere.'

I said nothing. He came up to the dice table, then stopped and turned to Bartsch's wife.

'You're sure?'

The lipstick poised in mid-air. She pursed her lips and checked the red bow of her mouth in the mirror before speaking.

'It was him. Almost three hours yesterday morning.'

'Tell me about you and Bartsch, Fraser. *Everything* about you and Bartsch.'

The unexpectedness of it caught me completely off balance. He waited, his stocky figure incongruous in the double-breasted dinner jacket, and when I still didn't answer he grabbed the front of my shirt and pulled me to him. His voice was a whisper of barely-suppressed rage.

'No back way out this time, Fraser. No toy guns, either.' He jerked his head in Annette's direction. 'The quicker you tell me, the better for her. You and Bartsch. The connection. *What is it?*'

The big, booming voice saved me from answering. Bartsch dragged his huge bulk up the steps, massive and malevolent, out of scale with everything else in the room. His wife's eyes opened wide with fear.

'Is that all you want, Weidemann? I'll tell you that, all right. But first things first.'

The blow was something between a slap and a punch, flat and loud, delivered with the speed of a man half his age. It smashed the make-up mirror into pieces against the wall and sent her sprawling across the floor. An angry red weal spread itself quickly across her cheek, but she said nothing. The old man took off hat and coat and laid them across the back of the nearest chair.

'Stupid bitch,' he said calmly.

The force of his personality filled the room and ruled it, immediately and absolutely. No one spoke. He looked at each of us in turn, then strode across to the canvas, perused it, and grunted with satisfaction. My mind began to recover from its state of atrophy as I watched his quick examination of the letters. I was the only one who knew the painting was a fake . . . Was there a way to use the fact? Absent-mindedly he stroked the metal of the projector as he read, as though his hand was an independent intelligence, capable of assessing the machine's value by touch alone. He put the letters down.

'Interesting, interesting.' For a second he gave the old machine his full attention. 'Antiques, eh? Didn't know that was your line, Weidemann. Something worth watching, I hope. Blue movie, maybe?' He looked down at the cowering figure of his wife. 'Keep her happy' anyway. But business must be worse than I thought.'

Icily, Weidemann's voice broke the spell. 'Enough theatrics, Bartsch. If you want to talk business, let's start with yours and Fraser's.'

The old man laughed and shook his head. 'There is no connection between me and Fraser. He held me up for information and I gave it to him.' He turned to me. 'Toy revolver, eh? Cheeky, that. But you're a stupid bastard all the same — could've made yourself a fortune. You're a dead man, now.'

I felt the tension rise with the admission that he'd talked to me. The butler subtly shifted stance to cover both Bartsch and me with the gun. Suddenly there was curiosity in Weidemann's voice.

'If you're not behind him, why are you here?'

Bartsch reached into his jacket pocket and pulled out a sheaf of papers. He held them up, smiling like a winner at the bookmaker's window. His voice was conversational.

'Interesting reading, this report. All about an incident up here yesterday afternoon. All about how your pet psychopath tried to shoot his attacker instead of arresting him like the police officer he's supposed to be. Then shot a dog, would you believe.' He shook his head, an indulgent grandfather remembering childish folly. 'The police chief wants the *Burgermeister's* opinion on how we should proceed with it.' The look of amused contempt turned itself on the figure by the mirror. 'Perhaps you should just keep him for teenage girls in future, Weidemann. People like Fraser seem to excite him too much.'

Everyone except Annette looked at Lemke. The red scar stood out against the pale flesh as though he'd been branded, but it was the only sign of his anger. Weidemann's face was a picture of disgust as he watched him.

Bartsch went on. 'And I wouldn't start making any arrangements for my sudden disappearance, either. That might be just too much of a coincidence — for my very good friend the police chief, I mean.'

There was no pause, no hesitation. Both of them knew Weidemann had to deal.

'What do you want?'

'In. A reasonable cut, no more.'

'That's not up to me, you know that.'

Bartsch gestured towards the telephone at the other end of the room. Weidemann walked across, lifted the receiver, dialled four digits, and waited. The conversation was too low for me to hear, but it was over in less than a minute. I felt Lemke's eyes upon me, and as I returned the stare his hand went to his jacket pocket. He was fingering the gun, I knew. It couldn't be long now before he was given the chance to use it on me. Weidemann strode back down the room.

'He'll talk to you.'

Bartsch sat down heavily on an ornate chair and folded the papers away again. He smiled. 'Good, good. But first I think I should know exactly what we're talking about. I've always been a curious man, Weidemann. Show me this film that's so important you have to watch it in the middle of the night.'

The silence was uneasy. I watched Weidemann, and found myself echoing the thought. What was so important about the film? It was obvious he didn't want Bartsch to see it, but it was also obvious he had no choice, for the old man held all the cards. Finally Weidemann signalled, and without taking his eyes from me, Lemke walked over to the projector. The lights went off, the ancient machine creaked into life. I heard Bartsch's muttered oath as he recognised the scene.

It was as Max had described it. Exactly: a smoky sky, the ruined street, the blackened remains of the buildings, the broken pillars of the shattered church . . . There was a second's haziness while the lens focused on the altar, then a blur of bodies and, finally, an awful clarity. Loathing swelled in me at the flickering black-and-white pictures. The woman lay like a broken puppet, her dress torn away, her wrists held down on the cracked marble by two swarthy, unsmiling soldiers, her head lolling backwards as though disconnected from the body that was being used so savagely. Her attacker's thrusting was relentless, merciless. A thigh twitched upwards. A black-gloved hand threw it carelessly to one side without breaking the animal rhythm. Another man looked on, uniform tunic unbuttoned, cap askew on his brown hair. Not even the jerky motion of the old film could disguise the calmness with which he was enjoying his cigarette.

Her hand broke free, reached out . . .

Suddenly Max was there with me, no longer just a memory. His disgust and fear were alive in me, they had become my own. I turned away, the projector's whirring roaring in my ears. Its light threw weird shadows round the room, making a cubist portrait of the planes of Lemke's face. The obscenity of his grin drove my eyes back to the screen. Once more I stared at the pain of the scratched images.

A pale breast, undulating . . . A white leg, bouncing gently against the front of the altar . . .

Again I forced my eyes away; again they found Lemke's face. His grin was beyond sadism now. For a second it fixed on Annette's blankness, and then he turned it towards me. It widened. I knew what he was telling me, I *knew*! I felt the tightness growing in my chest.

On the screen, the shoe dropped from the woman's foot.

Lemke laughed.

Something in me snapped. I found myself on my feet, stumbling forward, reaching out. Rage propelled me across the room. I heard the shot from the butler's gun and staggered as pain seared across my shoulders, but it didn't matter. Only one thing in the whole world was important — to crush the life out of Lemke! Two more shots rang out as I ran full-tilt into the projector. There was a blue flash as it hit the floor, then sparks showering round me as I flailed, clawing for his face. I had to stop his laughter! There was shouting, the sound of splintering wood in the darkness. I felt a body in front of me and lashed out as hard as I could with my fist. The lights went on again. The butler's face stared at me, open-mouthed, then fell slowly away to the side, the blood from the back of his head smearing a crimson curve on the wall between the brass light-switch and the carpet. For a second the sight paralysed me, and then I tried to get to my feet. My leg . . . It was trapped! Desperately, I struggled to free it from the remains of the table. Suddenly there was an acrid smell.

'*The painting!*'

It was Bartsch's voice. He held the smouldering

canvas in one hand, beating at the flickering edge of flame with the other. Weidemann ignored him, pulling at the film, tearing what was left of it free of the still-sparking projector. I began to lever myself up, but a hand caught my shoulder. I crashed back down to the floor and looked up.

I saw Lemke's enraged face, the jagged edge of the broken table leg, the beginning of its downward arc — but then there was a deafening blast. He seemed to blow away to the side. The makeshift club twirled harmlessly over my head, and wetness splattered me.

There was silence. I dragged my leg out of the tangled wood, and looked.

He must have died instantly. The force of the bullet had slammed his body across the room and brought it to rest at an impossible angle. It lay across the overturned chairs, one arm almost blown off, a darkening red mass where his chest used to be. The final twitch of a contracting nerve turned his head and showed me his face. I stared; the surprise of death had left him with an expression that verged on the angelic, I wiped the stickiness of his blood from my eyes, and looked at the gun.

The hand holding the snub-nosed pistol shook like a leaf. Her glazed eyes darted between the faces and the strip of film in Weidemann's hands. Then they went to the charred canvas, and finally to the bloody, grotesque thing that was sprawled across the golden chairs.

I got up. 'Annette, give it to me.'

For a second the smoking mouth fixed itself on me, and then it began to move — past the terrified figure of Bartsch's wife, past Bartsch himself. She couldn't control the nervous twitching of her face. The gun shook even more as she trained it on Weidemann.

'Don't,' I whispered. 'Don't shoot him.'

I walked towards her very slowly, and put my hand round the barrel. She made no attempt to stop me taking it. I kept it trained on Weidemann as I stood there, nerving myself up for what I knew had to be done next, and then I crossed to Lemke's body, forced my hand into his pocket and pulled out the automatic, slick with blood. Suddenly Bartsch's wife turned and ran. I put my arm round the girl's shoulders as we listened to the heels, stumbling down the steps, clattering awkwardly across the floor. Annette's eyes came back to the bloody torso, and her hand pointed as though it still held the weapon.

The calm voice was an appalling thing that had dissociated itself from her shivering body. 'He had to pay. For what he did.' It was her receptionist's voice. Her eyes shifted to Bartsch's massive figure. 'He should have paid.'

For the first time, I saw confusion in the old man's face. Her eyes looked through him instead of at him.

'Everyone has to pay. Mama says.' She turned to me. 'Even *you*.'

'Annette . . .'

I felt the strength go from her, and managed to catch her before she hit the floor. I eased her down, then looked across at Bartsch.

'Take care of her.'

He nodded slowly. I turned. Weidemann was sitting amid the débris of the projector, dabbing at the blood from his cut lip, his breathing laboured and heavy, a tangled mess of celluloid at his feet. It was hard to recognise him as the same man who'd threatened me such a short time ago, who'd terrorised me for so long; the dapper little anglophile was gone for ever. Bartsch put the painting down on a chair and began to inspect the damage.

'Don't bother,' I said. I heard the triumph in my own voice, and the bitterness. Weidemann stared at me. 'It's a fake.'

I saw the old man's fingers stiffen as though I'd insulted him, but he took only seconds to recover his composure. He looked pointedly at Lemke's corpse, then went over and prodded the wounded butler with his foot. The man groaned. Bartsch's voice gave no indication that my revelation had touched him any more than the death or the violence.

'Maybe it was this one that fired the shot. I never saw it, of course. I was asleep in bed — remember that.'

His fingers touched the charred edges of the canvas as he waited for my reply. I understood. It was his last offer, his last attempt at a deal . . . Reluctantly I nodded my agreement. If anyone could keep her out of it, it was him. I emptied the remaining bullets from the butler's pistol. The old man's eyes never left mine as I put them in my pocket and laid the weapon on the nearest chair. I turned back to Weidemann.

'Up.'

He rose. I put the blood-smeared automatic to his head.

'Take me to him. *Now.*'

The peaks had just begun to separate the sun's first rays into uneven purple and white spokes across the snow. I shivered, the freezing air stinging the bullet graze on my shoulders, but Weidemann gave no indication that the cold touched him as he trudged on ahead of me. The icicles on the heavy wooden door snapped as he pushed it, but it opened easily enough, and we passed through into the shelter of a white, domed archway. In the courtyard beyond I could see the glass and concrete of modern, unsentimental renovation; they were practical people here. A side door opened and a hooded brown figure emerged, carrying a tray with the remains of a breakfast. His face was veiled by the cowl, but I saw his eyebrows rise in surprise at the sight of us. I only just had time to get the gun out of sight into my pocket. I dug it into Weidemann's back through the cloth.

'Good morning, brother,' Weidemann said. 'Is the *Herr Direktor* awake yet?'

The monk perused us carefully. 'He is.' He walked away from us, then stopped and looked back. A smile played about the edges of his mouth as he delivered his mild reproof. 'And a happy Christmas to you, my son.'

Neither of us replied. I watched him cross the ice-covered cobblestones, and then Weideman led me into the corridor he had just left. It led to a single, oak-panelled door.

'In there?'

Suddenly his collapse was total — and frightening. Head bowed, he stared silently at the floor, his bloody lip swollen, the blonde forelock hanging limp and unheeded over one eye. I made him get down on the floor, and used his own handcuffs to fasten his wrist to the pipe that fed the radiator. He made no attempt at resistance. I went up to the door. It was Bartsch who was expected, and Bartsch would knock . . . It was an effort to make myself perform such a simple task gently.

'*Herein.*'

I pushed the door open. The man at the far end of the room wheeled round as I entered.

It was a face that could have belonged to one of the monks. The harsh shadows of the window's lighting made it ascetic, accentuating the sharp bones, the high brow, and even though I'd been watching it only moments before, I wouldn't have known him had it not been for the one feature that was impossible to disguise. I wondered fleetingly about surgery — but somehow I knew he would never have considered it. This man had found other ways to alter his past; he wore the black patch like a badge, exactly as he had done for the last fifty years.

The other eye belonged to a hawk rather than a man. He moved a yard or so forward to examine me, and I saw it focus in rapid succession on the salient points before it: the gun, my face, the despondent figure of his subordinate through the open door. He spun away from me, back towards the window, then pulled himself round to face me again. The dark cloth of the sober business suit seemed to negate the body between head and hands, and my eyes were drawn from the striking face to his fingers, long and bony, thin, white-knuckled as they gripped and pushed. Their work done, they rested above the black rubber like talons, ready for the next command. The solitary eye went again to the miserable figure in the corridor, then came back to the gun. He waited for me to speak, but I had no words; I hadn't expected the wheelchair.

'So.'

The tone was interested, reasonable, the word a quiet summation of the *status quo.* The skeletal fingers came together over his lap, pressing against each other in a speculative arch. In another man it might have been a gesture of prayer.

'You are a determined young man, Mr Fraser. A determined young man with courage as well as luck. I ask myself what your intentions are — to destroy our enterprise or to take it over?' The talons clutched. The wheels whirred as he propelled himself across the polished floor to me. 'A going concern. Everyone would prosper — you, the child . . . And yet the question is obviously rhetorical. You have not the vision to rise above the tedious confines of your own conscience. A great pity. What is to become of you?'

Even though I recognised the trick, I still had to force myself to ignore the presumption of command in his voice. I made myself speak. 'I don't call murder and rape 'vision', Falkenheim. Or is it Wertheimer?'

He laughed. The wheels whirred again as he returned to the window. 'As a matter of fact, neither is applicable any longer, but does it matter, Mr Fraser — or Mr Lawless? You are also no stranger to the necessities of deception. Deeds are more lasting than names.'

'I want to know how you got the land.'

Again the wheelchair spun round. He reached into the inside pocket of his jacket, then stopped as he saw the gun tremble in my grasp. Very slowly, the claw-like hand emerged again with a white handkerchief. He coughed into it, and the sound thrust a wedge of memories through the fabric of the scene before me. Suddenly I was back in Basel; it had all begun with my love and respect for another man who was old and sick . . . How would it end? I fought the unreality.

'The land. I want to know.'

He folded away the handkerchief and smiled coldly at me. The voice was a mockery of politeness. 'I understand you have met my wife.'

It took a moment for the full import of it to touch me, and then I remembered the crazy laughter, the pathetic old woman on the floor before me in the *Wasserburg*. Her words came back, their meaning clear now. My voice was unsteady as I repeated them.

'In the country of the blind . . .'

He ended it for me, his voice vibrant, '*The one-eyed man is king!*'

There was silence. He broke it by tapping on the eye-patch with a long forefinger.

'It was very simple, Mr Fraser. To share an affliction is the first step towards sharing an affection. Often the case, is it not?' His head shook in wry amusement as he watched my reactions. 'I didn't even have to resort to any of the persuasions I'd planned — the lady was only too grateful, I assure you.' He laughed again. 'After all, I did save the family name. I would hardly let it be known that my wife's brother was a homosexual who consorted with Jews. Her gratitude knew no bounds.'

'She married you,' I said dully. 'After you shot her brother, she married you.'

'Four days after I shot him, to be precise. A tragic accident, of course' — the mockery of his laughter rang round the room — 'but not without its fortunate side. Had Erich Von Laer been brought to trial as the criminal he undoubtedly was, his estates would have been confiscated by the Reich. My wife was anxious to avoid such a complication. The terrible accident of his death meant that the land reverted to her, but she agreed with me that a true German, a natural aristocrat, should have land of his own. Marriage had made me a Von Laer, after all . . . On the day of the ceremony I gave her a necklace I had acquired in Spain. This' — the claw left its perch to become an elegant hand in a gesture of ownership before settling again — 'was her wedding gift to me. Does that answer your question?'

Her loneliness, her obsession with the land of the Von Laers . . . Perfect raw material for his opportunism. A little kindness, a little attention . . . A marriage of the pathetic and the ruthless; it rang true. I said nothing. Again the laughter came, but it curtailed itself into a short bray of contempt as he read my expression. The wheelchair moved again, this time towards the cupboard that stood against the far wall.

'Stop,' I said quietly.

He did so. I went over and opened the cupboard to find ampoules, syringes, boxes and bottles of tablets. He smiled grimly as I examined them.

'You forget this is a clinic, Mr Fraser. A part of the profit from our business ventures goes towards its upkeep. People with cancer die peacefully here. How does your black-and-white morality deal with that?'

He took a capsule from one of the boxes and rolled once more to his favourite position by the window, his back towards me. I listened to the bubbling outbursts of his sarcastic laughter. The sound was all the more cruel for being so pleasant, so musical . . . It separated him from my memories of Max by a thousand lives.

I thought about cancer, the cancer of power. No matter how old he was, how sick, this man would stop at nothing to cling to power; it was an end in itself, the ultimate disease, the parasite which had long ago eaten away the last of his humanity. All his life he had nourished it — with barbarity, with rape and death. And even though his body was beyond the enjoyment of any of its fruits, he would still feed it with anything it craved. How many people had died because of this man? The laughter stopped. The cultured voice took on a new tone as it lifted the subject from me.

'Death,' he said, calmly. 'Death, Mr Fraser. You are no stranger to that, either. Your appearance is appropriate to your history.'

I looked down and realised I was still covered in Lemke's blood. The wheelchair began to move slowly across the room, towards the furthest corner. His voice went on, businesslike, precise.

'You are a hypocrite about death, Mr Fraser. You condemn me, yet you yourself are a convicted murderer.'

One part of my mind saw him heading for the desk in the corner; the other was in the grip of his voice, waiting for his judgment of me.

'*You beat your wife to death, Mr Fraser.*'

I flinched at the words. I felt blood rush to my face as the hypnotic voice went on.

'And yet you vacillate about executing me. How can that be? In your own eyes I am a hundred times more guilty than she was.'

The gun seemed to weigh down my shaking hand. He was almost at the desk now. Suddenly I knew.

'Falkenheim! *Stop!*'

His head shook in a decisive negative. The claw reached out, ready to alight on the handle of the drawer. I was sure there was a weapon in it. I heard voices, commotion, doors being thrown open, but his voice came out above it all with the final, paralysing goad. '*You haven't the guts.*'

I aimed the gun. I could feel neither rage nor fear, only shame. It was a simple, inhuman choice. If I didn't shoot him now, in cold blood, he would kill me. I closed my eyes and began to tighten my finger on the trigger, and then there were other voices in the room.

'*Freeze!*'

I turned to see two grey-clad Austrian policemen in the doorway. Both of their guns were trained on me, and there were others behind them. Then a slimmer figure broke through the press of bodies and came forward. A uniformed arm restrained her. She stared at the weapon in my outstretched hand, ready to execute a crippled man in a wheelchair. She looked at Falkenheim's calm face, then back at me again, and the horror in her eyes gave way first to sadness, then to pity. I was aware of the gun being taken from me, the sudden relief in the voices, and then the sound of bells — the monastery bells ringing out over the valley for Christmas morning. All I could see was Elly's shocked, pale face.

It was over.

Chapter 13
EPILOGUE
THE BUSKER

IN THE BIG hallway, the noise dropped to a quiet susurrus as we emerged. I took a long, deep breath. The cold air was a relief after the overheated drawing-room with its memories and the inane conventions of its formal conversation. Everybody stopped working and watched as we trooped down the stairs in an undignified gaggle past the oppressive line of pictures. The *Landesminister* stopped at every one, examining each face as though it belonged to a living constituent with a castable vote, and each time the procession came to an obedient halt around him. When we reached the last frame there were dismayed looks, then an angry, muted argument between two of the fashionably-suited aides. Finally one of them whispered deferentially into the Minister's ear.

'Ah . . .'

The quick political smile, impeccably timed, did its job. Its benign sweep favoured the entire room, covering his embarrassment, assuring all of us of his goodwill without promising any of us his support. It lasted long enough for the doors of the big reception chamber to open, and then the whole caravan followed him through, thankfully putting the awkwardness behind them in a babble of German, Dutch, Spanish and English. The legal staff and their helpers watched the doors close, then resigned themselves once more to their pens and clipboards. Slowly the hubbub built up again as they went back to the mammoth task of completing the castle's inventory. Only the two policemen and myself were left in front of the portrait, and as I looked at it I understood the recriminations. Someone has bungled; they hadn't been supposed to hang it again until officialdom had finished its visit and was long gone from Burg Laer.

'Remarkable what they can do now. Shouldn't we go in with the others?'

The young German detective's voice betrayed his nerves. It was understandable; when we'd first met I'd been chief suspect for a string of murders, and though I was now officially cleared, my change of status had been too rapid for him. The Austrian grinned frankly at his discomfort as the double doors opened again and Mary Wellbeck came out. The stooping figure by her side supported himself partly on her arm, partly on a stout ash walking stick. For a moment they joined us in our scrutiny, and then Peter Alvarez let go of her and held himself straight.

'Good painter. Strong line to that, don't you think? I'm glad they saved it, even if she was a monster. He wanted it kept, no doubt about that.' He turned briskly to me. 'A clever man, Fraser, don't you agree? A man with style. It must have taken a certain panache to paint a portrait of his sister over an old master. But he was right, of course. Best way to keep it out of Goering's hands. And it worked, it undoubtedly worked. Without the letters, we'd never have known it was there.'

'Why did he paint the copy?' I asked.

He leaned on his stick, peering at a detail of the canvas. 'Additional verification — insurance, if you like. He badly wanted the Van Dyck identified, and he wasn't sure if the photograph he'd sent to the Prado was good enough. It was only black-and-white, after all, and he knew he was a good enough painter to copy the original pretty exactly. My father's correspondence says he intended to send it, but he must have received my letter first. The reference had been found in the papers by then, so there was no real need.'

He waved his stick at the picture that had hung undisturbed at the foot of the marble staircase since nineteen thirty-nine. 'And then she got him! *Sold* him! Tragedy, that. To fight a country full of Nazis they needed men like him. Still do.'

The young detective's blush was painful to watch. Only one person had the courage to attempt a deflection of the conversation's course; Mary Wellbeck's iron diplomacy was the legacy of a thousand academic sherry parties.

'A pity he left nothing else behind him, Mr Alvarez.'

'*Nonsense!*' barked the old man. The force of his outburst silenced even the workmen. They stared. 'He left the finest thing he could. His example.'

There was a few seconds' hiatus before the chatter surrounded us again, and then he relented, patting Mary's hand to soften his bluntness. It was typical of him. He'd come to verify the handwriting of the letters I'd found in the round tin — the correspondence between Erich Von Laer and his father, Señor Ramon Alvarez, professor of fine art at Madrid university in the thirties, the man Von Laer had trusted to investigate the painting's history. The authorities had offered to take the letters to Peter Alvarez in England, but instead the old man had seized upon the opportunity of seeing an undiscovered Van Dyck for himself. I liked him. He proffered a trembling hand to me, but there was nothing at all querulous about its grip.

'I am very pleased to have met you, Mr Fraser.'

He accepted Mary's arm and they went towards the front door. He was leaving before the official handover, for he shared my distaste at what was happening here, and he didn't care who knew it. Somehow, despite the mismatch of her stately walk and his hobbling, arthritic gait, they made a natural couple.

'A character, all right,' muttered the Austrian.

One of his foul cigars appeared at the side of his mouth. He'd chain-smoked them all through my interrogation, and I was used to the smell by now, but the young detective cleared his throat and wrinkled his nose in distaste. The Austrian noted the fact and took great delight in ignoring it.

I looked again at the portrait of Ilse, Baroness Von Laer, and found myself sharing the German's admiration of the technology involved. Somehow they had removed the original painting, the hidden one, from beneath it, then transferred the top work to a new surface before reframing. But I couldn't look at the youthful confidence of the face without a chill going through me. Seen from this angle, she appeared a normal, attractive woman. Both deformities were hidden, soul and eye.

'What have they done with her?' I asked.

'Nuthouse,' replied the Austrian laconically. He gestured at all the activity around us. 'State of Nordrhein-Westfalen has appointed trustees for the estate. Usual vultures.'

The German shifted his feet uneasily at such forthright language.

'And the others?'

'Falkenheim's still with the monks, of course. House arrest till someone works up the guts to decide what's to be done with him. Weidemann —' he grinned at his young companion — 'is helping our friends here with their enquiries, prior to the locking up and throwing away of a very big key.'

'And it's all stopped now, the whole operation?'

The young German was unable to conceal his mounting dismay any longer. He broke in, earnest and concerned. 'I don't think, Herr Meyer, that it's wise to . . .'

The Austrian's grin widened. 'That's right, son. *Don't*

think. In fact, why don't you bugger off and liaise with somebody.'

The young face flushed crimson, but he knew he didn't have the authority to protest further; Meyer was a very high-ranking policeman indeed. We listened to his furious footsteps as he marched back to rejoin the main party.

'Fucking Germans,' Meyer said. 'You can see why they're going crazy, though — bent policeman running a forgery ring from headquarters! As well as this Lemke character strolling around for years, threatening people with one of their I.D. cards. *Dum-dum bullets in his bloody gun!* God only knows what slime-pit Weidemann dug him out of; he's not on anybody's files. Crazy isn't the word for it. They're *terrified*! The Bundesamt's asking me twice a day if we've found anything else.'

He drew a sheaf of photographs from his pocket and showed me the top one. 'Familiar?'

It took a moment. The hair . . . Why did it look strange? Finally I recognised the butler.

'Name of Frank Burton. Sheet on him at Scotland Yard's as long as the Old Testament. Forger, high quality stuff. Been singing like a bird ever since he got out of hospital. Apparently Weidemann had him by the balls, something to do with some other job, years ago, in England.'

The accent . . . I'd known it was odd. I remembered the report of Helga's private detective, the London forgery case that had made Weidemann's reputation. Meyer scratched at his unkempt grey hair with the hand that held the cigar and went on. 'He's given us most of it now. Turns out they had all sorts of bright capers going on, crooked betting and so forth, but apparently the counterfeiting thing was declining in importance for them, even though Burton had just started doing bond certificates as well as currency. Cash laundering, our friend Frank says, big money from the well-organised lads in Italy, that's what they were getting into. Turnover of millions, Fraser, millions. But they pinched pennies on the accountants. Didn't do the books well enough. Big demand for back taxes last year, capital transfer, capital gains from selling off chunks of the valley, stuff like that. Seems the tax boys were getting heavy, and Falkenheim was trying to sell the Italians a big slice of the whole deal when you blundered in. Must've put the cat right among the pigeons, that. But anyway, that's why the painting was so important. Not just money ...'

'But quick money,' I finished for him.

He nodded. 'Right. You were Tantalus, my friend, blessing and a curse at the same time. Falkenheim could never have sold anything to the Italians if it got out there was a threat to his ownership, and if he'd got his hands on the Van Dyck, he'd have had enough to get the tax people off his back. For a while, at least.'

He chuckled. One of the aides emerged from the big room, walkie-talkie in hand. He stalked past, murmuring into the apparatus, ignoring us. Meyer shook his head in disgust.

'Toys. My lot are just the same. Won't be long now before they've forgotten how to talk to something that can swear back at them.'

'There's only one thing I don't understand,' I began slowly. 'What . . .'

'Only *one* thing?'

The cheerful voice took on a sardonic edge as the policeman in him came back to the surface. He coughed gently on the smoke of his cigar and gave me a hard stare. 'There are so many things I don't understand, Fraser! Like how the hell you got from Münster to Neustift without so much as a sparrow hearing about it, much less a border guard, or where the Swiss girl is that Weidemann keeps bleating on about! Or why the gun that shot Lemke only has this character Burton's prints on it when we found you with a pocketful of bullets that fit it. Or why my so-called colleague in Neustift — who isn't fit to be in charge of an abattoir, never mind a police force — is so desperate to provide an alibi for one of the town's most prominent citizens!'

I said nothing. It was the first I'd heard of Bartsch or Annette. How had he got her away? And Helga . . . What had happened to her? Meyer began to button up his overcoat as he spoke.

'But it's enough for me that this bunch of animals is off my patch and you're not parading round the Tirol with toy pistols any more. I've learned never . . .'

'The film,' I said quietly.

'. . . to expect truth or justice to be as simple as a jigsaw puzzle, Fraser, no matter what the politicians would have us think. Always lots of pieces missing, lots of loose ends. Even big ones, like Falkenheim. What the hell are we supposed to do with him? The doctors give him six months at the most. What the hell do we do?'

I didn't answer. He came closer to me.

'I doubt if he'll even come to trial. Sticks in my craw, that does.'

'The film,' I repeated.

'Christ, but you're an obstinate bastard!'

He sighed, shuffling the photographs through his hands until he found the right one. It was a still from the film, grainy and scratched, much magnified, but precise enough — the face of the brown-haired officer who had so calmly watched the rape. Meyer brought another photograph out of his pocket, held the two together for me to compare, and I recognised the features of the politician whose posters had been so liberally plastered across the Bavarian town. Even allowing for the difference in age, there could be no doubt: they were the same man.

Meyer's voice was low, conspiratorial. 'Rising star in his party, if you can dignify that bunch of vermin with the word. Would've been a certainty for office in the next reshuffle down there. Grace and favour, Fraser . . .

Influence. Better than money in the bank, any day. Worth much more than the painting. In the hands of a man like Falkenheim . . .'

'What will you do with it?'

'Not my decision, thank God. But don't be surprised if you don't see the face at the next election. Come outside a minute.'

I followed him through the courtyard. The mist was rising, but the pale January sun wasn't high enough in the sky yet to melt the frost on the wooden bridge. A thin layer of opaque ice skirted the edge of the black water. He opened the car door and pulled out my fiddle case.

'Courtesy of a grateful Austrian republic,' he said, not bothering to hide the irony. 'Nearest thing you're going to get to payment for services rendered. Repaired in Mittenwald. Good as new.'

Awkwardly, feeling the familiar twinge of pain from my bandaged shoulder, I took the case. I didn't know how to phrase the thanks, for I knew that he'd done it himself, that the action was free of official stamp or knowledge. The voice took on a tone of gruff kindness as he climbed into the driver's seat.

'You're free, now, Fraser,' He nodded at the castle gate. 'You don't have to go back in there and put up with any of that shit. They asked me to get you here, but that's as far as I'll go for them. Official line is, they want to thank you for cleaning up their dunghill of a police department, but all they really want to do is put the arm on you to keep quiet. That's why they've wheeled out their tame Minister. Supposed to impress you . . . Up to you what you do, of course, but as far as I'm concerned you can walk away now.'

He didn't look at me. In the time I'd known him, the formal roles of suspect and interrogator had fallen far enough away for a mutual respect to grow, and we'd talked frankly; both of us knew there were other reasons why I had to go back inside. He held out an ancient, callused hand.

'Good-bye and good luck.'

I watched him drive away through the maze of official cars, then walked hesitantly back to the castle, listening to the echo of my own footsteps beneath the big arch. I felt tired, uncertain, very alone now that he was gone. In the hallway the inventory people were still scurrying around like diligent rodents, storing against catastrophe. But the catastrophe had already happened, I thought grimly, fifty years ago. I took a last look at the portrait, and found my eyes drawn to the unfinished corner. What had been missing in Ilse Von Laer? Why had she been left with a corner of darkness in her soul, and how much had Erich Von Laer known of what his sister really was? I knew Peter Alvarez was right, that he'd wanted the picture kept, for he'd deliberately primed the surface of the Van Dyck with a layer of *gesso*, so that both paintings could later be saved. I looked again at the face on the wall and found myself wondering whether he'd wanted to paint her as she should have been.

A whistling workman nodded to me as he passed. His carefree eyes followed my gaze back to the painting. 'Good looker, eh?'

I tried to smile, but I couldn't. *If only* . . . He went on his way, happily ignorant of what the woman meant to me and to others. There was a lesson in that, I decided — what she had unleashed on me was already history, and better left so. I went into the big room as quietly as I could.

People were clustered together in groups determined by professional allegiance rather than friendship or nationality, facing the big easel. The woman from the Dutch social work department gave me a brief, uncertain smile before turning away again. I was growing used to that smile. It was laced with superior professional regret. *Even though you meant well*, it said, *it would have been so much better if none of this had happened. If only you had gone through the proper channels* . . .

No one else noticed me. All eyes were on the Minister, the easel. The woman with the sash looked back at them across the centuries, aristocratic, serene and magnificent. The difference between copy and original was obvious now. To acknowledge the fact was no denigration of Erich Von Laer's skill; it was merely to see the difference between a good painter and a great one. The beauty of the portrait reached out to me, but as I looked at the other people I could see no one similarly affected. The eyes devoured her, but they measured neither her beauty nor the talent that had captured it; they measured the wealth her image had become, the power, and in the end that made them no different from Falkenheim. There was a brief flurry of brightly-lit photography, and then the Minister rose to speak. The voice matched the smile.

'Ladies and gentlemen, it gives me great pleasure today, on behalf of the state of Nordrhein-Westfalen, to assist in the return of a work of art to its proper home. The circumstances in which ...'

I felt a hand on my arm and turned to find Mary Wellbeck. Eyes upon the easel, she whispered, 'I was right. Late sixteen twenty, his first visit to London. Did Peter tell you the rest?'

I nodded and looked back at the portrait, at the device on the sash: the heraldic arms of Don Diego Sarmiento de Acuña, Count of Gondomar, Spanish ambassador to the court of His Majesty James the First of England. The papers of the Gondomar family told the story simply enough.

In sixteen twenty the young Van Dyck had come to London with an eye to entering the royal service. He already had a reputation as a brilliant painter, but he was by no means well off, and he was more than willing to accept the commission Gondomar offered him: to paint — in secret — a portrait of a young kinswoman of the ambassador, a member of his household. Gondomar presented the finished work to the man he knew to be the lady's admirer, to George Villiers, the all-powerful Marquis of Buckingham, James's court favourite. Buckingham was the avenue of all patronage at court, the man with the king's ear, and the painting was a part of Gondomar's continuing game of diplomatic intrigue, the sole aim of which was to influence English policy in a pro-Spanish direction.

In straight terms the painting was a bribe. The papers were quite specific on the point: Gondomar had wanted Buckingham to know that he would approve of a liaison — and that he would expect favours in return. The painting which was now valued in millions had fetched Van Dyck twenty guineas, and after its execution it had simply vanished from sight. No one knew if the bribe had been successful.

Mary gave my arm a gentle squeeze, and I saw sympathy light up her eyes as she whispered good-bye. I watched her go to the door; a remarkable lady, when all was said and done, and she'd proved a good friend. Again loneliness touched me; first Meyer gone, then her . . . I only became aware of the Minister's droning voice again once she was gone.

'. . . an era of better international understanding. The regrettable mistakes of the . . .'

I stopped hearing the words the moment I found the child's face through the throng of bodies. She didn't see me. She was more intent than I had been in her inspection of the faces around her, and there was neither humour nor shyness in her expression. The eyes went from person to person with a penetrating, sad stare that was too frank to be called curiosity. My heart sank as I realised what she was doing.

Lisa was looking for her parents.

There was a polite smattering of applause as the Minister finished his remarks, and she looked up as the two men on her left side bowed slightly. They were her guardians now, the envoys that had been sent from her new life. The taller of them gently patted her black hair, smiling down at her like some dark-suited, paternalistic raven.

They'd dressed her up for the occasion in a green velvet dress with a white collar. My eyes went back to the canvas on its easel, and I wondered if they'd deliberately made the child wear the same colours as the woman in the portrait — the woman who was her ancestor. As I saw them together, I wondered how I could have missed the resemblance. A dream on Terschelling had told me once, and Elly had tried to tell me in Neustift, on Christmas Eve. Even in Erich Von Laer's copy, it had been unmistakable.

I wondered what they would call her now, for the verification of the painting's pedigree had led to a family name. The woman Van Dyck had painted in sixteen twenty had been one Donna Maria de Acuña; it was a name she shared with the woman who had been raped on a Basque church altar in nineteen thirty-seven. The painting had been kept in that family for centuries, its value unheeded until the ravages of Spain's civil war had forced the modern Maria de Acuña, or Maria Ruiz, as she had become after marriage, to flee her home. She had been Lisa's maternal grandmother, but she had not been the last of her line. Relatives had been found in Spain, titled ones, elderly, childless, the only survivors of their generation of the family. No doubt they would care for Lisa well, but in order to care for her, they had to possess her. The girl seemed to belong to them now; she had become a property. She stood perfectly still, unconsciously assuming the pose of the portrait, a miniature of the woman she would become. She heard nothing. Neither did I.

She was heiress to a huge fortune in Spain. She was the owner of a great tract of land in the Austrian Tirol. My eyes were drawn to the crest on the wall behind her. One day, when a mad old woman died, she would be the owner of this castle, custodian of the black eagle and the white unicorn . . . What price the ginger kitten then? The child who was the last of the Von Laers and the newest member of a Spanish noble house continued her grave scanning of the faces, searching for a mother, a father.

Then she saw me, and tugged urgently at the hand that held hers.

The dress was simple, formal, beige silk, cut to disguise how thin she had become, and her face seemed unnaturally pale. In another woman the two things together would have marred the beauty, but in her the effect was merely to make it all the more striking. It gave prominence to the classic frame of the good bones and brought a delicacy to her features that made every other woman in the room look oafish by comparison. Only Maria de Acuña, safely immortal, could rival her.

But there was a defensiveness about her stance, a rigidity in the way she held herself, and I could see that her spirit was stretched to its absolute limit. Her whole body was taut with the effort of controlling her feelings. It was the little girl, the parting. This was their last day together. The bond between them was strong and simple, and the pain of its breaking would bury itself deep inside her. And there were other burdens: decisions loomed, big ones, made even bigger by the fact that they now had to be made around the void that losing the child would leave. I knew she had to wait until the cruelties of this long day were behind her before approaching them. Survival had its own priorities. Courage, even hers, was not an infinite thing, and coping with the loss had first call upon her store of it.

Courage . . . I wondered how much of it she would need to win through this one day. She had used up so much already. They'd kept us apart during the interrogation, and the fragility of her beauty now was a measure of just how much those two and a half weeks had cost her. But I knew she would still find the courage to make the decisions, and I knew that somehow I had to find it as well. Enough courage to match hers and make myself a part of them, to stop those two and a half weeks from turning into a lifetime. But not now, not today. Today she could absorb no more hurt.

Suddenly both of us felt the child's serious gaze upon us. Lisa examined each of our faces in turn, wisely, gravely, and to be aware of the scrutiny made the room's expanse too great to be crossed by our eyes. Elly averted hers, and the hair swept down across her cheek. She made to toss it away, then checked herself. It was a slow hand, determinedly calm, that brushed back the hanging brown wave. The other hand held on to Lisa as though the child was her last source of hope, of strength against the world.

Again her eyes found mine, and the rest of the room vanished as I watched her. I couldn't forget how she had looked the last time she had seen me. It was all so different now; the violence had been replaced by something called legality, but somehow the justice I had sought seemed as far away as ever. The other vision of her face, staring in horror at the gun in my hand, swam before me. Would that always happen? *Would I be there to know?*

Figures began to drift past, and I realised the ceremony was over. I couldn't move, couldn't take my eyes from her. Suddenly the Minister himself was standing squarely in front of me. The two aides collided with each other in their eagerness to clear his path. Folders dropped. A white flood of paper covered the floor. Both of them floundered around, trying to recover it.

Lisa's face . . . Elly's face . . . The dreams we'd had. What would fill the vacuum of their breaking? Not the people who were gathered here. They were merely the detritus of them. I wanted none of their pallid, institutionalised solutions, their nine-to-five social concern. I wanted the courage to choose, to make my own life, just as she would make hers. And I wanted it *now*.

The Minister frowned at me in bewilderment, unbriefed, unprepared. He looked around him for someone to ask the question, but there was nobody. He managed a ragged version of the smile.

'And you are . . .?'

I felt the weight of the fiddle case in my hand.

'I'm the busker,' I said.